"An Aztec priest of the dead tries to solve a murder mystery, and finds that politics may be even more powerful than magic. A vivid portrayal of an interesting culture in a truly fresh fantasy novel."
Kevin J. Anderson

"Part murder mystery, part well-researched historical novel and part fantasy… The fantasy element blends neatly with the other parts. 4****"
SFX Magazine

"From page one I was drawn into Acatl's world… a remarkable historically-based fantasy, using the myths and legends of the Aztec people as a background to a twisting murder mystery."
Speculative Book Review

"A gripping mystery steeped in blood and ancient Aztec magic. I was enthralled."
Sean Williams

"A strong debut, and a fascinating look at a culture and setting rarely used in modern fantasy."
Elizabeth Bear

"An amazingly fresh and engaging new voice in fantasy: the shadows of the Aztec underworld drip from these pages."
Tobias Buckell

ALIETTE DE BODARD

Harbinger of the Storm

Obsidian and Blood
vol. II

ANGRY
ROBOT

ANGRY ROBOT
A member of the Osprey Group

Lace Market House,
54-56 High Pavement,
Nottingham
NG1 1HW, UK

www.angryrobotbooks.com
Our father the sun

Originally published in the UK by Angry Robot 2011
First American paperback printing 2011

ISBN 978-0-85766-076-3

Printed in the United States of America

9 8 7 6 5 4 3 2 1

ONE

A Hole in the Fifth World

I felt it when it happened, even from where I was: sitting atop the platform of my pyramid temple, so high that the city below seemed a mere child's toy.

It was as if the entire world were exhaling: a slow, ponderous shift that coursed through the streets and the canals of Tenochtitlan, through the closed marketplace and the houses of joy – extinguishing the glow of the torches in the water, muffling the voices of the singers and the poets in the banqueting halls, and darkening the moon in the sky.

The Revered Speaker Axayacatl-tzin – the protector of the Mexica Empire, the link between us and our patron god Huitzilpochtli, the Southern Hummingbird – was dead.

I looked up at the Heavens. The sky was clouded, but a faint scattering of stars shone through, already smeared against the dark background, their light growing stronger and stronger with every passing moment.

They were coming down; the star-demons, eager to walk the streets and marketplaces of the city, to rend our flesh into bloody ribbons, to open up our chests with a flick of their claws and pluck out our beating hearts. Huitzilpochtli's divine power, channelled through the Revered Speaker, had kept them away from the Fifth World, the world of mortals.

But not anymore.

I took a deep breath to steady myself. It was not unexpected, by any means; but still... The boundaries between the worlds had become weak, effortlessly breached, and the work of summoners would be easy. Creatures would soon prowl the streets, hungering for human blood. Not a propitious time. We needed to brace for it; to be ready for the worst.

Footsteps echoed beside me: my Fire Priest, Ichtaca, second in command of my order. In one hand he carried a wooden cage with two white owls, their yellow eyes wide in the dim light. The other hand was tightly wrapped around the hilt of a sacrificial obsidian knife.

"Acatl-tzin," Ichtaca said, curtly bowing his head. The "tzin" honorific was muted, added to my name almost as an afterthought. In that moment, that I was High Priest for the Dead and he my subordinate didn't matter. We were both kindred spirits, both aware of the magnitude of the threat. Until a new Revered Speaker was invested, the whole of the Fifth World lay defenceless, as tantalising as feathers or jade to an indebted man.

I nodded. "I have to go to the palace." I had a place in the funeral preparations, small and insignificant. My patron Mictlantecuhtli, Lord Death, was not the god most honoured in the Empire. But, nevertheless, I couldn't afford to stay away at a time like this. "But let's see about the wards first."

Ichtaca didn't move for a while. On his round face was something very close to fear; unnerving, for Ichtaca had faced down gods, goddesses and underworld creatures without ever losing his composure.

"Ichtaca?"

He shook himself like an otter just out of a stream. "Yes. Let's do that."

We descended the steps of the pyramid temple side by side. The temple complex lay below us, low, one-storey buildings fanning out around the central courtyard, shimmering with the remnants of magic. It was not an hour of devotion, and most of my priests were sleeping in their dormitories. Everything was eerily silent, the examination rooms deserted, the bells sewn into the embroidered entrance-curtains gently tinkling in the breeze.

The pyramid temple was in the centre of the court-yard. At the foot of the stairs leading down from it was a large stone circle, engraved with the insignia of Lord Death: a skull, a spider and an owl. Dried blood stained the grooves, remnants of the previous times the wards had been renewed.

Ichtaca and I each took an owl from the cage before moving to opposite ends of the circle, I at the foot of the stairs, Ichtaca facing the temple entrance.

At my belt hung my own obsidian knife, blessed with the magic of Lord Death. I slit the owl's throat open, feeling its warm blood stain my hands. Then, with the ease of practise, I opened up the chest, and sought out the heart between the ribs, balancing it on the tip of the blade. The obsidian quivered, beating on the rhythm of coiled power. I laid the heart carefully on the boundary of the circle, and, with the blade dipped in blood, traced the contours of the circle with the knife. Blood pooled in the recesses of the carvings, shimmering like dust in sunlight.

Ichtaca started chanting:

"Above us, below us
The beautiful place, the home of our mother, our father the Sun

Above us, below us
The region of mystery, the place of the fleshless…"

It was nothing so spectacular as the aftermath of Axayacatl-tzin's death. Rather, green light slowly suffused the circle, a faint, ethereal radiance that carried with it the dry smell of dead leaves, the crackling noise of funeral pyres, the rank taste of carrion… the breath of Mictlan, the underworld.

I slashed both my hands, let them hang over the skull, as if in blessing.

"Above us, below us
An order as solid as a rock
The mountain upheld, the valley held in Your hand
We, Your servants, Your humble slaves,
We give our blood, our precious water
For that which maintains life
For that which maintains the Fifth World…"

The light slowly spread, sinking into the earth and the frescoes of the buildings until nothing but wisps remained hovering above the circle. Overhead, the stars were fainter, an illusion afforded by the protection, for nothing but Huitzilpochtli's power would banish the star-demons.

Ichtaca rose carefully, his silver lip-plug glistening in the moonlight. "It's done. Hopefully they'll last long enough."

I tore my gaze from the sky, unable to dismiss the heaviness in my stomach. If experience had taught me anything, it was that whatever could go wrong usually did so. "Let's hope they do. I'll leave you to wake up the priests while I go to the palace. Can you spare me Palli? I'll need an escort, if only to keep up appearances."

Ichtaca grimaced. He was much fonder of forms than I was. "It goes without question. You will–"

8

"Change into full regalia. Yes." I sighed. "Of course."

"And the rest of the priests?" Ichtaca asked.

"You know it as well as I do," I said, a recognition of competence, with no animosity. "Prepare the mourning garb and the chants."

"I'll see to it." Ichtaca's gaze was sharp again, his mind set on the tasks ahead.

Mine too, however, there was one significant difference. Ichtaca was looking forward to his work. I, on the other hand, had absolutely no wish to go into the palace – not late at night, not right after the emperor's death, when the infighting would have started in earnest. A Revered Speaker's successor was not determined by blood ties, but appointed by the council; and the council could be bribed, coerced or otherwise convinced to vote against the best interests of the Mexica Empire.

Not to mention, of course, the fact that more than half the people awaiting me at the palace despised or hated me, with the whole of their faces and of their hearts.

The Storm Lord strike me, it was going to be an exhausting night.

As I'd promised Ichtaca, I changed into full regalia before leaving. The owl-embroidered cloak and the skull-mask were definitely magnificent, calculated to impress even the most arrogant of noblemen, but it was a warm and sweltering night. I felt trapped in a portable steam bath, and it did not promise to get better any time soon.

Palli was already waiting for me in the courtyard, and he followed me in silence. It was scarcely a time for meaningless gossip. There was a hole in the universe around us, one that jarred with every heartbeat, every movement we made. Anyone with magical abilities could feel it.

Our temple, like all the major ones in Tenochtitlan, lay in the Sacred Precinct, a walled city within the city that made up the religious heart of the Mexica Empire. In spite of the late hour, most temples were lit. Most priests were awake making their usual devotions, though their blood penances and prayers had grown more urgent and desperate.

May the sun remain in the sky, may the stars not fall down into the Fifth World…

The palace lay east of the Sacred Precinct; we went through the Serpent Wall to find ourselves dwarfed by its sandstone mass. Torches lit up the guards who let us pass with a deep bow.

Like our temple, the palace was a mass of buildings, except on quite a different scale. A maze of huge structures opening onto courtyards and gardens, including everything from tribunals to audience chambers, warrior councils and workshops for feather-workers and goldsmiths.

I made straight for the Imperial Chambers, which overlooked a wide courtyard paved with limestone. Normally, it would have been empty of all but the highest dignitaries; now noblemen and warriors crowded on the plaza, a sea of gold-embroidered cotton, feather headdresses, jaguar pelts sewn into tunics, and the shimmering lattices of personal protective spells. But I barely had to push in order to make myself a passage. I might have been the least important of the High Priests, but I was still the representative of Lord Death in the Fifth World, wielder of magic beyond most people's reach.

Steps rose from the courtyard towards a wide terrace with three doors closed with entrance-curtains. The middle one was the Revered Speaker's reception room, the other two were rooms for the other rulers of the Triple Alliance when they visited the city. If they weren't there already, they soon would be. They had a place in the funeral rites, but more importantly, they would vote along with the council to designate a new Revered Speaker.

Indistinct speech floated through the entrance-curtain of Axayacatl-tzin's rooms. Two pairs of sandals confirmed I hadn't been the first one to arrive. Who would be inside? In all likelihood, my adversaries, here to remind me of my small place in the scheme of things…

No point in worrying before the sword strike. I added my own sandals next to those already there.

"Wait here," I told Palli.

I pulled aside the entrance-curtain in a tinkle of bells, and entered the inner chambers of the emperor.

I had never been there before. My work as High Priest had taken me as high as the audience chambers, but one had to be consort or wife to behold the Revered Speaker in his intimacy. But death took us all and made us all equal, our destinies determined only by the manner of its coming and, in its embrace, no privacy would remain.

It was a large, airy room, with a window at the back opening onto the gardens. There was little furniture, a handful of braziers, a few low chests, and a reed mat upon which lay the body. Frescoes wrapped around the columns of the room, representing animals from jaguars to the *ahuizotl* waterbeasts, all tearing apart small figures of men in a welter of blood.

"Acatl-tzin, what a surprise," a sarcastic voice said.

There were only three people in the room: the one who had spoken was Quenami, the newly appointed High Priest of Huitzilpochtli the Southern Hummingbird, his lean face suffused with the arrogance of the nobility and with the knowledge that, as priest of our patron god, he was our superior both in magic and

11

politics. I had disliked him from the first moment I'd seen him, and he was doing nothing to change that opinion. He wore the blue-and-black makeup of his god, his cloak was of quail and duck feathers, and more feathers hung from his belt, opening out like a turquoise flower.

Acamapichtli, High Priest of Tlaloc, scowled at me with undisguised animosity. I was not surprised. The Storm Lord had recently tried to seize power in the Fifth World, and I had played a significant part in foiling the attempt. Now Acamapichtli was in disgrace, and he blamed me for all of it.

I'd expected to see Tizoc-tzin, Master of the House of Darts, the heir apparent and favourite for the succession, but he wasn't there. I didn't know whether to be relieved or angry; my relations with him were icy at best, but his place was here with his deceased brother, not planning a gods-knew-what manoeuvre to secure his accession to the Turquoise-and-Gold Crown.

The last man, instead, was Tlilpopoca-tzin, the She-Snake and vice-emperor of the Mexica, a short, slight man wearing unrelieved black, and who was said to have played the game of politics from his mother's womb.

The She-Snake was also the only one who had not removed his sandals, a privilege afforded only to him. He and the Revered Speaker were two sides of the same balance, near-equals, one male, one female; one in charge of external policy and one keeping order in the city and in the palace, just as men waged war while women managed the daily business of the household.

I bowed to the She-Snake, and to everyone else in turn.

"My lords," I said. "I have come, as custom dictates, for the body of the Revered Speaker, Huitzilpochtli's chosen."

"We surrender it willingly," the She-Snake said, in

the singsong accents of ritual. His voice was grave, inviting trust. "We all must leave this world, the jades and the flowers, the marigolds and the cedar trees. Having nourished the Fifth Sun and Grandmother Earth, we all must leave the world of mortals. For those who died without glory, they must go down into the darkness, and find oblivion at the end of their journey. Let the Revered Speaker be no exception to this."

I did not know where he stood. Rumour had it that he opposed Tizoc-tzin, that he might even want to become emperor himself instead of the eminence behind the Revered Speaker. He probably believed in the gods only distantly – like his father, who had viewed religion as a tool, and not as the life and breath that kept the Fifth World whole.

"Let the Revered Speaker be no exception," I repeated, and broke off the ritual with a bow. Now that the formalities were out of the way, I could finally approach the body.

Axayacatl-tzin lay on his reed mat, relaxed as only death could make a man. His face – the face upon which no mortal had been allowed to gaze back when he had been alive – was slack, every trace of divinity long since fled. He looked much like any other corpse in my temple, save for the turquoise tunic that denoted him as Revered Speaker. He was painfully thin, the bones of his arms visible through the translucent skin, and his body smelled faintly unpleasant, the rancid odour of a man old before his time. He'd died of war wounds gone bad; of the decay that had settled into his bones and muscles. No foul play here. Not in a palace barricaded by protective wards, not under the watchful gaze of so many priests.

"Satisfied?" Quenami asked. The High Priest of Huitzilpochtli looked even more smug. I hadn't imagined that was possible.

"I expected to be," I said, turning back to face him. "You know that the corpse isn't the problem when a Revered Speaker dies."

Acamapichtli snorted. "The star-demons? You worry far too much, Acatl. Last time, the wards held for more than a month. And I should think our fighting abilities haven't diminished since then."

I wasn't a fighter, and he knew it. "When we are talking about beings that want to tear us apart, yes, I'd rather worry."

"Worry, then, if you wish. The interregnum will be short, in any case. We'll soon crown a new Revered Speaker, whom the Southern Hummingbird will invest with His power."

I turned towards Quenami, who made a small grimace. "Yes," he said. "It might be worth considering them. The palace wards will be reinforced."

He was young, newly come into his role, elevated from the nobility through connections and privilege and not from the clergy. He had no idea of the stakes. "You take this far too lightly," I snapped. "If you'd seen the creatures that prowl the boundaries, you wouldn't laugh."

Ahuizotls, creatures that feasted on the eyes and fingernails of drowned men; Haunting Mothers, who tore babies and toddlers into pieces; and star-demons, crouched above us, waiting for us to make a mistake, waiting for their time to come...

Gods, it wasn't a time for levity or carelessness.

"And *you* have no idea of the stakes," Acamapichtli said, with obvious contempt.

This, coming from a man whose god had tried His best to topple the Fifth Sun. "Do dispel my ignorance," I said.

Acamapichtli crossed his arms over his chest, looking down at Axayacatl-tzin with no expression on his face.

"He might not have been a great Emperor. He did not carve our territory out of the forsaken marches, or elevate us from tribe to civilisation. But he held us together."

What did he mean? "As will the next Revered Speaker."

The heron-feathers in Acamapichtli's headdress rippled in the breeze. "If he can be chosen."

"Tizoc-tzin was the Revered Speaker's choice," Quenami said, as seamlessly as if they'd planned it together. Considering the wide distance they kept from one another, I rather doubted it; but then again, Quenami had amply proved in the past that he knew how to sway a conversation. "His brother, the Master of the House of Darts, the commander of the regiments. He holds the loyalty of the army's core."

Politics. Power-grabbing. Always the same. "I still don't see what that has to do with us. Whoever becomes Emperor will want to maintain the boundaries. They will want the Heavens, the Fifth World and Mictlan to remain separate. They will want us to *survive*."

The She-Snake spoke up, in a calm, measured tone. "That's what they want to tell you, Acatl-tzin. That the council might dither. That it might not want to confirm Axayacatl-tzin's decision, that of a sick old man whose mind was halfway to Mictlan, after all." The She-Snake's voice carried the barest hint of sarcasm. He had to be one of the other candidates the council was split over; and his adversaries had just embarrassed themselves in front of him.

I thought of the stars overhead, growing larger with every passing moment. It would probably only be a few star-demons prowling the city, but even a few was too many. "If they wanted to dither, they should have done it before the Revered Speaker's death. It's too late now. Every passing day, the star-demons draw closer to us." There would be remnants of Huitzilpochtli's protection, tattered pieces, so easy to grind down to nothingness. There would be wards, such as the ones in my temples, drawn by devotees of other gods – the Flower Prince, the Feathered Serpent, the Smoking Mirror... But nothing like the impregnable wall that had been in place during Axayacatl-tzin's reign.

"Nonsense," Quenami said. "In the chronicles, they sometimes took entire weeks to decide on a new Revered Speaker. It never seemed to harm anyone."

"This is not a good time," I said. "The moon grows closer to the sun. The calendar priests have been warning about an eclipse for some time. We stand in its shadow, and this means that star-demons will be able to breach the boundaries."

As the moon loomed closer to the sun, eating into its radiance, She of the Silver Bells, the moon goddess, grew stronger; and her brother, Huitzilpochtli, our protector, weaker.

"In previous reigns, perhaps we were made of stronger stuff," I said, a slight jab at Acamapichtli and Quenami, who didn't react. "But today we are weak and defenceless. I have seen stars tonight, bearing down upon us. They are already coming to us. Have you ever seen a star-demon, my lords? You wouldn't laugh, believe me."

They were all looking at me with mild interest, as if I were trying to sell them a mine of celestial turquoise or a quarry of underworld jade. They didn't care. They thought it was an acceptable risk, so long as the end result allowed them to rise to greater power and influence.

They disgusted me more than I could express in words.

"My lords," I said, bowing. "I will attend to the body, and leave you to the mundane matters—"

16

I never finished the sentence. The entrance-curtain was cast aside in a discordant sound of bells slammed together, and someone strode into the room. "Acatl-tzin!"

"Teomitl?" My student, who also happened to be Axayacatl-tzin's and Tizoc-tzin's brother, wore more finery than I'd ever seen on him, a gold-embroidered tunic, a quetzal-feather headdress, and black and yellow stripes across his face. He clinked as he moved, from the sheer weight of jade and precious stones on his body.

Both the High Priests and the She-Snake bowed to him, deep. Tizoc-tzin had many brothers, but, should he attain the Turquoise-and-Gold Crown, Teomitl was likely to be anointed Master of the House of Darts in his stead, heir apparent to the Mexica Empire. Ignoring him would have been a mistake.

Teomitl made a dismissive gesture. "There's no time for pomp. Acatl-tzin, you have to come. Someone just killed a councilman. In the palace."

TWO

The Moon Hungers to Outshine the Sun

The murdered man did not live in the Imperial Chambers, or in those of the high nobility: his rooms were as far down the palace hierarchy as they could be without it being an outright insult. They were on the ground floor, opening up onto a small courtyard away from the bustle of palace activity with a very simple fountain to make up the garden. The walls were decorated with rich frescoes, but without the outright ostentation that marked the imperial family.

Somehow "killed" seemed a deeply inaccurate description of what had been done to the councilman. To say that he had been torn apart would also have been an understatement. There was no body left, not as such, just an elongated, glistening mass of bloody flesh with bits and pieces of organs spread all over the stone floor. Something which might have been an arm lay outstretched on one of the wicker chests; something else coiled around the braziers, and on the reed mat, lay the two globes of the eyeballs and an elongated shape that had to be the ripped-out tongue, somehow the most uncomfortable detail in the whole mess. A small obsidian knife lay near an out-flung hand, preceded by a trail of red.

Blood stained the room, stains of various sizes, all the way down to small drops marring the frescoes. It had not been quick, or easy.

Ordinarily I would have knelt, closed the body's eyes and said the death rites; this time, it seemed like the body was scattered over the whole room. So I just stood there, and said the prayers I always did.

> "We live on Earth, in the Fifth World
> Not forever, but a little while
> As jade breaks, as gold is crushed
> We wither away, like feathers we crumble
> Not forever on Earth, but a little while…"

Teomitl waited until I had finished before he spoke up.

"What do you think killed him?"

Given the remains, it was unlikely to be anything human. "Whatever you choose," I said, angrily. I hadn't expected the evening to go wrong, so fast. "Anything could have done it. With your brother dead, we're wide open to whoever feels like summoning creatures."

"Acatl-tzin," Teomitl said, with an impatient shake of his head. "I'm on your side, remember?"

I sighed. "Yes. I know."

The She-Snake had left after only a cursory glance inside; apparently he was going to interrogate the guards to know how such a thing could have happened. I'd sent Palli back to the temple to bring back priests and supplies, and begin the rituals over the Emperor's corpse.

The two other High Priests were outside trying hard to hide their nausea. Ironic, considering that they'd officiated at so many sacrifices. But the offerings to the Southern Hummingbird simply had their hearts removed and those to the Storm Lord were drowned. There was blood, but not that kind of butchery.

My order, on the other hand, dissected dead bodies to know how they died. This much frenzied bloodletting was unfamiliar; but the contents of a human body were almost like old friends.

And this particular one...

I knelt by the side of the largest mass, staring at it for a while with my priest-senses. "Tell me about him," I said. "The dead man."

Teomitl spread his hands, a little more defensively than I'd have expected. "Ocome. A minor member of the imperial family, perhaps descended from a Revered Speaker three, four generations ago. The blood ran thin."

"That's not really helping," I said, not looking away from the scattered flesh. Magic still clung to the room, the memory of a memory, faint and almost colourless, as if something had washed it away. "Any family?"

"Distant, I think. Ocome's wife died a while ago, and his marriage had not been fruitful. He'd be by far the most unsuccessful member of his family."

Aside, of course, from the position on the council.

So, probably not personal. I didn't feel any of the hatred which accompanied summonings done for vengeance. "Anything else?" I asked.

"Ocome was always trying to work out which side would win, so he could join them and be elevated still further." Teomitl spat on the ground. "No face, no heart."

"And lately?"

"He'd been supporting Tizoc," Teomitl admitted grudgingly. "Though it hadn't been for long."

Great. A professional waverer. His death was a message, but it could easily have been to Tizoc's side as to any of the other factions. Continually shifting allegiances meant Ocome must have made many enemies

– not much to be gleaned from here, not until I had a better idea of the sides involved.

"Hmm," I said. I fingered a spot of blood on the ground thoughtfully. Outwardly, everything seemed recent, except for the magical traces, which had faded much faster than they should have. "How long ago would you say he died?"

Teomitl had been standing by the entrance to the courtyard, looking away as if lost in thought. He turned towards the room, quietly taking in the scene, utterly unfazed by the gore. But then, he was a warrior who had already seen two full campaigns. He, too, had seen his share of mutilated bodies.

"They're clean wounds, and the blood is still pretty fresh. Two, three hours ago?"

The man had died in battle, no matter how unequal it had been. As such, his soul was not bound for the oblivion of the underworld but into the Heavens to join the dead warriors and the women lost in child-birth.

However, something bothered me about the body. The magic should not have been so weak. There could have been some interference from the wards, but the way it read seemed to indicate that the body had barely been alive in the first place – as if he'd come here wounded or already dying.

I supposed he could have been torn apart after his death; and, given the state of his body, we'd never know if he'd died before or afterwards. But most supernatural creatures didn't mutilate dead bodies. They found their thrills in the fear of the hunted, their power in the suffering of the tormented. Dead men could neither fear not suffer.

A human could have managed this, I guessed, but not easily. It would have taken time, and a great deal of dedication.

I could, however, think of a particular creature whose habits fitted this all too well, down to the fading magic over the remains.

And, the Southern Hummingbird blind me, I didn't want to be right. The star-demons couldn't be here, in the palace, not yet…

"I need your help," I told Teomitl. "Come over here."

He bounded over to me in a clink of jewellery and stood over a relatively clean patch of stone. He had magic wrapped around him like a cocoon, an intricate network of light that marked Huitzilpochtli's protection. It was that magic which I planned to tap in order to ascertain whether the councilman's soul had indeed fled into the Heavens. And, if it hadn't…

No, better not to think on the consequences of that now.

For the second time in the night, I slashed my earlobes open, and spread the blood around us in a quincunx, the fivefold cross, symbol of the beleaguered world of mortals. Then I started a chant to Tonatiuh, the Fifth Sun, the Southern Hummingbird's incarnation as the supreme light.

> "Dressed in yellow plumes
> You are He who rises, He of the region of heat
> Those of Amantla are Your enemies
> We join You, We honour You in making war…"

I slashed a wound in the palm of my hand, extended it to Teomitl, who had done the same. As we held hands, our blood mingled, trickled on the ground as one.

> "Dressed in paper
> In the region of dust, you whirl in the desert
> Those of Pipitlan are Your enemies
> We join You, We Honour You in making war…"

22

Light blazed across the pattern, spreading inwards, until it seemed that it would smother Teomitl for a bare moment, before his protection sprang to life again, an island of light within the light. Everything else faded into insignificance: the room, the frescoes, the grisly remnants outside and inside the circle. The colours were swept away, merged into the light; the faces of the gods and goddesses became the featureless ones of strangers.

The air was growing warmer, the ground under our feet was the red sand of the deserts, and a dry, choking wind rose in the room.

In the light was the huge visage of Tonatiuh the Fifth Sun, His war-painted face melding with that of a beast, sable hairs sprouting around His sharp nose, His cheeks still bearing the scars of His original sacrifice, His lolling tongue dripping blood. His eyes, slowly opening, were twin bonfires wrapped around the huge, hulking shape of a human being: the god Himself, still burning after all that time, endlessly burning to offer light and warmth to Grandmother Earth.

His gaze rested on us – a touch more searing than that of the wind – before moving away.

The wind died down, the desert retreated into the yellow stone of the room; the world sprang back into painful focus.

I exhaled burning air, gasping for the freshness of the mortal world. Teomitl's knees had buckled, and he was slowly pushing himself up again, with angry pride on his face. "Not a careful god," he said.

"No," I said. Teomitl pushed himself hard, but in return he demanded high things from everyone around him, gods included. "But that's bad."

"What?"

"He wasn't looking here," I said, trying to forget the icy void opening in my stomach. "No more than at any other place. It's not sacred ground. No soul has ascended into Heaven from here."

Teomitl looked puzzled. "The body…"

"I know," I said. In my head was running a chant we learnt in the House of Tears, the school for the priesthood: *The moon hungers to outrace, to outshine the sun; the stars hunger to come down, to rend our flesh; the stars hunger to fall down, to steal our souls…* "It's a star-demon, and it has his soul."

"That can't be–" Teomitl started. "They…"

They couldn't come here, not unless summoned; and, even then, it would require at least the lifeblood of a human being, spilled by a strong practitioner, in honour of a powerful god. We had a sorcerer loose in the city, one who wished no good to the Mexica Empire.

And then another, horrible thought stopped me. What if it was no sorcerer?

What if She'd got free?

"Come on," I said to Teomitl. "We have to check something. I'll explain when we get there."

To my apprentice's credit, he followed without demur, though I could feel him struggling to contain his impatience as we strode out of the palace.

"Where are we going?" he asked.

"The Great Temple." I headed back towards the Serpent Wall, though not before looking up. The stars were still there, still reassuringly far. It had to be a freak occurrence, had to be someone taking advantage of the current power vacuum to loose fire and blood upon us.

"You want to pray?" Teomitl shook his head. "This hardly seems the time, Acatl-tzin."

"I'm not planning to pray," I said. The Sacred Precinct opened up in front of us. Directly ahead was the Jaguar House, reserved for elite warriors, still lit up, with snatches of song and perfume wafting up to us. And, further down, the mass of the Great Temple, looming in the darkness like a mountain. "I'm going to make sure we don't have a bigger problem on our hands."

"In the Great Temple?" Teomitl asked. "It's just a shrine."

I shook my head. "Not only that."

Teomitl started to protest, and then he shook his head. His gaze turned towards the bulk of the Great Temple pyramid, looming over the rest of the Sacred Precinct. A fine lattice of light rose around the stone structure, flowing over the stairs and the double shrine at the top two mingled radiances, the strong sunlight of Huitzilpochtli the Southern Hummingbird, and the weaker, harsh one of the Storm Lord Tlaloc, tinged with the dirty white of rain clouds.

Teomitl's face twisted. A pale, jade-coloured cast washed over his features, until he seemed a carving himself. He was calling on the magic of his other protector Chalchiuhtlicue, Jade Skirt, goddess of lakes and streams. His gaze went down, all the way into the foundations of the Great Temple "Oh," he said. "I see."

What mattered was not the temple, it never had. What mattered was what it had been built on, Who it had imprisoned since the beginning of the Mexica Empire; a goddess who was our worst enemy.

It was the Hour of the Fire God, the last one before dawn; and the priests of Huitzilpochtli were already climbing the steps, preparing their conch-shells and their drums to salute the return of the Fifth Sun. The priests of Tlaloc the Storm Lord, much less numerous, had gathered to offer blood in gratitude for the harvest.

Neither order paid much attention to me or Teomitl; their heads turned, dipped in a bare acknowledgment

– tinged with contempt in my case, for they knew all too well what their own High Priests thought of me.

We climbed up the double set of stairs that led to the platform at the top of the pyramid, feeling magic grow stronger and stronger around us, the Southern Hummingbird's magic, a fine mesh of sunlight and moonlight slowly undulating like satiated snakes, descending around us, mingling with Teomitl's protection, resting on my shoulders like a cloak of feathers. It hissed like a spent breath when it met Lord Death's knives at my belt, but did not do anything more. A relief, since Huitzilpochtli's magic, like the god Himself, could be violent and unpredictable.

Atop the temple were two trapezoidal shrines, one for each god, from which the pungent reek of copal incense was already rising into the sky. Slightly before the shrines the stairs branched. On a much smaller platform to the right opened an inclined hole, the beginning of a tunnel that descended into the depths of the pyramid. The entry was heavily warded, with layer upon layer of magic, bearing the characteristic, energetic strokes of Ceyaxochitl, the old woman who was Guardian of the Mexica Empire, and the subtler ones of the previous priest of Huitzilpochtli. They parted around us, though with a resistance like the crossing of an entrance-curtain.

Beneath us was a flight of stairs going down into the darkness. A stone chest with its lid flipped open held torches, and a single flame was lit at the entrance. We both took a torch and set it aflame before going down.

It was damp, and dark, and unpleasantly cool. The deeper we went, the more the magic tightened around us – as if a snake, once pleasantly settled around the shoulders, had suddenly decided to constrict. Our breaths rattled in our chests until each inhalation burnt, and each exhalation seemed to leech heat from our bodies and from our hearts. Even Teomitl's light from his protective spell grew weaker and weaker; I could see him slowing down before I, too, adapted my step to his. Together, we moved through the growing thickness, moment after agonising moment.

We passed many platforms on our way. The Great Temple had been rebuilt several times, each incarnation grander and more imposing than the last, wrapping its limestone structure around the shells of all its predecessors. Altars shone in the darkness, faint smudges on them, the memories of previous sacrifices.

At last we reached the bottom of the stairs, the foundation of the Great Temple, and entered a wide chamber, its walls so covered with carvings that the eye barely had time to settle on one figure before another caught its attention.

At regular intervals lines had been carved into the stone, slight depressions linking the floor to the top of the temple, channelling the blood of sacrifices all the way down to pool on the floor. It reeked like a slaughter yard – even worse than an ordinary shrine, for there was almost no way for the air to escape such a confined space.

The floor itself was a huge painted disk, three times as large as the calendar stone that hung in the shrine above. It lay on the floor – in fact, it *was* the floor, for it filled most of the room from wall to wall, with only a little space for an altar at the further end. The carvings on it were almost too huge to be deciphered. I could see bits and pieces of them; an arm bent backwards, a severed foot, a gigantic head with a band and rattles, separated from the dismembered torso. There was a feeling of movement, as if all the pieces were still tumbling down from the original sacrifice. Blood coated everything, its power pulsating in the air above the disk like a heat wave.

I knelt by the disk, and carefully extended a hand to touch the edge. There was a slight sound, like the tinkle of silver bells, and I felt the stone warm under my finger, the only warmth in the room, beating like a human heart, pulsating with Her anger and murderous rage, an urge to water the earth with my lifeblood, to tear me from limb to limb and inhale my dying breath, to scatter my essence within Herself until nothing remained…

"Acatl-tzin?"

With difficulty I tore myself from the stone and looked up at Teomitl. "She's still sealed here," I said. Otherwise I wouldn't just be remembering Her rage, I would be dead. The wards still held. The blood magic, renewed with the daily sacrifices of prisoners, was still as strong as ever.

I'd have breathed more easily, had the atmosphere of the room allowed it.

"You're sure," Teomitl said. "It's…" He knelt in turn, though he was careful never to touch the stone. "If She were to break free…"

Then She would regain the control of the star-demons, the creatures She had made in the distant past. She would stride forth as in the days before the Mexica Empire, hungry for blood and human hearts, eager to erase from the Fifth World all memory of Her brother's chosen people.

All gods were vicious and capricious, but Coyolxauhqui – She of the Silver Bells, who had once been goddess of the Moon – was the worst. The others could be cajoled with the proper offerings, bribed into protecting us; we were weak and amusing, but it was our blood that kept the sun in the sky, and our blood that kept Them satiated and powerful. Coyolxauhqui – She was war and fire and blood, and She would not rest until the Fifth Sun tumbled from the sky, and darkness covered Grandmother Earth from end to end, as in the very beginning.

"I know," I said. "But She's not free." Not yet. It was not only the blood of sacrifices that kept She of the Silver Bells imprisoned, but also the Revered Speaker, the living embodiment in the Fifth World of Southern Hummingbird's power.

And, at present, we had no Revered Speaker.

"Come on. Let's go back up," I said.

The return journey was much easier, as we climbed the weight lifted from our shoulders, and the constriction in our chests and necks gradually eased. The air grew warm again, and we emerged under the grey sky before dawn feeling almost refreshed.

Unfortunately, that feeling of relaxation lasted for perhaps a fraction of a moment. "Acatl," a familiar, imperious voice said. "I had a feeling you might be the one getting past the wards."

Of course. I turned and beheld Ceyaxochitl, the Guardian of the Empire, the keeper of the magical boundaries, resplendent under her feather headdress. She leant on a cane of red polished wood that had to have come from the far south, deep into Maya land.

She did not look sarcastic, for once, but by the gleam in her eyes I knew I was in for trouble.

"Star-demons," Ceyaxochitl said, thoughtfully. She had dragged us back to the Duality House, where slaves brought us bowls of cocoa and a light meal of fried newts and amaranth seeds. We sat around a reed mat in a small room at the back of the House, which opened onto one of the more private courtyards, a garden of marigolds and small palm trees. It was silent and deserted even at this hour of the morning, when every slave should have been out grinding the maize flour for today's meals.

As was her wont, Ceyaxochitl did not sit down. she remained standing, towering over us. The slaves finished laying out the meal on the mat, and withdrew, drawing the entrance-curtain closed in a tinkle of bells.

"Star-demons are to be expected," I said. But it was much too soon for them.

"Yes, yes," Ceyaxochitl said. "However, strictly speaking, the heart of the Great Temple is the province of Southern Hummingbird's High Priest, Acatl. Not yours."

"It doesn't seem like Quenami is over-preoccupied with star-demons," I said, with a touch of anger.

Ceyaxochitl sighed. "These are difficult times, Acatl. Fraught with intrigue."

"I know. That doesn't mean I have to like it," I said. Especially not when it risked supernatural creatures in the palace, or in the streets of the city.

"You never did," Teomitl said, with some amusement.

I threw him a warning glance. He might be making progress with the magic of living blood, but we were going to have to work on the respect side of things. "Apart from the impressive costume, you don't look very involved in the succession either."

Teomitl didn't react to the jibe. "I'm not in a position to influence that, so I just keep my head down."

"You're Tizoc-tzin's brother," I said. "Master of the House of Darts, if all goes his way." Though I still couldn't quite reconcile myself to the idea of Tizoc-tzin's ascension.

"Perhaps." Teomitl fingered the jade beads around his wrist – an unusual evasion for him, who always spoke his mind without worrying about the consequences.

Ceyaxochitl banged her cane on the ground. "Let's keep to the original subject, please."

I winced. Our relationship had always been rocky and had not improved much in the past year. When Ceyaxochitl set about to helping you, she would do what she judged best for you, whether you agreed or not. Needless to say, I seldom shared her point of view.

"What more do you want?" I asked. "Someone summoned a star-demon and tore a councillor to death in a heavily warded place. I had to make sure that it didn't come from She of the Silver Bells."

Ceyaxochitl nodded, but it took her some time. "A good idea. But still—"

"Look," I said, determined to put an end to that particular matter. "I know it's the province of the other two High Priests. Right now, they're too busy trying to influence who will become Revered Speaker, or overconfident. I'd rather do it on my own than have the star-demons loose around us. You know that we're wide open now, vulnerable to pretty much anything. People will want to take advantage of that."

"I suppose," Ceyaxochitl said. She did not look overly happy. "Still, I have other things to do."

As Guardian of the Mexica Empire, she was the agent of the Duality, the source and the arbiter of the gods. Her work was to protect the life of the Revered Speaker and, when that life was ended, to set wards around the Empire in order to keep the star-demons and the monsters of the underworld at bay.

"Then, if you're busy, just leave me in peace," I said.

"Not so fast, Acatl." She banged her cane on the ground again. "You must know where this is going."

I raised an eyebrow. "If it's not She of the Silver Bells, then it's a sorcerer, determined to sow chaos among us. The first of many. It's not the grievances that lack." The Mexica Empire was made of subjugated populations from whom we demanded regular, sometimes exorbitant, tribute; and foreigners were many in

Tenochtitlan, though most would be slaves or under some form of indenture.

It could also be someone trying to influence the succession by other means. But still, you'd have to be mad to do it by decimating the council, not when there were so many other means of influencing it.

"And how do you plan to find such a sorcerer?" Ceyaxochitl asked, shaking her head.

As usual, she called my competences into question. "I am not without resources. Magic, especially magic that powerful, will leave a trail."

"Yes, yes," Ceyaxochitl said, shaking her head as if I were still a wayward child. "You need help, Acatl."

"I have my order."

The corner of her lips curled up in a smile. "You do. But I was thinking of more massive resources."

Over the course of the night, I had faced two High Priests and a vice-emperor, our most powerful god, and His imprisoned sister – not to mention that my last hour of sleep had been in the evening. I didn't have the patience to play along with her games of dominance any more. "Are you offering your help?"

"Of course. In recognition for past wrongs." She turned, and glanced through the entrance-curtain. The grey light was subtly changing colour, sunrise was not far away.

"Past wrongs?" A year ago, Ceyaxochitl had embroiled me in yet another set of intrigues, involving one of my brothers. She had not seen fit, though, to provide me with all the information at her disposal, or with more than a token assistance. The resulting conflagration had almost levelled Tenochtitlan; it had cost the life of my sister-in-law, and had tarred my family's reputation so thoroughly we were going to require years to even start our rehabilitation. "You'll excuse me if I'm not entirely ready to believe you're offering only out of remorse."

Her lips curled up again. "As I said before, you may not think it, but I always do things for your own good, Acatl."

And *that* was the problem. "Of course," I said. But I could ill afford to refuse her. "What did you have in mind?"

Ceyaxochitl had the grace not to look triumphant. "We'll keep a watch on the situation at the Imperial Court."

"You have information?"

"A little," Ceyaxochitl said. "I can tell you of the factions I know at court. Tizoc-tzin, the She-Snake, several of the princes, and the other rulers of the Triple Alliance, of course."

"Of course." Our brothers, our co-rulers in the Mexica Empire, dreaming, no doubt, of the day when they headed the Triple Alliance instead of being subservient to it. "They'll have sent runners to them."

Teomitl looked up from his bowl of cocoa. "It was done before you arrived, Acatl-tzin."

A blare of conch-shells and wooden drums cut us off. The Fifth Sun had risen outside. There was a pause, during which we all scratched our earlobes and spilled blood to honour His return, to pray for His continued existence and protection, even though Axayacatl-tzin's death had severed him from the Fifth World.

> *"In the place of light*
> *You give life, You hide Yourself*
> *In the place of clouds*
> *Mirror which illuminates things*
> *Follower of the Heaven's Path*
> *Mirror which illuminates things…"*

When it was over, Ceyaxochitl came back to the

original discussion as if nothing in particular had happened – and, for her, perhaps it was the case. The Duality had no favourites. "The other two Revered Speakers of the Triple Alliance will be here in one, two days. The other rulers might take slightly longer, but then they don't have a vote in who wears the Turquoise-and-Gold Crown."

"But they still might be behind this, or give it their support."

"It's still only one isolated incident," Ceyaxochitl said carefully.

"Yes," I said. "It might be personal. It might be isolated. But the odds are that it won't remain so for long. Other people will emulate it. The usual barriers against summonings are weak, and everyone will know that." The emptiness in the fabric of the Fifth World was still there, an itch at the back of our minds – a hole that would only be filled by a new Revered Speaker.

Teomitl spoke in the silence with the voice of one used to command. "We must show our strength. And fast."

I thought of She of the Silver Bells, of Her hunger, of Her rage that we still dared to be alive, to imprison Her anew with every sacrifice, every drop of blood we shed in honour of Her brother Huitzilpochtli.

We had to show our strength, or we would be broken without recourse.

THREE

The Threat from Within

We walked out of the Duality House into a beautiful morning, the sun overhead already warming our limbs. It was the dry season, a time when we should have been preparing for war, but the death of the Revered Speaker had slightly postponed the preparations. The next war we launched would be the Coronation War, when the new ruler would prove his valour on the battlefield.

The Sacred Precinct, like most of its priests, awoke early. Because of Axayacatl-tzin's death, the plaza was already crowded. Novice priests scurried on errands to the marketplace. Some had already come back, carrying cages with offerings ranging from rabbits to monkeys. Nearby a fire priest and two offering priests led a chalk-painted sacrifice victim to the altar. The man walked with casual arrogance, proud of being selected for a glorious death, eager to rejoin the Fifth Sun's Heaven.

"I'll see you home," Teomitl said.

"I don't need–"

He smiled, in familiar, dazzling arrogance. The sunlight caught the gold on his wrists and around his neck, and mingled the blinding reflections with the radiance of his magical protection. In that moment, he did indeed look imperial, as if some of his brother's glory had rubbed off on him, some radiance passed between them. "We have star-demons among us."

"Just one so far." I hoped fervently there wouldn't be more.

Teomitl spread his hands. "You walk like a dead soul, Acatl-tzin. If anything happened…"

"I seem to remember you're the student, and I the teacher," I said, somewhat acidly.

Teomitl's smile was wide and innocent. "Isn't that proper respect? Attending to your master's needs?"

And I was the Consort of the Emperor. "Walk with me if you want. But for company, not for protection." Or, Duality forbid, for mothering me.

"As you wish." Teomitl fell in step by my side. People turned as we passed. I was still in full regalia, and the refined costume Teomitl wore could only have come from the Court.

"So," I asked. "How is Mihmatini?"

Teomitl had met my younger sister a year ago, and had been immediately attracted to her, and she likewise. I had grudgingly given my approval to the relationship, suspecting all the while that it would go nowhere. An imperial prince was not free to marry as he chose. Teomitl's principal wife would likely come from one of the neighbouring cities, as a token of goodwill and good conduct.

But, to my surprise, it still seemed to be holding, a year on, despite Mihmatini's acid tongue and Teomitl's carefree manners.

However, when I asked that question, Teomitl grimaced.

"Trouble under Heaven?" I asked.

He waved a hand, airily. "Nothing that need concern

you, Acatl-tzin. Your sister is as lovely as ever."

And she'd likely tear his head off if he attempted flattery like that. "Teomitl."

His gaze met mine, defiant. "I will soon be Master of the House of Darts, member of the inner council. No one can tell me what to do."

My heart contracted. I couldn't help it. Reason told me that, of course, someone would step in, someone would want to bring the wayward prince back into the norms, but still… Still, whenever she thought of him, Mihmatini's whole demeanour would soften, and her face shine like marigolds in the gloom. Teomitl would make excuses to leave our magic lessons early, so he could casually drop by the house and see her, even if it was with a chaperone. "Someone doesn't agree," I said.

"I could fight one man." Teomitl's voice was low, intense. "Barring a few who are much too strong. But it's bigger than that, Acatl-tzin."

"The Court?" I asked.

Teomitl shook his head, and wouldn't answer no matter how hard I pressed him. Finally, he changed the subject with a characteristic, airy dismissal. "Enough about me. This isn't the time. More is at stake than my pathetic little self."

I had to admit that he was right, though I didn't like the way he was behaving. Teomitl was honest and loud, and seldom held grudges. If he was bitter, it was never for long, his natural resiliency allowing him to get past it without trouble. This time it sounded as though they had got to him, whoever "they" were.

We'd reached my house. Unlike the residences of the other two High Priests, which were within the palace, mine was a small adobe building set around an even smaller courtyard with a lone pine tree over a covered well. The only concession to my status was the two-storied house. Tall houses were reserved for the nobility or the high ranks of the priesthood.

"I'll see you at the palace, then," I said.

Teomitl shook his head. "I'll be outside, Acatl-tzin."

I started to protest, but he cut me off. "I know you. You'd just sneak out in a few moments if I left. Go get some sleep."

"And you?"

Teomitl eyed the exterior of the house. "It looks like a comfortable adobe wall," he said, deadpan.

"With your finery? I'd be surprised."

"It's just cloth and feathers," Teomitl said, with the casualness of those who had never lacked for anything in their lives. "The imperial artisans can weave them again."

"I'm sure," I said. My bones ached, and my hands were quivering. I wasn't sure how long I could argue with him successfully, especially since, even awake and fresh, I always found myself losing. Teomitl was very persuasive, and as stubborn as a jaguar tracking prey. "Fine. I'll be kinder to your clothes than you seem to be. You might as well come inside."

I'm not sure what Teomitl busied himself with when I was sleeping, but I woke up to find him still sitting in the courtyard, glaring at the lone pine tree as if it had personally tarnished his reputation.

I itched to put on something simpler, but since we were going back to the palace, I couldn't shed the regalia. I did tie the skull-mask to my belt, in a prominent position that left the hollow eyes and sunken cheeks visible: it would remain visible, but not hamper me any longer.

We went to Lord Death's temple first, where I checked with Ichtaca that things were going on as foreseen, the suspicious deaths investigated, the funeral vigils taken care of, the illegal summoners arrested and tried. I mentioned, briefly, the body of the councillor. Ichtaca frowned. "That's trouble. Do you want more people?"

I shook my head. Many of the priests were already at the palace, taking part in the elaborate rituals that would culminate in the Revered Speaker's funeral. "You're overstretched already. I'll take those at the palace."

We took a brief meal in the temple with Ichtaca, maize flatbreads with spices, and a drink of maguey sap. Then Teomitl and I walked back together to the palace. I couldn't help casting a glance in the direction of the Great Temple, but the only activity going on seemed to be the usual sacrifices. The altar was slick with blood, and the body of a man was tumbling down the steps, its chest gaping open. Blood followed it, a slow, lazy trail that exuded a magic even I could feel. But I could see the other magic, the white, faint radiance trapped underneath, the anger that possessed Coyolxauhqui. She of the Silver Bells would not forgive, or forget, or relent in any way.

It was past noon. The Fifth Sun overhead battered us with His glare. On the steps leading up to the palace massed a group of priests clad in blue cloaks, embroidered with the fused lover insignia of the Duality. They were tracing glyphs on the ground with a set of twined reeds. Most other orders would have shed blood, but the Duality deemed blood offerings unnecessary.

At their head was a man I knew all too well: Yaotl, Ceyaxochitl's personal slave. He'd never looked less like a slave, though; his neck was bare, unencumbered by any wooden collar, his cotton cloak was richly embroidered, his cheeks painted blue and black, the same colour as the priests' cloaks.

"Ah, Acatl," he said, his scarred face splitting into a smile. He did not venture any explanation, which did not surprise me. Like his mistress, Yaotl often kept me in the dark, but made no pretence of altruism; it was purely for his own amusement.

I summoned my priest-senses, and took a look at the stairs. The glyphs drawn before the entrance shone for a moment, before sinking into the stone. A fine coating of light had always hung around the palace, the protective wards that kept the high nobility safe, but now the light was growing warmer, clearer. The stone under us was quivering with power, like a heart barely torn out of a chest.

"Reinforcing the wards?" I asked.

"I see your observation skills are as keen as ever." Yaotl cast an amused glance to the sandstone face of the palace, with its frescoes depicting the end of the migration from the heartland, and the founding of Tenochtitlan on the spot where the Fifth Sun's eagle had perched on an agave cactus, gorging himself on a human heart.

"Why now?" I asked.

"As a precaution," Yaotl said. He shook his head, as if to clear a persistent thought. "Huitzilpochtli is already watching here, but He is weak. Mistress Ceyaxochitl thinks help wouldn't hurt."

"Where is she?" I asked. "Inside the palace?"

Yaotl nodded. I looked again at the light. It was now tinged with the blue, peaceful radiance of the Duality, but the structure underneath, the magic of the Southern Hummingbird woven in daily layers, was more than solid. Even weakened by Axayacatl-tzin's death, it was impregnable.

"It doesn't need help," I said, aloud. "They hold."

"Observation at work once again," Yaotl said.

No, that wasn't the problem. "It was summoned inside the palace."

"The star-demon?" Teomitl asked.

I nodded. I had been wrong. It wasn't just some foreign sorcerer with a grievance against us. It had to be someone who had access inside.

To be sure, there were means to bribe palace servants, but this wasn't just a matter of someone scouting out the weaknesses of the palace guard. The summoning had to have been done inside the wards, from beginning to end, which implied two things. First, the summoner was enormously skilled, which only confirmed what I already knew. Second, the field of suspects had just been drastically limited. The pillars of the entrance were enchanted, and a sorcerer without Court accreditation wouldn't have been able to pass between them.

So, not just any sorcerer, but a member of the Court with access to magic. I would need to check who was on the list of accreditations.

I added this to the growing number of things I was going to need men for. I hated taking people away from the Revered Speaker's funeral, which should have been my priority, but if there was a summoner of star-demons loose in there…

Teomitl turned, to look at the protective spells over the gates with a dubious frown.

The Storm Lord blind me, whoever had done this was extremely well prepared. Not only had they managed to find someone on the inside, but they had also been ready to do their summoning in the hours that had followed Axayacatl-tzin's death.

I didn't like the sound of that.

The first thing I did upon entering the palace was to go to the Revered Speaker's rooms. I found the guards at the gates in a state of alert. I assumed they had been apprised by the She-Snake on the murder, and were holding themselves ready for anything.

Inside, the burly offering Priest Palli was watching as two dozen priests for the Dead prepared the corpse for its funeral. A quincunx of blood spread across the tiled floor, with the faint greenish tinge of Mictlan's breath. The priests were all chanting hymns, calling on the minor deities of the underworld; except two, who were busy undressing the former Revered Speaker. Clothing was all-important: the mummy bundle that would be burnt would be made of dozens of layers of many-coloured cotton, each added with the proper beseeching to the gods, each garnished with gems, amulets and gold and silver jewellery.

Palli nodded to me when I entered, but waited until the current hymn was finished to move outside the blood quincunx. "Acatl-tzin. As you can see, we have matters well in hand."

I nodded. The forms looked to be respected. The room itself was pulsing with a presence like a burst dam, the breath of the river that separated the under-world from the Fifth World. Everything was well taken care of. "No doubt of that." I hesitated; but it was still something that needed to be done. "How many could you spare?"

Palli looked dubious. "I could without half, but the rituals would progress more slowly…"

"No matter," I said. "The funeral isn't going to be for a while anyway." Not if the other High Priests had their way.

"It's about the body, I assume."

I nodded. "It looks like the summoning of what killed that man was done from inside. I need one person sent to the registers, to check up on the accreditations of all the sorcerers."

"You don't mean—"

"I'm not sure what I mean," I said, darkly. "But watch your step, definitely."

Palli nodded. "I can do that, but…"

"I know." It was going to be a long list. Most noblemen had access to magic, if only for their protective spells. If they didn't have a pet sorcerer, they were sorcerers themselves; and that didn't count the numerous priests and magistrates who came here, either in the service of their temples or in the service of the Imperial Courts.

"And the others?" Palli asked.

"I want them to search the palace. If a summoning was done here, it should show." The magic wouldn't be washed away, not so easily. "Every room, every courtyard. There has to be a place we can find." It was the timing I didn't like: the murder of Ocome had taken place barely one hour after the death of the Revered Speaker. This suggested… planning. Someone, somewhere had held themselves ready for an opening, knowing it couldn't be long until the ailing Revered Speaker passed into Mictlan.

Palli grimaced again, an expression he was a little bit too fond of. "I'll see who I can spare. For the ritual's end…"

Only the High Priest for the Dead could ease a soul's passage into the underworld. "I'll be there." One way or another. I wouldn't rob a dead man to serve another one.

I just hoped the corpses would stop arriving.

Teomitl and I dropped briefly by Ocome's room, which still stank of death. Two guards were keeping watch by the entrance-curtain, looking as if they would have given anything to be elsewhere.

In the room itself, there was not much new to see: the magic was slowly dissipating, absorbed by the wards. I'd expected the scattered gobs of flesh would have started to rot, but they remained in the same state, as if the star-demon's removal of the soul had put a stop to the decomposition process.

I'd made more cheerful discoveries. No matter; he would still burn on his funeral pyre as well as any corpse, provided we could scrape the flesh from the floor and from the walls. For once, I was glad to be High Priest, which meant someone further down the hierarchy would do the exhausting, distasteful work.

When we came out in the courtyard in the dim light of late afternoon, I turned towards the burliest of the guards. "How long ago were you assigned to this room?"

I could see him hesitating, his eyes roving over my regalia, weighing the possibility that he could get away with a lie.

It was his companion who spoke, a much thinner man, with the white lines of scars crisscrossing his legs identifying him as a veteran of some battlefield. He held his *macuahitl* sword – a wooden club studded with obsidian shards – with the ease of those who had carried it nearly all their lives. "We've been guarding this place for three weeks."

"I see," I said. And, as casually as I could, "I take it you weren't standing guard when this happened?"

The burly guard grimaced. "We thought we heard something on the other side of the courtyard, so we went to investigate."

"And didn't come back?" This from Teomitl, who had been standing with one hand on the entrance-curtain.

The guard grimaced again. "It turned out to be nothing, but we still wanted to make sure. I went to ask the others who were on guard in the next courtyard." He wouldn't meet my gaze, but in any case I knew he was lying. His companion the veteran was even less talkative.

"Really?" Teomitl started, but I lifted a hand.

"Someone called you away?"

The burly guard had the grace not to answer; the veteran shifted uncomfortably. There was a light in his eyes I couldn't read, anger or fear, or a bit of both. What had been promised to them, in exchange for their silence?

I sighed. Whoever had done this had influence, a currency I was short on. "You do know who this is?" I asked, pointing to Teomitl, who stood up even straighter. "Tizoc-tzin's brother, who will soon become Master of the House of Darts. Do you truly wish to lie to him?"

The burly guard shook his head, a minute gesture that he stopped before it became too visible, but it had already betrayed him. He didn't believe in Tizoc-tzin; or at least, didn't want him to wear the Turquoise-and-Gold Crown.

I didn't know whether to be relieved I wasn't the only one to dislike Tizoc-tzin, or terrified that the divisions within the Court ran so deep.

"I can have them dismissed," Teomitl said. His gaze was on me, his whole stance had hardened. This wasn't my student anymore, but the man who would one day become Revered Speaker. "Master of the House of Darts or not, I'm still imperial blood."

The guards' faces did not move, but the veteran's hands clenched around his *macuahitl* sword, slightly tilting it towards us. The obsidian shards embedded in the wood glinted in the sunlight.

"My lord," the burly guard said, cautiously. "We don't seek to deny you, but surely you must understand that there are higher powers–"

Teomitl cut the guard off with a stab of his hand. A pale green light was dancing in his pupils, the power of Jade Skirt, his protector. The Duality only knew what

45

he thought Chalchiuhtlicue could accomplish in this situation. She was more subtle than her husband the Storm Lord, but not by much.

I was slightly taken aback, but not surprised. Teomitl had absolutely no sense of humour when his face and his heart were questioned, or his reputation cast in doubt.

Better stop this before it went too far. Given the tense atmosphere of the palace, I had no intention of explaining why my student had attacked two guards. "Teomitl."

He lifted his eyes – ageless, cruel, malicious – towards me. "They're wasting our time with lies."

"Yes," I said, carefully. "I think dismissing them would be enough, don't you? There's been a lot of blood shed."

For a moment I saw not him but Jade Skirt in the murky reflections within his eyes, in the way he seemed to grow taller. "There is never enough blood, priest," She whispered, Her gaze piercing my flesh, holding me squirming like a fish on a pike. Distant, rhythmic voices whispering in my mind, like songs through underwater caves and then She left, the divinity draining out of Teomitl like water through a pierced vessel.

If I was shocked for a moment, and had to pause to recover my breath, it was nothing compared to the guards. The colour had gone from their faces, leaving them as white as sacrifice victims or drowned bodies.

The veteran looked from his colleague to Teomitl, and finally spat on the ground. "Who cares about her?" he said. "She's not even Mexica. It was Xahuia-tzin, my Lord. She asked us."

Xahuia was one of Axayacatl-tzin's oldest wives, the daughter of Nezahualcoyotl, former ruler of our neighbour Texcoco, given to the Mexica Revered Speaker in marriage to cement the Triple Alliance. Her father had been a canny politician, and he had no doubt taught her all she would need to survive at Court. I was a fool; I had been so obsessed on imagining foreigners within the city that I had forgotten the most obvious, those already in the palace.

"What did she want?" I asked.

"An interview with Ocome," the veteran said, cautiously. "She had an offer to make."

"And she asked you?" Teomitl's voice was contemptuous.

The burly guard, still visibly shaken, said, "Xahuia-tzin wanted us to let her inside, and leave her alone with him. She said he wouldn't dare throw her out if she could find her way into his rooms, that turning her away at the door was one matter, but once inside, she'd have enough time to speak to him."

I didn't ask what Xahuia had wanted to speak to him about; it was obvious. Ocome, as Teomitl had said, was small and insignificant, a failure by his family's standards, except now, at the one moment when his opinion would make a difference.

"So Xahuia came here," I said. "And you left?" The body had been discovered in the middle of the night, around the Hour of Lord Death; but the death could have occurred well before that.

The guards glanced at each other. "Yes, soon after nightfall. She said she'd warn us when she was done."

And they hadn't returned until the She-Snake sought them out, which made a good four hours unaccounted for. Four hours left unguarded.

By their gazes, they knew they'd made a mistake; and I didn't need to tell them. I wondered how much Xahuia had offered, what riches she'd turned their heads with. And why she'd wanted them away, at all costs. What was it that she'd done, that warranted total privacy?

The answer seemed obvious, a little too much so.

"I see," I said.

"About the dismissal–" the burly guard started, but the veteran cut him off.

"There is something else you should know, my Lord."

I wasn't quite sure if he'd addressed me or Teomitl; but Teomitl was the one who reacted fastest, inclining his head towards the man in a grave, regal fashion. The feathers of his headdress bent, like hundreds of birds bowing at the same time. "What is it?" he asked.

"He was a man much in demand," the veteran said. His lips curled into a smirk. "Many people came to see him, the other councilmen, Tizoc-tzin, Quenami-tzin, and Acamapichtli-tzin."

The Master of the House of Darts, and my two peers. Not much surprise here.

"There were envoys, too," the veteran said. "They came two or three times, and they didn't look very friendly."

"What envoys?"

"They had blackened faces, and heron-feathers spread in a circle around their heads. It was silent inside when they came." He paused, and smiled without much amusement. "I imagined they didn't find it necessary to talk much."

"Intimidation?" Teomitl asked. The wrath of his protector Jade Skirt was creeping back into his features. Had the boy learnt nothing in a year? He seemed barely able to control his powers tonight.

"It's to be expected," I said, more dryly than I'd intended to. "Threats or rewards are the way you move the world." Even with gods – the only thing that changed were that the stakes, desires or fears had nothing in common with mortals. "When was the last time they came?"

The veteran thought for a while. "Three, four days ago. They might have come while we weren't on guard, though."

Odd. Why had they ceased coming? Had they got what they wanted?

"How long ago did Ocome shift his allegiance?" I asked Teomitl.

He made a dismissive gesture. "More than ten days ago, Acatl-tzin. That's not it."

It didn't quite make sense. Was there yet another faction, or had one of the visitors decided to send others to intimidate instead of coming in person?

Teomitl nodded to the veteran. "Thank you," he said. He looked at both of them, his eyes narrowing. "Which doesn't excuse the fault."

"My lord–" the burly guard started, but the veteran shushed him.

"I'll take it into consideration," Teomitl said. "In the meantime, you'd better think on what you've done."

He waited until we were out of earshot to speak. "Gods, what fools."

I didn't know why I felt moved to defend them. "You don't know what she offered them."

"I can guess." His face was still as harsh as carved jade. "Gold, feathers, silver. They're no better than Ocome, they'd rather trample their faces and hearts than be destitute."

"Many men would," I said, at last. As High Priest for the Dead, I oversaw inquiries into all kinds of suspicious deaths; and I knew all too well the depths to which the human soul could sink. "Not everyone has your fortitude." Or his fortune, indeed.

"That's no excuse," Teomitl said, a trifle abruptly.

I had seldom seen him like that; it was in moments like these that I felt much younger than him, less hardened to life at Court. I knew that his tutors

49

at the palace had taken him back in hand since last year, but it was as if his brother's death had cracked open a shell, revealing a pearl stuck inside, so luminous and warm that it would burn whoever touched it.

"Well, I hope it's not Xahuia," I said, as we walked out. It was evening, and the palace bustle was slowing down; the braziers' red light shone in the rising gloom. Time to find some dinner, and then head home. It had been a short day which had started late, because of the sleeplessness last night.

"Why?" He looked puzzled. "That would finish the investigation quickly."

"And launch us into a war with Texcoco." The Revered Speaker of Texcoco, Nezahual-tzin, had acceded his throne when young with the support of Tenochtitlan. At sixteen, he remained a beleaguered young man eager to prove himself to his detractors. If we executed his sister, he would at the very least want compensation for her death, if not use the pretext to unify his people against us.

"We'd win the war in any case," Teomitl said. He sounded smug. "We have twice their strength, and the better men."

"I don't think we need that kind of war on our hands right now." As usual, he thought like a warrior first and I, no matter how high I'd risen, would always think like a peasant. His numbers presumed every single able man was pulled from the fields, which would be disastrous for the harvest. Glory was all well and good but not even the warriors would have food if the harvest was not gathered.

"Acatl-tzin." He shook his head, mildly amused. I wasn't entirely sure I liked the way his careless arrogance was turning into something much more contemptuous.

But, then again, I knew exactly who he was borrowing from, and I'd never liked the man's arrogance.

His brother, Tizoc-tzin, perhaps our next Revered Speaker.

I shook my head. "In any case, we need to arrange protection for the remaining councillors." I would have done it myself, but my patron Lord Death wasn't exactly a god of protection against anything.

Teomitl barked a short laugh. "I'm not a priest."

"You're watched over by a goddess, though," I said, but I knew he was right.

Teomitl looked dubious. "I'm not really sure…"

I shook my head. "No, you're right." Any spells Teomitl worked were likely to be large and unsubtle, and shine like a beacon. They might protect, but they'd also draw unwelcome attention. "We'll offer them protection from the Duality." I was sure Ceyaxochitl wouldn't mind. She might groan and protest a little theatrically if she was in a bad mood, but she would understand the stakes.

She always did.

There were many feasts that night in the palace, loud and boisterous, the various candidates for the Turquoise-and-Gold crown showing their largesse and gathering their support. Teomitl, who disliked pomp, led us to the courtyard just outside his rooms, where we sat under the night sky, eating a simple meal of frogs and amaranth dough.

Afterwards, I headed back to my house to sleep – deeply and without dreams. The trumpets of the Sacred Precincts proclaiming the return of the Fifth Sun woke me up just before dawn. I got up, dressed, and found Teomitl already waiting for me, as much at ease as if it had been his own inner quarters he was sitting in, instead of under the lone pine tree in my courtyard.

"I could have picked you up on my way," I said.

He smiled at me sweetly, innocently. "The palace is a dangerous place, Acatl-tzin."

I snorted, but made no further comment.

"Where to?"

"The council," I said; time to see if we could get answers out of them.

We entered the palace through the gates, where Yaotl's wards shone in the sunlight, and headed towards the state room. We were perhaps halfway to it, bypassing the House of Animals where cages held everything from webbed-foot capybaras to dazzling quetzal-birds, when someone called out.

"Acatl!"

It was Quenami. The High Priest of Huitzilpochtli the Southern Hummingbird appeared to have found another set of ceremonial clothes: a heavy feather headdress falling on his back, and huge plumes hanging from his belt, spread like the wings of a hummingbird. He smiled at me with paternal condescension, never mind that he was the younger one here. "Just the man I wanted to see. Come, we need to see the council, and reassure them that nothing is wrong."

Treating me like a peer when it suited him, not that I was surprised. "We were already on our way."

If I'd expected to faze him, I was disappointed. "Perfect. Then let's go together."

I hid my grimace of distaste as best as I could, and fell in step next to him. He was going to be surprised, though, if he thought what I had to say was going to reassure the council.

We had a powerful summoner within the palace, capable of calling star-demons, and ruthlessly determined to influence the succession. Unless things went their way, I very much doubted that they would stop at the murder of one councilman.

Our only hope was to catch them before they struck again.

FOUR
The Council's Quarrels

The state room was on the ground floor, below the Revered Speaker's reception room. To reach it we crossed the courtyard, which, in daylight, was now deserted, order having presumably been restored by the She-Snake's men.

By the noise that came through the entrance-curtain, the council was locked in a bitter discussion. I did not relish having to take part in it, but I also knew that anger made evasions more difficult. I might learn things I wouldn't have found out from clear-headed men.

Teomitl touched my arm as Quenami lifted the entrance-curtain. "Acatl-tzin."

"Yes?"

"I won't be much use in here." His eyes were fierce, still lit with something close to battle-frenzy. "I'll go ask around, to see whose envoys they were. There aren't that many liveries in the palace."

I doubted that whoever had sent the envoys would have been so transparent, but, then again, I might be surprised. Subtlety wasn't the hallmark of the nobility. They were all warriors, over-obsessed with their faces and their hearts. I nodded. Teomitl straightened up in a brief salute, and strode away.

Lucky man. I'd have given much not to have to face the whole council. With a sigh, I followed Quenami inside.

Like the reception room, the state room had been calculated to impress, painted with rich frescoes of Huitzilpochtli striding forth on the battlefield, holding four spears in His left hand, and a reed shield in His right. The Southern Hummingbird's face, arms and legs were painted the deep blue of imperial tunics, and a huge eagle hovered over Him, its wings spread out over the whole of the Heavens.

The council sat on reed mats spread around the room. In the centre was a light lunch of maize wraps with mushrooms and frogs.

They were all men, most of middle age or older. One of them in particular looked old enough to have seen the founding of the Triple Alliance. He sat like a king, wrapped in intricate magical protections that clung tight to his body. No doubt he was the council's leader in magic, if not in politics.

Tizoc-tzin was still nowhere to be see, but furthest away from the entrance was the She-Snake, engaged in what looked like a heated debate with his neighbour, a middle-aged man with a round face and traits reminiscent of an older Teomitl.

Quenami released the entrance-curtain. Whatever I thought about the son of a dog, I had to at least admit that his sense of timing was impeccable. The bells jangled and jarred against each other, and every gaze in the room turned towards us.

"Ah, the High Priests," the She-Snake said. He gestured towards us. "Why don't you sit down and join us?"

"I think not." Quenami's voice was as cutting as cold obsidian. "We're not here to pour chillies on the fire."

"Are you not?" The She-Snake's voice was measured and pleasant, much in the same way that the song of an *ahuizotl* waterbeast was pleasant; a prelude to being dragged down, drowned and torn apart. "You're not part of this council, Quenami."

Quenami did not give ground. "I stand for Huitzil-pochtli, and you would do well to remember it."

The She-Snake raised an eyebrow. "So do I. Have you forgotten? In the absence of the Revered Speaker, the She-Snake is the ruler of the land. If it helps make the point, I'll start eating behind a golden screen, and forbid any man to look me in the eye. Though I'd prefer not, it would be unseemly."

During his speech, I'd been surreptitiously looking at the council, trying to gauge their mood. They sat unmoving, their gazes alternating between the She-Snake and Quenami. The overall atmosphere was tense, far too tense. Several of them were sweating, as if in fear for their lives. No wonder, with a summoner of star-demons loose in the palace.

Quenami glared at the She-Snake, obviously preparing a withering response. "Look," I started, at the same time as the She-Snake's neighbour, the round-faced man, got up.

"I don't think this petty quarrel is the reason you came here," he said, and he was looking straight at me. Now that my attention was focused on him, I could remember seeing him several times at Court. His name was Manatzpa, a brother of Axayacatl-tzin's father, making him therefore Teomitl's and Tizoc-tzin's uncle. He was Master of the Worm on the Maize Blade, among his duties was the collection of the tribute from the conquered provinces.

I shook my head. "I came with questions. As you all know, there has been a death in the palace tonight."

Several members shifted uncomfortably. Manatzpa

nodded. "Ocome. Not a popular man."

"I take it you didn't like him?" I asked him, bluntly. He sounded congenial enough, and I doubted he'd be vexed by my honesty.

"None of us did. But I, no." Manatzpa smiled. "You'll discover soon enough that I threatened to dismiss him from the council."

"Something you had no right to do." Quenami's face was filled with self-righteous outrage.

"Oh, Quenami," the She-Snake said with a shake of his head. "You're far too concerned with propriety."

"Propriety?" Quenami drew himself to his full height. "You speak of the rites of Huitzilpochtli? They have kept us alive. They have allowed us to survive She of the Silver Bells, and a century of migration in the marshes. They will allow us to survive those shadowed days, if we're willing to follow them."

More than a few council members looked embarrassed. Quenami, as subtly as ever, had reminded them that, in the first days of the Mexica Empire, the Revered Speaker had chosen his heir before his death, and the council's role had only been to approve that choice. By that logic, Tizoc-tzin should have been elected Revered Speaker without much fuss. But, over the years, the councilmen had gained influence and prerogatives, and now they would not be content with merely confirming Axayacatl-tzin's opinion.

Well, at least I knew exactly where Quenami stood. Not that I was surprised, since Tizoc-tzin had appointed him in the first place.

Manatzpa's face had turned smooth, unreadable. "Believe me, the last thing we want is chaos, Quenami-tzin." He turned again towards me. "Acatl-tzin, I imagine you still have questions?"

If glances could kill, Quenami would have struck me dead on the spot. Then again, the man had asked me to come with him, so he had only himself to blame.

"Yes. You said you had tried to get Ocome dismissed from the council. Why?"

"Oh, come, Acatl." Manatzpa smiled. "By now, you must know what Ocome was like. He was a liability to this council. His only use was as an indicator of which direction the Fifth Sun would shine. We're the high council, not stalks bending to the slightest breath of wind. He made us all a disgrace."

I could see his colleagues as he spoke, several of them nodding to the rhythm of his words, others carefully unreadable. Very few people seemed to disagree outright.

It looked like I was not going to lack suspects.

"It's hardly a reason to commit murder, though," Manatzpa said. "There are more civilised ways to solve our quarrels."

"Even when precedents aren't on your side?" This from Quenami, who had obviously not forgotten his curt dismissal.

Manatzpa did not even bother looking at him. "Not everyone considers death a viable solution. Believe me, if I'd really wanted him out of this council, I'd have found a way. Enough pressure in the right places…"

"Such as envoys?" I asked.

Manatzpa looked puzzled. "I don't understand what you mean."

"Someone sent envoys to Ocome regularly," I said. "With threats, in all likelihood. And the chances are it's someone in this room."

Or Tizoc-tzin, or Acamapichtli, or Xahuia, the princess from Texcoco. But I didn't say that aloud. I just watched them. Several members of the council were looking distinctly uncomfortable, bearing the waxy hue typical of guilty men.

There'd only been one set of envoys, though. Why

did so many of them look so nervous?

"Look," I said. "I need to speak with you, that's all. Work out where you're standing."

"That doesn't concern you." Manatzpa's voice was hard.

"It might," I said. "Someone is obviously trying to meddle in the succession. I wouldn't care if they had poisoned Ocome or stabbed him, or crushed his head. But they summoned a star-demon to do it, and that comes within my province." And Quenami's, and Acamapichtli's, but neither of them had made much effort to deal with that so far.

Manatzpa eyed me for a while, as if gauging my worth, but he did not move. At length he relented. "I suppose," he said. "But let's do this somewhere else, Acatl-tzin."

Manatzpa and I repaired to a smaller room in an adjacent courtyard, an almost bare affair, with only a few frescoes showing our ancestors within the seven caves of the heartland, before Huitzilpochtli sent them on their migration to found a city and an empire that would spread over the whole Fifth World.

He sat for a while, cross-legged, as impassive as a statue of a god or an obsidian mask, waiting for me to make the first move. I sat down on the other side of the reed mat. "You look like one of the most active members of the council."

Manatzpa inclined his head, gracefully. "If you mean that I view this appointment as more than a sinecure, yes." He must have seen my face, for he laughed. "Expecting more evasions? I dislike deception, Acatl-tzin."

I very much doubted that he'd risen so high on honesty alone. Teomitl was the only member of the imperial court I'd met who preferred bluntness to flattery, and while I couldn't help but like him for it, I was also aware that it made his survival at court much more difficult. "Let's say I believe you," I said. "If you're determined to be so honest, tell me this. Who do you support as Revered Speaker?"

Something like a smile lifted up the corners of Manatzpa's thin lips. "Tizoc-tzin is a weak fool. He has the support of the army's core, but not much else. He lacks the... stature to fill the role he wants to claim. The foreign princeling – Xahuia's son – he has her support and that of her followers, but he is a spoiled brat, nothing like the ruler we'd wish for.

"The She-Snake," and here Manatzpa sounded almost regretful, "he has the ambition, and the greatness within him. But it would set an uncomfortable precedent. His father refused the honour of the Turquoise-and-Gold Crown, and justly so. There is a place for the She-Snake, and one for the Revered Speaker. Male and female, violence and order-keeping; you cannot mix both."

"And the High Priests?" I asked, fascinated in spite of myself.

"We both know where Quenami stands." Manatzpa sounded amused. "Especially after tonight. You, Acatl-tzin, obviously have no ambition. " He lifted a hand to forestall any objection I might have. "Understand me, I say this as a compliment. To keep the balance is knowing your place in the order of things. I respect this."

That we could agree on, if nothing else. "And Acamapichtli?"

"Tlaloc's High Priest is also ambitious. The Storm Lord made a grab for power last year, after all. Though Acamapichtli's participation has not been proved, I wouldn't swear that he has the best interests of the Fifth World at stake."

Me neither. Last year, he had also been quite busy

trying to convict my brother Neutemoc on false evidence. I'd have to speak with him, if I could keep my calm long enough to do that. Better purge the abscess before it could fester.

"So you stand for no one?" I asked. "To have no candidate–"

"Is to wish for the star-demons to walk among us, I know. But consider, Acatl-tzin. The Revered Speaker is the embodiment of Huitzilpochtli, the vessel through which the Southern Hummingbird's divine powers can spread into the Fifth World. A flawed vessel just means a flawed protection. Is that what you wish for?"

"No," I said. It was one of the reasons I couldn't wholly support Tizoc-tzin, even though I knew he had been Axayacatl-tzin's choice of heir. "But still, every day that we temporise looking for perfection…"

Manatzpa inclined his head. "Make no mistake. If I can't have what I wish for, I'll settle for a flawed vessel rather than none at all. But I'd rather try to sway the council towards a more suitable choice of candidate."

"Who?" I asked. I couldn't see any other suitable candidate, anyone who'd have the stature of a Revered Speaker.

Manatzpa looked away. "Forgive me. To name him would be pointless, since he has so little support."

I frowned. "I don't want mysterious factions within the council, Manatzpa-tzin. I need to know–"

"You need to know who killed Ocome," Manatzpa said. "I can give you my word that my candidate isn't involved in this. He couldn't have been, since he doesn't even know of my support for him."

"Your word?"

"As I said, I despise deception. I'll swear it by my face, by my heart. May I lose both if I have been deceitful."

I watched him, trying to gauge his sincerity. His eyes shone in his moon-shaped face, burning with a fire I wasn't sure how to interpret. "Fine," I said, not sure if I could believe him. "But if it comes to a point when I need his name…"

"Come back and speak with me," Manatzpa said. "I'll help you. My word."

"I see," I said. "What else can you tell me about the council?"

He appeared relieved by my change of subject, and launched into a tirade on the various members, dissecting them in small, neat sketches. He was obviously a keen observer of men, and he had had enough time to read the currents of the council.

There wasn't much to be learnt. The council was nearly evenly split between the She-Snake and Tizoctzin, with a few supporting Xahuia. It was a bleak picture, promising endless days of debates before a clear vote could even be reached, days during which the star-demons would grow closer and closer to us, not to mention opportunities for the summoner to call more demons to roam the palace.

"You have no influence…" I started.

Manatzpa spread his long, elegant hands on the reed mat, palms up in a gesture of powerlessness. "I'm just a man, Acatl-tzin. I speak for the council in matters of law, which makes my word respected. But, at times like this, it's not enough to make them remember anything but their own good."

Great. I prayed that the Duality was indeed watching over us, because the days ahead promised to be fraught and messy at best.

"And about Ocome?" I asked.

"I've told you what I knew about Ocome. Truth is," he smiled at that, "most people would have leapt at the chance to get rid of him. A vote is a vote, but one you can't trust..."

"Did anyone have a quarrel with him?" I asked. "I mean, more than usual?"

Manatzpa thought for a while. "I know the She-Snake had words with him. But then again, he had words with everyone."

Clearly, Manatzpa liked the She-Snake. I could understand his argument why he didn't want the She-Snake to claim the Turquoise-and-Gold Crown, but all the same, it must have pained him, because here he was, still trying to defend the man in spite of everything else.

I didn't trust the She-Snake, who was far too smooth and too ruthless. And I was definitely going to make sure I caught him and asked him about this quarrel with Ocome.

"I see," I said. I talked more with him, but got nothing else that was useful. "Thank you. Can you see if the other councilmen will speak with me now?"

Several hours later, I had not learnt much more. Most of the council members were of the same mould as Manatzpa, men of imperial blood bypassed by the succession and either proud of or resigned to their subservient roles.

Of the frightened ones, the only thing I was able to find out was that there had indeed been threats. The same envoys, perhaps, though they wouldn't admit to anything. Except for Manatzpa and the old magician, they seemed in fear for their lives. Hardly surprising, when one has enjoyed all their lives the riches and privileges of power without responsibility, to suddenly face that much danger must have been sobering.

The old magician was much calmer, and even his protective spells were nowhere as powerful I'd originally thought, mainly for protection against human attacks, nothing that would stand against a star-demon or other creature.

"I grow weary of the strife," he said to me, bending to lift his bowl of chocolate.

"It's not really going to get better as time passes," I said.

He shook his head, a little sadly. "No. Men have always loved power. I've seen many things in my years, Acatl-tzin."

His name was Echichilli, and he was Master of Raining Blood, keeper of the rites and ceremonies, another watcher who made sure the balance was respected. He was a risen noble – a man who had joined the council on battle prowess and not birth – and he insisted on calling me by the honorific "tzin", even though he was my superior both in position and in years. In many ways, he reminded me of my old mentor, a man long since dead. In other circumstances, I might have been glad to call him a friend.

"I need to know what's happening," I said.

He merely shook his head again. "The Turquoise-and-Gold Crown is a powerful lure, and there are many factions."

"One of them killed Ocome."

He closed his eyes for a brief moment and his face pulled up in genuine grief. "I know. But I can't help you there, Acatl-tzin."

"Can't," I said, "because you don't know, or because you don't want to?"

He looked at me, thoughtful. "He bent the way of the wind, and made many enemies. His death isn't surprising." And that was all he would say, no matter how hard I pressed him.

It was predictable, but neither Quenami nor the She-Snake were of much use – beyond the latter's oral confirmation that he was indeed setting himself up as a potential candidate for the Turquoise-and-Gold Crown, an admission made with a shrug of his shoulders, looking me in the eye as if it was the most natural thing.

As to his quarrel with Ocome, the She-Snake admitted it in much the same careless fashion, in such an uninvolved way that, in spite of knowing how good an actor he was, I still found it very hard to believe he cared about Ocome at all – about his vote, or indeed about the man. It was as if Ocome had been too small, too petty to even register in the She-Snake's field of view.

By the time I wrapped up the last abortive interview, evening had fallen. The stars shone in the sky, larger and more luminous than the night before, an unwelcome reminder of the chaos and devastation that would lie ahead if we didn't act soon.

After a brief and very much belated meal, I was speaking with Manatzpa about possible security measures, up to and including the use of Duality spells, when the noise of a commotion reached us, loud voices and angry tones, coming from one of the nearby courtyards. Given the funereal quiet of the palace, that was surprising…

"Acatl-tzin," Manatzpa said, his voice cutting through my thoughts. "You'll want to head over there."

"I don't understand…"

And then I caught a familiar voice, raised in withering anger.

Teomitl.

What in the Fifth World had he got himself embroiled into this time?

He was easy enough to find: the noise came from the Imperial Chambers, at the entrance of which had gathered a crowd of curious onlookers; noblemen made idle by the absence of the court, wearing all their jade and feather finery, a mass of protective spells jostling each other on the narrow adobe staircase leading up to the terrace.

The She-Snake and his guards were pushing them back, attempting to maintain order within the palace, but curiosity was the worst emotion to hold at bay.

Snatches of the argument drifted my way: "...as weak as a dog...", "deceived us..."

I had no idea what was going on, but obviously my place was upstairs, before Teomitl committed the irreparable.

I slashed my earlobes, muttered a brief prayer to my patron Mictlantecuhtli, and let the cold of the underworld spread like a cloak around me – the keening of ghosts, the embrace of Grandmother Earth, the descent into flowing waters, the freezing winds atop the Mountains of Obsidian and the ultimate cold, the one that seized the souls in the presence of Lord Death and His consort.

Thus armed, I pushed my way through the crowd. The protective spells hissed and faded away at my touch, and more than one nobleman grimaced as the cold, skeletal fingers of Lord Death settled on the back of their neck, a reminder of the fate that awaited them should they fail to die in battle or on the sacrificial altar.

The She-Snake nodded grimly at me as I cleared the top of the stairs, an unspoken acknowledgment that I was responsible for my student, and that this was the only reason his guards were letting me pass.

Inside, the body of Axayacatl-tzin looked intact – a relief, I had feared the worst. My priests had scattered to the corners of the room, with the pale faces of the powerless. The offering priest Palli, who had been in charge of the ritual, stood a little to the side with his hands clenched, trying to decide if he should intervene.

At the centre before the reed mat stood two men, glaring at each other like warriors about to launch into battle.

One, as was already clear, was Teomitl, with the harsh cast of the goddess Jade Skirt subtly modifying his features, and one hand already on his *macuahitl* sword. The other was Acamapichtli, High Priest of Tlaloc, who looked as if he'd been mauled by a jaguar, and intent on striking back. The air around him was as dense and as heavy as before a storm.

I couldn't stand Quenami, but I had to admit he had a point about the power of entrances. I released the curtain with as much force as possible, sending the silver-bells sewn in it crashing into each other, a noise that could not be ignored. Only then did I stride into the room to confront them.

They had both turned to face me with murder in their eyes. I might have shrunk before their combined might, if I had not been so angry. "What in the Fifth World do you think you're doing?" I asked, looking from one to the other. "For the Duality's sake, this room belongs to Lord Death now, for the vigil, and I won't have you desecrate it with whatever quarrel you have with each other."

"Acatl-tzin." Teomitl was quivering with contained rage. "You don't understand."

I was getting tired of that particular line. I jerked a finger in the direction of the entrance-curtain. "You have the whole palace gathered outside, wondering what all the shouting is about. And, as a matter of fact, so am I."

"He–" Teomitl started, but Acamapichtli cut him off.

"Your student," he said with freezing hauteur, "your student has just accused me of a grave crime. I cannot tolerate such groundless persecution." He looked at me as if the whole blame for that rested solely on my shoulders.

"Groundless?" Teomitl snorted. "Look at me, Acamapichtli, and tell me you don't know about the envoys."

"I sent no such people," Acamapichtli said.

I was slowly beginning to work out what this might be about, even though I wasn't sure how we had got to this place.

"Dark blue paint and heron feathers in a circle around the face," Teomitl said, with the deceptive stillness of the eagle before it swoops down. "It's an old uniform that hasn't seen service since the days of Revered Speaker Moctezuma. But my comrades have a good memory." His hand, wrapped around his obsidian-studded sword, lifted slightly, as if to draw it out. "And now I find you performing magic in this room, over my brother's corpse?"

Magic? The room appeared normal, with no trace of the faint white-and-blue which was associated with Tlaloc's spells.

"I assume there is an explanation for all this," I said, slowly.

But Acamapichtli was not going to let me play peacemaker. He lifted his chin in a supreme expression of offence. "I'm not obliged to provide any explanation."

I'd started by feeling angry at Teomitl for the wholly unsubtle approach, but by now I was beginning to understand how matters might have degenerated. Acamapichtli had a very easy way of grating on one's nerves, and Southern Hummingbird blind me if I let him get away with it.

"As a matter of fact, you do have to explain things," I said. "In the absence of goodwill from either you or

Quenami, I'm the sole person responsible for the keeping of the boundaries. And anyone who has been in contact with Ocome could be the key to solving his murder." A small, tentative way of soothing his wounded pride; I very much doubted it would be enough, and I was right.

Acamapichtli wrapped himself in his cloak, and strode towards the exit, not looking at me or at Teomitl. "I owe no explanation to anyone, Acatl, and least of all to *you*." He all but spat the name. "The Fifth World is far more resilient than you credit."

"As you would know, having tried to unseat it," I snapped, unable to contain myself.

Acamapichtli's gaze froze. I had gone too far. "I serve my god. I uphold the Fifth World's law. You won't accuse me of anything beyond that."

"You're not exactly making efforts to defend yourself."

"An innocent man shouldn't have to," Acamapichtli said.

This time, he was the one who went too far. "I don't read minds. And there are no innocents. You're all embroiled in one intrigue or another," I said, more forcefully than I'd intended to. "Don't you dare parade your purity before me."

"And you your sickening self-righteousness." Acamapichtli spat on the ground, without even a gesture asking for the forgiveness of the dead Revered Speaker, whose funeral room he had just soiled. "You're no better than the rest of us, Acatl."

"Of course he is," Teomitl said, in the growing silence.

I stood unmoving, trying not to give in to the wave of contempt and hatred which spread over me for this man, who was not even fit to wear the robes of the lowest priest in the service of Tlaloc, not even fit to sweep the floors of the Great Temple. But this was not the time for such divisions, not a time for quarrels, not the place. I couldn't afford to be sucked into his game.

My nails dug into my hands, sending spikes of pain up my arm. "If you persist in this obstruction, I'll have no choice," I said, more calmly.

"You have no choice," Acamapichtli said.

Other than letting him go? I didn't think so. I went on, as if heedless of his words, "I'll refer this to the She-Snake, as current head of the state, representative of the Southern Hummingbird amongst us." I didn't trust the She-Snake; but I'd already seen that he didn't support Acamapichtli.

Acamapichtli's beady eyes widened slightly, but then he laughed. "Do try, Acatl, do try. I'll enjoy seeing you making a fool of yourself."

Then he swept out, the curtain falling back over the entrance in a slow, almost peaceful tinkle of metal bells.

And that might have been it, save that, in the brief moment before the curtain swept down, I caught a glimpse of the silhouette standing at the entrance, which slouched too much to be a guard, and was much too tall to be the She-Snake.

"Acatl-tzin," Teomitl started.

I lifted a hand to silence him. An uncomfortable few moments passed; and then the watcher outside grew bored of our inactivity. The entrance-curtain lifted again to admit Quenami in all the finery of his rank as High Priest of Huitzilpochtli, smiling as widely as a jaguar that has found prey.

"Acatl," he said. "What a coincidence to find you here."

"Indeed," I said. And, tired of evasions, "how long have you been outside, Quenami?"

He smiled even more widely. His teeth were the same deep blue as his costume, meticulously dyed. "Long enough."

"Playing spy like a merchant looking for a bargain?" Teomitl asked.

I lifted a hand again before the insult went too far. Quenami looked entirely too satisfied, which meant nothing good for either of us.

"Confirming an opinion. But, as they say, the game was played long before I got here." He looked at both of us in turn, his eyes narrowing in what might have been disapproval, or disappointment.

I hadn't thought anyone could get on my nerves more than Acamapichtli, but Quenami was running a close second. "What do you want, Quenami? There's no need to dance around each other like warriors on the gladiator stone."

He pretended to look thoughtful, even though he had to know he couldn't keep us waiting forever. "No, there might not be. A message was entrusted to me, and I pass it on to you both. Tizoc-tzin will see both of you."

"It's evening now," Teomitl pointed out. "Surely my brother can wait—"

Quenami shook his head. "Now, Teomitl-tzin."

Given the unhealthy joy that danced in Quenami's eyes, I was certain that Tizoc-tzin would not congratulate us. In fact, I might be happy to get out of there with my rank intact. With Axayacatl-tzin's demise, both he, as Master of the House of Darts, and the She-Snake received the right to name High Priests. While the She-Snake would keep me around for the sake of appearances, Tizoc-tzin, who hated anything to do with the clergy, would leap at the first chance to dismiss me.

FIVE

Imperial Blood

Tizoc-tzin's quarters were in a courtyard on the same layout as the Imperial Chambers: a wide terrace over two state rooms where his followers sat, gorging themselves on amaranth seeds, and cooked fowls. It was... not exactly indecent, I guessed, not exactly forbidden, but still unseemly, with the palace in mourning.

Upstairs massed mostly warriors – Eagle Knights in their cloaks of feathers, and Jaguar Knights in full regalia, with their helmets in the shape of a jaguar's head. They watched Quenami and I pass by with predators' smiles. The division between priests and warriors ran deep. They saw us as uptight fools, we saw them as arrogant men obsessed with appearances. Even Teomitl, who paid less attention to this than other warriors, proudly bore the orange scorpion cloak and the shaved head that denoted him as a Leading Youth.

The entrance-curtain was wide open, even though the evening was colder than usual. Inside, bare-chested warriors lounged on mats, picking frogs, fish and other delicacies from bowls set in front of them.

Quenami wove his way through the crowd with supreme ease, stopping here and there to greet a particular table, ignoring their gazes of frank contempt. Teomitl's face was frozen in ill-concealed anger, and he walked with the haughty pride of a sacrifice victim.

At the back of the room, five windows opened on another courtyard, a garden from which came the chatter of birds. The wind, blowing through the apertures, brought in the smell of the distant jungle, strong enough to overwhelm the aroma of copal incense.

Tizoc-tzin was seated on a mat behind a wooden screen so polished it shone with yellow reflections. Beside me I felt Teomitl stiffen. "Does he wear turquoise too?" he whispered angrily.

As it turned out, Tizoc-tzin – a middle-aged man with sallow skin – did not wear turquoise, but a deep blue that was uncomfortably close to the imperial colour. I couldn't help but notice that several of the warriors we'd passed had also removed their sandals out of reverence.

"Ah, our High Priest for the Dead. What a pleasure," he said. He dismissed Quenami with a wave of his long fingers, and then turned his attention back to me.

He had never made me comfortable, but in a very different way than the She-Snake. I could trust the She-Snake to act in his own interests; but with Tizoc-tzin I never knew if he was going to do something just out of caprice.

His eyes were two small, black beads that pierced me like a spear. He considered me for a moment with growing anger. "I've always known that priests couldn't be trusted. You have just exceeded my expectations."

"The star-demons –"

"Save your breath." His voice had an aura of command: cutting, merciless. "I know all about the star-demons, Acatl."

"Then you'll know this isn't the time for quarrels."

"On the contrary." Tizoc-tzin smiled, an expression that didn't reach his eyes. "This is a time of flux. What better opportunity for change?"

Oh by the gods, what a fool. But a scrap of self-preservation prevented me from saying that aloud. "My Lord—"

"I know everything there is to know about you, and you have gone too far."

"Too far?" I asked. I might have, with Acamapichtli, but there was no way he could know about that, not unless Quenami could communicate by thought alone.

Tizoc-tin's gaze moved to Teomitl. "Don't act so innocently, Acatl. Did you think I would never realise? A prince will marry a noblewoman or a princess, never the daughter of peasants."

So *that* was what it was all about. How dare he? "If you refer to my sister," I said, coolly, "she is no longer the daughter of peasants. She is the sister of a Jaguar Knight, and of the High Priest for the Dead."

Teomitl's face had gone pale. I had to admit we did not have much to stand on. Mihmatini would have made a wonderful concubine, but to reach any higher would have been the worst kind of arrogance.

"The daughter of peasants," Tizoc-tzin repeated. "And you... you have the audacity to think her fit to join the imperial family? It is not enough to have my brother in your thrall, always following you. You must have more, Acatl. You place your pawns everywhere advantageous and hope that I won't notice. Well, I'm no fool, and I have seen."

I'd listened in growing perplexity, and then anger. "You accuse me wrongly. I have never had any intention of holding power in this court."

"That was the game you played at first." Tizoc-tzin's face had turned the colour of muddy earth. "Last year, when you came before me, having never set a foot at Court. But that's no longer true."

"I have the best interests of my order and of the Fifth World at heart."

"No doubt, no doubt." His face was creased in a smirk I longed to wipe off.

Star-demons take the man, how could he not see that I was sincere? Out of all those he had to face within the Imperial Court, I was possibly the one with the least reason to set myself against him…

Except, of course, for the treacherous little voice that kept whispering that the She-Snake and Manatzpa were right, that he was no man fit to be Revered Speaker, no man fit to rule Huitzilpochtli's empire.

"My Lord…"

His eyes were on me. I saw then that he'd dismiss me. That out of his rivals, I was the one enjoying the least support, an isolated priest whom no one would miss. That was the reason why Quenami, the Storm Lord's lightning blind him, had looked so happy, one fewer man in his path.

"Enough."

It was Teomitl who had spoken. For the first time since entering the room, his voice had the same cutting edge as Tizoc-tzin's. "Brother, look at you. You disgrace yourself."

"So says the man who follows him," Tizoc-tzin snapped.

"So says the man who sees clearly," Teomitl said. "Do you truly wish to dismiss the High Priest for the Dead, at a time like this? What an auspicious way to start your reign."

Tizoc-tzin did not move, but his whole stance hardened. "You're young," he said to Teomitl. "You understand nothing of politics."

"No," Teomitl said. "And I'm not sure I ever will."

Tizoc grimaced. "You'll have to. Can't you see?" His voice softened, no longer the ruler chastising his subjects. "In less than a week, you'll be Master of the House of Darts. In a few dozen years…"

"The Revered Speaker is anointed by Huitzilpochtli," Teomitl said, at last, and Tizoc-tzin, who believed more in men than in gods, grimaced. "He leads us forth into battle, to extend the boundaries of the Mexica Empire from sea to sea. This isn't about politics."

"You'd marry her, then?" Tizoc-tzin's lips had thinned to a slash across his face. "The little peasants' daughter?"

If that was intended as a reconciliation – a shared moment of prejudice – it failed utterly. Teomitl's face froze, took on the cast of jade. I reached out and squeezed his arm hard enough to bruise. "No, you fool," I whispered.

"What I choose to do or not to do does not belong to you," Teomitl said. "Nothing has been decreed yet, brother."

"It will not be long." I wondered where Tizoc-tzin's confidence came from, when the council was so split, and one of his own followers had just been slaughtered?

"I thought you'd know," Teomitl's voice could have frozen water, "you who will dedicate yourself to the Southern Hummingbird, to the Smoking Mirror, the gods of all that is fluid and impermanent. Nothing in the Fifth World is ever certain."

"Oh, you're mistaken." Tizoc-tzin's smile, for once, was sincere, and quietly confident. "Very much mistaken, brother."

"Then we'll see, won't we?" Teomitl put his hands palms up; and then turned them towards the floor in a clink of jade and metal. "How the dice fall. Meanwhile–"

Tizoc-tzin's gaze rested on me, dark and angry. "Meanwhile, I will let things rest. But be assured, Acatl, I won't forget."

Neither would I.

I came out of our interview with Tizoc-tzin shaking like reeds in the wind. Teomitl, who viewed all such displays as cowardice, appeared unmoved. It was only when he stopped in a small courtyard and just stood there, staring at the sky, that I knew he had not been unaffected.

"He's not a bad man," he said.

Around us, the night was cold and heavy, the stars above pulsing softly, the owls hooting in the night, the faint smell of copal and scented sweatbaths. "I'm not sure," I said.

"You don't know him. He was always like this." His hands clenched. "He can't see the world through other people's eyes, but he knows his own faults, all too well."

No, I didn't know Tizoc-tzin. But, somehow, I doubted that Teomitl, who was ten years his junior and had grown up in the seclusion of a priests' school, would know him any better. "He's your brother," I said. I'd do the same for any of mine. Heavens, I'd even defended my brother Neutemoc last year, even though I'd believed him to be as guilty as the evidence indicated. "Your loyalty–"

"It's not about loyalty." Teomitl paced in the courtyard, around a small basin decorated with coloured stones. His eyes were still on the sky. "I know how he is."

"You didn't grow up together–"

"No, of course not. But he's grooming me to be Master of the House of Darts in his stead."

"That doesn't mean–"

"I'm not a fool!" He stabbed the empty air with his right hand.

"I never said you were." I'd never seen him in such a state, and it worried me. Throughout the previous day, he'd gone into the palace, more or less picking quarrels with everyone he met. He seemed to have reverted to the prickly boy Ceyaxochitl had entrusted to me a year ago, one who had "grown up like a wild flower", as she had said. It was as if all my teachings, all my exercises, had been for nothing. Was it Axayacatl-tzin's death? His brother had been Revered Speaker for most of Teomitl's life. It would be hard to admit the world was about to change irretrievably.

"You don't understand. I take his lessons, and I learn." His voice was softer now, almost spent.

I asked the question he wanted me to ask. "And what do you learn, Teomitl?"

"Not the lessons he wants to teach me." He stopped pacing, and would not look at me. "I learn that he stopped trusting others a long time ago. I learn that he has enemies and sycophants, but no friends. I learn," and his voice was a whisper by now, "that power took him and gnawed him from the inside out, and that he is but a frightened shell, that the only goal he can still dream of is to sit on Axayacatl's mat. Everything else tastes like ashes."

I was silent for a while. "That's what you learnt. But not what I see." Not to mention that this gave him a motivation to influence the vote, perhaps to the point of using supernatural help to do it.

"Acatl-tzin–"

I had always been honest with him, and even when it came to this moment, I could not give him some comforting lie. "No," I said. "I can only believe what I see."

He looked at me for a while. His hands were still, preternaturally so. "I see. I see."

"Teomitl–"

"No, you're right. It's not that at all, and I am a fool. Good night, Acatl-tzin."

"Teomitl!"

But he was already gone.

I remained for a while, sitting in the courtyard, wondering what I could have said that would have made things go differently. I didn't like those bleak moods, or the quick way he took offence. He'd always been susceptible, but tonight he had looked as though his nerves were rubbed raw.

Something was wrong, but I couldn't work out what.

Footsteps on the stones tore me from my reflection. Looking up, I saw Ceyaxochitl looming over me, her slight silhouette highlighted by moonlight. "I thought I'd find you here."

"Here?" I said, gesturing to the small courtyard. The only remarkable thing about it was that it contained us both.

"In the palace." She grimaced, and slid to sit cross-legged next to me on the warm stones. "I've told you before: you don't get enough sleep."

"I should think I've outgrown the need for a mother."

Ceyaxochitl's gaze grew pensive. "Yes, I should think you have. Most impressively."

A small, almost muted jab. Even though they'd both been dead for years, my parents had loomed large over my life, until the previous year, when I'd finally realised I was no longer beholden to them. "What do you want, Ceyaxochitl? I assume you didn't come here to talk."

She shrugged. "Perhaps I did. Perhaps I do care about your welfare."

Now she scared me. The last time Ceyaxochitl had interfered in my life, she'd got me nominated as High Priest, a position I didn't want and didn't particularly appreciate. That I'd grown into it over the years didn't change the original intent. "You can't get me higher than this," I said. I tried not to think of Teomitl, my student, the boy-prince who would one day become Revered Speaker.

Ceyaxochitl smiled, the lines of her face softening in the moonlight. "We'll see."

I hesitated, loath to break the moment by focusing on murder and intrigue once again. "I promised the councilmen protection from the Duality, for those who desired it."

"We can provide," Ceyaxochitl said. "Though I imagine many of them will already have their own protections."

"Echichilli?" I said, thinking of the old councillor.

"He was always a strong magician." There was an expression on her face I found hard to read in the moonlight, and then I realised it was nostalgia. "A good man, one of the few on the council."

"The others…"

"The others like the sound of their own voice, and the power they hold – at ordinary times, and in circumstances like these. But you knew this already."

"Perhaps," I said, non-committal. "What did you find?"

"Not much. Quenami moves to Tizoc-tzin's tunes, but I shouldn't think this is much of a surprise. The boy always did like power and pomp."

I wondered who in the palace she didn't know – whom she couldn't dissect as effectively as she dissected me. It was a terrifying thought.

"How goes the courtship?" she asked.

There was only one courtship I was aware of. "Well, I suppose," I said, cautiously. I had not seen Mihmatini in a while. "Enthusiastically, knowing Teomitl."

"But Tizoc-tzin doesn't approve, does he?" Ceyaxo-chitl's flat gaze bored into mine.

"I shouldn't think you need to be a calendar priest to divine that," I said.

"He's a fool, Acatl." She appeared unconcerned by the fact she'd just uttered treasonous words. "The Master of the House of Darts is a military leader, first and foremost. He plans our campaigns, he oversees the movements of troops within and without the capital. Tizoc-tzin uses it for prestige, and as a stepping stone to the Turquoise-and-Gold Crown."

"He'll be Revered Speaker, soon," I said slowly.

"Yes." She closed her eyes. "Yes. There is that. Well, there isn't anything you or I can do about that, sadly." She rose and walked slowly, leaning on her cane, which rapped on the ground. She'd always looked old and frail, but I'd never seen her move so cautiously. "Ceyaxochitl?"

"Yes?"

"Can you do it?" Could she hold us together, keep the star-demons from the Fifth World?

The woman I'd known all my adult life would have shaken her head and berated me for being a silly, sentimental fool. This one – the old, weary one by my side – simply shook her head. "I don't know. Things have changed. The previous Guardian was still young when Moctezuma-tzin died, and her husband was still alive."

"Husband?" I asked, startled. Most priests were celibate. I'd assumed the Guardian would be, too.

"Of course." Her voice was light, ironic again. "The Duality is male and female, the creator principle that drives the Fifth World. Guardians can marry."

"And you–"

She shrugged. "When I was very young. But it didn't last."

I tried to imagine her with a man in tow, an equal, not a slave, a man she'd have loved. My mind refused to wrap itself around the idea. I had always known her old and single, as a quasi-mentor figure. It was hard to discard all this. "Did he die?"

"Weak heart."

"I'm sorry–"

"Don't be, Acatl." She didn't sound grieved; but of course it would have happened decades ago.

"But there is only one Guardian. I've never heard–"

"He was a symbol," Ceyaxochitl said, patiently. "Of the male principle. Not a Guardian, not even a priest. But when you don't have the luxury of living blood, symbols turn out to be important. Vital."

"And…"

"And the signs are here," Ceyaxochitl said. "As I told you. I'm an old, lone woman past childbearing age. Hardly the ideal vessel for the Duality's powers."

"We've always held." I didn't need to say "because of you", because she already knew it.

"We have. And everything comes to an end, as you are uniquely placed to know."

"Don't mock me," I said. "The stakes–"

"The stakes will always be high," Ceyaxochitl said. "But I might not rise to it. Be prepared, Acatl."

She left the courtyard without looking back. I stood there, shaking, a hollow opening in my belly. If the Guardian couldn't hold us…

In my temple, I found my second-in-command Ichtaca anxiously waiting for me outside. "Palli has been looking for you all over the palace and the Sacred Precinct. He says he has some information you sent him for."

The sorcerers on the registers, and the room search.

"I'll see him now," I said. I was tired, but this was more important. I had to see Palli or I'd lose his respect.

Ichtaca led me through the courtyard, past the numerous examination rooms that opened into the frescoed walls. Students were crowding around one of the entrances. I could hear snatches of sound from inside, a lesson on how bodies changed after death, and how to look for the signs of poison.

"How did it go?" Ichtaca asked.

"Not well." I couldn't quite keep the frustration out of my voice. "They're all bickering about who gets to be Revered Speaker."

Ichtaca's gaze drifted upwards, towards the star-studded sky.

"I know about the star-demons. But they don't seem to." There was one star there which shone more brightly than the others: He who was the Evening Star and the Morning Star, Quetzalcoatl the Feathered Serpent, the God of Knowledge and Creation – the god of all priests, whoever they served. He was the only one on our side, but His powers, like those of all the gods, were constrained in the Fifth World.

"Not a time for games," Ichtaca said. "But, if that's their will…"

I had no constructive answer, merely a prayer to the Duality that we weather the transition without too much bloodshed.

Palli, the offering priest in charge of Axayacatl-tzin's funeral, was waiting cross-legged in one of the smaller examination rooms, under a fresco that showed the progress of the soul through the levels of Mictlan, from the river that marked the boundary, to the ninth level, to Lord Death's throne. The god sat, bathed in blood, on a chair made of bones, skeletal and hunched, with his ribs poking out of His chest, His clawed hands empty.

Palli rose when we came in. "Acatl-tzin. Ichtaca-tzin."

I bowed, a fraction, as befitted our respective functions. I hated the formalities, but I knew he and Ichtaca lived by them. "I apologise. I ran into some trouble in the palace, but that's not an excuse."

His gaze suggested, very clearly, that I was High Priest, and that it wasn't his place to question me, an attitude I'd always found unhealthy. At least Ichtaca always made it clear when I erred. I sighed. "What have you found?"

He handed me a list written on maguey paper in a neat hand, every glyph aligned and detailed, as if it had been written by a high-level scribe. Names and dates.

"I thought you might need to know birth-signs," Palli said.

A man's birth-sign determined his access to different kinds of magics and his innate talent. I had been born on a day One Reed, which put me under the gaze of the Curved Point of Obsidian, Lord of Justice, of the Feathered Serpent, and of course of Lord Death.

I scanned the list. Many names I knew. The She-Snake was near the top, as was Echichilli the old councilman; and even Manatzpa. In fact, most of the council was.

There were some notable absences, though. "Xahuia?" I asked.

Palli shook his head. "The Texcocan wife? She wouldn't be in here, Acatl-tzin, and neither would her retinue. They seldom get out of the women's quarters, and never out of the palace, so there is no need."

No need to register them, because they'd never need to enter the palace again. I smoothed the paper carefully. "I see." One name caught my attention. "Who is Pezotic?"

Palli bent over me, trying to read the glyphs upside-down. I turned the paper towards him, and pointed to one name near the bottom.

"Master on the Edge of the Water?" Palli asked. "That's a councilman's title, isn't it?"

"It sounds like one," I said, slowly. "But I would have remembered if I'd interviewed him." And I had interviewed the whole council. Manatzpa and Echichilli had told me as much.

"There are many other names on the list," Ichtaca said, in a conciliatory tone. "Surely you need not waste your time with this one."

"If he's a councilman and he's not there anymore, then I want to know. And I want to know why." Quenami had made it clear one did not demote councilmen, but it seemed like this had in fact happened. I'd have to ask Manatzpa next time I saw him.

I looked over the list some more, but I couldn't see anything else that was surprising. "Thank you," I said to Palli, and folded the paper back into a fan-shape. "What about the rooms?"

Even before he grimaced, I'd guessed what his answer would be. "I can only spare six or seven priests, and it's a large palace. If you want, I can get more. "

"No," I said. "I appreciate it, but we can't afford to let the Revered Speaker go without funeral rites, or leave the city unattended. Do what you can."

Palli nodded. "I might be able to send more priests if we rearrange the rituals a bit," he said thoughtfully. "Make sure that there's someone on guard all the time."

We left him to think things through. Ichtaca and I walked back to the circle we'd drawn on the ground on the previous night, a lifetime ago, to check on the wards. As Ichtaca said, best make sure the city stood; we could see about the Court later on.

After we were done I checked on the temple's doings – on a few ongoing investigations into suspicious deaths, the death-vigils and the few offerings we got from the living. But my mind was elsewhere, and I retired to my house soon after the Hour of the Lord of Princes, with the night still young. Teomitl had been right about at least one thing – better get some sleep while I could.

I woke up briefly to the blare of conch-shells that announced the rise of the Fifth Sun then sank back into darkness.

When I woke again it was mid-morning, and the bustle of the Sacred Precinct filtered into the courtyard – the prayers and the chants, the drum-beats that accompanied the sacrifices, the familiar smell of incense mingling with that of animal blood.

I knelt and sliced my earlobes to make my own offerings – to Lord Death, and to the Fifth Sun, He who would see us through those difficult times, for it looked as though His human servants were sadly lacking.

I sat for a while in the courtyard, under the lone pine tree, chewing a day-old maize flatbread, the only edible thing I had left in the house. I should have thought of asking Ichtaca for supplies on the previous evening, but I had been too preoccupied with Teomitl.

The Storm Lord blind him, what was wrong with the boy?

Perhaps he had outgrown me. After all, I had known that he couldn't remain my student – or, indeed, Mihmatini's suitor – forever, that he was destined for politics and war, wholly outside my purview. Tizoc-tzin had taken him under his protection, and was teaching him what was necessary.

Still, it wasn't as if I could shed my responsibility when it suited me. A man who would pick quarrels with the most powerful individuals in the Mexica Empire was not yet an adult and would not rise far, even through feats of arms. If even Tizoc-tzin, a canny politician, could not teach Teomitl that then it was also my responsibility to try. Perhaps he would listen to me more than to his brother.

Admittedly it did not look very likely at this point.

The sky was clear and blue, its colour as crisp and as vivid as a new fresco. I walked to my temple, intending to pick up Palli before going back to the palace. Instead, the first person I saw when entering the courtyard was Yaotl, Ceyaxochitl's personal slave, in the midst of a conversation with Ichtaca.

My sandals on the paved stones of the entrance made enough noise that they stopped talking. "There he is," Ichtaca said.

Yaotl turned, his embroidered cloak rippling in the breeze. "Acatl-tzin."

I braced myself for more sarcasm, but his face under the blue-and-black paint was grim, an expression I had never seen on him before.

Fear reached inside my chest and closed a fist around my heart. "What is it?"

"It's Mistress Ceyaxochitl. She's been poisoned."

SIX

Princess of Texcoco

The Duality House, unlike the palace, was silent and dark, and those few priests we crossed were in court-yards, down on their knees to beseech the favour of the Duality for their ailing superior.

"She came back from the palace late at night," Yaotl said. "Everything was fine at first but then she started complaining of tingling in her hands and feet. And then it spread."

"Something she came into contact with?" I asked. I had seen her yesterday, and she had seemed tired and weary, but I had attributed it to a long day, not to poison.

Would it have changed anything, if I had noticed?

I hoped it wouldn't have. I needed to believe it would make no difference. Regrets wouldn't serve us now; what we needed was to move forward.

We reached the main courtyard of the shrine, a vast space from which rose a central pyramid of polished limestone. Ceyaxochitl's rooms were just by the stairs. Their entrance-curtain, usually opened to any suppli-cant, was closed, unmoving in the still air.

Inside, Ceyaxochitl was propped up against the wall, her skin sallow, her whole frame sagging. A frowning physician was holding a bowl of water under her chin.

"No shadow. Her spirit is still unaffected," he said. "It's a physical poison."

"You know about poisons," Yaotl said.

I couldn't help snorting. "Yes, but after death. Generally, I don't have patients. I have corpses."

The physician withdrew the bowl of water. "That's as close to a corpse as you can get to, young man. Nothing is responding. She can't speak, or move any muscle." He turned to Yaotl. "I'd need to know the day and hour of her birth, to know which god is in charge of her soul."

Yaotl's hands clenched, slightly. The physician's asking for her nameday could only mean that he intended a full healing ritual, which in turn meant the situation was desperate. "Quetzalcoatl. The Feathered Serpent." God of creation and knowledge, and the only other god to accept bloodless offerings. I couldn't say I was surprised.

"I'll send for supplies, then," the physician said.

I knelt and touched Ceyaxochitl's warm skin. Nothing responded. Her heartbeat was fast and erratic, as if the organ itself were bewildered.

"She's in here," the physician said. "Conscious. It's just that her body is completely paralysed."

About as cowardly and as nasty a poison as you could think of. They could have had the decency to make it clean, at least.

"Acatl-tzin," Yaotl insisted.

"Do you have any idea what she could have been poisoned with?" I asked the physician. He was the expert, not I.

"What other symptoms have you seen?"

Yaotl thought for a while. "She was rubbing at her face before the numbness came. And having some difficulty walking, as if she'd been drunk, but Mistress

Ceyaxochitl never drinks."

Indeed not. She might have been old enough to be allowed drunkenness, but she'd always seen that as a sign of weakness. She'd always been strong.

Gods, what would we do without her?

"Something she ate, then, in all likelihood," the physician said.

"Something?" I asked. Surely things hadn't degenerated so fast at the palace that food and drink couldn't be trusted anymore? "Can't you be more precise?"

"Not without a more complete examination," the physician said. His voice was harsh. "But I think you'd want me to see if I can heal her first."

"Yes," Yaotl said. "But I also want to make sure that the son of a dog who did this does not get away with it."

The physician looked at Ceyaxochitl again and scratched the stubble on his chin. "I seem to remember a similar case some time ago. I'll send back for my records, to see if anything can be inferred from it. In the meantime the best we can do is keep her warm."

And breathing. It didn't take a physician to know that if the paralysis was progressing, the lungs would stop functioning at some point, not to mention the heart.

I moved my hand from Ceyaxochitl's hands to her chest, feeling the heart within fluttering like a trapped thing. "I know you can hear us. We'll find out who did this. Stay here. Please."

Please. I knew we'd had our dissensions in the past, our disagreements on how to proceed, but they had been spats between friends, or at least between peers. To think that she was dying, that she might not see the next day…

The Flower Prince strike the one who had done this, with an illness every bit as bad and as drawn-out as the poison that now coursed through Ceyaxochitl's veins. "Did she say anything?" I asked Yaotl. "Any clues?"

Anything we could use…

He shook his head. "Not that I can remember. She complained about the whole afternoon having been a waste of her time."

But she must have seen something, or suspected something after the fact. Otherwise why take the risk of poisoning her? The penalties for such a crime would have been severe, death by crushing the head, at the very least.

"Nothing at all?"

The physician, who was lifting the entrance-curtain in a tinkle of bells, stopped, and then turned back towards me. "When I was first called, the paralysis hadn't quite reached everywhere. She managed to say something, for what it's worth."

"Yes?"

"Well, her lips were already half-paralysed, but I think it was something about worshipping bells."

Yaotl and I looked at each other. "Acatl-tzin?"

Bells. Silver Bells. Huitzilpochtli's sister Coyolxauhqui, She of the Silver Bells, who waited under the Great Temple for Her revenge.

"I don't know if it makes any sense," the physician said.

I withdrew my hand from Ceyaxochitl and carefully stood up. "It does make sense. Thank you."

"Not to me," Yaotl said.

"Silver Bells. She's been poisoned by a devotee of Coyolxauhqui," I said, and watched the pallor spread across his face.

Our enemies were indeed in our midst. One person, or several, were worshippers of She of the Silver Bells; summoners of star-demons, harbingers of chaos, determined to sow destruction among us.

The only question was who.

• • •

I ate a sparse lunch in my temple with my priests: a single bowl of levened maize porridge, flavoured with spices. Then, instead of going straight back to the palace, I detoured through the Wind Tower, the shrine to Quetzalcoatl. Like the other shrines it stood on a platform atop a pyramid; unlike the other shrines, which were squat and square, the Wind Tower was made of smooth black stones and completely circular, offering no sharp angles or purchase. For Quetzalcoatl was the Feathered Serpent but also Ehecatl, the Breath of Creation, and to hinder Him in His passage through His own shrine would have been an unforgivable offence.

And He was the Morning Star and the Evening Star, our only ally in the night skies in those dangerous times.

I could have prayed to Lord Death in Ceyaxochitl's name, for He was the only god I claimed, as familiar as a wife to a husband or a digging stick to a peasant. But, somehow, it felt wrong to appeal to Him to keep a soul out of His dominion.

I stood for a while on the inside of the shrine with pilgrims crowded around me, unsure of what to say. I did what I had always done. Kneeling, I pierced my earlobes with my worship thorns, and let the blood drip onto the grass balls by the altar. The Feathered Serpent took no human sacrifices, but only our penances and our gifts of flower and fruit. He had given us the arts and the songs. He had once descended into the underworld for the bones of the dead, had braved death and darkness so that humanity might be recreated.

"Keep her safe," I whispered. *"Please.*
You who know the metals in the earth
The jade and the flowers and the songs
You who descended into Mictlan

Into the darkness, into the dryness
Please keep her safe."

I wished I could say that He'd been listening, but the shrine remained much the same as ever. I was not His priest, I did not have His favours. My prayer was no doubt lost among the multitude.

I walked back into the palace in an even bleaker mood than I'd left it. As fate and the Smoking Mirror would have it, the first person I met in the corridors was Quenami, the High Priest of Huitzilpochtli, who looked unusually preoccupied.

"Acatl." He frowned. "I haven't seen you this morning."

"I had other business to attend to." I was not in the mood for niceties. "Did Ceyaxochitl come to you yesterday, Quenami?"

There was a brief moment before my words sunk in, which I could almost follow by looking at his blue-streaked face. "The Guardian? She might have. I don't remember."

"Only a day ago, and you can't remember? What a fickle mind you have."

"I thought yesterday's little interview would have removed your inclination to insult your peers or your superiors." Quenami's voice was cutting.

So many things had changed since yesterday. "Perhaps. That was before someone poisoned Ceyaxochitl."

"Poisoned? That means—"

"She's dying," I said, curtly. I tried not to think of her warm, unresponsive skin under me, of the feeling of her heartbeat lurching out of control. She'd been at my back for as long as I could remember. We'd fought, but I'd always known she'd be there when the Empire truly needed her. "And whatever happened, it was in the palace."

"Do you have any proof of that?" Quenami appeared to have recovered from his shock, feigned or genuine I did not know.

"Who else would dare poison the Guardian?"

"More people than you'd think." His voice was condescending again. "Foreign sorcerers–"

"The only sorcerers of any note are in this palace," I snapped. "And I'm going to make sure they can't do any harm anymore."

Quenami's face was frozen into what might have been anger or fear. "So you'll just badger us into confessions? You're making a mistake."

"Why? Because I'm impinging on your privileges? Look, I'm not intending to probe into secrets or shatter your face and heart in public, but you must realise that someone tried to kill the Guardian of the Sacred Precinct – agent of the Duality in this world, the keeper of the invisible boundaries. If they dare to do that, then no one here is safe."

Quenami's face shifted to disdain. He was going to tell me that he was High Priest of Huitzilpochtli, that out of all people, he should be safe.

I forestalled him. "It was poison poured into a meal, or a drink." I kept my voice as innocuous and as innocent as possible. "That could happen to anyone. Even if you could have your meals tasted by a slave, it was slow-acting. She didn't show any symptoms until a few hours after the poisoning."

"What poison?"

"I don't know," I said. "But a nasty one. The muscles refuse to obey. You're trapped as a prisoner in your own body, until your lungs or your heart give up. It's not a pleasant way to go." Not to mention pointless. Sacrifices and wounds dealt on the battlefield were painful, but this pain was an offering to the gods, the whole body becoming a sacrifice. But, for Ceyaxochitl

94

there would be no reward, no justification for enduring this slow slide into oblivion.

"Fine," Quenami said. "What do you want me to do, Acatl?"

"Just answer a few questions. Did you or did you not see Ceyaxochitl yesterday?"

"Yes," Quenami said. "Very early in the morning."

"And?"

He hesitated for a while, trying to see what he could and could not tell me. "She kept insisting to know where I stood."

"Not surprising."

"I suppose not," he said with a trace of the old haughtiness. "But still, she was annoying."

That I had no doubt of – she could be. "Did she eat or drink anything while she was with you?"

He looked at me for a while. "I could deny it, but I think you wouldn't believe me." His face creased into an uncharacteristic smile. "She had maize porridge, brought by the slaves."

"Your slaves?"

Again, Quenami hesitated. "Yes."

I made a mental note to see if any of that maize porridge was left. There were spells to detect the presence of poison, although they took a long time to be cast and could be finicky. "And what about Ocome?"

"What about him? I barely knew the man."

"I think you're lying."

"And I think you're trying to draw me out." He looked me in the eye, his aristocratic face exuding casual pride.

"I know you came to see him."

"Who wouldn't?" He made a dismissive gesture. "The man had a vote, and he was selling it. Who wouldn't leap at the chance?"

"An honest man," I said, a little more acidly than I'd meant to.

Quenami smiled pityingly. "It's a wonder you've remained High Priest so long, Acatl."

And it was a wonder he'd become High Priest at all. But I held my tongue.

"Seriously," Quenami said. "You know who I support, and who Ocome supported. Why would I kill him?"

"Because you couldn't trust him not to change sides?"

Quenami snorted. "Murder is a serious matter, not decided so lightly." For once, he sounded sincere. Not that it changed anything. I could well imagine him planning a murder with much forethought, and though it looked as though he'd become High Priest only through his connections, I very much doubted his magical abilities would be insignificant.

"I see," I said. "What do you know about Coyolxauhqui?"

"My, my, just full of questions today, aren't we? I can't possibly see what I can tell you about She of the Silver Bells that you don't already know, Acatl. Sister of the Southern Hummingbird. Creator of the star-demons. Rebelled against Him during the migration to found the Empire. Defeated, and imprisoned beneath the Great Temple." His tone was bored, as if he were reciting something learnt by rote. But, if he had been worshipping Her all along, he would have learnt to hide his allegiance.

"That's all you know?"

"What else would there be?" He lifted a hand, thoughtfully staring at his tanned, long fingers, covered with jade and turquoise jewellery. "I can still feel Huitzilpochtli's power, so She's still imprisoned. And we're warded against star-demons."

He was, as usual, far too confident. He had not even bothered to check.

But still, as High Priest of Huitzilpochtli, he made a poor candidate for a secret worshipper of She of the Silver Bells. He had passed both the initiation as a priest, and the investing with the Southern Hummingbird's powers, all of which would have been difficult to do with conflicting allegiances.

After I was done with Quenami, I could have gone back and seen the council; but there was one person I had not interviewed at all, and who appeared far from uninvolved in the whole business – Xahuia, the princess of Texcoco who had sent away the guards at Ocome's door on that fateful night, and who had either been the last person to see him alive, or worse.

Accordingly I crossed the palace to the women's quarters and asked for an audience, which was granted immediately, a welcome change from the current trend.

The women's quarters were at the back of the palace, protected by a stout wall adorned with red snakes, and a large image of Chantico, She Who Dwells in the House – with a crown of thorns and a tongue twisting out of Her mouth, as red as the paprika She held in Her cupped hands. Those quarters were, more than anywhere else, a place of seclusion. The courtyards I crossed were small, the rooms that opened into them had their entrance-curtains all drawn closed, and I saw no one but the slaves that accompanied me.

Xahuia's audience room was on the ground floor. I wasn't sure if that was her choice, or merely a statement that, as a foreigner, some imperial privileges were denied to her.

Xahuia herself was in a shadowed room separated from the courtyard by pillars carved with glyphs and abstract patterns. She was sitting cross-legged on a reed mat, playing *patolli* with three of her women; winning, too, by the look of the pawns on the brightly-painted board. Hers were nearing the end of the quincunx-shaped circuit.

"My Lady," one of the slaves said. "The High Priest for the Dead, Acatl-tzin."

She raised her head. Her face was smooth and beautiful, painted with the yellow of corn kernels, cochineal spread on her teeth to give them the colour of blood. Her eyes, underlined by a slight touch of black, were wide, the pupils shimmering like a lake at night. "I see. Leave us, will you?"

The slaves scattered like a flock of parrots, leaving me alone, facing her across the *patolli* board. "Xahuia-tzin."

She laughed, like a delighted child. "Oh, please. You flatter me by using the title, but no one else uses it."

"You're of the Imperial Family."

Xahuia's thin lips turned upwards, her gaze creased in amusement. "Of Texcoco. Of Tenochtitlan – only by marriage, and you must know it." She did not say that was why I was here. She did not need to.

"My Lady," I said, finally. "You know there has been one murder, and one murder attempt, in this palace."

Her face went grave again. "I know only of one murder. Who is the second?"

"The Guardian."

"Really." She did not look or sound surprised. Her face had gone as harsh as an obsidian blade.

"You expected this?"

Xahuia was silent for a while, her hands automatically picking up the beans from the board. "She behaved as if the whole palace was hers. It's not a good time for that kind of attitude."

"She came to see you yesterday," I said, voicing the obvious.

Xahuia made no attempt to deny it. "In the afternoon, in the hour of the Storm Lord."

"And?" I asked.

"We talked for a while."

"Around refreshments?"

"Of course." She smiled. "I'll have the slaves bring some to you as well, don't worry."

I forced a smile in answer. Given what had happened to Ceyaxochitl, that wasn't exactly the most promising invitation I'd ever received. "You do know that she was poisoned."

Xahuia shook her head. "Of course not. I've just told you I didn't even know about the Guardian's attempted murder." But she did not ask any more questions. Not what I would have expected, had she been truly ignorant.

"Let's say you don't," I said. "You can't deny you knew Ocome."

"The little councilman?" She laughed again, the strange, careless laughter of a girl. "Of course not. Who did not know him?"

Who indeed.

"I heard he was quite in demand," I said, keeping my face expressionless. Nearby, a quetzal bird took flight, its call harsh and unforgiving, as raw as a burnt man's scream.

"A voice that can be swayed. A voice that can be bought. Of course he'd be quite in demand, as my brother would say." She looked up, straight at me. "But of course you've never met my brother, Acatl-tzin."

"I can't say I have," I said, cautiously. I was starting to feel I was losing the control of the conversation, assuming that I'd ever had it.

"Nezahual has always been the canniest among us.

They say he was blessed by The Feathered Serpent, too, able to foresee the future. He's more than fit to rule Texcoco."

As far as I could remember, Nezahual-tzin had been but a child when his father had died, leaving him legitimate ruler of Texcoco. Three of his elder brothers had conspired to depose and kill him, and Nezahual-tzin owed his Turquoise-and-Gold Crown only to Axayacatl-tzin's intervention . The young prince had been sheltered for a while in Tenochtitlan, before coming back to Texcoco under the hungry gaze of his many brothers and cousins. That he was still Revered Speaker said something, indeed, about his political acumen. "And you're his sister," I said. Fine. I had had my reminder of who she was, of whose support she could enjoy. But the Storm Lord blind me if I was going to let that stop me. More than Tenochtitlan or Texcoco were at stake.

"Let's go back to Ocome," I said.

The women came back. One of them cleared away the *patolli* board, the other laid down a tray of newts and frogs with amaranth seeds, and slices of tomatoes and squashes.

Xahuia reached for a tomato, and nibbled at it for a while. "Not hungry?"

"Not right now."

Again that laugh. "I'm not going to poison you, poor man."

"You'll forgive me if I don't feel reckless."

She nodded, a hint of amusement across her features. "What do you want to know about Ocome?"

"Who killed him."

"That's usually a good start. I'm afraid I can't help you."

"I think you can."

"Do tell me."

"You were the one who sent the guards away that night, weren't you?" And, when I saw that I had shocked her into silence, "The last one to see him alive."

"I should think not." Her voice was clipped, precise, with a hint of a foreign accent. "That honour would be reserved for his murderer."

"Which you deny being."

"Of course." She picked up another tomato slice. "I won't deny the part about the guards, though."

"Then perhaps you can explain to me what you hoped to achieve."

"Oh, Acatl-tzin." Xahuia shook her head, a trifle sadly. "Are you such a naïve fool? When you're a woman in a world where men are empowered to make the decisions, you learn to use what weapons you have." She bent forward slightly, and all of a sudden I became aware of the curve of her shirt above her breasts, of the luscious hair falling down her bare neck, of her hands, long and soft and capable…

I closed my eyes, but it was too late to banish the images she conjured.

She went on, as if this was nothing out of the ordinary. "Of course, you have to make sure it happens late enough at night that your husband won't ever hear of it."

"So you sent away the guards." My voice was shaking. Did the woman have no shame? Her husband was dying, and all she could think of was how to best sell herself?

"Yes, I did. I'm sorry for Axayacatl, but I have to think of myself and of my son, and of what happens when he's no longer there to protect us." Xahuia shifted to an upright position again, and now I saw only a queen in her palace, receiving a supplicant. "You disapprove. I'm not surprised. Most priests are too uptight for their own good."

Uptight, perhaps, but at least I knew where the dividing line lay between right and wrong. "Tell me what happened," I said through gritted teeth. "Did Ocome reject you? Did he laugh at you, and tell you that he had already made his decision? How much did you hate him?" Was that why he had died?

I don't know why I expected her to leap up at me with her nails extended like a jaguar's claws, perhaps too much familiarity with goddesses who seldom could stand being mocked, but I found myself braced for an attack.

Instead, she reached for a newt, carefully picking it out of the tray and bringing it to her mouth, swallowing it in two bites. "As you said, he had made his decision. But with men like Ocome, decisions are seldom final."

I had to close my eyes again. "You–"

"Don't be a fool. I offered both; pressure, and pleasure. I could make life very unpleasant for him, and he knew it."

"More unpleasant than Tizoc-tzin or the She-Snake?"

Xahuia smiled again. "As much. But I could promise him one thing they could not. Once my son had risen to power, I could make sure his rivals both died."

And, of course, neither Tizoc-tzin nor the She-Snake could make that promise for she was a princess of Texcoco, and unless either one of them was willing to break the Triple Alliance, they could not kill her – not when young Nezahual-tzin was so desperately in need for something he could turn into a show of strength. "I see. And he accepted your offer." I still could not quite believe it, she lied as easily as she breathed, told me exactly what she wanted me to hear. Her father had indeed trained her well.

She inclined her head, gracefully. "Of course he did. He made me a promise."

"One he wouldn't go back on?"

She smiled. "You underestimate me, Acatl-tzin. I am no fool. The moment he revealed his allegiance, others would court him. So I made him promise not to say anything until it was time."

"And he accepted?" Of course, if he had given in to her seduction, she would have had her blackmail tool. The Revered Speaker might have many wives, but they were not for ordinary mortals.

"Of course."

"You trusted him?"

"Not any further than I had to," Xahuia said, with that same smile, revealing the darkened red of her teeth. "But I made him swear a solemn vow before a priest of Quetzalcoatl."

A canny move, for oaths sworn before Quetzalcoatl were sacred – the Feathered Serpent Himself, scourge of falsehood and deception, being called to witness them. Such a priest wouldn't have been easy to find at this hour in the palace. But, then again, she was a princess of one city and an empress of another. Who would not come, if called?

"I suppose you won't want to tell me the name of that priest?"

"Why should I not? Every word is true; besides, the fool is dead." And, for a moment, her mask of beauty and power slipped, revealing a face as cold and as merciless as that of an executioner.

In that moment, she frightened me as no one else had. I saw that just as she had told me, she would not hesitate to do what was necessary for her own good. That she would not hesitate to remove a Guardian, perhaps, who was too curious, or even a High Priest.

My hands shook, and even the sunlight seemed cold on my brow. "I see," I said, but I still had my duty. "Do you know a man named Pezotic?"

She looked genuinely puzzled. "It's not a familiar name. Who is he?"

"A member of the council," I said. I'd been a fool. I should have asked Quenami, but I had been too busy fencing with him to think of that particular question.

"Oh. There are far too many of those." She laughed, careless once more. "I can't say I remember him at all."

"I see," I said. I would have pushed, but her puzzlement and surprise had been so obvious I didn't think she knew him. "I'll take the name of that priest of Quetzalcoatl, if you please. The one Ocome swore an oath before."

"Of course." She gave me a name, telling me he officiated at the Wind Tower, the same place I had gone to pray for Ceyaxochitl's sake. "Will that be all?"

The food sat between us. I had not touched it, and all she had taken were the tomatoes and a newt. Her teeth, when she smiled at me, were the red of spilt blood; and her eyes shone with the light of the moon, of the stars which belonged to She of the Silver Bells, now and forever. A light which grew stronger and stronger, starting from the pupils and slowly consuming the irises and the whites, a great sea of light in which I drowned.

"That will be all," I said, forcing the words between my teeth. I could hear footsteps in the distance; the slaves, coming to escort me out. All I had to do was to get up; to put myself outside of her influence…

"Ah, my dear," Xahuia said, from far away. She turned away from me; and, in that moment, broke the eye contact between us, and whatever spell she had been weaving. "What a pleasure to see you."

Shaking, I pulled myself to my feet, and met the curious gaze of a youth. He looked to be even younger than Teomitl, with a round, open face reminiscent of a rabbit, with the soft folds of flesh of one who had never had to work a day of his life.

But it was his companion who caught my gaze, and held it. He was much taller, as rake-thin as a pole, his face crossed by a single black stripe. His right foot trailed slightly behind him, to a rhythm as erratic as a dying man's heartbeat.

"You haven't met my son, Zamayan," Xahuia said, but I was barely listening.

The stripe and the foot were enough clues of the god the man served. Even without those I could not have mistaken him for a mere slave, for magic hung thick and strong around him, an angry, pulsing network of grey and black as deep as night, and the smell of blood wafted from him, as strong as that of an altar.

He was a servant of the Smoking Mirror, the lame god of sorcerers and dark magic, He who delighted in souring men's fates.

And not just any servant, but someone so wreathed in power that summoning a star-demon would have been a trifle.

SEVEN
The High Priests

I must have said something – even if I had no memory of anything besides standing frozen in the courtyard – for Xahuia's son moved away from me, leaving me facing the sorcerer.

He inclined his head. "The High Priest for the Dead. I have heard much about you."

"I, on the other hand, have heard nothing about you." His hands shimmered in the heat, shifting colours between dark brown and red. The strong tang of blood wafted from his clothes, as if even washing could not remove it anymore.

He bowed, as he would before a king. "My name is Nettoni. I am but a humble servant of My Lady."

I did not need to look behind me to know Xahuia would be smiling. "I have no doubt that you serve well." Sweat was running down the nape of my neck. Nettoni meant nothing more than "mirror", and it was what he had fashioned himself into, the living image of his god in the Fifth World, a vessel most suited for receiving His powers. The blood that hung around him would be that of a hundred sacrifices and, unhampered by any of our scruples, he would use pieces of human corpses for curses, raid the tombs of women that died in childbirth for their nails and the locks of their hair, and breathe in the power of those touched by the gods.

"I take it you are from Texcoco as well."

"It is my honour." Nettoni smiled. His teeth were black, shining like polished obsidian. "Now, if you will excuse me, My Lady and I have business."

I did not need to be told twice. I made my exit as fast as I could without seeming churlish, and I could feel his eyes – and hers – following me all the way out of the women's quarters.

Ceyaxochitl might have been able to fight him; I could not. Even rested and refreshed, and even with the whole of my order behind me, I would not be able to even dent his protection. Nettoni had accrued enough power to leave us looking like ineffectual fools.

And, if Ceyaxochitl, agent of the Duality on earth and vessel for Their power, was his only adversary, wouldn't he want to remove her from the board?

I'd said it to Teomitl already, but now I *really* hoped that Xahuia was not the culprit. Together with Nettoni, they made a formidable team, one it would take all our forces to defeat.

And, so far, for forces, we had two High Priests more obsessed with placing their own pawns than with the approaching star-demons and a distant She-Snake, whose guards could barely maintain the order in the palace.

Not to mention a dying Guardian.

The day felt markedly darker as I made my way deeper into the palace.

Palli's messenger found me in the kitchens, where I was examining some of the maize porridge Ceyaxochitl had consumed.

"Acatl-tzin?" It was Ezamahual, a lean, dour-faced

novice priest, a son of peasants who moved through the vast rooms as though he trespassed.

"Here," I said.

The porridge was set in a beautiful blue-and-black ceramic bowl, with golden trimmings. Clearly, Quenami had spared no expense. A brief invocation to Xolotl, Bearer of the Dead, had confirmed that, sadly, it was as innocuous as it was beautiful. Whatever Ceyaxochitl had been poisoned with, it wasn't that.

Ezamahual bowed. "Palli sent me to tell you the ritual is almost complete."

I looked up from the courtyard. The sky was still the brilliant blue of late afternoon. "Tonight, then," I said. Passages into the underworld took place at sunset or at night, when the Fifth Sun itself was underground. "Tell him I'll be there. I have a few things to take care of first."

The first thing I took care of was dinner. I'd had a sparse lunch, but given how long the night was going to be, I didn't hesitate to ask the kitchen slaves for the best they had. I consumed a whole fish with crushed calabash-seeds, and a handful of maize cakes.

Then I went back to the council room, where I found Manatzpa in discussion with the old man Echichilli, the magician of the council. Their servants lounged nearby on a stone bench, watching the courtyard, bored.

"Ah, Acatl-tzin," Manatzpa said. "We have taken the security measures you asked for."

I stilled the shaking of my hands. "I fear it's too late for that."

"Oh?" His eyebrows rose.

"We have no Guardian at present." I thought I could say this with the same calm I'd pronounced the previous sentence; that Xahuia and Nettoni together would have drained me of all fears. But my voice still shook.

Manatzpa's face darkened. "What happened?"

"Poison," I said, curtly.

"Is she…" He paused, letting me fill in the rest.

"Not dead," I said. "But very ill."

"It's dangerous business," Echichilli said, querulously. "The world has changed too much. The young just don't remember how fragile the balance is."

"Did she come to see you yesterday?" I liked Manatzpa, but that did not mean I was going to act as a fool where he was concerned.

"He and the rest of the council." His voice was thoughtful. "She asked us many questions. A canny one, that Guardian. Her heart and soul were in the right place. A pity."

Not so much a pity as a crime, and one that I was going to make sure was punished. "I see." I remembered the question I'd failed to ask Quenami. "Does the name Pezotic mean anything to either of you?"

They shared a glance, a distinctly uncomfortable one. For the first time, Echichilli looked angry, a slight tightening of his wrinkled, sun-tanned face, but an expression that was almost shocking coming from him.

"Yes," Echichilli said, looking me in the eye all the while. "He had a disagreement."

"With whom?" I asked. Manatzpa, too, looked distinctly exasperated, as if some boundary had been breached. What bees' nest had I sunk my hands into?

Echichilli shook his head. "With the council. He was dismissed."

"I thought you couldn't dismiss anyone," I said, very slowly. But it was Quenami who had told us that. Quenami, who wasn't a member of the council, who interfered where he wasn't needed.

"There are exceptions. What he did was unforgivable."

Manatzpa shook his head. "You know it wasn't."

"Wasn't it?" Echichilli looked him in the eye, until

109

Manatzpa's glance slid away, towards the painted floor at our feet.

"What in the Fifth World are you talking about?"

Manatzpa shrugged, but the taut set of his shoulders made it all too clear how angry he was. "Pezotic was worse than Ocome – or more honest, depending on how you view matters. He couldn't stomach the threats, the constant intimidations."

"He ran away?" I asked. It seemed too simple, too innocent. Or was I becoming as paranoid as Tizoc?

"Yes," Echichilli said. "Rather than face his responsibilities." It had the ring of absolute truth – no evasion, no attempt to look aside, or to look me too much in the eye – a simple fact, and one that both saddened and angered him. "I had thought him a better man."

"He was a clever man." Manatzpa's voice was bitter. "He knew where this would lead us."

Echichilli said nothing. Both he and Manatzpa looked drained, their skin as paper-thin and as dry as that of corpses, their stances slightly too aggressive. I assumed there had been further threats, further attempts to bring them to support one candidate or another. But that was one area I couldn't help with. My hands were full enough as it was.

I thought again on what Xahuia had told me – the priest's name branded into my mind. I could assume it was bluff and go question him, but I would have to get out of the palace and back to the Wind Tower, and this would take me time, time I might not have. Ceyaxochitl's removal suggested that the summoner of the star-demons was readying himself for another strike.

So, start out by assuming Xahuia had told the truth; and I couldn't imagine she'd tell a lie, not on something so easily verifiable. Assume she had got Ocome's promise that he would shift sides to hers, without revealing to anyone where he truly stood.

Then the one person who stood to lose the most was the one whose side Ocome had supported, Tizoc-tzin, the heir-designate.

Unfortunately, he was also the man who had threatened to have me dismissed from the court altogether. And, without his brother Teomitl to stand for me, any audience I sought would end in disaster.

But still, he might well be behind it all, and I couldn't stand by while he swept to power under the cloak of Axayacatl-tzin's approval.

How would I face Ceyaxochitl, if she ever recovered?

What I needed was an ally, or at any rate someone who made sure that I came out of Tizoc-tzin's chambers without losing anything. Manatzpa was not nearly powerful enough; it had to be one of the other contenders for the turquoise-and-gold crown.

My heart was not up to asking Xahuia or Acamapichtli. Given how my last interview with the High Priest of the Storm Lord had ended, pacifying him would be nigh impossible.

The She-Snake, then.

I headed towards the She-Snake's quarters. They were in a courtyard symmetrical to the imperial chambers, on the other side of the palace – as befitted the symmetrical roles of the Revered Speaker and the She-Snake.

Unfortunately, when I arrived there, the She-Snake had left for his evening devotions. I asked when he would be back, and was met only with a shrug.

"I wouldn't bother, if I were you."

I turned, slowly. Acamapichtli was standing behind me in the courtyard, dwarfed by his headdress of heron feathers. "Why?" I asked. The last time I had seen him had been his argument with Teomitl, which had ended with his walking out of the room. He seemed calmer now, although he still appeared tense.

He made a quick stab of veined hands. "He won't see you. He doesn't receive anyone but his followers."

"And you don't count yourself as such."

Acamapichtli rolled his eyes upwards. "That much should be obvious."

"Which side are you on, Acamapichtli?"

"I don't think I'm obliged to say that to you."

"It might demonstrate goodwill," I said, a little sarcastically.

His eyes narrowed. "I'll admit I was wrong to leave yesterday. But I didn't have to answer those questions, especially not in the way your student asked them."

His admission was bald, made without a trace of shame, and it was like a blow to the solar plexus. Out of all the people I'd expected an apology from, he was the last.

Since I remained silent, he went on, "I'm not trying to overthrow the Fifth World. I never was."

"You act oddly for someone who isn't."

"Allow me a little mystery." His voice was sarcastic.

"This isn't the time for that."

"What do you want to know?" He drew himself up, wrapping his blue cloak around him. "That I'm ambitious and do things for my own benefit? That is true. That I don't approve of Tizoc-tzin or the She-Snake?" The way he spat the words left little doubt as to what he thought of them.

"I can't take your words on this," I said.

"Then take my acts."

"Fine," I said. "Then tell me about the envoys."

He smiled, and bowed, a little ironically. "Perhaps you could call them mine. I wouldn't swear to anything before any god or any human court, of course."

I fought to keep my fists from clenching. "Suppose they were yours. Why would they come back so regularly?"

"He was a man who needed watching."

"Even if he wasn't yours?"

"Especially if he wasn't mine," Acamapichtli said. "You seem to overestimate the council, Acatl. They might have responsibilities and grand-sounding names, but in the end, they're nothing more than men too old to go to war."

"Tizoc-tzin isn't old," I said. And Teomitl, if he became Master of the House of Darts, wouldn't be either.

He tapped his head with a finger. "Not old in body. Old where it matters. They don't like risks anymore. They don't throw the bean and wager on the outcome. They want safety, at any cost. One way or another, they were all like Ocome, and they knew it. They all watched him, to determine what they should do." His voice was far too bitter for a simple statement, as if he'd gone against them, and found them lacking. What had happened?

"They weren't anxious for whatever gamble you had in mind?" I asked, not bothering to disguise my hostility.

"My own business," Acamapichtli said, a tad acidly. "But it doesn't have anything to do with his death. I'll swear it on any god you want."

"You're easy with your promises. For all I know—"

"For all you know, even Tizoc-tzin might be implicated." His voice was mocking.

"And you don't think he is?" That surprised me.

"Tizoc-tzin is a weak fool, but he's too much like you. He wants stability under the blessing of the Southern Hummingbird, with magic kept to the world of the gods. He would never summon any creatures, or anything that might look like a spell." He spat on the ground. "Fool. As if others wouldn't feel free to use magic."

I decided not to react to the obvious insult, to focus on the information he had just given me. "You seem very sure."

Acamapichtli laughed, a wholly unpleasant sound. "Remember last year, Acatl. Remember how much he hated the lot of us, standing before him. That's how much trust he puts in magic."

A year ago, I had appeared before Tizoc-tzin to bargain for my brother's life, and I had almost failed to walk out of the Imperial Courts. What Acamapichtli wasn't saying was that he had been the one trying to convict my brother; and that Tizoc-tzin, seeing this as a quarrel between High Priests, had taken hours of convincing that either of us was saying anything of value. "That was a year ago," I said, slowly. "People change."

"That's Tizoc-tzin's failure." Acamapichtli's lips compressed to a thin line. "He can't change."

"I can't just take your word," I said. But in truth, he was so obviously hostile to Tizoc-tzin I couldn't see why he would lie to me about this.

"Think about it. You're a smart man." His voice made it clear he didn't believe a word of it. But still...

He'd been walking back to the council rooms; I'd followed him through several courtyards, half-fascinated, half-horrified by his spiteful allegations. The palace was preparing for the night. The magistrates were heading out of the courts, back to their own houses; the warriors were in finery, ready to attend feasts.

"I don't think you quite understand what the Fifth World is, either you or him." Acamapichtli's voice was quieter. "You think of it like Mictlan, a static universe where change would be deadly. But we change every day, and we endure. Worshippers shed their blood, and the Southern Hummingbird wraps us in His embrace. We will endure."

I wished I could be so convinced. "Last year…"

Acamapichtli shrugged. "Tlaloc attempted to wrest power from Huitzilpochtli. One more wave in a storm-tossed lake. It's not because of that boats will sink."

"And you truly think the situation is the same here?" I couldn't quite keep the anger from my voice. "People have died–"

"One, so far."

I cut him. "There was another murder attempt."

He looked so genuinely surprised it was hard to believe it an act. "The Guardian Ceyaxochitl was poisoned."

His face did not move, but I could have sworn his skin was slightly paler. "I see. It still doesn't prove anything. People have died in successions before, Acatl. You may not like it, but it's the way things work."

"You're right," I said. "I don't like it." I'd almost preferred him when he was hostile, and not trying to reason with me. Every one of his words made me feel soiled.

We walked the rest of the way to the council rooms in silence. It was empty now; but Quenami was still in the courtyard, his head cocked as he stared at the sky.

He turned when he heard us. "What a coincidence."

I no longer believed in his "coincidences", which came too conveniently for him. Either he was good at turning the situation whichever way he wanted, or his spy network was much, much better than I had thought. Either way, not a pleasant thought.

"I have been to see the Guardian," he said. "You were right." His tone said, subtly, that he had not quite believed me before.

"And?" I asked, more acidly than I'd have wanted. "Any thoughts you'd care to share?"

Even without a spell of true sight on me, I could feel the strength of his wards, the slight heat that emanated from him.

"Poison," he said.

"What a feat of observation," I said, echoing Yaotl's muted sarcasm of the day before. "And what else?"

His face shifted, halfway to an awkwardness I'd never seen in him. He had been brash before, always in control; now it looked as though he was staring at some profoundly unpalatable meal. "I'm no maker of miracles."

"You are—" High Priest of Huitzilpochtli, the strongest among us, the one for feats of valour, and turning the impossible commonplace.

"I know what I am." His voice was as cutting as obsidian shards.

"Representative of the sun, of the light within us," I said, not without bitterness. "Of what keeps us all alive."

"He's powerless." Acamapichtli's voice was filled with malicious amusement.

"He can't be—" I started, and then saw Quenami's face, and it was as if someone had sunk a knife into my gut.

"The sun is strong at its zenith, but at dawn and at dusk its light is all but useless. So it is with Huitzilpochtli." Quenami sounded as if he were giving a lecture, save that the smugness had been scoured from his voice. "Now is dusk, the time of coyotes and jaguars."

The time of Tezcatlipoca the Smoking Mirror, of Coyolxauhqui of the Silver Bells. "I still don't see how the god can be powerless," I said. "We see evidence of His presence every day above us."

"Tonatiuh the Fifth Sun is still here," Quenami said. "But Huitzilpochtli has retreated to the heart of his strength, bracing Himself for our defence."

He sounded as though he only believed half of it, and that was more frightening than His previous arrogance had been. What would we do, if the Southern Hummingbird could not protect us against His sister.

"The heart of his strength," Acamapichtli said, thoughtfully. "The heartland."

Quenami grimaced. "Yes."

The heartland. Aztlan, the White Place, where our seven ancestors had emerged from their caves into the burning light of day, and where the Southern Hummingbird had promised them they would crush the world under their sandaled feet if they followed Him. Our place of birth, our place of origin.

"Why the curiosity?" I asked.

"Nothing." Acamapichtli made a dismissive gesture. "Just making sure what help we could expect."

For all His reassurances, I didn't like Acamapichtli's probing: the heartland was also where Huitzilpochtli was, diminished and less powerful than his usual.

The perfect time to put an end to the reign of a god.

Quenami made a dismissive gesture. "The Southern Hummingbird will be here when He is needed, Acamapichtli, you can be sure of it."

Acamapichtli bowed, but his gaze was mocking. "As you wish. Meanwhile–"

"Meanwhile, we keep this palace warded." Quenami's voice was firm. "We make sure everyone is safe."

"Safe?" I all but choked on the word. "This is the second murder, Quenami. I'd say it proves beyond a doubt that we can't keep ourselves safe."

"Not so fast, Acatl. The first murder was a star-demon, but the second attempt… I grieve for Ceyaxochitl-tzin, believe me, but this was purely mundane."

117

Mundane – this was how he would dismiss her? "She had found a devotee of the Silver Bells," I snapped.

"Still mundane." Acamapichtli sounded angry, as if he couldn't believe my foolishness. But I wasn't able to let *him* cow me into silence.

"Heavily linked to the first," I said. "Enough to make it necessary to hunt down whoever is summoning the star-demons."

"And we will," Quenami said.

"I've already said it, you put far little trust in our resilience," Acamapichtli said. "We have always endured. We will this time, too."

Quenami said, smoothly, "But your investigation is important too, Acatl."

Another way of saying he had no intention of helping. "Quenami."

"Acatl." Quenami's voice was firm. "We have reached a decision."

"You have," I said.

"No, we," Quenami said. "Do you forget? We are the High Priests. We make the decisions as a group."

Only when it suited him. But I couldn't say that. Teomitl might have, in my stead, but I was just a peasant ascended into the priesthood, with no influence or powerful relatives to shelter me. With Tizoc-tzin and Acamapichtli against me, I could not afford to gainsay Quenami. I clenched my hands. "Fine," I said. "Now if you will excuse me, I have a body to prepare for a funeral."

They could not contradict me on this, and let me walk away without another word.

One man with too much confidence in his wards, and another who kept insisting that the Fifth World would resist anything, as if he still wanted to find out how to break it once and for all. That was what we had, for High Priests, Duality curse me.

Should another star-demon come down, they would be useless.

I, on the other hand, was determined not to be.

EIGHT
On Mictlan's Threshold

I entered the Imperial Chambers with more reluctance than the last time, remembering the unpleasantness of my previous visit.

I passed them with a deep bow, and divested myself of my sandals in the antechamber. Everything was silent; not the hostile, pregnant atmosphere everywhere else in the palace, but a final silence I knew all too well, one that could not be appealed against or dissipated.

My six priests had withdrawn against the wall as I entered. Palli bowed to me, the blood on his pierced earlobes glistening in the dim light. "It is done, Acatl-tzin."

The body of the Revered Speaker lay on the reed mat, dressed in multi-coloured garb, the knees folded up until they touched the chin. A golden mask with a protruding tongue, symbolising Tonatiuh the Fifth Sun, covered his face, and his body had been painted red, the colour of the setting sun. A jade bead pierced his lips. When I touched it, it pulsed with magic.

As befitted that part of the rites, they had brought a cage containing a yellow dog. It lay curled on the ground, its short-cropped fur completely still save for the slight rise of its breathing, its large head nestled between its paws in a strange pose of resignation.

A faint odour of rot wafted from the body, sour and sickly – nothing I couldn't handle. I knelt in preparation for the ritual, and was about to open the cage, when I saw the traces. There had been other rituals before mine, spots of black and grey peppered the ground, along with scratches like the traces of a knife blade. Whatever it was, it had been cleaned, but not well enough. I drew one of my obsidian blades from its sheath, and scratched at it in turn. It was hard, not like congealed blood or sloughed-off flesh, but more like solidified stone, and it wouldn't yield. I managed to take only a small scrap of it, which lay cold and inert in my hand. Tar? Why would anyone want to use tar?

"Palli?" I asked.

He and the other priests had been quietly leaving the room, for this was a moment for the High Priest alone. When I spoke, he turned around. "Do you know what this is?" I asked.

He walked back, carefully navigating around the accumulated traces of magic in the room. "Tar?" he said.

"That's what I think, but–"

"We didn't use tar," Palli said. "It must have been here before. But it's odd."

Decidedly odd. Tar was an uncommon ingredient to use in a ritual, save for very specific gods; and why use it in the imperial chambers themselves?

"Do you want me to look into it?" Palli asked.

"Yes," I said. "Later, though." Whatever ritual had been accomplished, it was old. I couldn't detect any traces of magic, and the spots of tar didn't look as though they would interfere with the spell I was about to cast. "Now isn't the time."

121

I waited until Palli had left the room to open the cage. I held the dog by the neck and, with the ease of practise, brought the blade up to slice its throat. It gave a little sigh, like a spent hiss, as it died. Blood ran down my hands, warm and beating with power, staining the blade and the stones of the floor.

I used the knife to draw the shape of a quincunx around us: the five-point cross, the shape that symbolised the structure of the world from the Heavens down to Mictlan.

I sang as I did so, the beginning of a litany for the Dead.

"We leave this earth, we leave this world
Into the darkness we must descend
Leaving behind the precious jade, the precious feathers,
The marigolds and the cedar trees…"

The familiar green light of the underworld seeped into the room, hanging over the stone floor like fog. Shadows moved within, singing a wordless lament that twisted in my guts like a knife-stab.

"Past the river, the waters of life
Past the mountains that crush, the mountains that bind
Past the breath of the wind, the breath of His knives…"

The frescoes and the limestone receded, to become the walls of a deep cenote, at the bottom of which shimmered the dark waters of a lake that had never seen, and would never see, the light of day. Small figures moved over the water, growing fainter and fainter the further they went – first they had faces and features that looked almost human, and then they were mere silhouettes, and finally they seemed as small and insignificant as insects, vanishing into the darkness at the far end.

Cold crept up my spine, like the fingers of a corpse or a skeleton. The air became saturated with a dry, musty smell, like old codices left for too long, or the cool ashes of a funeral pyre.

And, abruptly, I was no longer alone.

It was a faint feeling at first, that of eyes on the nape of my neck, and then it grew layer by layer, until, turning, I saw the faint silhouette of a man by my side, shimmering in the darkness like a mirage. Though I could barely see his face, I could guess the outline of a quetzal-feather headdress, spread in a circle around his head and hear the swish of fine cotton cloth as he moved.

"Priest?" he whispered. His voice seemed spent, as if it had crossed whole countries to reach me.

I bowed, as low as I could. "Revered Speaker."

"I feel so cold," Axayacatl-tzin whispered. "Cold…"

I reached with my hands, spreading a little of the blood on him. He rippled, as if I'd drawn the flat of my palm across a reflection in the water. "Priest…"

I started chanting again, the words that he needed to make his way across.

> "Past the beasts that live in darkness, that consume hearts,
>   Into the city of the streets on the left, the city where walk the Dead
> We must go, we must find the way into oblivion…"

The scene shifted as I spoke. We were in the middle of the lake, on a boat that held its steady course, and he was by my side, darkness sweeping over his face. The headdress vanished, as did the cotton clothes.

> "The region of mystery, the place of the fleshless
>   Where the strength of jaguars, the strength of eagles
>   Is broken and ground into dust…"

Then we stood on the other shore of the lake, dwarfed by a huge mass of rock. Ahead of us was darkness, and the faint suggestion of a gate. The Dead passed us by, shambling on, unaware of our presence.

I lowered my hands, and let the blood drip onto the ground. Each drop fell upon the other and stuck, so that little by little a darker mass detached itself from the ground, the faint shape of a dog, shining yellow in the darkness, like a pale memory of sunlight or of corn.

"I give you the precious life, the precious water
The Fifth Sun's nourishment, Grandmother Earth's sustenance,
All of this, I give you as your own
To guide you, to take you down into darkness."

When I finished chanting, the dog sprang to life, running around the shadow like an excited puppy, its tinny barks the only sign of life around us. Its paws struck up dust where it passed.

"It's time," I whispered to Axayacatl-tzin.

"I see," the former Revered Speaker said, and his voice was clearer, stronger than on the other shore. He was among his own kind now, in the only place where his existence still had meaning. He turned towards me, a featureless shadow among featureless shadows. "Thank you, priest."

I couldn't help a slight recoil of surprise. The Dead tended to be tremendously self-focused – for such was the nature of death, which severed all bonds of the Fifth World – and I had never had any spirit turn back and thank me before setting on.

"I am Revered Speaker, Huitzilpochtli's own agent." There was a hint of self-deprecating humour in Axayacatl-tzin's voice. "I have known propriety all my life, in death I will not forget."

Though I'd only seen him from afar when he was

alive, already I liked him, more than any of those who would claim his ruler's mat. "I am honoured," I said, bowing. "But I was only doing my work."

"And you do it well." If the Dead could look amused, he would have. "I'll leave things in your capable hands."

I could not help a slight grimace, and he was shrewd enough to see it. "Do you not think yourself capable?" His head moved, slightly. His eyes shone yellow, the same colour as the dog at his feet, a memory of the sunlight that had once been poured into him. His features had been completely washed away, so that he seemed to have become the mask they had put onto him. "Ah, I see. It's others you don't trust."

Tizoc-tzin had been his choice and he would have approved the nomination of the other two High Priests – not to mention of Xahuia, favoured enough to bear him a son. "I apologise–" I started.

"No need to." He sounded amused again. "I'd always known there would be a rift when I died. But only for a time. I've made sure it will close itself."

"How?"

His head cocked towards me, a fluid movement like a bird's. "Let that be a surprise, priest."

"Someone poisoned the Guardian," I said, the words torn out of me before I could think. "A devotee of She of the Silver Bells."

"The Silver Bells? Her worship should be dead." His eyes blazed, touched for a bare moment with all the might of Huitzilpochtli.

"So you don't know who it could be?" I was pushing my luck. One did not interview the Revered Speaker – even less so the soul of the dead Revered Speaker – as if he were a witness in a courtroom.

He was silent for a while. At length, he hunkered down on the dry, dusty earth as if he were still sitting in judgment. "I didn't know in life, and so wouldn't

125

know in death. But…" he paused, as if admitting something painful. "The She-Snake has always had unorthodox worship practises. Not surprising. His father used religion as a tool, and made the worship of Huitzilpochtli into a political act."

"You think he's reacting against that?" I asked. A touch of Mictlan's cold went down my back. If the She-Snake was worshipping She of the Silver Bells, things had just escalated. His men were all over the palace, keeping watch over all the key areas – not only of the palace, but also of the Sacred Precinct and of the city itself. All the temples, and all the Houses of Darts, the arsenals where we stored weapons.

"I don't know," Axayacatl-tzin said. "But I can tell you this, priest – beware of him. He can act with the best of them, and you'll only know he's lied to you after he's twisted the knife in your chest and taken out your heart for his own purposes."

I nodded. That would teach me to trust a pleasant face. I hesitated; but there was too much at stake. "Your wife Xahuia–"

"I remember Xahuia." His eyes softened.

"Do you remember her sorcerer?" I asked. "Nettoni?"

"Dedicated to Tezcatlipoca, the Smoking Mirror? Yes," Axayacatl-tzin said. "An ambitious man to serve an ambitious woman. His ally, for as long as their goals overlap." He rose, turned back towards the waiting darkness. "But I don't think–" He paused. A thread of cold light wrapped itself around his waist; climbed, snake-like, to his ears, as if to whisper words I couldn't hear. "Ah, yes. A reminder, worthy to be heeded, priest. It's the star-demons who will end us, coming down from the sky to devour us, swarming over Tonatiuh until His light is extinguished and the age of the Fifth Sun comes to an end."

"And?" I asked, but I had remembered, too. I knew what Lord Death had told him, nothing more, nothing less than what I had already known.

If Axayacatl-tzin still had a mouth, he would have smiled. "The Smoking Mirror is the Sixth Sun. It is His destiny to climb into the sky and take His place as supreme god of the new age."

And His desire, perhaps, to see the Fifth Age, the age of the Fifth Sun Tonatiuh and the Southern Hummingbird Huitzilpochtli, end much sooner than it should.

"I see," I said. The cold was in my bones and in my heart. "I see. Thank you, Axayacatl-tzin."

When I opened my eyes, I was back in the Fifth World within my blood-quincunx, the potency of which was slowly leeching away. Axayacatl-tzin's corpse still sat facing me, but something seemed to have gone out of him, some bright, subtle light that even death had not extinguished. His soul – his heart, the divine fire which animates us all – had passed into Mictlan, never to return.

But what he had left me with was troubling. I had forgotten that the Sixth Sun was Tezcatlipoca, and that the devotees of the Smoking Mirror would therefore have ample motivation for ushering in chaos – a chaos that would lay the ground for their god's rise to power. They might not worship She of the Silver Bells, but did it matter, as long as they could control the star-demons?

But still, that would require the devotees of both gods to be in collusion. It wasn't uncommon. The previous year I'd uncovered a plot between Xochiquetzal, the Quetzal Flower, Goddess of Lust and Desire, and Tlaloc, the Storm Lord. But it still seemed a very complicated conspiracy, if conspiracy there was.

I sighed. The light that filtered through the entrance-curtain was the pale, grey one before dawn. as expected, the ritual had taken all night. There would be time, later, to reflect on the consequences of what I had learnt. What I needed now was rest.

I made it home just in time for the blast of conch-shells and drums that announced the rise of the Fifth Sun, did my offerings of blood; and fell on my sleeping mat.

When I awoke, the sun was slanting towards the horizon, bathing everything in the room in warm, golden light. I shook my head, trying to clear my thoughts.

Outside, I half-expected to find Teomitl waiting for me, but though there was someone in my courtyard – which could hardly be called "private" anymore given the sheer flow of visitors that came through it – it wasn't my student.

"Yaotl?"

Ceyaxochitl's slave was still dressed sumptuously and his eyes shone with a resolution I'd seldom seen, though his face was haggard beneath the makeup. The eagle feathers of his headdress drooped, as though he'd walked through a squall; and his embroidered cotton cloak was slightly askew on his shoulders. Any humorous remark I might have made about his intrusion died on my lips.

"What observation skills," he said. It started bitingly, and then became toneless as he remembered the seriousness of the situation.

"Any news?"

He shook his head. "The physician said that she might live if she can survive the next day. Her body might purge the poison on its own."

One day. Fourteen hours. We both knew this

wouldn't happen. Though she lived and breathed, Ceyaxochitl was as dead as the Revered Speaker.

"You haven't come here for that," I said.

A shade of the old sarcasm shone in his eyes. "No. I came to tell you we know what poisoned her."

"So?" I asked.

He raised a hand. "All in good time." There was a gleam in his gaze that suggested that what he had to tell me was of much more import than the nature of the poison – Storm Lord blind him, this wasn't a time for his usual equivocations.

"Yaotl–"

"It's obscure," Yaotl said. "The physician looked through all his notes, and finally found a case that was similar."

"You're enjoying this, aren't you."

He looked up at me, and let me see for the first time what lay beneath the mask of irony – an anger that possessed him to the bones. "She's as good as dead, Acatl-tzin. Doomed. Gone from the Fifth World. She took me from the marketplace, and turned me from a slave into her assistant. She gave me status and riches. And you think I don't want her murderer punished?"

"She helped me too," I said.

Yaotl's face clearly said that I couldn't understand – that I'd been a priest long before Ceyaxochitl took an interest in me. He had been a captive destined for a life of drudgery. He breathed in, once, twice. I could almost feel the air trembling in his lungs. "It's a newt. A fiery-looking critter with a red-belly and stripes across the back. Rather distinctive. They secrete a poison that acts that way, shutting down the muscles one after the other."

A newt. I thought, uneasily, of all the times in the palace I'd eaten one. Why, I had taken some from the kitchen only a few hours ago. "That wasn't all you had, was it?"

Yaotl's smile was like the rising of a star, as red as blood and as bent on causing chaos. "They're uncommon. Finding them takes work. Except–" he brought both hands together with the finality of a book closing. "Except that they flourish on the lake shore near Texcoco. Xahuia-tzin asked for them specifically last week. She said it was for cosmetics."

And what interesting makeup those would make.

Yaotl, predictably, was eager to take a troop of Duality warriors into the palace and bodily arrest Xahuia.

I, on the other hand... I could remember Xahuia's spell, and the aura of power that hung around Nettoni, enough to make me a lot less eager than Yaotl. "Tlaloc's lightning strike you, I need to think! We can't possibly barge in there that way."

"Why not?"

Because... Because, if Axayacatl-tzin was right, the She-Snake might be complicit, or at the very least sympathetic. Because Xahuia and Nettoni, between them both, had enough power to level this palace twice over.

"There's too much at stake," I said. "This is going to be a declaration of war against Texcoco."

Yaotl shrugged. His stance said, very clearly, that if I cared about such trifles I was an ungrateful fool.

I could guess what Tizoc-tzin's reaction would be, if we brought him the news. Sarcasm, and perhaps even a declaration that he cared little about the Guardian's fate. But we needed allies, and they were in short supply. We needed someone to give us their support.

"We need Manatzpa," I said. This was political and if we had it wrong, if Yaotl's guesses and my circumstantial evidence gathered from Axayacatl-tzin's vague memories were just coincidences, then the Triple Alliance would tear itself apart for nothing.

That is, if we survived the arrest at all. I doubted

Xahuia or Nettoni would go down peacefully.

"That's not his place," Yaotl said, sharply.

"This is a princess of Texcoco. Not just some grubby little summoner in a peasant's hut in the Floating Gardens." I hated politics, but I could see the shape of the game, all too clearly.

Yaotl watched me for a while, and relented. "Fine. But if you're not here at the Hour of the Earth Mother, my men and I will go in regardless."

For once, I was lucky. Manatzpa and Echichilli were both in the council room, going over some papers.

"See, the province of Cuahacan hasn't delivered their tribute of jaguar pelts," Manatzpa was saying.

"I think it was waived this year," Echichilli said, his wrinkled face creased in thought. "Let me see…" He reached for some of the other papers in the pile, and stopped when I entered in a tinkle of bells. "Acatl-tzin?"

He looked up when I came in, genuinely surprised. "Acatl-tzin?"

"We need your help," I said.

"Our help?" Manatzpa sounded sceptical.

"I know who poisoned Ceyaxochitl."

"That's a grave accusation," Echichilli said. "Do you have evidence?"

"Yes." I outlined, briefly, what had led us to this.

When I finished, Echichilli did not look satisfied. "It's scant. Too scant."

"The Guardian was poisoned," I said.

"But if you're wrong… It will mean war with Texcoco."

"I know." I wanted to scream, but I had more decorum than that. "But we can't let that kind of thing go unpunished. Otherwise, who knows what else might happen?"

Echichilli looked at Manatzpa for a while. At length, the younger councillor set aside his writing reed. "I think it's enough," he said. "It's a presumption, to be sure, but we can find a way to apologise if it doesn't turn out the right way. The presence of a strong sorcerer inside the palace at this juncture is enough to be suspicious."

"You were always good with words." Echichilli sounded sad. "See how we can tear ourselves apart."

"I wasn't the one who started." Manatzpa sounded angry. He rose, wrapping his cloak around his shoulders. "I'll go with you, Acatl-tzin."

He and Echichilli both looked polished and clean, their ornaments from embroidered cloaks to feather-headdresses impeccable, suited to attending the imperial presence. Manatzpa himself would be all but useless in a fight, merely giving us his support, but little else.

I needed Teomitl. "We'll need to collect someone first," I said.

The palace was a big place, and it seemed even bigger when searching for someone. We headed straight to Teomitl's rooms, a small courtyard by the side of where Tizoc-tzin was holding court, where the entrance-curtain fluttered orange in the breeze, the same colour as Teomitl's cloak. Unlike Tizoc-tzin's, the room was on the ground floor, but then, Teomitl had never cared overmuch about pomp. He applied his own exacting standards to himself, and the opinions of his peers mattered little to him.

At least, that was what I'd thought before Tizoc-tzin started teaching him.

"Teomitl?"

No answer came from within. I'd expected guards, or at the very least a slave, but nothing moved beyond the curtain. I debated whether to enter, and finally settled for silently drawing the curtain aside, to make sure that Teomitl was not sleeping inside.

I had been in the courtyard outside those rooms, but in the year I'd taught him Teomitl had never invited me inside. The room was decorated with rich frescoes in vivid colours, depicting our ancestors in Aztlan, the fabled heartland of Huitzilpochtli's strength. Fish and leaping frogs filled water as clear as that of a spring, and little figures withdrew nets under the gaze of the god and of His mother Coatlicue, a wizened, harsh-looking woman wearing a dress of woven rattlesnakes, her large breasts obscured by a necklace of human hands and hearts.

The furniture, however, was at odds with the wealth of the decoration. A single, thin reed mat lay in the furthest corner, turned yellow by age. A stone box, a shallow vessel in the shape of an eagle, a three-legged clay pot with a chipped rim and two worn wicker chests completed the furniture. It would have seemed almost unlived in, save for the three grass balls pierced through with bloody thorns.

Carefully, I released the curtain; I couldn't help feeling embarrassed at discovering more of Teomitl's intimacy that he'd ever revealed to me.

Well, he was not here, that was certain. Where in the Fifth World could he have hidden himself?

I cast a hesitant glance towards the south, where the red-tinged silhouette of Tizoc-tzin's chambers towered over Teomitl's small courtyard. Could he be at Court with his brother? If that was the case, we were lost. I couldn't risk coming back, not on such stakes.

The hollow in my stomach wouldn't close, an unwelcome reminder of how anchorless the Fifth World had become with the death of the Revered Speaker.

Manatzpa had been waiting politely for me at the entrance to the courtyard. He bent his head towards the sky, where the sun was climbing into its apex, a graceful way of suggesting we needed to hurry without actually saying the words.

We walked out again, and attempted to locate the youths of imperial blood.

I found them lounging at the exit of steam-baths, lazing in courtyards over *patolli* games, listening to slaves playing rattles and drums. None of those I questioned – smooth-faced and careless, with the easy eyes of people who had never had to wonder about their next meal – could tell me where Teomitl was. And time, through it all, kept steadily passing, each moment bringing me closer to Yaotl's deadline.

At length, a fist of ice closing around my heart, I headed back towards the entrance, Manatzpa in tow.

As I passed the House of Animals, I caught a glimpse of orange in the darkness.

I slid inside, unsure whether I had truly seen anything. The House of Animals spread over several gigantic courtyards, cages of woven reeds held rare or beautiful animals, from emerald-green quetzal birds to the graceful, lethal jaguars; from web-footed capybaras munching on palm leaves to huge, slumbering armadillos curled against the bars.

The flash of orange came again, in the direction of the aviary, where the Revered Speaker kept the birds with precious plumage that could be turned into feather regalia. I crossed the arcades of a gallery, and found myself facing a couple of quetzal birds and, through the bars of their cage, Teomitl, who stood watching them with the intentness of a warrior on a reconnaissance mission.

"Acatl-tzin?" He sounded shocked and not altogether pleased. But our grievances could wait.

I raised a hand to forestall him. "I need your help," I said. "To prevent Yaotl from getting into trouble."

"Trouble?" Teomitl's face focused again on the present.

"Arresting a sorcerer," I said, curtly.

"But surely Ceyaxochitl–"

"Ceyaxochitl is dying," I said. This time, my voice did not quiver. I felt terrible, as if uttering the words to him finally made them reality.

Teomitl's gaze hardened. "Who? The sorcerer?"

I nodded.

He wrapped his cloak around his shoulders, casting a last, regretful glance at the birds. "I'm coming."

When we reached the entrance neither Yaotl nor the Duality warriors were there.

"Acatl-tzin?" Teomitl's voice was slightly resentful, as if he expected me to apologise for the disturbance.

The Storm Lord strike me if I gave in, though. This was not a time for indulging his pride. "They're inside," I said. "If we hurry…"

But, even as we ran towards the women's quarters, the sounds of battle cut through the courtyard. We were going to be too late.

NINE
Fire and Blood

Teomitl, Manatzpa and I took the courtyards at a run, heedless of the hissing noblemen who barely made an effort to move out of our way. The sound of fighting got closer all the while – obsidian striking wood, obsidian striking obsidian, the familiar cries of the wounded and of the dying.

By the wall that marked the boundaries of the women's quarter, a guard in the She-Snake's black uniform lay choking in his own blood. Teomitl knelt by his side, assessing the wounds with an expert gaze. He shook his head. His face was still, strangely frozen in a moment between human and divine, half brown skin, the colour of cacao, half the harshness of jade, hovering on the verge of taking over.

"…by surprise…" the guard whispered. Froth bubbled up from between his lips. His gaze rose towards Tonatiuh the Fifth Sun who hung over the courtyard, swollen with the red of evening light.

"Spare your effort." Teomitl's voice was curt, an order that could not be refused. "Acatl-tzin?"

I shrugged. "We go in." I reached up, and fingered the wounds in my earlobes. The scabs easily came off, and my fingers came with blood pooling at their tips.

I knelt by the dying man, and drew the glyph for a dog on his forehead, whispering the first words of a litany for the Dead, to ease his passage into the underworld.

> *"As grass becomes green in spring*
> *Our hearts open and give forth buds*
> *And then they wither*
> *This is the truth*
> *Down into the darkness we must go…"*

Teomitl watched me in silence, though his whole stance was that of a snake coiled to strike, eager to draw blood.

"Let's go," I said, with a curt nod.

Inside, every courtyard was deserted, the entrance-curtains drawn. From time to time the pale faces of women peered at us through the cotton. The sounds of battle were dying out. Whatever had happened, it was over.

As we approached the courtyard where Xahuia had received me, the air became tighter, as if we were tumbling down a mountain towards denser climates – and magic saturated the air, an unhealthy, suffocating tang that crept over my whole field of vision. I could have extended my priest-senses, but I already knew what it was – Tezcatlipoca's touch, a miasma that rose from the deep marshes, from corpses and from rotten plants.

Teomitl's face seemed to be made of jade now, as he ran forward.

But, in the last courtyard, all that we found was an exhausted Yaotl, standing over three bodies. Two were Duality warriors, and the third I would have known anywhere, even without the aura of sorcery that hung around him.

Something had changed with the courtyard. It took me a while to realise that a new entrance-curtain had appeared where there had been only a frescoed wall. It opened in the midst of a fresco depicting the Southern Hummingbird. As the curtain fluttered in the breeze I saw that it was only the start of a series of holes pierced through several walls, a path that led through courtyard after courtyard, until...

"Where does it go?" I asked.

Yaotl nodded, grimly. "I sent the remaining warriors to check, but I would think outside."

Manatzpa bowed, briefly, to Yaotl, and wandered near the entrance-curtain to get a better look.

"Of course it goes outside." Nettoni's voice was a spent whisper. "Don't be a fool like them, Acatl."

I knelt by his side. He had no wounds, and the strength of his magic was still gathered around him, potent enough to give me nausea. And yet... his face was as pale as muddy milk, his mouth curled back, showing the blackness of his teeth. "That's where you sent Xahuia."

His lips moved, as much a grimace of pain as a smile. "I told you. I was privileged to serve her."

Axayacatl-tzin had told me otherwise; that they only served each other because their goals lay in the same direction. But he could have been wrong.

Nettoni grimaced again. "Not much point, in any case. You'd have caught me easily enough. Sometimes, you have to admit defeat."

Teomitl's hand brushed Nettoni's forehead, and withdrew as if scalded. "Acatl-tzin."

"She's not a goddess of healing," Nettoni said. The whites of his eyes were slowly filling with blood – red at first, and then darkening as if it was drying

138

inside. "She's never been. And She's not your servant."

"I'm not naïve enough to think She is," Teomitl snorted.

We had other things to worry about than Jade Skirt's motivations. "I think it's your god we should be talking about, Nettoni. The one you tried to help."

He smiled again, and it looked like the death-grin of a skull. "That I tried to help? In many ways, I was as ineffective as you were, Acatl."

"We put Xahuia to rout, and killed you. I hardly think that's ineffective." I kept nothing back; there was no point in being polite or kind – not to a dying man, not to a servant of the Smoking Mirror.

He snorted. His eyes were now as black as obsidian, glimmering with the same harsh light. "Then perhaps I've been more ineffective than you."

"You killed Ceyaxochitl." Yaotl's voice was harsh. "You poisoned her, you son of a dog."

Nettoni smiled again. "Have you understood nothing?" His hand closed around my wrist before I could pull away – his touch burnt, and cuts blossomed everywhere he touched me. "You fool..."

I tried to free myself, but every movement I made widened the cuts. I sucked in a breath against the myriad pinpricks of pain climbing up my arm. "Let me go, the Southern Hummingbird blind you!"

Yaotl and Teomitl moved, each seizing their obsidian weapon, but Nettoni just smiled, his face taking on the harsh cast of one possessed by the gods. The shadow of black and yellow paint hung on his features, and, like Axayacatl-tzin, I could guess at the shape of a feather-headdress, crowning him in glory. "You're a fool, then... But even fools can learn... Do you not see, Acatl? Do you not see?"

Teomitl's *macuahitl* sword swung down, connecting with Nettoni's arm just below the elbow. It sheared through the skin and bone as if through air. Blood spurted in a warm fountain that sank into my clothes. The smell of sacrifices filled the air. Nettoni's face went a little paler, but his smile did not diminish.

"Not too late…" he whispered, "My Lady…" The blood flow was pouring from him into the beaten earth, power shimmering over it. He whispered a string of syllables I could not understand, and then his eyes closed, as if peacefully asleep, and the light fled from him. His hand and lower arm fell, limp – the fingers opening up, were studded with shards of obsidian like a sword, but, as I watched, even they faded away, until nothing but the severed hand of a corpse remained.

The sense of coiled power, of wrongness, died with him. I breathed in a burning gulp of air, feeling lighter already.

"Acatl-tzin." Manatzpa was frowning down at me. "We have to hurry."

I couldn't understand his urgency. "The Duality warriors have got a head start on us. If they can't find Xahuia, then it's likely we won't. I'm touched by your confidence, but…"

He cut me with an impatient shake of his head. What in the Fifth World was wrong with him? "Didn't you hear, Acatl-tzin?"

"I heard a lot of allegations, and most of them were too cryptic for their own good."

His eyes were wide in the dim light. "The name he said, at the end… Echichilli. Echichilli is in danger."

Not for the first time we found ourselves running through the deserted courtyards of the Imperial Palace. This time, though, we had Teomitl with us. My apprentice might not have had any idea of how to steer a boat or negotiate at the marketplace, as he had amply proved in the past year, but he did know the palace layout by heart.

Night had fallen. The stars overhead glittered down upon us like the eyes of a thousand monsters and the hole at the centre of the Fifth World was growing larger and larger, a sense of emptiness that pulsed in my chest, in my hastily bandaged wounds.

"Do you know where he is?" I asked Manatzpa, after what seemed like the tenth near-identical courtyard.

He made a short, stabbing gesture with his hands. "My rooms. That's where he was meant to wait for me."

"It might be a false alarm," I said. "A plan to get us away from the hunt."

"He doesn't need that." Teomitl's whole stance radiated an unearthly confidence – in the straightness of his back, in the calm shake of his head. "He's beaten us on that already."

We had left Yaotl behind, to continue the hunt for Xahuia. But whether Nettoni had cared for Xahuia or not, or had been allied with her and chosen to sacrifice himself in order to further the chaos in the Fifth World, if he had been the one to organise her escape, he would have gone about it methodically, secure in his god's favour. I very much doubted we would find her or her son.

"Then why warn us at all?" He hadn't cared a jot for us; for any of us. He was Texcocan, and he had tried to destroy us. Unless… unless he'd hoped we would die with Echichilli, thus giving him his revenge from beyond death.

I didn't like the explanation, but nevertheless I had to make room for it, in order to be ready.

"I don't know why he warned us," Teomitl said, frustrated. "Can you let me focus on where we're going?"

I bristled, but now wasn't the time to berate him for

his lack of respect. "And once we've found them, then what?"

He turned, briefly, looking genuinely surprised. "I thought you'd know."

I hadn't really had time to think about it either. It was night, which meant the outside would afford us no extra protection. "There are enough wards on the outside walls to blast even a beast of shadows into oblivion," I said. "For all their power, I don't think the star-demons will be able to cross that line."

"So we take Echichilli outside?"

"The Duality House," I said, curtly. It was either that or the shrine of Huitzilpochtli at the Great Temple; but Quenami had made it abundantly clear that the Southern Hummingbird was all but powerless, merely awaiting a new agent to invest with His powers. "It's always a safe haven."

It would be, even with Ceyaxochitl's illness.

What we needed was to buy time, to slow down the star-demons.

We needed The Wind of Knives: the keeper of boundaries, the enforcer of the underworld's justice.

He'd have come on His own, if the boundaries between the Fifth World and the underworld had been breached. But the star-demons came from the Heavens, which were not His province.

However, He could still be summoned, by the adepts, or the foolhardy.

With any other minor underworld deities, I would have drawn a quincunx in blood, and stood chanting at the centre. But I had once merged my mind with the Wind of Knives, to bring down a god's agent in the city; and the link had remained.

As we ran, I slashed my earlobes, and let the blood pool into my hands, warm and pulsing, an anchor into the Fifth World. I sent my mind questing high above the deserted city, past the Houses of Joy and the warriors' banquets, past the peasants' dwellings squatting at the river's edge and the myriad reed boats bobbing at their anchor, down, into a dark cenote where rainwater pooled, away from the sunlight and the warmth of the Fifth World.

There was a shock, as if I'd run into a wall. *Acatl*, a voice like the keening of dead souls said. *You are timely. The boundaries are breached. I am coming.*

I could feel Him, gathering darkness into Himself, emerging from the cenote, wisps of shadows and fog trailing behind Him. He was flowing up the canals like a miasma, covering in instants what would have taken hours for a man on foot.

"Bad news," I said to Teomitl.

"What?"

"The boundaries are breached." The summoner, whoever he was, was already in the process of calling down a star-demon into the world.

Teomitl's face shifted, became the colour of jade. "Then I'm summoning the *ahuizotls*."

The *ahuizotls* were Jade Skirt's creatures, small and wizened beings which lived at the bottom of Lake Texcoco, dragging men down into the water to feast on their eyes and fingernails.

I shook my head. "They won't be effective." The palace was on the main island of Tenochtitlan, as far away from the water as it was possible to be in a city of canals and boats. Even accounting for the *ahuizotls'* supernatural speed, they wouldn't be here for a while, assuming they managed to get past the wards at the palace entrance.

"Do you have a better plan?"

Then again, the Wind of Knives probably wouldn't be here on time, either.

At length, we reached a courtyard much like

Teomitl's, a quiet, secluded place where only a few slaves swept the ground. I glanced upwards: the stars remained in the same position, and there was no gaping emptiness. For once, we were on time.

The Wind of Knives was in my mind, a pressure like water against a dike, a whistle like the passage of air through obsidian mountains, a grave voice tearing at me like a grieving lament. *Acatl. I am coming.* He was flowing up the stairs of the palace now, the guards scattering in His wake like a flock of parrots.

Almost there…

I knelt, and collected more blood from my earlobes to trace a quincunx on the ground. "Acatl-tzin!" Teomitl said, exasperated.

"You heard me," I said. "The boundaries are breached. I'd rather have protection."

I started a litany for the Dead:

"In the region of the fleshless, the region of mystery
The dead men go forward
They crawl on bleeding feet, on bleeding hands
Forward into darkness
Away from the Fifth World's reach."

A veil fell over me, darkening the courtyard, and the stars in the sky receded, became as insignificant as scattered bones. The world shifted and danced, and the faces I glanced at – Teomitl's, Manatzpa's – seemed those of old men. Teomitl's voice came to me, tinny and weak, the veil leeching all resonance, all warmth from his words.

Gods, I hated that spell.

"Acatl-tzin!"

"Let's go," I said.

Teomitl pulled the entrance-curtain aside and strode in, barely holding it long enough for me to enter in turn.

The room stretched before us, as long and narrow as a fishing boat, interspersed with carved columns. Its walls were painted a vibrant ochre, engraved with leaping deer and jaguars.

Near the centre, Echichilli was seated on reed mats a half-consumed meal before him maize flatbread, tomatoes and the bones of fowl.

"Manatzpa?" His wrinkled face looked puzzled. "I thought–"

"Later," Manatzpa said. Teomitl had his *macuahitl* sword out, the obsidian shards glinting in the reddish lights of the brazier. "We need to get you out of here. Now."

I'd expected Echichilli to protest. He certainly had not been shy about his opinions beforehand, but he remained silent, his eyes fixed on the nibbled fowl-bones. "Venerable Echichilli?" I asked.

He smiled, revealing a few yellowed teeth stuck haphazardly in his mouth. "I think it's too late for that, isn't it?"

"What do you mean?" I asked. But, as I did so, a cold wind lifted the entrance-curtain, and I felt the hole in the Fifth World widen. Something pressed down upon us. Cracks appeared in the roof, fragments of adobe rained down, and the stars shone through the cracks. One of them was falling, straight towards us, growing larger and larger…

"Teomitl!" I screamed.

The rattle of shells filled the room and a shadow stood before us, its hundreds of eyes shining malevolently in the dim light. No, not eyes but stars, scattered at the knees, elbows and wrists of a vaguely humanoid creature – stars that, if you looked into them for long enough, were also demons, smaller monsters with talons and fangs and necklaces of human hearts…

It brought with it the emptiness of the night sky, a cold so intense that my teeth seized up, chattering unstoppably. My limbs shook, started to twist out of shape, and all I could feel was the frantic beating of my heart.

Its eyes, the deathly blue of stars, rested upon me for a while, and I felt as if fingers were closing around my throat, as if hundreds of cold stones pressed against my skin. My veil of protection buckled and shattered, leaving only a cold feeling. My vision started to blur, my corneas burning as if someone had thrown chilli powder into my face.

Where was the Wind of Knives?

The star-demon's gaze moved away; I was not its target. My limbs, now utterly out of control, twisted each in a different direction, leaving me on my knees, struggling not to fall further.

Manatzpa had risen, arms crossed against his chest. "This isn't your place." His voice rang with confidence. How he could still be standing, facing *that*?

The star-demon made a sound which might have been laughter. I heard only the rattle of shells, of yellowed bones shaken together in a grave, my own bones, grinding in the agonising mess of my chest.

"Manatzpa." Echichilli's voice was quiet. "Some things cannot be fought against."

Manatzpa's face twisted in uncharacteristic anger. "You say this like you approve."

I didn't hear Echichilli's answer. My legs were quivering, threatening to slip away from me, and it took all my concentration to remain upright.

The star-demon was moving, flowing towards the two councilmen with the inevitability of a flood. Manatzpa's hand strayed towards his knife, but the clawed hands batted him aside as casually as a child might hurl a toy. He flew towards the wall, hit it, and slumped at the feet of the frescoes, bleeding from a dozen cuts.

That left only Echichilli. The old councillor stood, watching the star-demon come with an odd, melancholy smile on his face. "For everything a price," he whispered. He bowed his head, and did not move.

The Duality curse us, why wouldn't he fight? Why wouldn't he use magic, anything to save himself from the gruesome death facing him?

I slid my hand towards one of my obsidian knives. It was like moving through thick honey. My fingers kept jerking out of the way, and my progress was agonisingly slow, finger-length by finger-length, knuckle by knuckle, every movement a supreme effort.

The star-demon's body blocked my sight of Echichilli. Its back was a dark cloak rippling in the wind, shimmering to reveal row upon row of skulls. Shells as white as bone, sewn into the hem, rattled as it moved.

My fingers hovered over the handle of the knife, closed over empty air. The Duality curse me, I needed...

Echichilli screamed once, a sound abruptly cut off by the wet sound of flesh being torn apart. Hundreds of droplets splayed into the room; organs and blood, spattering my face and hands.

No...

I managed to close my fingers over the knife. The familiar emptiness of Mictlan arced up my body, stretching into my lungs and throat. The sensation of twisting diminished. I pulled myself upwards on shaking legs, the knife handle digging into the palm of my hand, a persistent, known pain that anchored me back to the Fifth World.

"Acatl-tzin." Teomitl had got up with me, his hand still affixed to my shoulder. Chalchiuhtlicue's magic wrapped around him gave a green, rippling cast to his cloak and headdress. "They're coming."

The *ahuizotls*. I knew; and I also knew that they would be too late.

The Wind of Knives, however, wasn't.

His weight in my mind grew excruciating, like a white-hot spear driven into my head. Darkness flowed into the room, bringing with it the deep, teeth-chattering cold of the underworld, and He was standing by my side as if He had always been there. Light glittered on a thousand obsidian planes, caught on the black points like beads on a necklace's thread.

His hand rested lightly on my shoulder, balanced on a dozen obsidian shards as sharp as the points of knives and a tight, cool feeling spread from the points of contact, enough for me to focus again. "Acatl. I am here."

I managed to utter words, through chattering teeth. "You can... see."

"Yes," the Wind of Knives said. His voice was like the water of the cenote, dark, without warmth or sunlight. "I see."

Before I could say anything more, He flowed, fluid, inhuman, towards the star-demon.

The creature had turned, its pale head shifting between the Wind of Knives and Manatzpa, who had pulled himself on an elbow and was daubing Echichilli's blood into the beginning of a huge arc around himself, chanting all the while in harsh words I couldn't make out. The dim light glinted against the tears in his eyes.

The Wind of Knives met the star-demon with a screeching sound, obsidian blades sliding on shell rattles. They fought each other, flowing across the room in an embrace. Obsidian shards glinted. Here and there pale fragments of skin flashed blue in the darkness as they moved past, again and again, spraying drops of Echichilli's blood all over the room like warm rain. It was almost hypnotic, that play of colours, of darkness on light, if the consequences hadn't been so absurdly terrifying...

"Acatl-tzin!" Teomitl screamed.

With growing horror, I realised that the star-demon was coming straight at me. Behind it, the Wind of Knives lay pinned to the floor by something jagged and white – a huge fragment of shell under which the Wind struggled to free Himself.

Of course. It thought to kill me, and thus cut the Wind of Knives' link to the Fifth World.

It was almost close enough to touch, Its eyes held me, and my hands started to shiver and contract. I held onto the knife, to the stretched emptiness of Mictlan, the only part of my body that seemed not to writhe in pain.

Teomitl bypassed me, his *macuahitl* sword at the ready. He moved more slowly as the star-demon's gaze transferred to him, but his features became harsher, the whites of his eyes glazing into green. His sword came up, hundreds of obsidian shards glittering in the light, ready for a strike.

The star-demon was faster. It sidestepped in a rattle of shells, and threw itself at me.

I went down in a tangle of flailing limbs, fighting to regain control of my own body. Up close, it seemed almost human, its face as pale as a corpse, with the bluish tinge of death, its cheeks swollen and tinged with black spots, its eyes without corneas or pupils...

The Wind of Knives was still down. Manatzpa was still chanting, but it did not seem to be having any effect on the star-demon. I was the only one who could save myself...

Fighting all the while, I raised the knife, sank it into whatever I could reach. It howled, but remained upon me. I watched its hands rise as if from a great distance. The fingers curled into claws as sharp as broken obsidian, tiny stars at the joints that were also the eyes of monsters. The claws fell, and swiped across my chest, opening my flesh in a flower of pain.

The star-demon howled, shaking its head. Through the growing haze, I saw Teomitl's face, transfigured into jade. He was going to strike again, and I couldn't remain inactive. I tried to roll over, but my chest felt as if it was splitting open. I raised my hand again, flailing, desperately trying to focus on what I needed to do. The blade of the knife quivered in a blur of black reflections as I drove it up to the hilt into the star-demon's chest.

The blade slid into its flesh without resistance, as if there had been no substance to it at all. Something warm and pulsing fell over me, a suffocating river that smelled of cold, dry earth, nothing like blood. Every one of its eyes closed for a moment, leaving us in darkness, and then they opened again, and its claws swept down, faster than I could follow.

Everything went dark in a burst of pain.

TEN
Aftermath

I woke up, tried shifting, and almost screamed when the pain in my chest flared again.

"Don't move, Acatl-tzin." Teomitl's face swam into focus, his skin dark brown again, all traces of the goddess purged from him.

I managed to shift my gaze down to see my chest swathed in a mass of bandages. That feeling of emptiness was still there, and I wasn't sure any more whether it was the hole left by Axayacatl-tzin's death, or simply a remnant of the magic of Mictlan that had arced through me as I stabbed upwards.

"If I'm still here, I imagine it's gone?"

Teomitl nodded. "Disappeared the moment it was stabbed. Couldn't have done it without the Wind of Knives, though."

The Wind. I could no longer feel Him in my mind. He had vanished at the star-demon's death.

I lay back, and breathed a sigh of relief.

Teomitl's face hovered between horror and fascination. "That's what we have to deal with?"

"A lot more of them, yes," I said. If only Quenami had seen that, even he would have had to admit that this was a genuine threat.

I pulled myself upwards cautiously. The surroundings were unfamiliar. Frescoes depicted the triumphant march of Huitzilpochtli across the marshes, our enemies trampled underfoot, the sorcerer Copil vanquished and his heart torn out, the founding of Tenochtitlan after two hundred years of wandering and our rise to glory. "Where–?"

"Manatzpa's rooms," Teomitl said. "A different part. Now, if you'll excuse me, I have some *ahuizotls* to send away." He frowned. "The other High Priests are at Tizoc-tzin's banquet. I've sent for a priest of Patecatl. He'll be here any moment."

Healing spells required a heavy sacrifice to obtain, their cost all but restricted their use to the Imperial Family. "I'm not sure…"

Teomitl's face was pale, but determined. "You're High Priest for the Dead in Tenochtitlan, Acatl-tzin. Of course he'll come."

Of course. I lay back, feeling infinitely weary. "Thank you. Just go see to those *ahuizotls* before the screaming starts."

I watched him leave and reflected that he could have sent the *ahuizotls* away from the room; this meant he had something else to do, something he didn't want me to be privy to. I wasn't sure I wanted to know, in my current state.

A tinkle of bells at the entrance-curtain heralded the entrance of Manatzpa, who was carrying a tray with two bowls of warm chocolate. His own wounds were bandaged, but he walked very carefully, as if the least sudden movement would take him apart.

"I thought you worse off." I managed to pull myself up into a sitting position, wedged against the wall.

He didn't smile. "We both have looked better." He set the tray between us, and sat down facing me. "But, no, it just knocked me out." His lips curled upwards. "A good thing your student is strong."

There was an expression in his eyes I couldn't quite read; as if he had some strong feeling that he was trying to hide from me, either hatred or fear or… "He's your candidate, isn't he?"

Manatzpa looked away. "He's young." His voice was toneless. "A minor, inexperienced member of the Imperial family, with only one prisoner to his name, and a reputation as an uncontrollable element dabbling in sorcery. And he won't have a chance to improve it before the coronation war."

"So you won't vote?"

"You already know what I think of the other candidates." Somehow my questioning appeared to have put him off. He pushed a bowl towards me. The bitter smell of cacao, mingled with that of spices and vanilla, wafted up to my nostrils, tantalising.

"And you know…"

He made a quick, stabbing gesture with his hand, and grimaced as he was reminded of his wounds. "I know, Acatl-tzin, I know. But, as I said before, I'd rather have a good leader than the first that came to mind."

"Even after seeing this?"

For a moment, anger stole across his stately features. "I won't forget what happened to Echichilli, or leave it unpaid. But I'll stand by what I believe."

Perhaps I was deluding myself, then. If even such a measured man as Manatzpa could bring himself to wait, having seen what a star-demon could do, then how would I stand a chance of convincing Quenami or Tizoc-tzin that we had to choose a Revered Speaker *now*?

Manatzpa drained his bowl in one gulp. He still appeared angry; at my questions, or at Echichilli's death?

"I disturb you. I'll leave you to your rest. We'll have visitors soon enough."

Left alone, I drank my own chocolate, enjoying the familiar hint of bitterness taste on my tongue before the chilli overwhelmed it. Manatzpa's rooms were as devoid of furniture and ornaments as Teomitl. No wonder he liked his nephew enough to support him for the Turquoise-and-Gold Crown.

All the same…

Something felt wrong, and I couldn't have said what. A premonition, such as the ones the adepts of Quetzalcoatl sometimes received? But I did not worship the Feathered Serpent, or claim any more than a distant allegiance to Him. Perhaps just the wounds and the lightness in my whole body, which would have been enough to make any man feel moody? But, no, it wasn't that.

My mind could not seem to focus on anything. It drifted, watching the frescoes blur and merge into each other. Huitzilpochtli's blue-striped face loomed larger and larger, shifting into the grin of a star-demon, and the darkness swarmed over me and swallowed me whole.

In my dreams, I stood on one of the hills around Tenochtitlan, garbed as a High Priest in my cloak embroidered with owls and the skull-mask over my face.

By my side stood other High Priests, Quenami in jaguar skins and Acamapichtli with his heron-plumes, and others, lesser ones I could not recognise. Above us were the stars, blinking slowly and coldly; and they were coming down, one by one, trails of light against the dark sky, growing larger and larger, until we could see the eyes in the joints of their elbows and knees, feel the cold of their passage. The sun had faded into darkness, and the earth underneath rumbled, splitting itself apart…

There was a chant, in the background, harsh, sibilant words in a language that I had heard before and couldn't place. And then, as everything split apart in a shower of sparks, I could finally make it out.

"From darkness I call you
For the broken, for the discarded
For the imprisoned, wailing in the world below
The world is desiccated bones, twisted and gaunt faces
It is the time of my mastery
The opening of my reign."

And I knew, too, where I had heard them: they were the words of the invocation Manatzpa had been attempting to make to defend himself against the star-demon – words no one but a devotee of She of the Silver Bells should have been able to use.

I woke up with a start, my heart hammering painfully against the confines of my chest. I felt stiff and sore; but when I attempted to move I only felt the dull, distant pain of healed wounds. It looked as if the priest of Patecatl had indeed come, and healed me while I was asleep – leaving me whole but weak and drained of everything. Great.

The dream remained hovering at the edges of my mind. But, like ice brought from the mountains, it thawed, leaving its revelations mercilessly clear.

Manatzpa. No wonder he had been angry when I had questioned him about his allegiances; no wonder he was willing to temporise, if it would buy the return of his goddess – to lie, to smile, to poison Ceyaxochitl to prevent her from prying any further.

Which meant…

I cast a glance at the empty bowl. I wasn't feeling any worse, but Ceyaxochitl had not felt the symptoms for a few hours after her return. There was no telling–

Enough. If he had poisoned me – and I could not see why he would take such a risk, not when he had defused my suspicions so deftly with the mention of Teomitl – then there was nothing I could do. Yaotl had said there was no antidote.

In the meantime… in the meantime, I lay alone, exhausted and defenceless with a sorcerer, a murderer and a poisoner as my sole company.

The Duality curse me, where were the other High Priests when you needed them?

There was no way in the Fifth World I could get out discreetly. In my current weakened state I wouldn't stay up long, and Manatzpa would catch up with me fast.

Not to mention the possibility he'd summon a star-demon, of course. But, even keeping to mundane happenings, the odds did not look good.

If the priest of Patecatl had already come, then the only person I was still waiting for was Teomitl – but he still hadn't come back.

I was going to need all of the gods' luck if I wanted to survive the night.

I must have slept, sliding in and out of consciousness, waking up with a vague dread before remembering my predicament, muttering confused prayers and letting darkness overtake me again. I dreamt of coldly amused stars watching me, of the gods turning Their faces away from the city, of Tizoc-tzin's coronation under the Heavens where shone a bright, cold moon that kept growing larger and larger against the thunderous rattle of huge bells…

I woke again, and the sky through the pillars was grey. Huitzilpochtli grinned at me from the frescoes, far away and powerless, resting in the heartland with no care for us. The air was bitterly cold. I shivered, and drew my cloak closer around me.

"I see you're awake."

I had half-expected the voice, what I had not expected was that it would come from so close to me. It took all the nerves I possessed not to jerk in surprise. "Manatzpa?"

He was sitting across from my sleeping mat. A bowl of maize porridge lay between us, along with dried algae. His face in the dim light was unreadable. "I brought you breakfast."

"Someone…" I fought to part my tongue from the palate where it seemed to have become stuck. "Someone has come."

Manatzpa looked curious. "Yes. The High Priests, the She-Snake and the Master of the House of Darts. They brought a priest of Patecatl with them, but couldn't wake you up even after the healing. I told them it wasn't worth disturbing you."

Quenami, Acamapichtli, the She-Snake and Tizoctzin – all the help I could have expected, but he had sent them away. No one would come back before daybreak. "And Teomitl?"

Manatzpa's eyes narrowed. Did I seem too eager to leave? He could not possibly have guessed that I knew. "I feel like I'm imposing on you," I said, with what I hoped was my most embarrassed smile.

"Not at all." His lips curled up, in that peculiar approximation of a smile. "Anything for the High Priest for the Dead. It's people like you that keep us safe."

He would know, of course. I lowered my gaze, as if embarrassed. In reality, I was wondering if Teomitl had come or not, if I could expect him.

Not that it mattered. I made as if to rise, but could not find the strength.

"Acatl-tzin." Manatzpa shook his head. "Surely you can't think of leaving so soon. Look at yourself."

"I have duties," I gasped, falling back on the sleeping mat.

"Your duties can wait." His eyes were dark, knowing. "Have some maize porridge."

And some poison? "I don't feel very hungry," I started, but when I saw the shadow steal across his face, I knew I'd gone too far. If he hadn't been suspicious before, he was now. "But I do appreciate all the trouble you're going through for my sake." I reached across, took the bowl, and raised it to my lips, hoping that I wasn't courting my own death.

The porridge was hot and spicy; my lips tingled from the first sip, but surely it was just my imagination? It couldn't possibly be that fast-acting.

Better not tempt luck, though. I took a few sips, made a face like a sick man who has discovered he can't stomach food so soon, and carefully laid the bowl down again. "I'd have thought a man of your stature would have slaves," I said.

Manatzpa shrugged, an expansive gesture that racked his whole frame. "I have several, but they're often on errands. I'm young enough to take care of myself, Acatl-tzin."

He sounded uncannily like Teomitl. If circumstances had been different, I might even have liked him. As it was...

Manatzpa was looking at me, his gaze thoughtful, as if trying to work out something. "Is anything wrong?" I asked.

His lips thinned to a pale brown line against the dark skin of his face, as if he were angry, or amused. "Nothing is wrong, Acatl-tzin. I just have many things to do, as I have no doubt you have."

I inclined my head, inhaling the sharp, spicy smell

of the maize porridge. "I have no doubt the council will be in a panic after what happened last night."

Manatzpa's face did not move. "Two deaths in so little time. Yes, that would be cause for concern." He gestured again towards the bowls. "You've barely eaten anything, Acatl-tzin. Please."

His eyes were too eager, too hungry. That was when I knew for sure that there *was* something in that porridge, something he wanted me to consume. My lips itched again, as if blood had just returned to numb flesh. Was that what had happened with Ceyaxochitl? "I've already told you," I said, very carefully. "I feel like my stomach has been overturned." I pointed to the bandages on my chest. "That tends to cut the appetite." It was hardly a lie. In the past few moments, the feeling of emptiness had seemed to increase a hundredfold – not like the coming of a star-demon, but as if the existing hole in the centre of the Fifth World had spread – had become a maw, sucking me into its depths.

"I see." Manatzpa's lips curled up again. He didn't believe a word of it. "But you need it, believe me." His voice was flat, his eyes as dull as quarried stone. "If necessary, I'll force it down your throat."

My heart missed a beat; I tried to convince myself I'd misheard, but I knew I hadn't. "Manatzpa."

He knew. The sensation of emptiness was increasing in my chest. A hollow grew in my stomach, as if dozens of lumps of ice were forming there.

Manatzpa's face had changed; contempt and hatred filled the emptiness of his eyes, but he had it under control again in a heartbeat, becoming once again the harmless, round-faced man I'd first met. That was more frightening than anything I'd seen that night. "Let's not dance around each other like warriors at the gladiatorial sacrifice, Acatl-tzin. You know I can't possibly let you walk out of this room alive."

There was nothing here I could use; my weapons had been stripped from me, and none were in evidence. He had me backed against a wall, sitting between me and the only exit. Even if I hadn't been wounded…

The sensation of emptiness was becoming as crippling as the wounds. If I didn't act now, I never would.

I reached out in a heartbeat, the side of my hand catching the bowls of warm porridge and sending them flying into his face. Then I was up, ignoring the weakness that knifed through me, and running towards the exit with agility I hadn't known I possessed.

From behind me came curses, and the tread of heavier feet. He was wounded too, but I was drained. He would catch me…

I ran, pain beating like sacrificial drums in my chest. I swung the entrance-curtain out of the way in a jangle of bells, plunged into the courtyard and towards what I hoped was the exit.

I didn't look back, but I knew he was getting closer.

Another room; another set of entrance-curtains; another courtyard. I wasn't going the right way.

"Acatl-tzin. This is pointless," Manatzpa said behind me. His voice quivered, on the edge of breathlessness. "You cannot hope to get out."

I didn't bother to answer, just tried to run faster. But he caught the hem of my cloak, sending me sprawling to the ground. "You fool."

He stood over me in the courtyard under the red, swollen gaze of the Fifth Sun. Obsidian glinted in his hand; a knife. "This is going to be much harder to explain…"

The emptiness in my chest flared to life, a huge fist punching through the confines of the Fifth World. The air around us rippled, the sunlight dimmed, and a cold wind blew through the courtyard, prickling our skins like shards of obsidian.

"What?" Manatzpa asked, the knife pausing in its descent.

I didn't spare time to think. I pulled myself upwards again, and half-crawled, half-ran towards the entrance-curtain. There were voices, close by, indistinct murmurs that sounded like a lament for the dead.

I burst out of Manatzpa's rooms into the courtyard, and all but crashed into Teomitl.

"Acatl-tzin?"

He wasn't alone. A group of guards accompanied him and, just next to him, were a priest of Patecatl, and my sister Mihmatini, pale and wan and looking as though she wanted to tear me to shreds for deliberately splitting my wounds open again. "Acatl!"

I struggled to speak, the air in my lungs like searing fire.

The entrance-curtain tinkled again and Manatzpa staggered out, still holding the knife. It took him a moment to understand what he was looking at; but then his lips curled into a bitter smile, and he threw the knife away. "I see," he said. "It was good game. A pity I lost."

Teomitl looked from me to Manatzpa, but he had never been a man to hesitate for long. "Arrest him." He half-turned towards me. "And there had better be some explanations."

Explanations. Yes. I looked up, at Tonatiuh the Fifth Sun, Whose light was once more bright and welcoming. But I was not fooled. The hole in the Fifth World had widened again; and it could only mean one thing.

The Guardian of the Sacred Precinct – Ceyaxochitl, agent of the Duality in the Fifth World, my friend and mentor – was dead.

There were explanations; or, at any rate, all those I could offer Teomitl, given my current knowledge. He all but carried me to his room, where he insisted I lie down.

"You need rest," Teomitl said, fiercely. "You shouldn't over-exert yourself."

"As if he'd do it," Mihmatini said, from where she was sitting, in the furthest corner of Teomitl's room. "My brother is one of those men who can kill themselves quite effectively by sheer exertion."

Teomitl raised a hand. "Not now." He turned back to me, his face hardened into stone. "I want to know what happened."

He listened to my increasingly confused explanations, his face growing darker as I spoke. "The Guardian is dead?"

"I'm not sure. You could send to the Duality House." But I *was* sure, and the emptiness in my chest, the tightness in my eyes, weren't only because of the hole in the Fifth World. Ceyaxochitl had loomed large over my life, and, much as I wanted not to believe that she had gone, I had seen enough people deny Lord Death's grip on their lives, and pay the price for their blindness. Death should be accepted, and the living should move on.

I knew this. But still, I couldn't keep my voice from shaking, couldn't stop the prickling in my eyes.

"And Manatzpa is the summoner?"

"Yes," I said. "And the man who killed Ceyaxochitl." But it made no sense. Manatzpa's life had been as much in danger as ours and he had seemed genuinely angry at Echichilli's death. And, to cap it all, he had not been able to cast out the star-demon. "I'm not sure, actually. Some things just don't fit."

"I see." Teomitl's gaze was dark and thoughtful. "I'll ask Tizoc if I can interrogate him, then."

"He's in Tizoc-tzin's hands?" I asked. If he'd been in any hands but Teomitl's, I'd have expected the She-Snake's.

"Those were his guards." Teomitl sounded genuinely surprised. "Do you think I have my own?"

"You're Master of the House of Darts."

"Not yet." His voice was low and fierce. "I have to be worthy of it first."

"I should think you've proved yourself amply."

He sighed. "You're not the one who makes the decisions, Acatl-tzin."

A fact I knew all too well. "Still…"

"Still, I'm a troublemaker." His lips twisted into a smile. "Not ready for politics. But with Tizoc's help, this should sort itself out."

"You went to see him yesterday," I said. "When you said you were going to dismiss the *ahuizotls*."

"What of it?"

"Nothing," I said. "Except that you could have told me the truth."

"I know how you feel about my brother." Teomitl's face had grown cold again.

Silence stretched, tense and uncomfortable. It was Mihmatini who broke it. "Teomitl," my sister said. "He needs rest. Honestly."

Teomitl looked up and down. His gaze darkened, as if he didn't like what he saw. "Yes, you're right." He rose, stopped by her side to run a hand on her cheek. "Take care of him."

She smiled. "Of course."

A tinkle of bells, and then he was gone, leaving me alone with my sister. Somehow, I wasn't sure this was an improvement. "Acatl–"

I raised a shaking hand. "I know what you're going to say. I need sleep, I need my wounds to close; and I need to stop traipsing around the palace on too little food."

"See? I don't even need to say it." Her face went grave again. "Seriously, Acatl."

"Seriously," I said, pulling myself up against the wall. "You shouldn't be here."

She puffed her cheeks, thoughtfully. "Why?"

I wasn't deceived. I might not have been a big part of her childhood, since more than ten years separated us, but I knew all her ways of deflecting my attention. "You must know that you're not welcome here." That you weaken Teomitl's position – that you open him wide to Tizoc-tzin's accusations, however unfounded they might be...

But I couldn't tell her that. I couldn't repeat the horrors Tizoc-tzin had said about her.

"Acatl." Her gaze narrowed. "My brother is gravely wounded. I don't care what it looks like. Knowing you," she said, darkly, "you might have killed yourself before I got there."

Manatzpa had almost taken care of that. "Look–"

"No, you look. I'm not a fool. I know who doesn't want me here; and I know that he's not Revered Speaker yet."

"He's still powerful enough to cause you a lot of trouble."

"What's he going to do?" Her gaze was bright and terrible, and for the first time she looked more like a warrior-priestess than my smiling, harmless sister. "I don't have a position at Court, or anything he can touch. He can order me not to see Teomitl again–" she stopped, her eyes focusing on me. "Oh."

I shook my head. "No. He wouldn't dare displace me. Not now." I wasn't so sure, but it was reassuring that more than a day had elapsed since my interview with Tizoc-tzin, and that I was still High Priest for the Dead.

Or perhaps Tizoc-tzin was just biding his time. I didn't know. I'd never pretended to understand how his mind worked.

I steered the conversation to another, albeit related, subject. "Teomitl has been different lately."

Mihmatini sat by my side with a sigh. She wore her black hair long in the fashion of unmarried women, it fell back from the smooth, perfect oval of her face. that is, until she spoiled the effect by grimacing. "He has a lot to face. He might be Master of the House of Darts in a few days, one of the inner circle, moving in the wake of power."

"I didn't think that would frighten him," I said, finally.

"No. But you know how he is." She smiled, a little self-consciously. "Always trying to be the best at everything, always judging himself to have fallen short."

Was that the only explanation? "And that's why he talks to Tizoc-tzin."

"You might not like him," Mihmatini said, and the tone of her voice implied she didn't much care for him either. "But he's still Teomitl's brother. They still share something."

"I guess," I said, finally. Out of all my brothers, the only one I saw semi-regularly was the eldest, Neutemoc, a Jaguar Knight and successful warrior elevated into the nobility. But our understanding was recent and fragile, and I couldn't say he'd ever been much of a confidante.

If anyone had filled that role, it had been Ceyaxochitl.

"Acatl?" Mihmatini asked.

"It's nothing." I watched the light glimmer across the entrance-curtain, and wondered if things would ever feel right again.

I couldn't believe they would.

ELEVEN

The Obsidian Butterfly

I must have slept again. The priest's healing spell was more effective than bandages, but still no miracle. I woke to the bright light of early morning. A whole day had elapsed, lost to my healing.

Teomitl was nowhere to be seen; not surprising, given my student's inability to sit still at the best of times.

Mihmatini lay curled up in sleep behind me, looking oddly young and innocent – she who was eighteen, almost too old to be married and have children of her own already. I revised my opinion of Teomitl's disappearance. I wouldn't have been surprised if he had slept elsewhere, rather than cast a slur on my sister's virginity.

Good.

Everything ached, from the ribs in my chest to the stiffness in my legs, and I felt even more empty than before, as if hope and joy had drained out of me into the hole in the Fifth World.

I got up. My head didn't spin, a vast improvement over my previous awakening, and I could stand steadily on my legs. Slowly, carefully, I dressed again into something suitable for the High Priest for the Dead, and went back to the Revered Speaker's room.

The room was subdued, the few priests for the dead left were renewing the blood around the quincunx with their own, making sure that nothing untoward could follow the Revered Speaker into the underworld. Palli himself was sitting cross-legged at the centre of the quincunx, watching a silver plate which depicted the progress of the soul through the nine levels of Mictlan. From time to time, his lips would move around an incantation, and he would nod. Everything appeared under control.

I leaned against a wall, watching them, the familiar chants and litanies washing over me, reassuring and unchanged. For all the chaos and the uncertainty, death remained constant, always by our side, something to be relied on no matter what else might transpire.

A refuge, a goddess had once told me accusingly. I'd flinched at the time, but now I knew that she was right, and that it was nothing to be ashamed of. Everyone had a refuge: some in pomp, some in family. Mine was a temple and chants and bodies, and the god that was everywhere in the Fifth World, underlying even the most boisterous songs, the most vivid flowers.

At last, there came a pause in the rituals. Palli looked up, and his eyes met mine. He gestured to another of the priests, and motioned him to take his place at the centre. Then, carefully, he stepped out of the quincunx and walked towards me. "Acatl-tzin."

"Tell me what's going on," I said.

"Revered Speaker Axayacatl-tzin is on the third level," Palli said. "Nothing unexpected so far."

The third level was the Obsidian Hills, still a relatively friendly place by underworld standards. If something bad happened, it would be on the deeper levels, where the beasts and creatures of the under-world prowled. "And the search?" I asked.

Palli grimaced. "For the place of the star-demon summoning? I put all the priests the order could spare into this. So far, no one has reported anything useful."

I suppressed a curse. A full dozen priests searching the palace, I knew the place was huge, but they had the help of spells, and surely one of them would have found something useful by now. "I see. Send to me the moment they find something."

Palli nodded. He hesitated, then said, "Acatl-tzin, one more thing. You remember the tar you noticed on the floor?"

I had to cast my mind back a day and night, to the ritual in which I'd spoken to Axayacatl-tzin. It seemed a lifetime ago. "Yes," I said. "It seemed odd, but…"

Palli's face was pale. "I did think it was familiar," he said. "Someone died in this room."

"The Revered Speaker," I said carefully, without irony.

"It's an older death. A… sacrifice."

In the Revered Speaker's private rooms… Not in a temple, not on an altar?

"An older death," I said, slowly. "A powerful one, then, if you can still detect it." I thought, uneasily, of the missing councilman both Manatzpa and Echichilli had been angry about, the one that seemed to have vanished from the records and from the palace. What had been his name again?

Pezotic.

"Yes," Palli said. "A powerful death." His lips twisted. "I'm not sure, Acatl-tzin, but something is wrong about this."

"What?"

"Too much power," Palli said.

I bit my lips. There were ways and means of ampli-fying the power received from a human sacrifice, but almost all of the ones I could think of required a High Priest's initiation. "Can you look into this?"

Palli grimaced. "I can try," he said.

A full human sacrifice. An old, powerful death. Something was going on in this palace. Something… untoward. Even before the Revered Speaker's death, then. But he'd died of natural causes; we were sure of that, at least.

Then what was happening? Some ritual to undermine the Empire at its core? "Do you know what they used the magic for?"

Palli shook his head. "Something very large."

"But not the summoning of a star-demon." If that had been the case, he'd have told me long beforehand.

"No. The magic's wrong for that," Palli said. "It feels beseeching. Desperate."

"Hmm," I said, thoughtfully. I didn't like this; I couldn't see how it fitted in with anything – with Manatzpa, with Ceyaxochitl's death – but it didn't augur anything good. I added it to my questions for Manatzpa, once I managed to see him.

I finished with Palli, and wrote a message to Ichtaca, asking him to send someone to the Duality House in order to prepare the funeral rites for Ceyaxochitl.

Then, still weak and trembling, I went to see the She-Snake, the only person who might have an idea of what was going on in the palace.

I'd expected to have much further to go, but I found him in the council room, sitting on the reed mat at the centre, eating a meal. As he ate he listened to a report from one of his black-clad guards. His round face was grave.

"Acatl?"

I didn't feel in the mood for apologies or pomp, but I did gingerly bow.

"Glad to see you recovered," the She-Snake said. He dipped his chin, and the guard moved away slightly. I was left with the full weight of his gaze on me. It was peculiar, he was soft, and middle-aged, and I would have expected him to be drab. But the gaze, piercing and shrewd, gave him away.

"I, er, understood you visited me," I said.

"Indeed." His voice was grave. "Had I known about Manatzpa, I might have done more than visit. But no matter. It is done now."

I waited, but nothing more seemed to be forthcoming. "I need your help," I said.

"My help?" He sounded mildly amused.

"You keep the order in the palace. Don't tell me this situation makes you happy."

His lips thinned to a muddy line, but his expression didn't change. "I expected trouble when Axayacatl-tzin died. I'm not surprised."

I doubted much would ever surprise him. "But you want the attacks to cease?" I pressed. I remembered, uneasily, what Axayacatl-tzin had told me about the She-Snake's unorthodox manner of worship. But even if it was true, he would want to be seen maintaining order.

"I see. What did you have in mind?"

"I want men."

"They are in short supply."

"Look," I said. "Those star-demons, they're being summoned here, inside the palace wards. Someone, somewhere, has converted a room for the purpose."

He was quick to seize my meaning. "And it's a large palace."

"I've had my priests search it, but we're not enough."

"Surely, you would need magical training to find such a spot."

I shook my head. "It's going to be large, and bloody, and definitely not discreet." Not given the amount of power that had been expanded to call so many star-demons down into the world in such a short time.

"I see." The She-Snake pressed both hands together, thoughtfully. "I see." At length, he looked up, and fixed me again with his gaze. "I'll send the men I can spare. Was there anything else?"

"Do you know where the other High Priests are?"

That same mirthless smile quirked up the corner of his mouth. "Quenami is with Tizoc-tzin. Acama-pichtli… I fancy we won't see much of Acamapichtli in the days to come."

"I don't understand."

"Oh, come, Acatl." His gaze was pitying. "He threw his weight behind the Texcocan princess. Gambled it all, and lost it all."

"He's…" I started, and stopped. Nothing short of death or treason could remove a High Priest from his post.

"He's in disgrace, if that's what you mean. Not that he wasn't before, mind you."

The whole business with the Storm Lord trying to take over the Fifth World. Acamapichtli seemed to have a singular gift for backing the wrong person or god.

I'd have pitied him, if he hadn't been the man who'd tried to condemn my brother to death. "If we were to arrest all the men who backed the wrong person in this struggle, the palace would empty itself fast," the She-Snake said. He still sounded amused, as if he secretly relished the chaos.

I didn't trust him. I couldn't.

"Arresting the waverers might give people a reason to stop playing," I said darkly, and took my leave from him.

• • •

I made my way back to Teomitl's room, where I found Mihmatini still sleeping. Thank the Duality; if she'd woken up and found me gone, I might not have survived her sarcastic remarks.

I looked up at the sun. It was almost noon, and I'd eaten nothing all day. I managed to find a servant in one of the adjoining courtyards, and sent him to the kitchens for a meal.

While I waited for his return, I mulled on what Palli had told me.

A death – a powerful one – and star-demons. Perhaps a last entreaty against chaos, made by a desperate man? But why tar, and why the Revered Speaker's rooms? There was a place for rituals like this, in the Great Temple, the religious heart of the city. Why there, unless it was something specifically connected to the Imperial family?

The bells on the entrance-curtain tinkled. "Come in," I said, keeping my voice as steady as I could.

It was Yaotl, still garbed in his warrior's costume. He looked worse than before. The blue paint did not mask the dark circles under his eyes, or the paleness of his face. He cast a distant glance in Mihmatini's direction, but made no comment. "I heard you got into more trouble," he said.

I said nothing. There was nothing I could say. In the light, his eyes were huge, a reservoir of grief that spilled over into the Fifth World.

"She died just after dawn." Yaotl did not bother to sit. I thought he didn't want to remember that he was my social inferior; not now, not when his whole world seemed to come undone around him.

"I felt it," I said. I hesitated. I knew all the words, all the empty things one could say when Lord Death has taken his due. They meant nothing save comfort to the living. But Yaotl served the Duality, and he would know that death was part of the eternal balance, that destruction and creation were entwined like lovers, making and annihilating the world in an endless dance. "I can't believe she's gone," I said, settling for the truth.

Yaotl's lips thinned to a line. "Me neither. I keep expecting her to rise from her funeral mat and take charge." His gaze wandered again. "I hear you arrested the poisoner?"

"I think so," I said, cautiously.

"It's all over the palace." Yaotl's voice was grim.

"And Xahuia?" He didn't look as though he had caught her, but one never knew.

"Gone to ground, too well hidden."

I nodded. "Even if she wasn't guilty, I don't think her activities were entirely lawful."

Yaotl barked a short, unamused laugh. "Resisting arrest alone would have been enough. We found the paraphernalia of sorcery in her private rooms: mummified animals, dried women's hands, arms preserved in salt baths…"

"The Smoking Mirror?" I asked, thinking again of Nettoni's touch on my skin.

"Yes," Yaotl said. "But nothing tied to the summoning of star-demons."

"I think that was Manatzpa," I said, feeling less and less convinced the more I thought about it. "You need to find her."

"I'm looking for her." Yaotl could barely hide his exasperation. "It's a big city, as you no doubt know."

I suddenly realised how we looked – two men meant to be allies, tearing at each other, no better or no worse than the rest of the Court. "Forgive me," I said. "It's been a long couple of days."

"For both of us." Yaotl smiled, a pale shadow of the terrible, mocking expressions he'd throw at me. There was no joy in it whatsoever.

Then again, I guessed I didn't look much better.

The heavy silence was broken by the jarring sound of bells struck together. Teomitl had lifted the entrance-curtain with his usual forcefulness, and was striding back into the room. He was followed by the servant I'd sent for a meal, who appeared much less eager.

"Acatl-tzin," Teomitl said.

I rose, gingerly, leaning on the wall for support. "I take it you were able to speak to him."

Behind him, the servant moved, to lay his tray of food on one of the reed mats. He bowed, and was gone.

Teomitl barely noticed any of this. "I spoke to Man-atzpa, yes." He looked a fraction less assured, a fraction less angry. The arrogance I'd seen over the past few days had almost faded away, leaving only the impatient adolescent, as if whatever Manatzpa had told him had shattered Tizoc-tzin's influence.

"And?" Yaotl asked, shaking his head impatiently. "Did he confess?"

Teomitl looked at him blankly.

"The murder of Guardian Ceyaxochitl," I prompted him.

"Oh." He did not look more enlightened. "We didn't talk about that."

"Then what about?" Yaotl was fuming by now.

"About the star-demons." Teomitl's face was hard again, on the verge of becoming jade. "He's said that he'll only talk to you, Acatl-tzin."

I briefly woke Mihmatini to let her know where we were going. She made a face of disapproval I knew all too well, a mirror image of Mother's when my brother or I had broken a dish or muddied a loincloth. "You haven't eaten anything."

I pointed to the tray the servant had left. "I had maize soup. And a whole newt with yellow peppers."

Her gaze made it clear she wasn't fooled. "Acatl, you're in no state to walk."

"I feel much better." And it was true; utterly drained, but much better. The pain was gone, leaving only the dull feeling that nothing would ever be right again.

Mihmatini made a face that told me she didn't believe me. "I should come with you," she said.

Teomitl put a hand on her arm gently. "No. Not now."

"But–"

"Out of the question," I said. My judgment might be a little shaky now – a little pale and empty like the veins in my body – but there was no way I would let her walk into Tizoc-tzin's chambers.

"Acatl-tzin is right," Teomitl said. "My brother won't be happy to see you, and this isn't the time for this."

"Teomitl…"

He shook his head again. "No."

And that effectively ended the conversation, though Mihmatini glowered like a jaguar deprived of its prey. "I'll be waiting for you," she said, and the way she spoke made it doubtful she'd hand out hugs or flowers.

I could feel Yaotl's amused gaze on my back all the way to Tizoc-tzin's chambers; but he said nothing.

I wondered what Manatzpa could have to tell me. How he could not hate me, when I had been the one who had brought him down? Most likely he would taunt me. I doubted that he would bend. In that way, he was very much like his nephews Tizoc-tzin and Teomitl. But there might be something to be gleaned, information that would help us. For if my gut feeling was right and he was not the summoner of star-demons, then we still had someone out there, busily plotting our ruin.

I'd expected some silence in Tizoc-tzin's courtyard; or at any rate, some mark that something was wrong

175

with the palace, but it seemed like nothing had changed. Warriors gathered on the platform, laughing among themselves. Noise floated from Tizoc-tzin's rooms, the singsong intonations of poets reciting compositions, the laughter of warriors, the deep rhythm of beaten drums. But underneath, in the wider courtyard, were other warriors, dressed far more soberly, their long cloaks barely masking the whitish scars on their limbs. They talked amongst themselves, casting dark glances at the finery on the platform; the other part of the army, the true warriors, the ones who would support only a veteran, not a mediocre fighter like Tizoc-tzin.

If nothing else, things were starting to get ugly here, with factions openly declaring themselves.

Teomitl, oblivious, strode into a smaller courtyard, a mirror image of the House of Animals, loaded with exotic trees and bushes. It seemed as though we had stepped into another world altogether, a land to the south where the heat was stifling and quetzal-birds flew in the wild, raucously calling to each other. Cages dotted the landscape at regular intervals, huge, empty, their wooden bars almost merging with the foliage of the trees. The air smelled of churned mud, with the faint, heady fragrance of flowers. What was not expected, however, was the reek of magic, so strong it burnt my lungs.

"Something is wrong," I said, but did not have time to go further.

She stepped out of the caged wilderness as if She belonged within it; tall, Her skin as black as the night sky, and stars scattered at Her elbows and knees, stars that were also the eyes of monsters. Her cloak spread behind Her – no, it was not a cloak, but wings made of a thousand shards of obsidian, glinting in sunlight – and her face was pale skin, stretched over the hint of a skull, with bright, malevolent eyes that held me until I fell to my knees, shaking.

"Priest. Warrior. Slave." Her gaze swept through us all. I clenched my hands to stop my fingers from shaking. "You're too late," She said.

Something shone clung to Her wings, a light that was neither sunlight nor starlight; the memory of something that had once belonged in the Fifth World. A soul, ripped from its body.

Manatzpa.

She threw me a last searing glance, and leapt over me with an agility I wouldn't have expected from something so monstrous.

And then She was gone, with only the reek of magic to remind us of Her presence.

My obsidian knives were warm, quivering under my touch, as if She had affected them too. I looked around. The air smelled of charnel and blood, and the single cage ahead of us had its bars broken.

We'd arrived too late.

Both Yaotl and Teomitl had gone down. Yaotl was still shaking, and Teomitl was pulling himself up, with the wrath of Chalchiuhtlicue filling his face.

"What was that?" he asked.

"I–" She had looked like a star-demon; but different, too: not a mindless thing, but a goddess in Her own right, unmistakably female. "Itzpapalotl," I said, fighting past the constriction in my chest. "The Obsidian Butterfly, Goddess of War and Sacrifice." Leader of the star-demons, She who would take us all into Her embrace, when the time came.

"That's impossible," Yaotl remained sitting in the mud, oblivious to the growing stain on his cloak. "She's–"

"I know." Imprisoned, like Coyolxauhqui of the Silver Bells, like the star-demons.

"Why now, Acatl-tzin?"

"Because someone did not want Manatzpa to talk." A chill had descended into my stomach and would not be banished. Because he had known something, because he would, indeed, have revealed it to me?

Whoever it was they were in the palace, and aware of what was happening in Tizoc-tzin's closest circle. Either Xahuia still had agents inside, or...

Or it was someone else entirely.

"Acatl-tzin!" Teomitl's voice was impatient. "Come on."

I must have looked blank, for he shook his head impatiently, the whites of his eyes shifting from jade to white and back again as he did so, an eerie effect.

"It's still in the city. We have a chance to catch up to it. Come on!"

Still in the city? Why hadn't it–

No time to think. I picked up my cloak from the ground, shook some of the mud loose, and ran after Teomitl.

As we exited the palace, running down the stairs leading up to the Serpent Wall and the Sacred Precinct, the *ahuizotls* came, slithering out of the canal besides the palace. Their faces wrinkled like those of a child underwater for too long, their tails curling up into a single clawed hand, which opened and closed as they moved.

On ground, they looked wrong, as black and sleek as fish out of the water, crawling on their four clawed legs like salamanders or lizards, and yet still moving with a fluid, inhuman speed that seemed to surprise even Teomitl.

The star-demon was ahead of us, moving through the Sacred Precinct. The crowd fought to avoid Her, the pilgrims elbowing each other, sacrificial victims being pulled aside by their keepers, the priests hastily kneeling on the cleared-out grounds, fighting to trace quincunxes and circles in a vain attempt to slow Her down or banish Her.

Teomitl, who was younger and much fitter than me, was already ahead, the *ahuizotls* fanning around him in a grisly escort. He moved in the trail left by the star-demon, widening the circle of emptiness she had left around Her.

I cast my mind out, trying to summon the Wind of Knives. Up and up it went, over the crowded plaza, over the houses of noblemen, past the canals and the islands on the outskirts, into the cenote, until His presence went up my spine, straightening it with one cold touch.

Acatl. I am coming.

I ran after the star-demon as fast as I could, my lungs burning, my chest itching, the presence of the Wind of Knives in my mind growing larger and larger…

For all of Teomitl's speed, he never quite managed to catch up to the star-demon. She strode through the plaza of the Sacred Precinct without pause, Her gaze stubbornly fixed ahead.

There was only one place She could be heading. "Teomitl!" I called in the eerie hush that had spread over the Sacred Precinct.

He flicked me a quick backward glance; I pointed towards the bulk of the Great Temple, yelling at the top of my voice. Teomitl nodded, and resumed the chase.

The presence in my mind grew to a spike and suddenly the Wind of Knives was there, standing by my side. "Acatl."

He threw one glance at the situation, and moved, fluid and inhuman, towards the Great Temple, with barely a glance backwards in my direction. Where He passed, the air seemed darker, and even the sunlight, catching the thousand obsidian shards of His body, became dimmer, shadowed by His presence.

Priests had already gathered on the steps of the Great Temple; two cohorts, one on each of the twin stairs, their obsidian knives at the ready. Magic clung to them, shimmering in their blood-matted hair, on their dusty skins, in the very structure of the temple, sunk as deep as blood into limestone. Here was our strength; here was the heart of our Empire.

The wind of Her passage brushed the priests as She headed up the stairs. Everything shattered.

The priests' hair became dull and rank, like that of filthy animals; the stone lost its lustre and became the grey of ash and dust. The veil of magic over the temple tore open like a stretched spider's web, with a sound as stilling and as deafening of that of the earth splitting itself apart.

Itzpapalotl ran, one clawed hand scattering the priests across the stairs, sending them tumbling down, as bloodied as sacrificed victims. Teomitl followed, the *ahuizotls* sliding upwards like fish through water; the Wind of Knives overtook Teomitl on the stairs, but did not quite manage to catch up with Itzpapalotl.

I reached the bottom of the stairs, and paused for a moment to catch my breath.

One of the priests lay beside me, his blood shimmering in the sunlight, a source of power calling out to me. His eyes were open, already glazing over.

"Forgive me," I whispered, dipping my hand in the warmth of his blood. "She has to be stopped."

He must have nodded: I couldn't be sure, but the blood under my fingers became warmer, beating like a living heart, like that used for a penance or daily offering.

There was little time. Itzpapalotl was almost at the top of the stairs, and Teomitl lagged behind Her. I hastily traced a quincunx around myself, and said the shortest prayer I knew, one to my patron Mictlante-cuhtli.

> "We all must die
> We all must go down into darkness
> Leaving behind the marigolds and the cedar trees
> Nothing is hidden from Your gaze."

A thin layer of light shimmered into existence, an overlay over reality, nowhere near the level of detail of the true sight, but still more than I would have got from my priest-senses. The stairs of the temple turned a reddish black, like clotted blood, and every step I took sent a little jolt through my body – I could feel the magic bleeding out of the temple with every passing moment, like water draining out of a sieve.

At the top of the stairs, Ceyaxochitl's wards, once a shimmering blue, had also darkened, and the ragged hole in their centre marked the place Itzpapalotl had crossed them. Priests lay on the stairs, some dead, most unconscious.

I couldn't see Teomitl anywhere, but I assumed he'd have gone on without waiting for me. I hoped he was still alive, and in a state to fight.

I'd have had the same thought about the Wind of Knives; but I very much doubted anything could stop or incapacitate Him for long.

The stairs leading down to the temple's heart were silent, magic lazily bleeding out of them, a widening stain that was spreading within the Fifth World. The air was stale, dried-out, as if Itzpapalotl had drained everything out of it while descending.

I found Teomitl in the room near the foundations, the *ahuizotls* curled up at his feet like pet monkeys. He was watching the central disk with a scowl on his face.

The Wind of Knives stood a little to the side, His head turned towards me when I arrived, a glimmer of obsidian that pierced me to the core.

"I arrived too late," the Wind of Knives said.

Storm-Lord blind me, She was fast. "Is there anything–"

He shook His head in a shivering of dark light. "Not until She breaches the boundaries again." He seemed almost disappointed – unusual for Him. "Call me if you have need, Acatl." And then He faded away, the monstrous head slowly shimmering out of existence, the welter of obsidian shards receding into nothingness, until nothing was left but the faint memory of a lament.

Teomitl pursed his lips. "She just crossed to the centre, laughed at me and vanished."

I could tell that it was the laughter that bothered him most. Contempt, even coming from a star-demon, would have hurt him more than claw-swipes. But that wasn't what we needed to focus on now.

"Vanished," I repeated. I knelt by the side of the disk, cautiously extending one hand across it. The stone was warm, angry. Such anger, that of a caged being hurling itself against the walls of its prison, again and again until something yielded… Something had to yield, something had to crack, and She would be free to walk the world again, to watch humans scatter like insects, to drink our blood like stream-water…

I pulled my hand away, coming back to the Fifth World with a start. "Still imprisoned," I said aloud. Itzpapalotl had been summoned, like the rest of the star-demons. She hadn't spontaneously moved out of the stone disk; she hadn't been under any orders from Her mistress, She of the Silver Bells…

But I did not move. I crouched, watching the stone disk. The blood in the grooves had dimmed and dulled, too, as if its potency had been absorbed. And I couldn't be sure, but I could make out a hand and an arm, and a headdress with crooked edges – more details than before, as if everything were re-knitting itself together.

She of the Silver Bells was still imprisoned, but the Duality knew for how long.

I got up. Teomitl was still watching me with that peculiar intensity. "I should have known," he said, finally. "If I'd guessed Her destination earlier–"

"You can't rewrite the past," I said. "And if you hadn't launched in pursuit, we wouldn't even have known where She was going."

The stone disk lay at our feet, huge and monstrous, a gate to another country, a world waiting only to tear us apart and consume us. And Manatzpa was the only one who could have shed some light on how and when it was going to happen.

"I'm going to need something from you," I said.

He pulled himself straight, like a warrior standing to attention. "Acatl-tzin."

"You were the last person to see Manatzpa alive. I need you to tell me everything that he said when you interviewed him."

"Uh." Teomitl's face fell. "I don't exactly–" He shook himself and frowned. "A lot of things that didn't seem relevant."

I lifted my chin in the direction of the disk. "At this stage, it's safe to assume that anything might be relevant. We've had three deaths in the palace in a matter of days. At this rate, we'll be lucky to still have a council by the end of the week."

Teomitl shifted. One of the *ahuizotls* did the same, lazily raking its clawed hands on the stone. Nausea welled up in my throat, harsh and uncontrollable. I kept telling myself that, one day, I was going to get used to the creatures moving as though they were part of him; but it had been a year since Teomitl had acquired their services, and it still didn't get any better.

"He liked me." Teomitl appeared halfway between embarrassment and anger. "I thought it was a façade, but he didn't really need to pretend anymore, did he?"

"He might have hoped for your mercy."

"No." Teomitl shook his head, quick and fierce. "I've seen that happen, too, and it wasn't anything like that. More," he spread his hands, frustrated, "more like having someone you admire fighting for the other side. You know you'll never stop trying to capture each other, but still…"

I thought of Manatzpa's face when he had admitted Teomitl was the candidate he favoured above all others. I had assumed it to be a lie after he had revealed himself as a worshipper of She of the Silver Bells, but perhaps it had been more complex than that. "I see. What else?"

Teomitl grimaced. "He was unhappy about Echichilli's death."

I wanted to say it was obvious, but stopped. I couldn't possibly hope to get anything out of Teomitl if I was putting my own words in his mouth. "How so?"

"He…" Teomitl floundered for a while, before collecting himself. "I tried to tell him allying with star-demons was a foolish thing to do, that this needed to stop before the whole Fifth World crumbled. And he said something about duty. About how I was being so impressively dutiful, but that duty had killed Echichilli, and that he was done with duty himself."

Echichilli? I tried to remember who he had favoured. No one, as far as I could recall. He had been the oldest member of the council, aggrieved that no arrangement could be reached. "Duty to whom?"

"He didn't say," Teomitl said. "I'd guess either the She-Snake or…" He paused for a moment, and went on, "My brother. They're the only two to whom Echichilli could possibly have a duty."

Xahuia did seem like a pretty unlikely candidate. But we would gain nothing by being too hasty. And I had yet to understand how duty to anyone could have led to a star-demon killing Echichilli.

Unless he had been doing someone else's dirty work?

But no, he couldn't be the summoner of the star-demons, or, like Manatzpa, he would have been able to banish the one that had killed him. Instead, he had bowed to the inevitable...

"He knew something, too," I said. "Whatever it was. And he was killed for it."

"That doesn't really help, does it?"

"It might," I said. So far, I'd assumed the killings of the council had been random, intended to throw us all into chaos. But if both Manatzpa and Echichilli had been killed to silence them, then something else was going on. It was no longer exclusively a matter of making sure the council wouldn't select a Revered Speaker. There was something else going on; something much larger. "There has to be a reason behind the sequence of the killings. Something we're missing."

Teomitl grimaced again. "And?"

"I don't know." I was feeling increasingly frustrated. "All the dead men have been taken by star-demons. They're out of Mictlantecuhtli's dominion. I can't even hope to summon them and make them talk."

The usual way to get the ghosts of people who did not belong to Lord Death was to go into the lands of the god to whom they belonged, either Tlaloc the Storm Lord, or Tonatiuh the Fifth Sun. However, with star-demons, that was the epitome of foolhardiness. There was no way in the Fifth World I would elect to go into the empty spaces of the Heavens where they roamed, or into the prison the Southern Hummingbird had fashioned for His sister.

"Anything else?" I asked. It looked as though Itzpapalotl had done Her work well, we would not find any evidence left behind by Manatzpa.

"He said he wasn't the one summoning the star-demons, but that one seems obvious," Teomitl said, biting his lips to the blood. "No, not much else." He paused, his face unreadable. "He said other things, too."

He would not look at me; and given how Manatzpa had felt about Tizoc-tzin, I could guess what he had told Teomitl; something about being his own man, about stopping listening to his brother's voice.

To be honest, I doubted it would work. Teomitl might be thrown off for a while, bewildered by what appeared sincere admiration, but the fact remained that Manatzpa had been trying to take apart the Mexica Empire. Teomitl loved his country, and he would never forgive Manatzpa for that.

"I see. And Xahuia?"

Teomitl's face fell. "I didn't have time to broach that subject, Acatl-tzin…"

I raised a hand to cut him off. "No matter. You did great work. Come on. It's time to get some sleep."

TWELVE
The Coyote's Son

When we came back, late in the following morning, the palace was still in shambles. The She-Snake's guards strode in the corridor, trying very hard to look in charge but only managing a particular kind of extreme bewilderment. They looked at Teomitl as though he might have the answers to their aimlessness; but Teomitl glared at them, and even without the *ahuizotls*, he looked daunting enough that no one wished to approach him with trivial matters.

I probed at the wards on my way in. They still seemed solid and reassuring, but there was something, some yield to them, like pushing against taut cotton. They might hold, but they could be torn.

Ceyaxochitl could have woven more, but she was dead, and Quenami had made it clear he couldn't or wouldn't help.

"Where to?" Teomitl asked.

I shook my head. "Manatzpa's rooms. I'll met you there. I have something else to check first."

What I did was brief: I merely checked with Palli that the search was progressing as foreseen – and that the

187

She-Snake's promised guards had indeed arrived. There were more of them than I expected, though most of them were young, callow youths who still seemed to remember the feel of their childhood locks.

I guessed the She-Snake had a sense of humour.

"I've had better subordinates," Palli said with a sigh. "More respectful, too. But I guess I shouldn't complain."

"We'll take everything we can," I said, finally. "Everyone else seems to have other priorities at the moment." I hadn't seen my fellow High Priests in a few days. I couldn't say I missed their company exactly, but imagining what else they might have done did go a long way towards making me nervous.

Palli spread his hands, in a gesture that seemed an eerie mirror of mine. "We'll make do, Acatl-tzin."

And I had to be content with that.

"On another subject," Palli said, "I've found something about the tar."

"The stains on the floor?" I asked, suddenly interested again. They seemed to fit into the larger puzzle, though I wasn't sure how.

"Yes," Palli said. "Tar isn't exactly common in the palace."

I couldn't even think of where the nearest tar pit might be, or what they would use it for. "And?"

Palli grimaced. "You know Echichilli-tzin?"

The dead councilman? What had he got to do with it? "Yes, but..."

"He was the one who asked for it, about fifteen days ago. And..." He grimaced again, a nervous tic. "He asked for a lot of it, Acatl-tzin."

A lot of things hadn't made sense lately, but this was firmly near the top of the list. "A lot?"

"Ten full jars," Palli said.

My mind balked at the mental picture. It did have

cosmetic uses, but ten whole jars seemed excessive. "And what happened?"

"They came in. Echichilli-tzin sent his slaves to collect it. I've asked them. All they know is that it was brought here to the Revered Speaker's room."

"While he was still alive."

"Presumably with his consent."

"Hmm," I said. "Thank you. This is… intriguing." To say the least. "Let me know if you can find out more." Where had those jars gone, and what had they been used for? The only use that came to mind was seal the hull of a boat, and the thought of building a boat right in the Revered Speaker's rooms was absurd.

What was going in this palace? Whatever it was, it had started before the Revered Speaker's death, and it looked like we were the ones caught up in the consequences.

I fully intended to make sure the consequences weren't drastic.

I found Teomitl outside Manatzpa's rooms, in conversation with a stern, middle-aged woman who introduced herself as Manatzpa's wife. They'd had five children, the two eldest of whom were away, educated in the *calmecac* school. The three youngest were much too young to have noted much of importance; and Manatzpa's wife wasn't much more useful. She had barely known anything of her husband's affairs; the household policy had apparently consisted of "to each their own". She had not spoken of matters of domesticity; he had kept whatever business he had with the council and the Revered Speaker's election private.

The gods were decidedly not on our side.

We made a cursory examination of the rooms which didn't yield anything useful, and moved onto Manatzpa's private quarters.

In daylight they seemed much smaller than in my fevered imagination. They did wrap around two courtyards, but even the largest of them barely covered the surface of the Imperial Chambers. They had loomed much larger in my frantic flight of the night before.

As I had already noticed, the rooms were bare, with few ornaments. Manatzpa might have been a nobleman, but he had not believed in pomp any more than Teomitl. A few wicker chests and a few circular fans, carelessly tossed in corners where the feathers had creased, their colours all but faded; thin and simple reed mats, serving as little more than places to sit; and two unlit braziers.

I opened the wicker chests to find piles of vibrantly-coloured codices, ranging from lists of rituals to the tribute of the provinces. In the chest after that was poetry, carefully re-transcribed. Pride of place was given to a volume collecting the poetry of Nezahualcoyotl, the previous Revered Speaker of our neighbouring city Texcoco. The codex had been well-thumbed, but the glyphs were intact with no markings on the paper, the treasured possession of a man who seemed to have had few of them.

Altogether they painted the picture of a man whose interests had been broad, a scholar, an intellectual whose curiosity extended to everything and anything. A man I might have appreciated, more than I ever had Quenami or Acamapichtli, had the circumstances been otherwise.

Teomitl was rummaging through another chest, shaking his head as he discarded clay vessels and worship thorns. At length he crossed his arms over his chest. "This is pointless, Acatl-tzin."

I couldn't help shaking my head in amusement. Teomitl might have had the raw power and the fighting spirit, but the minutiae of investigations would always be beyond him. "Have a little patience," I said, pulling aside a third chest to reveal treatises on medicine. "Whatever he left behind, he wouldn't have wanted us to find it. It's likely well hidden."

Teomitl frowned and moved to stand against one of the frescoes, his head at the level of Huitzilpochtli's angry face. "We're wasting our time while they move against us."

I lifted an almanac on plants and their uses, and moved to the rest of the pile. "The problem is that we don't know who 'they' are."

"Too many suspects?" Teomitl shook his head.

"Too many agendas," I said. It was a given that everybody was dabbling in magic or planning political moves against their opponents. The question was whose moves included star-demons. Manatzpa had sworn it wasn't him; and his death tended to prove it. But Xahuia was still on the loose; not to mention those who still remained within the palace compound.

And, the Duality curse me, I still had no idea of how it all intersected or made sense. A plot to bring the star-demons down shouldn't have had this many complications, this many people dying to prevent them from talking. Whatever else I might have said about She of the Silver Bells, She'd always been straightforward, much like Her brother. No tricks, just fire and blood and war.

"I see." Teomitl was silent for a while. "Acatl-tzin, I wish to apologise."

I turned, genuinely surprised. "What for?"

"For the other night."

It took me a while to see what he was referring to. Ages seemed to have passed since that night when he had walked away from me in the wake of our interview with Tizoc-tzin. "Don't mention it. We have bigger problems on our hands."

"It's the little cracks that break obsidian. The flaws that undo jade," Teomitl said. He looked me in the eye – proud, unashamed, his was as unlikely an apology as I had ever seen, and yet oddly touching. "You have your opinion about my brother, and I have mine."

"Yes," I said, cautiously. I wasn't quite sure of what opinion to have about Tizoc-tzin anymore, except that we were still at each other's throats.

"Let it remain that way." Teomitl made a small, dismissive gesture, a command that could not be denied. "Let's not talk further about this, or we'll disagree."

Probably, but I didn't say this. "As you wish."

I lifted another medicinal codex. I was almost at the bottom of the pile now, and still had nothing to show for my labour. The Southern Hummingbird blind us, it looked like Manatzpa had been prudent to excess.

Wait.

The second-to-last paper in the pile was much smaller, a single sheet of maguey fibre. The writing on it was the neat, elegant hand of someone used to glyphs, every colour applied with a sense of context and decorum that could only belong to a temple.

"Ueman, Fire Priest of Quetzalcoatl, the Feathered Serpent, the Precious Twin:

"On this day Ten Flower in the year Two House, Councilman Manatzpa gave the temple ten rolls of the finest cotton cloths, fifty gold quills and one bag of quetzal tail-feathers, in exchange for the Breath of the Precious Twin."

The Breath of the Precious Twin was a costly protective spell that put the holder under the personal gaze of the god. Along with the Southern Hummingbird's protection, it was one of the most effective wards a man could barter for. I was wary of using it. Mictlan's magic was not compatible with Southern Hummingbird's spells, and while the Feathered Serpent might be one of the most benevolent deities, there was something inherently disturbing about having His eye permanently on me.

I hadn't seen it, but then he'd have taken precautions so it wasn't obvious. He had been a canny man – save, I guessed, when he'd started to resort to murder to have his way.

Mind you, the protective spell had not helped him much. The Obsidian Butterfly Itzpapalotl had sheared through it as though it barely existed and taken his soul with Her as easily as a man might take a basket of herbs.

The priest's name at the top of the paper was the same one Xahuia had given me. His title was given as Fire Priest, the second-in-command of the Wind Tower.

I turned the paper over thoughtfully. Ten Flower. Seven days ago. And the spell had not come cheap, either. Even for a man as rich as Manatzpa, the price was a fortune. Even before Echichilli's death Manatzpa had already been looking for protection, as if he had already known that something was going to happen. How had he known?

What in the Fifth World was this secret that star-demons killed for?

Behind us, the bells tinkled: one of the slaves, wearing the elegant collar of the palace servants around his neck. "Master, there is someone who wishes to see you."

"Us?" Teomitl stepped in.

The slave shook his head. "He asked for the High Priest for the Dead."

Someone I didn't know, then, not any of the players still remaining, who would have summoned me instead of coming here. But why me?

The youth who strode into the courtyard was a sight. It was not that he was richly dressed, with an elaborately embroidered cotton tunic, a plume of heron feathers at his belt and another set of feathers bending from the back of his head towards his neck. Rather, it was the state of the regalia – the feathers were torn, their white tarnished with blood, and dark splotches stained the tunic all around the collar line. He held his *macuahitl* sword a little too casually, as if daring an invisible watcher to attack him, and the shards shone a sickly grey-green in the sunlight.

Behind him were two Jaguar Knights in full regalia, the costume made of a jaguar's pelt and the helmet shaped like the jaguar's face, their heads protruding from between the jaws of the animal. They looked a little better, though their hands shook and their skin was the colour of muddy milk.

The youth looked at me. His eyes were an uncanny colour, a shade between grey and green. His gaze was piercing, not hostile, but stripping me of all pretences, like a spear breaking the skin and burying itself in my heart. "Acatl-tzin," he said thoughtfully. "High Priest for the Dead in Tenochtitlan. I have come to you for an accounting."

"An accounting?" Teomitl shifted, to stand between me and the youth. His hand had gone to the hilt of his *macuahitl* sword; and the planes of his face had started to harden.

The youth bowed, slightly ironically. "I am Nezahual, Revered Speaker of Texcoco. Where is my sister, Acatl-tzin?" His voice was harsh.

He couldn't be. I looked again, but he stood alone in the courtyard, with only two Jaguar Knights as an escort, casual and undisturbed, his dignity no less than it would have been had he sat in his own audience room. "Revered Speaker–"

"There is no point in dissembling. I know you were the one who ordered the arrest." Nezahual-tzin's face was harsh, unforgiving.

Teomitl shifted. "This is the High Priest for the Dead, one of the three who keep the balance of the Fifth World. You will show him respect."

Nezahual-tzin's gaze scoured him. A smile creased the corners of his broad lips. "A pup with a bite, I see." Sunlight fell over him in swathes, highlighting the blood on his clothes and on the obsidian studs of his *macuahitl* sword, and became a white, searing light strong enough to blind.

I remembered what Xahuia had said, that her brother was favoured by Quetzalcoatl, god of Creation and Wisdom. I had taken it as a grand boast, but quite obviously Nezahual-tzin had been brushed by the Feathered Serpent Himself. He might not have been an agent, the sole repository of the god's power, but he still had enough magic to make trouble if he wished to.

"Your god won't protect you." Teomitl's voice was scornful.

"Neither will your goddess, when it comes to this," Nezahual-tzin said.

I'd never thought I'd see two young men fight like cockerels, an unseemly spectacle, witnesses or not. "Enough."

The light dimmed. Nezahual-tzin still stood as straight as a spear, waiting for my answer. "Your sister engaged in sorcery," I said, carefully.

"So does most of the Imperial Family."

"Not that kind of sorcery. The sorcerer in her service was named Nettoni."

Nezahual-tzin's eyes narrowed. "Mirror" could only refer to one god – Tezcatlipoca, the Smoking Mirror and eternal enemy of his own patron god Quetzalcoatl. "You lie."

"Ask around the palace," I said as casually as I could. I already had enough enemies without adding this cocksure boy to the list. "He was well-known."

Nezahual-tzin was silent for a while, pondering, giving me enough time to consider what would happen if he held me responsible. Enough unpleasant things to make me regret Tizoc-tzin's threats of dismissal.

Then he turned to the two Jaguar Knights who had escorted him inside. "Is this true?" he asked, bluntly.

The Jaguar Knights looked at each other. "Yes."

"I see." The light around him contracted as if someone had enclosed it in a fist. "Where is she, Acatl-tzin?"

It wasn't quite the same tone, though he still didn't look happy. Not that I could blame him, though I doubted it was affection that prompted his question. To lose her would be a fatal admission of weakness to the Texcocans.

I, on the other hand, didn't care much about losing face. "I don't know. Nettoni sacrificed himself to let her and her son escape. Presumably they found refuge somewhere in the city." And presumably she was still weaving her webs of intrigue. She was a determined woman.

"I see." He said nothing for a while. "Then my men and I will join the search for her. Let it not be said that a Texcocan can escape justice."

Teomitl stiffened in shock. "She's–"

"A political tool," I cut in.

Nezahual-tzin smiled, without much joy. "You still have much to learn, pup."

"Pup?"

"Teomitl," I said, warningly.

"He's the one picking the quarrel."

"No, he's the one provoking you. You don't have to answer."

I glared at Nezahual-tzin, daring him to counter with some mocking remark about how to keep my pup on a leash. But his face was serious again, and he was

196

watching me with a gleam in his eyes I didn't care much for, like a snake making up its mind about a rodent. "Don't let me detain you," I said. "You must have plenty of rituals to attend, and respects to pay."

Nezahual-tzin smiled, that same thin, unamused smile I had seen on the face of the She-Snake. "No doubt." But he did not move, still considering me in that unnerving way of his.

"You owe respect to my brother," Teomitl cut in.

Nezahual-tzin's gaze moved, slightly. "The living one, or the dead one?"

"You know which one." Teomitl's face was flushed.

"The dead one." He turned to me, slightly bending his head, looking for all the world like a snake or a bird. "Apologies, Acatl-tzin. I knew him well in life, and I don't think he would begrudge me a little delay."

Of course, Axayacatl had been the one to save Nezahual-tzin, to cast down the over-ambitious brothers and bring the young Revered Speaker to Tenochtitlan. Which also meant he would know Tizoc-tzin and the She-Snake, and it did not look as though he was eager to see either. "The Dead can wait," I said, bowing my head in return. "But not on a caprice."

Nezahual-tzin shifted slightly, the obsidian shards of his *macuahitl* sword glinting in the sunlight. "Paying my respects is all I've come to do, after all. I'm Revered Speaker of Texcoco, and will not play a part in whatever squabbles Tizoc and the She-Snake have. But you don't look like a man likely to be caught in their games."

I wasn't sure whether to be embarrassed by his accuracy, or annoyed at the distant, unconcerned way he considered us all. Teomitl had no such scruples. "You look like a man too cowardly to be caught in anything, Nezahual-tzin."

Nezahual-tzin's lips curved around the word "pup", but he did not say it aloud, and luckily Teomitl didn't see it. "I've learnt to see where the priorities are " His gaze narrowed again, becoming infinitely distant, as if he held all the knowledge of the world. "For instance, you must have been wondering for a while where all the blood on us comes from."

Teomitl snorted. "What I've been wondering for a while is how you enticed the Jaguar Knights to follow you."

"Enticed? Hardly." Nezahual-tzin did not turn around. "But you're right, they're not my men."

I looked at the Knights again. My mistake, I should have known that Texcoco had no Jaguar House. Teomitl was obviously more knowledgeable about warrior orders than me, "Then…?" I asked. If he wanted to toy with us, fine. He was the Feathered Serpent's favoured indeed, enigmatic, taking advantage of the only thing he had, which was knowledge.

Nezahual-tzin made a gesture – satisfaction, annoyance? "Three star-demons. In the Jaguar House."

In daylight. Outside the palace wards. I scrabbled for words that seemed to have fled. "Did they kill anyone?"

I'd expected him to be triumphant at the shock he'd caused, to revel in our ignorance; but he looked serious again, like a commander on the eve of battle. "No. There are worse places where they could have appeared than a House of trained warriors."

It could have been worse. Much, much worse. The marketplace, the Houses of Joy…

I took a deep breath, hoping to close the hollow in my stomach. It didn't work. "So far, they've only appeared within the palace wards." It could mean the sorcerer was outside the wards, like, say, Xahuia, but then why had the Obsidian Butterfly, Itzpapalotl, been able to appear inside the palace and carry off Man-atzpa's soul? No, the most likely explanation was that the Southern Hummingbird's protection was diminishing, and that the star-demons had grown stronger in the Fifth World.

Nezahual-tzin exhaled, in what was almost a hiss. "And one at a time?"

He was quick, the Revered Speaker of Texcoco, lithe and smooth like the snake that symbolised his protector. "Yes," I said.

It *was* getting worse. The boundaries between the worlds were slowly and irretrievably caving in. "I don't suppose you had a councilman or someone important inside the House at the time?"

"Besides myself?" Nezahual-tzin asked.

"They didn't attack you, did they?"

He shook his head, quick and annoyed. "Not any more than any of the other Knights. And the answer is no. Even the Jaguar Commander was absent."

No, not worse. Disastrous.

Teomitl was looking from Nezahual-tzin to me, back and forth, with growing determination on his features. "Then my brother has to be told. A new Revered Speaker must be chosen."

His naiveté was heartbreaking. "Teomitl, it's not that simple…" The problem wasn't only Tizoc-tzin. We would have to convince the She-Snake, as well as every single remaining member of the council. Tizoc-tzin wasn't popular enough to force the delayed vote.

"I don't see what's complicated. The Fifth World stands in jeopardy. Any personal interests must be set aside."

"If only." Nezahual-tzin's voice was sad, much older than his years.

Besides, even if a vote could be forced, it would take at least a day to set up, and further time to prepare the rituals of accession, time we no longer had. Star-demons on the loose, outside the palace, meant a greater threat than ever before. They had come not because they had been summoned, not because they had someone to kill, but of their own volition; for their own amusement.

Which meant the path to the Fifth World was wide enough to let them pass; and that we would see many more of them before the sun set.

"It's not a matter of days," I said. "Or even of hours. We have to do something, and we have to do it now."

"I imagine you know what?" Nezahual-tzin asked.

"Of course he knows," Teomitl snapped.

How I wished I did. Doing something. Doing… I racked my brains for an answer. My protector Lord Death had made it abundantly clear that He would not interfere in the affairs of humans. The Fifth Sun and the Southern Hummingbird had already demonstrated how weak they were. I held neither the favour of Tlaloc the Storm Lord, nor or his wife Chalchiuhtlicue, Jade Skirt, and I did not trust those two more than I had to. The Smoking Mirror, god of Fate and War, was to become the Sixth Sun, and could not be relied on, not to mention that he had tried to topple the Fifth Sun more times than I could count. Among the powerful gods, it left only the Feathered Serpent, to whom I did not have any particular ties. Perhaps Nezahual-tzin, who stood under the shadow of Quetzalcoatl, the Feathered Serpent…

On the other hand, I didn't see why I'd trust the boy just yet, with something that important. And yet…

I closed my eyes. The Duality was the source and arbiter of all the gods; our protector, the keeper of the souls that would be reborn under the Sixth Sun. Ceyaxochitl had been Their agent, and no new one would be invested for a while, not until the rituals for her succession could be completed; but it didn't mean They had withdrawn from us. Their wards around the palace, flimsy as they were, were probably our last possible defence.

But there had to be a way...

I was a priest for the Dead, and I did not know much of Duality lore.

But I knew someone who did.

"You cannot be serious." Yaotl's lips had thinned to a harsh line, the same colour as heart's blood.

"Do you see a better plan?" I asked.

We had left the boy-emperor of Texcoco to make his own way into the palace, no doubt clamouring for an absent Tizoc-tzin. He had looked at me thoughtfully as he left, a gaze that promised something I couldn't quite interpret: another meeting, or a challenge? He had more depths than I could probe currently, and since his protector god was not involved in the ongoing troubles, I was going to leave him well alone for now.

But I had little doubt we would meet again.

We had made our way into the Duality House, where we had found Yaotl having his noon meal. He had invited us to join him, though he surely had to be changing his mind, now that he knew what we were asking for.

Yaotl shook his head. "No. But it's not–"

"Ideal? I think we're well past that stage."

Yaotl sighed. "Fine. I already have all the priests I can spare warding the major temples of the Sacred Precinct. But it's not going to be enough."

"Then what would be?" I asked. "A new Guardian?"

"You don't become Guardian that easily." Yaotl's voice was grave, measured, carefully counting words, not focusing on their meaning. "The rituals of the investiture take time."

In other words, what I had known all along: it would be too late by the time the Duality could intervene. "There has to be a way we can get more than wards," I said. "Their equivalent of living blood." For any other god, it would have taken a human sacrifice: a removal of a heart, a drowning, a stabbing, the offering of a whole life and vessels brimming with blood. After all, the gods were dead, Their blood drained to feed the sun at the beginning of this age, Their own hearts long since torn out and burnt in honour of Tonatiuh the Fifth Sun. Only through living blood could They exercise Their power.

Yaotl grimaced. His eyes, wandering, fell on Teomitl; he stopped then, stared at the fresco behind Teomitl, which depicted the Fifth Sun rising from His pyre. "Wait here," he said, and was out of the room before either of us could stop him.

When he came back, he had two old priests in tow, a man and a woman who moved in precise, economical gestures. They wore the regalia of high-ranking clerics, a headdress of heron and duck feathers, and black cloaks with a blue hem depicting the fused-lovers symbol of the Duality. The priests looked at Teomitl speculatively for a moment, and then gave Yaotl a curt nod.

Teomitl, for whom patience was an alien word, wasn't about to be cowed, old priests or not. "Well?"

"There is a way," Yaotl said, slowly. "You're not going to like it."

That he said it in such a fashion, with no attempt whatsoever at sarcasm, was possibly the most worrying thing.

"Tell us," Teomitl snapped.

"You mentioned a new Guardian."

"To which you said it wouldn't help."

"They wouldn't have the Duality's powers, no," Yaotl said. "That takes time. The Duality doesn't choose

Their agent on a whim. But, symbolically…" He pursed his lips. "Guardians are still the representative of the Duality in this world. The right choice, accompanied by the right rituals, could be the equivalent of a magical statement."

"The right choice," I said, slowly. "I don't understand what you're trying to say."

"Imperial Blood," Yaotl said. "To signify the tie between the Duality and the Fifth World. And a young woman, to remember that the Duality is the source of all life. The creator principle, male and female…"

"I don't understand," Teomitl said.

I did, and I didn't like where this was going. I remembered Ceyaxochitl's late-night confidences, that she had been married once, which had made her into the living symbol of the Duality. "You're jesting. Surely–"

"Of course I'm not jesting." Yaotl's lips curled up in a savage smile, and for a moment he was once more the insolent slave I'd known all my life.

"There is a chain of succession," I said. "Proper forms. You just can't choose a Guardian like this! You–" I stopped, then, for I'd been able to accuse him of being a mere slave. That would have been a mistake. Here in this room he was not my social inferior, but Ceyaxochitl's assistant, the man who held the order together.

The old priestess spoke up. "Ceyaxochitl-tzin had been watching the young woman for a while. She's impulsive, and untrained, and inexperienced, but all these can be remedied."

"Look," I said, feeling I was fighting against the lake's current in the rainy season. "Ceyaxochitl wasn't young. She made plans for her succession. There is a second-in-command, or someone like this, who's been waiting for years to claim the place. You can't…" You can't just go and give it to my sister, who's never asked for it in the first place.

"Our order will take decisions as it sees fit," the old priestess said, with the same authoritarian tone as Ceyaxochitl in her worst moods. "Our charge is the boundaries of the Fifth World, not politics."

And they were naive if they thought politics didn't apply.

"You don't even know if she's willing."

"Her wishes," the old priest said, firmly, "are the least of our concerns."

Clearly they didn't know Mihmatini at all, to say that. "There has to be someone else–"

"No." Yaotl's voice was firm. "It has to be a virgin of childbearing years, with magical knowledge, and associated with another virgin of Imperial blood. Can you think of anyone else, Acatl?"

I would have liked to, but no matter how much I racked my brains, I couldn't think of another name. For the sake of the Fifth World...

I made a last attempt to stem the tide. "You do know Teomitl is linked to another god."

The priest sniffed. "To two gods, as a matter of fact. But we're not asking him to be Guardian."

"You're still asking him to be a Guardian's husband," I said.

The priestess looked Teomitl up and down, clearly more for show than for anything else. Her mind seemed to have been made up before she entered the room. "We've discussed it. It's somewhat problematic, but the other benefits outweigh the risks."

The words weren't said, but I could hear them all the same; they would be naming a Guardian with a husband who would become Revered Speaker, master of the Empire's policy. Influence could flow both ways.

Gods, Mihmatini was going to flay us all. "What rituals did you have in mind?" I asked. "Another symbol? A wedding, a coupling?"

Yaotl grinned. "Close enough."

Exactly why I didn't want to go ahead with this. "Yaotl," I said, firmly. "There has to be someone else. I know Teomitl is convenient right now–"

"It's not a matter of convenience," Yaotl said. "It's a matter of *need*." His voice was low and fierce, and utterly serious. "If the star-demons are walking among us, then the end has already started. We have to buy time, and we have to buy it now. We're not going to go through all the imperial princes looking for virgins."

How could Yaotl even be sure Teomitl was a virgin?

But my student was sitting very straight, and he hadn't protested; I knew that, if he hadn't, it meant that it was true. "Acatl-tzin," Teomitl said. "We can at least ask her. Yaotl is right, there is too much at stake." He didn't sound wholly happy about that, and no wonder. Quite aside from my personal objections on the matter, Mihmatini was going to tear his head off.

"Look," I said. "It's all good theory, but…" But, the Storm Lord smite me, it was my sister we were talking about, not me or Teomitl. She was no priestess or imperial princess, just a normal girl readying herself for marriage and children. No one had pledged her to the defence of the Fifth World.

Yaotl, Teomitl and the priests were watching me, their faces as expressionless as those of carved statues.

"Acatl-tzin," Teomitl said. "I swear to the gods I'll marry her within the year. No matter what my brother thinks." His face was set in a fierce scowl, moments away from invoking Jade Skirt's presence. "It's the only right thing I could do, anyway."

"I don't want you to do the right thing," I said. "I want her to–" And then I stopped, realising I was making all the decisions for her, that I might have accused Tizoc-tzin, the She-Snake and the rest of the council of endangering the Fifth World through the selfishness of their acts, but, really, was what I was doing any better? It might not have been about power or influence, but I was still placing myself and my blood above the sake of the Fifth World.

"You win," I said with a sigh. "Let's go ask her. But you're doing the talking."

The fleeting grimace on Teomitl's face was a small but satisfactory victory, the only one I was likely to get all day.

We found Mihmatini still in Teomitl's rooms, staring at the frescoes as if she could peel the paint from the walls.

"I was starting to worry about you," she said, getting up. Her gaze descended to my scuffed sandals. "You look like you've been mauled."

"Close," I said.

"I had no idea Tizoc-tzin was so fierce," Mihmatini said, deadpan. She raised her eyes; Yaotl had just entered the courtyard. "And you would be...?"

Yaotl bowed, somewhat perfunctorily. "Who I am doesn't matter much at this juncture."

"I beg to differ," Mihmatini said, somewhat acidly. She puffed her cheeks, apparently considering something. "All right. What is it that you're not telling me?"

I'd never thought I'd actually see Teomitl embarrassed. If he could have turned crimson, he would have. But, as it was, he merely shifted slightly, as if he didn't quite know where to stand. "We, er..." He shook his head, and plunged on again. "We need your help."

She was silent for a while. "I see. What wonderful plan has Acatl come up with?"

Teomitl shook his head. "It wasn't his plan. Look, there are star-demons outside the palace..." He trailed off into silence; she let him flounder, without a word.

"How interesting," she said. "So many words to tell me nothing."

Teomitl blushed. I'd never seen such a sheepish expression on his face. "We need to keep them at bay, and, well…" He took a deep breath, started again. "They need to designate a new Guardian. Us. I mean, you, on account of the imperial connection and the virginity…"

Mihmatini raised an eyebrow. I winced, wishing I could look away. I knew that expression all too well.

Teomitl, too, apparently, for he hurriedly got a more coherent explanation of why we needed a new Guardian, and why it needed to be her. "It's symbolic. They need a couple who can stand for the Empire in the eyes of the Duality, and we don't have much time to find one. And, well, Ceyaxochitl had had an eye on you for a while, and thought you might be suitable for the job anyway…"

When Teomitl was finished, Mihmatini was silent again, deep in a dangerous kind of musing, just before she lashed out. She'd never shied from telling me or my brothers exactly what she thought of our heroic acts, and I had no doubt she would.

"I presume you're desperate," Mihmatini said, finally. "If you're coming to ask me."

I could imagine the smile on Yaotl's face without turning around.

"I'm not doing this for pleasure."

"Oh, for the Duality's sake, don't be so serious," Mihmatini said.

"It is a rather serious matter," Teomitl said.

"Most things are." She smiled again, half-amused, half-angry. "But you have no sense of humour, either of you. You should give some thought to working on that, Acatl. It's clearly missing from his education."

"Much as I love your wit–"

"I know, I know." She was sober again. "It's not exactly innocuous."

"Most of it was my idea," Yaotl admitted behind me. "If it helps."

Dear gods, we must really have been desperate, as she was saying. Since when had Yaotl owned up to having an opinion of his own? It was more sobering than I'd ever imagined it would be.

"No, it doesn't." Mihmatini's voice was low and dangerous now, as cutting as a jaguar's claws. "Let me make matters clear. I'm not a tool to be used at your convenience, just because there's a need for a well-connected virgin. I'm not a fool either, and I know what you're asking."

"Mihmatini–" Teomitl started.

We were asking her to step into a position equivalent to that of a High Priest, to take Ceyaxochitl's place, for the rest of her life.

"Look," I said. "I know you wanted to get married–"

"It doesn't seem to be incompatible," Mihmatini said, dryly. "But I'm not a fool. Whatever is needed is bad, if it's got both of you pushing for me to accept."

Teomitl tried speaking again, a little more forcefully. "I told Acatl-tzin I would–"

"I can guess what you told him. We both know it's not what you want that matters most," Mihmatini said, with a small sigh. "Otherwise it would have gone differently. Courtships don't last a year, Teomitl."

This time, he reddened. "I'll find a way."

"I don't see what would make it different."

"You think I'll renege on a promise?" Teomitl drew himself to his full height, Jade Skirt's magic hovering around him, lengthening his shadow on the ground.

"I think you'll do what you can," Mihmatini said. "I very much doubt it will be all you want, but it doesn't matter. Come on, Acatl, let's go."

She walked out of the courtyard without a backward glance for the spluttering Teomitl. Yaotl followed, leaving both of us alone under the Fifth Sun's gaze.

"She's angry," I said. "She doesn't mean what she says."

Teomitl's face was dark with something more than anger. "I think she means exactly what she says when she's angry, Acatl-tzin. That's always been the problem. But it doesn't matter. This is a promise I intend to keep." His hands had clenched into fists, so tightly his nails had drawn blood.

Not for the first time, I wished – desperately – that I could believe him.

The ritual for Mihmatini's designation was a fairly lengthy one; not quite as complicated as the investiture of a new Revered Speaker, but still heavy enough to need a night and a morning to be prepared.

We arrived at the Duality House early on the following morning. While the priests explained the ritual to Teomitl and Mihmatini, I excused myself; and went inside Ceyaxochitl's rooms to pay my respects.

My second-in-command Ichtaca sat cross-legged on the ground by the side of the funeral mat. His lips moved, silently intoning a litany for the Dead; he looked up at me when I came in, but left me time to contemplate the corpse.

Ceyaxochitl had been washed and garbed in many-coloured cotton. The jade bead had been threaded through her lips. In death she looked small and pathetic, her vibrancy extinguished. Yaotl had said he kept expecting her to rise and take charge. Looking at the thin, bloodless lips, at the pale, blue-tinged face, I knew she wouldn't come back. She was down there in the underworld, making her slow way to the throne of Lord Death, just as the rest of us would, someday.

It was unfair; she had been so much more than the rest of us.

"Acatl-tzin." Ichtaca bowed to me.

I nodded, briefly. "Thank you for undertaking the vigil."

His gaze suggested that I didn't need to thank him; that he was doing nothing more than his work.

"She will be missed," Ichtaca said. His round face was grave, and he wasn't talking about sentiments.

"I know," I said. She had held us together. No matter how abrasive, or authoritative, she had cared for all of us.

"You could…" He swallowed. "You could summon her."

I shook my head. "Not until her vigil is complete." I *could* go down into the underworld to hunt her soul, but it was starting to be dangerous. I could feel the world, lurching slightly out of kilter. To further breach the boundaries at this stage might not be a good idea. Not to mention a summoning would force Ceyaxochitl to turn aside, slowing down her progression in the underworld. I had no wish to make her stay there longer than it had to be.

I spoke a little more with Ichtaca, mostly over administrative matters; and left the room in a much worse mood than I'd entered it.

The shrine to the Duality was atop a pyramid, like the shrine in my own temple. From the smooth marble platform, I could see all the way into the courtyard, into the silent room, its entrance-curtain fluttering in the breeze, where Ceyaxochitl's body would be resting, washed and garbed for her funeral vigil. And, further on, into the city, the canals glittering in the afternoon sun like strings of jewels, the houses of noblemen gradually giving way to the high, steepled roofs of peasants' dwellings, all the heart and blood of our empire, as vulnerable as a jaguar with its throat bared.

Below, in the courtyard, most of the high-ranking priests had gathered, dressed in sober blue and black, a dizzying sea of feather-headdresses and ash-stained faces.

There were stars overhead, pinpoints of lights in the sky that were the eyes of monsters, shining in full daylight with no fear of the Fifth Sun. Yaotl was right, the end had already started.

I was High Priest for the Dead. I could do no less, no more than I was doing. But...

Behind me, on either side of the platform, stood Teomitl and Mihmatini. They were garbed like a couple for a wedding; Teomitl in a bright new cape, and my sister in a cotton blouse with a very simple embroidery pattern around the neckline, her hair hidden under a flowing head-cloth. Yaotl had spread cochineal red around her mouth, and given her a basket of fruit and tamales which she held with a slightly sceptical air.

I was suddenly, absurdly glad I wasn't the only one who couldn't feel the seriousness of the occasion.

The altar was bare, shining golden in the sun. The air seemed to shimmer with power, the priests of the Duality had been chanting for hours. The two elderly priests who had made the decision to name Mihmatini Guardian-designate stood on either side of the altar, their faces grave.

"Acatl-tzin." Teomitl held a jar of *pulque* alcohol with an utterly serious air. I was sure he was more used to attending dubious rituals.

"I know, I know." I *was* used to rituals; but it galled me to have to be a spectator on this one. At least I'd managed to bargain for the right to stay. It seemed a

High Priest could attend on the pyramid platform, even if they took no part in the ceremony.

"Look," Mihmatini said, with an impatient shake of her head. "If you're going to ruin my life, you might as well not keep me waiting, Acatl."

"I…" I couldn't. There had to be some other god, some other ritual we could call on, some other solution that would keep the star-demons at bay, that would shelter us for a while more. There had to be…

I was grasping at maize seedlings, hoping they'd be strong enough to bear my weight. Pointless. We had already gone beyond the point when we could back out of this. Stifling a sigh, I moved to the edge of the platform, and watched the two priests officiate.

"Even as the maguey
You form a stalk, you are to ripen,
Taking root into the earth, you will hold up the sky
Your heart is jade, your heart is a precious green stone
Still virgin, pure, undefiled…"

Mihmatini shook her head; and in a fluid gesture removed the cloth over her hair. It spilled down her back in a flood to sit like the feathers of a raven. She approached the altar, her seashell bracelets tinkling with every step, not like the deep, ominous ringing of Coyolxauhqui's bells, but a light, airy sound like hundreds of footsteps following in her wake.

"Let us not go weeping forever
Let us not die in sorrow
Let the Fifth World be peopled, let the penance-born endure
Let us join together like the Lord and Lady of Duality…"

Teomitl set the pulque jar by the altar, whispering

a prayer. Carefully he reached over to Mihmatini, and helped her into the altar. Then, still as tentatively as if every gesture would break a fragile balance, he reached out, and tied a knot between his cloak and her blouse. The sun outlined its contours, sloshed into the folds of the cloths; the knot seemed to sparkle as if studded with gold or jewels.

He paused for a while, staring at her, and it didn't seem a ritual anymore, just part of their relationship, something I had no right to intrude on. I averted my gaze, staring at the floor. Dots of lights were running along the marble, joining together to form larger stains, like blood pooling in the hollows of an altar.

"I lie down with you, I arise with you
You are the quivering in my heart
The shaking of the earth, the storm-tossed sky…"

I couldn't tell how long I stood there looking down, at stone that gradually became translucent, as if some inner light were springing to life underneath. The air was charged, heavy as before a storm, and yet it was as light and as pure as that of a winter day, smelling of cut grass and algae, and of scattered marigolds.

When I raised my eyes they were kissing, and the sun seemed to have descended into the Fifth World. The white light bathed them, outlining the shape of their clothes, their two faces, like images in some distorted mirror, the knot, into which radiance pooled like water from streams, two bodies, pressing more tightly against each other. The stains of light contracted and shuddered and, in one sweeping movement, converged on Mihmatini and Teomitl, washing away their features until all I could see were two darker silhouettes, like shadows on limestone.

Light arced from the altar into the heavens, spreading upwards, the opening of a huge flower, petal after iridescent petal shimmering into existence above us. The flower stretched, lost its shape, and the light died.

When my eyes had accustomed themselves again to the dimmer light I saw, against the Heavens, the glowing shape of a dome, and felt a faint pressure at the back of my mind, like a reminder of its weight. The stars shone in the sky, but they were only pinpoints of light, and the air still smelled fresh, like the marshes after the rain, like the first flowering of maize.

Teomitl and Mihmatini sat on the altar, pale and drained, their skin an unhealthy white. Mihmatini had closed her eyes; Teomitl sat as straight as usual, but his quivering muscles betrayed him. The two priests had taken a step back. Their faces were mostly dignified, but not without smugness.

I approached the altar, the marble warm under my sandals, the stone beating triumphantly, like a living heart.

Safe. We were safe for a few more days, if nothing more. The word beat in my chest, wove itself in my brain, over and over; a litany, a prayer.

"Can you stand?" the priestess asked.

Teomitl gently teased the knot open. Light spilled from the folds of the joined cloths, like a scattering of gemstones into a sunlit stream. He pulled himself up, one articulation at a time, with none of his usual speed. He winced as his feet touched the floor. "Mostly," he said. His face shifted from brown to the green of jade, and back to brown again. He couldn't quite control Jade Skirt's gift. He seemed to realise this, and shook his head in annoyance. "I've never had so much taken from me."

"It's because you've never asked for so much power."

Mihmatini had not moved; she still sat on the altar, her hair unbound like that of a sacred courtesan, the red around her mouth smudged like the maw of a fed jaguar.

"Did it work?" she asked. Light still clung to her, a stubborn radiance that coated her skin and reflected itself into her eyes.

She frightened me more than I could put in words.

"Yes," the priest said. "Wonderfully."

"Thank the gods." Her voice was low, carefully pausing between words, as if unsure of the right one. Her hands shook. "If I'd gone through this for nothing, there would have been words, Acatl."

"I can imagine." The dome overhead pressed down on my mind, the words merging with each other in my thoughts. Safe, safe, safe.

I wondered why I couldn't feel any happiness over it.

"Come on," I said, ignoring the tightness in my chest. "Let's get you cleaned up."

By the time they'd dressed in everyday attire again, I'd seen that the light around Mihmatini did not diminish in intensity. It remained around her body, and a thinner thread linked her and Teomitl, like a reverse shadow on the ground, beating ponderously like a man breathing in his sleep.

A remnant of the Duality's touch, marking their new Guardian. As if we didn't have enough problems already.

They were waiting for us at the entrance to the Duality House, a group of warriors in Jaguar Knight livery; exquisite, from the jade rings on their fingers to their turquoise lip-plugs, their *macuahitl* swords casually hefted in their hands.

THIRTEEN

Master of the House of Darts

Tizoc-tzin's quarters were, surprisingly, almost deserted, compared to what I had seen last time. A handful of richly-attired warriors lounged on the platform outside, and the inner chambers held only the remnants of a feast, the smell of rich food turning sour in the gold and silver vessels.

It smelled of neglect, and of fear, like the house of an old man facing Lord Death at the end of a long sickness. I half-expected to find a corpse somewhere; but the only occupant of the room was Tizoc-tzin, still sitting behind his polished screen.

He looked furious, his face pale and set, his hands clenched around a feather-fan as if he could grind it into dust.

"They haven't bared their feet," he snapped to the warriors behind us.

"My Lord–" The lead warrior sounded embarrassed, and perhaps a little contemptuous. I couldn't be sure.

"You're not Revered Speaker." Teomitl's voice held the edge of broken obsidian.

Tizoc-tzin's gaze moved to him. His eyes were deepset in the paleness of his face, as dark and as bruised as those of a corpse. "And you're not Master of the House of Darts." His tone implied Teomitl would never be so, not as long as he had a voice.

Teomitl shrugged. "That's your threat?"

Tizoc-tzin smiled, uncovering a row of blackened teeth. "I can think of others. For now, I'll settle for explanations." He jerked his chin at me, in a movement so convulsive and unnatural that I took a step backward. "Try voicing them, *priest*." The contempt in his voice could have frozen Lake Texcoco.

I took a deep breath, composing myself. Tizoc-tzin was right. Teomitl wasn't Master of the House of Darts, Keeper of the Bowl of Fatigue, or Cutter of Men – he had no title, no official recognition save for his imperial blood, and the Revered Speaker had had dozens of brothers who had not amounted to anything. He couldn't defend us. No one could.

"There was need." I pitched my voice as low as I could, grave and determined. "The stars are shining in the sky, my Lord, and the demons walk in daylight, in the Jaguar House. They'd have overwhelmed us. We needed…" I tasted bile in my throat, swallowed. "We needed the protection of the Duality."

Where was Quenami? As High Priest of the Southern Hummingbird, he would have understood, at least, though he might still have disavowed me if it suited him.

"And so you thought of a ritual? How clever."

"The Duality takes no human sacrifices."

"Of course They don't." Tizoc-tzin moved back, so that his face was wreathed in shadows. "I've warned you before. I've warned you about her."

I guessed more than saw Teomitl put a hand on Mihmatini's shoulder, preventing her from speaking out. In the dimness of Tizoc-tzin's rooms, she still shone with the light of the ritual, and the thin, radiant thread curled on the ground between them, visible to all.

"Well, priest?"

I could think of no answer that wouldn't be an insult. "You did warn me," I said, cautiously. "But the ritual required both of them." I didn't tell him what else we'd done, it would take a while to fully invest Mihmatini as agent of the Duality, and the later he found out about this the better off we'd be.

"You lie!" The feather-fan trembled in Tizoc-tzin's hands. "I've seen you, priest. I know what you are, you and your kind – always hungry for power, always grabbing for more. Linking them together, parading them both in this palace, like a warrior and his courtesan, you spoiled him, too, took his potential and wasted it and turned it against this Court…" He was almost weeping now, the words tumbling atop each other, as fast and chaotic as waves on a stormy lake.

Teomitl's face twisted; the light of his patron goddess Chalchiuhtlicue, which had been surrounding him, died away. "I'm not against you, brother."

Tizoc-tzin raised his gaze to look at him, and I had never seen anything so frightening as the hunger spread on his features, hollowing his cheeks and his neck, pushing the eyes further back into his dark sockets. "I am the one," he whispered. "The one Axayacatl promised the Empire to. Fit to rule, to bring us the spoils of war and the tributes of provinces. He promised me. You know this. You know I'll do the right things."

"I'm not against you," Teomitl repeated. "I never was." His eyes glimmered in the dim light. It was Mihmatini, now, who had a hand extended, wrapped around his shoulder. "Brother…"

I had never seen him weep before.

Tizoc-tzin held Teomitl's gaze for a long while. He breathed in frantically, as if air had gone missing. At last he appeared to compose himself, and said in a much cooler voice, "Of course. Blood stands by blood."

"Always," Teomitl said.

I didn't like the sudden coolness, or the way his gaze moved around the room, transfixing all of us. We had seen him lose face and heart, reduced to an incoherent, weeping wreck of a man. Knowing him, he would never forgive us. Teomitl was family, but Mihmatini and I...

I could tell by Mihmatini's taut pose that her thoughts ran close to mine.

"Then set her aside." Tizoc-tzin's gaze was malicious. Mihmatini's hand tightened around Teomitl's shoulder, hard enough to bruise.

Teomitl's face was set. "That has never been a possibility."

"Who do you think you're convincing?" Tizoc-tzin laughed, a joyless sound that would have frightened even Lord Death. "She will forever be a peasant's daughter. You are imperial blood. You will be Master of the House of Darts. Do you think it's so easy to renounce your rank?"

"Perhaps, when I see what it's made of you. Look at you, brother. Look at you." Teomitl's voice was almost a cry. "You're a warrior and you cower in your own rooms."

"I'm not a warrior." Tizoc-tzin's voice was quiet, an admission of defeat. I looked up, caught Mihmatini's eye. There had to be a way we could make a graceful exit, before either of them remembered we were there. They were both behaving as if they were alone, baring more of their hearts and faces than I wanted to see.

Unfortunately, Tizoc-tzin caught my movement. "I'm not a warrior," he repeated, "but I'm not about to forget how your priest behaved."

"He's not mine," Teomitl said stiffly, and then realised what he had done – openly admitted I was not under his protection. He opened his mouth to speak again, but I shook my head to silence him. Tizoc-tzin would have attacked me, one way or another.

"Then he can speak for himself."

"What do you want to hear?" I asked. I hadn't meant to be so insolent, but I couldn't quite contain myself. He was behaving like an intoxicated jaguar, clawing at everything before his eyes – his own brother, my sister… "I can't offer anything but the truth."

"I've already heard your 'truth'." Tizoc-tzin waved a pale hand. "I have no interest in that."

"Then what else do you want to hear?" I wasn't quite sure I could contain myself. "My Lord, we have star-demons waiting for a lapse on our part, ritual or not. We need a new Revered Speaker."

His face twisted, in what might have been pain. "And you'll have one."

How had he changed, so quickly? The man who had screamed at me and accused me of nepotism had shrunk to this… this wasted thing crouching in the shadows, this living corpse whose every protestation of life rang false.

But he still had claws. He could still see me thrown out of Court, if the fancy took him.

He appeared to focus his attention on the ground, for the moment. "I admit I may have erred in ignoring the star-demons. Or, at the least, being unable to foresee what kind of carnage you'd wreak in the palace during your investigation."

The admission of weakness was surprising; the sting in the words that followed was not. "I've told you before," I said, unable to contain myself. "Someone is summoning star-demons, and they'll go on summoning them until they are stopped."

"Someone." His gaze rose, transfixed me, gaunt and dark, like the depths of Mictlan itself. "Who?"

If only I knew. But why was he so interested, all of a sudden? I couldn't understand what had changed. "That's why I'm investigating," I said, cautiously. "Your brother's wife Xahuia might have had something to do with it."

Or, at the very least, she would have ideas. I had little doubt she'd had spies all over the palace. But, if she was the guilty party, which sorcerer had she suborned? She needed to cast a spell within the palace where she no longer was; and her own sorcerer lay dead. I made a note to ask Palli about the women's quarters, to see if they could find anything in there that might be of use.

"Xahuia..." Tizoc-tzin rolled the word in his mouth, as if breathing in its taste. "She destroyed most of the women's quarters in her escape."

"Yes," I said, not knowing what else to say.

"I see." Tizoc-tzin's voice was distant again. "Whoever it is, they seek to undermine us, to make us as nothing. Never forget that they are dangerous, Acatl-tzin."

It was dishonest, it was disloyal, but I couldn't help compare this nervous man who presumed to give me curt orders as if he were Revered Speaker already to Axayacatl-tzin's graceful thanks and amused humility, his deep understanding of the rituals that had shaped his life. The Duality curse me, I just couldn't do otherwise. Manatzpa-tzin, for all his faults, had had the most accurate judgment of him, Tizoc-tzin didn't have the stature of a Revered Speaker.

"I will not forget," I said.

"Good." He nodded, as abruptly as a disjointed sacrifice. "Sometimes, better to take them dead than to run the risk of coming to further harm."

Surely he was not suggesting. "My Lord... " We would never find out the ramifications of the summoning that way, if we killed on sight.

"You heard what I said." He nodded – again, that movement so abrupt it seemed barely human. "Who else is involved?"

My lips formed the answer though my mind was elsewhere. "Councilman Manatzpa-tzin knew, but he is dead."

"How convenient."

No, not convenient. He had been killed for it, and so had Echichilli, because they had known *something*.

I had to ask, the Storm Lord blind me. Even if he arrested me for that, I was High Priest for the Dead, and it was my duty. No, it was my duty as a mortal of the Fifth World. "Echichilli died because of what he called duty," I said, carefully. "We thought that you might have an idea..." I let the sentence trail, braced myself for further abuse.

But Tizoc-tzin merely shook his head. "He wasn't a supporter of mine."

He *had* been a supporter of Axayacatl-tzin, though, hadn't he? Wouldn't he at least support the former Revered Speaker's choice of heir. "He did serve your brother," I said.

"He never liked me." Tizoc-tzin's voice was bitter. "Never mind, priest. This isn't something I can help you with."

"And Ocome?"

"Ocome. He was mine indeed. A poor kind of supporter, truth be told, bending to whoever shone brightest. Not a great loss."

I took in a deep breath, and said, "Xahuia claimed she had turned him to her side."

Something flashed in his gaze, a light in the hollows – anger, rage, guilt?

"Perhaps. I wouldn't have known." I could have detected the lie, even in a worse state than I currently was.

"There have been three deaths. One of the dead men had betrayed his allegiance to you," I said. "Another was neutral, and the third was your deadliest enemy."

"You accuse me?" There was something niggling at me, coiled at the back of my mind like a snake. Something obviously wrong, other than the sick fear, other than the diminishing of his whole being, But, try as I might...

"All we want is answers," Teomitl said, a little too hastily. "Brother, please. Crimes cannot go unpunished."

Tizoc-tzin's face was a death-mask. "Crimes? I am the Master of the House of Darts, priest. I answer to no one – certainly not to the priests who swarm around this court like flies, polluting us with their pretences of humility."

"You can at least explain to us..."

"Get out." Tizoc-tzin's voice was bright and false, with the same edge as a chipped blade. "I don't have to explain myself. Get out before I have you arrested, all of you."

I didn't need to be told twice. I carefully retreated, pushing Mihmatini ahead of me. Teomitl remained for a while, staring at Tizoc-tzin with pity on his face.

It wasn't until he joined us outside that I realised what had been staring me in the face all along. It was almost evening, the sky was pink and red, but the stars were already out, visible through the dome of the Duality's protection. "Star-demons," I said.

"What?" Mihmatini asked.

"He reeked of magic, as if he'd brushed one recently."

"That would explain his state," Teomitl said, curtly. "A narrow brush with death..."

It could have been that, a perfectly plausible explanation. But there was an equally plausible one, that he smelled of them only because he had consorted with them, and that the whole thing was a feint to purge the council, force them into a vote from which he would emerge the victor.

Storm Lord blind me, was that what we were facing?

I left the two of them in Teomitl's room, impressing upon him to bring Mihmatini home, trying not to think of that thread stretching all the way across the city, laid over the buildings and the canals, a trail everyone would be able to see. So much for discretion. Then again, I had known about this when we had first set out to do the spell, so it wasn't as if I could complain.

Then I went to check on Palli.

I found him sitting on the entrance platform of the Revered Speaker's rooms, looking despondent. "Acatl-tzin," he said.

I handed him one of the maize flatbreads I'd taken from a nobleman's kitchen. "Here, have some food. I take it the search isn't progressing."

Palli took the flatbread, but did not bite into it. "It's worse than that," he said. "We've checked almost everywhere, Acatl-tzin. The storerooms, the treasury, the armouries, the tribunals…"

"The women's quarters?" I asked, thinking of Xahuia.

Palli smiled, briefly. "Those, too. But it's useless. There is nothing that looks even remotely like a summoning place."

"You haven't finished," I said, trying to be encouraging. In truth, I wasn't feeling optimistic. If Palli thought there was nothing, then it was likely to be the case.

Palli's eyes drifted into the courtyard, staring at the beaten earth. It was almost dark, now "It's just a handful of rooms, and they're used by everyone. If there was a summoning..."

"I see," I said. I tried to hide my disappointment. There must be some place they had missed, some obvious location...

But, with so many people helping out, I doubted it was the case. Which left me with a problem – how in the Fifth World were the star-demons getting past the palace wards?

I mulled the problem over as I walked out of the palace, but could find no satisfying solution. With a sigh, I headed back to the Duality House.

After all the animation of Mihmatini's designation, it seemed oddly deserted, as if night had robbed it of all vitality. Only a few priests were there, kneeling in the dust to beseech the Duality's favour for the Empire and the Fifth World. I found Ichtaca where I had left him, watching Ceyaxochitl's corpse. His face lit up when he saw me. "Acatl-tzin. I see you're still–"

"Alive? I guess." He had seen me taken away by Tizoc-tzin's guards; no wonder he'd worried.

I sighed. Now that I was back in a familiar setting, all the fatigue of the previous days was making itself felt; the lack of sleep over the previous night, the barely-healed wounds on my chest, the hasty meals – all of it came like a blow.

Ichtaca pulled himself straighter. "I've received word from the temple, while you were out. There is something you need to know about the order of the deaths."

"The... order?" It hadn't occurred to me that there was something to check there.

"We checked the records. They only give the days of the religious calendar, but we can work out the correspondence with the year count."

He made it sound easy, but it was far from it. The religious calendar was two hundred and sixty days, while the year count followed the sun's cycle. They over-lapped, but working out dates from one to the other required patience and a talent for mathematics.

Ichtaca was pursing his lips, as he often did when contemplating a difficult problem. "The date of birth of Ocome-tzin was the Second Day of the Ceasing of Waters, that of Echichilli-tzin the Fifteenth day of the Ceasing of Waters, and Manatzpa-tzin was born on the Third Day of The Flaying of Men. All those dates are in the first or second month of the calendar."

"Coincidence?"

"I don't think so." Ichtaca rose, bowing to Ceyaxo-chitl's corpse, and turned to face me. "Or, if it is, too much of one. I took the liberty of checking the names of those councilmen I did know. Their dates of birth are all posterior to the dead ones."

"Said otherwise, they're dying by chronological order." I bit my lip. As Ichtaca had said, too much of a coincidence. It might explain why Echichilli had known his death was coming. But why?

The year had started on the day Two Rain, a time of unpredictability, a time of divine caprices. It was heading towards its end on the day Two House, and the *nemontemi* – the five empty days – a fearful time during which children were hidden out of sight, and pregnant women locked in granaries for fear that...

For fear that they would turn into star-demons. Oh no. "They're trying to hasten the end of the year, aren't they."

It wasn't a question, and Ichtaca did not treat it as such. "That seems a likely explanation. The five empty days would suit them."

These weren't just random summonings then, but I had been suspecting that for a while. This was organised, meticulously so, part of a ritual from beginning to end.

"This isn't good." I breathed in, trying to still the frantic beating of my heart. "If I give you the names of all the councilmen, can you work out who comes next in the order of deaths?"

"Yes," Ichtaca said. "But–"

"I know. It takes time. You've already done a great deal of work."

"I do my duty, Acatl-tzin. As we all do. I will have all the offering priests we can spare doing calculations. That's the most I can do. The novices don't know enough about the calendars. I wish the calendar priests were available, but they're overworked as it is, planning the funeral and the coronation."

"I see. Thank you." I gave him all the names of the council; they were not that many of them, and I had interviewed all of them.

Something occurred to me as I was about to walk out: the tar Palli had found in the Imperial Chambers. "Ichtaca?"

"Yes?"

"What does tar evoke to you? Magically speaking."

He looked thoughtful for a while. "Tar? It's not a common ingredient."

"No," I said. "But I have reasons to think it was used in a ritual in the palace. Something large."

"Tar is thick, and chokes. It can't be washed away with water."

"The Storm Lord?" I asked. Acamapichtli was away from Court, trying to make us forget he had supported Xahuia. But he could have done something beforehand. "Dying of the water, but not of it." The oldest rite, asking for His blessing on the crops.

"The Storm Lord's sacrifices tend to use rubber," Ichtaca said. "I suppose they might turn to tar, if rubber wasn't available." But he didn't sound convinced.

I thanked him, and walked out onto the Sacred

Precinct in my bleakest mood yet. It didn't seem like Tizoc-tzin was to blame, after all. If he truly wanted to become Revered Speaker, then he would not have any interest in hastening the end of the world.

On the other hand, he was acting most suspiciously. What was he not telling us?

Or was there some other purpose to the order of the deaths, something I hadn't seen?

FOURTEEN
Darkness

Even though I'd only been a participant, the Duality
ritual – and its stressful aftermath with Tizoc-tzin – had
drained more out of me than I'd expected. I went to
bed at a reasonable time, for once, early on in the
night, and woke up to find it was already early afternoon.

I reached up, touched my earlobes, which bore fresh
scabs. I must have done my devotions to the Fifth Sun
in a trance, barely realising what I was doing.

Nevertheless, better to be sure. I slit my earlobes
open again, and did the blood offering and the hymn
singing properly this time.

For once no one was waiting for me in my courtyard. I might have smiled, but I didn't feel in the
mood.

Since I had a little time to myself, I went back to the
Wind Tower with a chest of offerings, and asked to see
the fire-priest. I was in full regalia, my owl-embroidered cloak spreading behind me like the wings of a
bird, the skull-mask precariously balanced on my forehead, my sandals, as white as bone, making my tanned
feet seem pale. The priest watching over the pilgrims

took one look at me, bowed very deeply, and sent someone to fetch him.

I laid the chest by my side and waited, sitting on the platform where the Wind Tower stood. It was warm out there, with the Fifth Sun overhead, the stone glimmering in the harsh light, and the Sacred Precinct spread out before me, the mass of temples and priests' houses that made up the religious heart of the city. The canals behind the Serpent Wall seemed very distant, another world entirely, far removed from our problems.

I hoped they would remain that way.

"Acatl-tzin?" A tall man with pale skin and gaunt, hollowed-out cheeks, stood by my side. He wore a simple green tunic, and a long, trumpet-shaped wooden beak, which he'd set aside to talk to me, all that marked him as a priest. His hair, cropped short, was a shock of black. Unlike the other priests, he didn't mat it with blood, or weave in any kind of ornaments.

"I am Ueman," he said, bowing. "Fire Priest of this temple. I was told you wanted to see me?"

"Yes," I said. I didn't touch the basket by my side, and he didn't ask about it. "You're aware of the deaths in the palace."

"A little," he said, cautiously. "This place is far away from the centre of power."

Since the days of Tula, centuries ago, the Feathered Serpent Quetzalcoatl had not held power in any city and, in a day and age where the gods of War and Rain watched over us, He had faded into obscurity, His benevolence gently scoffed at, treated like an aged relative with no sense of the realities of life.

"Far away, perhaps," I said, "but it still dragged you in."

Ueman grimaced. He sat down by my side, carefully and easily, as if rank didn't matter. "We're a place for knowledge and healing, Acatl-tzin. We hold the Feathered Serpent's trust. We worship Him as the Wind, as the Precious Twin, as the king that was and will return. But some think only of knowledge as a weapon."

"Princess Xahuia came here," I said.

"With a councilman. For an oath." He didn't even attempt to evade the questions. Clearly, he'd have preferred to wash his hands clean of the whole business.

What he told me was brief, but it confirmed Xahuia's story that she'd convinced Ocome to swear an unbreakable oath of loyalty to her. Not that I had doubted it, but still...

Now Tizoc-tzin, the She-Snake and Acamapichtli were the ones with the strongest motive. Tizoc-tzin, strongest of all.

"Did you see other councilmen?" I asked.

"Of course." I'd half-expected he'd deny that, but he was an honest man, a breed all too rare in the palace.

"Manatzpa?"

"Among others." His voice was cautious again.

Others? "What do you mean?"

Ueman's gaze drifted towards the expanse of the Imperial Palace, which appeared small and pathetic from such a height. "I've had ten councilmen come to me since the beginning of the month, Acatl-tzin."

Ten was about the whole council, minus the inner circle. "I don't understand. What did they want?"

"The same thing Manatzpa wanted. The Breath of the Precious Twin."

There was a fist, slowly closing around my lungs, cutting the breath through my windpipe. "All of them? They all came to you for protection?" Still, there had been star-demons loose in the palace. Ocome had died, and they were under threat. Surely it was enough of a reason to buy a spell?

"Yes."

"When?" I asked.

My heart sank when he gave me the dates, which all predated Ocome's murder. Manatzpa had been the first to come, in the wake of Axayacatl-tzin's death; the others had followed in small groups, almost jostling each other on the temple steps.

"This makes no sense," I said.

"I can't give you sense," Ueman said, stiffly. "All I can tell you is what I witnessed."

"I know. My apologies. I didn't mean to impugn your honesty." For once somebody wasn't trying to defraud me or lie to me. It was a feeling I'd forgotten, and that was disturbing. The palace had its own rules, and it had slowly sucked me in, to the point I hardly was aware of what was normal.

Never again. As soon as this sordid business was finished, I'd go back to my temple, with only the occasional visit to the palace. Yes. I'd do that.

But, coming back to the matter at hand... I hadn't been mistaken, back when I had interviewed all the councilmen: they had all been deathly afraid. There had been mundane and magical threats. But this huge, complicated, expensive spell... It seemed almost too much.

It was almost as if they had known the star-demons would come for them.

But how could they have?

It made no sense.

"I see," I said to Ueman. I pushed the basket towards him. He took it with a puzzled frown, and opened it to peer at its contents.

Butterflies and jade ornaments, and the feathers of quetzal birds, as green as emeralds. "What are those for? Surely you're not—"

"Paying you for your answers?" I shook my head. "Of course not. Those are for the god."

"Have you a question, then?"

"No. I have a soul to entrust to His keeping."

"I see." His eyes were wide, his gaze as tender as that of a mother for her son. "The Feathered Serpent doesn't own the Dead, Acatl-tzin. You should know that better than I."

"He–" An unexpected obstruction had welled up in my throat, making the world swim. I swallowed. "He went down into the underworld once, for the bones of the Dead. He came back."

"Yes." Ueman closed the basket, but did not look away from me. "It was a long time ago. The Fifth Age hadn't yet started, and the gods still had Their full powers."

"Surely…"

"I can ask." His voice was quiet, gentle. "He is benevolent and wise. It cannot hurt."

But he wasn't sure whether it would help. I hadn't thought it would, but it was worth a try. Ceyaxochitl had deserved better than the darkness, and the cold, and the dust. "Very well. Thank you," I said, and rose, and walked away from the Wind Tower, trying to forget the sting in my eyes.

I was hoping to catch Teomitl in the palace, and work out some plan for dealing with Tizoc-tzin, but I couldn't find him anywhere. So instead I headed to the council room.

The funeral rites were underway, the palace rang with the lamentations of my priests, and everything smelled of incense and burnt paper. From far, far away, I caught a hint of a litany for the Dead:

"We leave this earth
This world of jade and flowers
The quetzal feathers, the silver…"

The council as a whole had nothing more to tell. They huddled amidst copal incense in the depths of their rooms, as if sunlight itself had become a blight, as shrunken and diminished as Tizoc-tzin, as if they were already funeral bundles arrayed for cremation after a long wake.

They wore the Breath of the Precious Twin. They had paid for it, most of them. But why?

Something *was* wrong, it was more than star-demons poisoning the atmosphere of the palace, but the more I pressed them, the more I got the feeling of standing amidst an elaborate pageant like a sacrifice victim, already removed from the preoccupations and the cares that plagued every other participant from the priests to the worshippers.

The Duality curse me, what was I missing?

There was not much to do for it, I would *have* to see the She-Snake again. He was the only one who might still cooperate. Quenami had become just an extension of Tizoc-tzin's will, and Acamapichtli, the High Priest of Tlaloc, was following his own purposes away from Court, which worried me, but I couldn't do much about it. The She-Snake's guards were all over the palace, and he had to have some inclination of what was going on. The only question was whether he would share it with me.

I headed to the half of the palace which held the She-Snake's quarters.

"Acatl-tzin!"

I turned, half-expecting Quenami again but instead I saw Nezahual-tzin, the boy-Emperor of Texcoco. He had changed into the regalia befitting a Revered Speaker; a turquoise cape, its hem embroidered with hundreds of tiny eyes, though he still carried his small shield with him, emblazoned with a coyote woven of feathers, the emblem of his father, and his *macuahitl* sword, its embedded shards shimmering with green and red light, the touch of the Feathered Serpent. Two warriors followed him, not the Jaguar Knights he'd had with him before, but I presumed Texcocan elite guards.

"I need to speak with you," he said. It was an order as much as a request, coming from a man with whom no one dared argue.

Of course, I had no choice.

He walked me back to the courtyard of the imperial chambers and climbed the steps to the terrace, where he chose one of the other two doors, the apartments held aside for the rulers of the Triple Alliance, Texcoco and Tlacopan.

Inside, frescoes spread across the walls, depicting the descent of Quetzalcoatl, the Feathered Serpent, into Mictlan and His return, with the broken bones of the Dead made whole by the shedding of the gods' blood. The braziers burnt copal incense, but not a variety I recognised, a more spicy, tangy smell than what I was used to, almost as if some medicinal drugs had been added to it. I could only hope they were not meant to induce visions, for as a High Priest, my mind hovering on the boundaries of the Fifth World already, I would have little defence against those.

Nezahual-tzin sat cross-legged on a low-back chair without much ceremony, though the setting was imperial – a jaguar pelt under his feet, a turquoise cloak, negligently wrapped around the wicker back, and a golden cup of steaming chocolate set before him on the dais. Something glimmered behind him, the limned maw of a great snake, the collar spread like blossoming daffodils, the pearly fangs closing just above his feather-headdress. Quetzalcoatl in the Fifth World. I had been wrong: Nezahual might actually be the agent of the Feathered Serpent on earth, the repository of all His wisdom.

"What did you want to ask?" I said. I stood; for he had not invited me to sit down.

"I have an offer to make you." Nezahual-tzin considered the chocolate in front of him, as if it held the key to the Fifth World.

"An offer?" He made it sound like something illegal. "In exchange for my support?"

He smiled, looking like a younger version of the She-Snake. The Duality take him, he had learnt politics at the She-Snake's knee; not the current one, but his father before him, the man who had forged an insignificant city into a wide-spanning empire. "Don't be a fool, Acatl-tzin. I have enough trouble in Texcoco without adding more."

But of course he'd be interested in having a sympathetic Revered Speaker, one who would respect his place in the Triple Alliance.

"Actually, what I wanted to offer was my assistance in tracking down Xahuia."

"We've already got men after her," I said. I had no doubt he would sacrifice her to further his own ends. He would not have survived for so long, or remained Revered Speaker in his own right and not a vassal of Tenochtitlan, if he had been naïve. But I didn't know what his own ends might be.

"Efficiency does not appear to be a quality of your men." He sounded amused. "She's disappeared for four days. Knowing my sister, she's already making other plans, and you won't like them."

"We're doing what we can," I said, stung.

"Of course you are." Nezahual-tzin lounged on the chair looking thoughtful. The smell of incense grew stronger as if he had fanned it himself, prickling my nostrils. "But still, you are not blessed by the Feathered Serpent."

"So you are His agent?" I asked. No point in dancing

around each other like fighting jaguars. Diplomacy had never been my strongest quality.

"Perhaps." Nezahual-tzin smiled again. His grey eyes rolled up, revealing eerily white pupils, filled with a single pinpoint of light. I did not back down, having been expecting something like this for a while. Besides, whatever he looked like paled beside star-demons. "I have quite enough power for this, I assure you."

"But I have no idea what you're using it for," I said.

"Fine. Let's be blunt with each other, then. It ill suits me to see the Fifth World endangered. I have vested interests in seeing who becomes Revered Speaker, I will confess, but being torn apart by star-demons is not part of my plans, now or in the future."

Everything about him sounded or looked older than he was. I couldn't be sure if being Revered Speaker had aged him, or if Quetzalcoatl, the Feathered Serpent, was indeed speaking through him. Either way, he worried me. I could deal with Teomitl's brash innocence, but with Nezahual-tzin I kept thinking I was speaking to a spoiled adolescent, but he wasn't one. He had probably never been.

"And you're offering–"

"You know true sight," Nezahual-tzin said. "You've probably used it."

"Of course." It was one of the rituals anyone could use without being a devotee of the Feathered Serpent, not one of the god-touched mysteries.

"There is another ritual." Nezahual-tzin's voice dropped a fraction, echoing as if through a great cavern. "A deeper, more ancient one from the Second Sun, of which the true sight is but a faint remembrance."

The Second Sun had been the Age of Quetzalcoatl, presided by the Feathered Serpent in all His glory until the Smoking Mirror, Quetzalcoatl's eternal enemy, had changed mankind into chattering spider-monkeys. "That's what you want to do? If it was that simple–"

"Oh, no, it's not that simple." Evening had come and Nezahual-tzin's teeth shone white in the gathering darkness. Slaves moved to light the braziers, the smell of charcoal overwhelming that of copal for a brief moment. "The Feathered Serpent does not require human blood, but he does ask for penance, and preparation."

"Fasting, and meditation," I said. "I'm not totally ignorant."

"Good," Nezahual-tzin said. He pushed the cup of chocolate aside. "A full night's vigil is what is usually required, from the emergence of the Evening Star until the Morning Star's dawn."

Another way of telling me he needed my answer now, or we would have to wait another day to track down Xahuia.

Teomitl had not trusted him, but Teomitl's judgment was hardly impeccable. Still...

"I'm not your enemy, Acatl-tzin," Nezahual-tzin said. "I assure you."

"You..." He was a politician; a born liar. "I can't trust you." The words were out of my mouth before I could think.

He looked at me, his eyes rolling up again in that eerie way. Had he been Tizoc-tzin, I'd already have been on my way to the imperial cells but instead he said nothing. Silence spread in the room, grew oppressive.

"Nezahual-tzin..."

"No, I understand your reluctance. But understand, Acatl-tzin, as long as Xahuia is loose in Tenochtitlan, I am at risk. I am her countryman; worse, her brother. If she is accused of destructive sorcery, then..."

"I shouldn't think your reputation was so bad."

"It has been better," Nezahual-tzin, with not a trace

of humour. "As you said to the pup, I know who to sacrifice, and when. Xahuia has done her time."

I wasn't sure whether to admire his frankness, or to despise him for his calculations. I said the first thing which came to mind. "You underestimate Teomitl."

"Perhaps." He did not sound convinced. The ghostly serpent behind him swayed in a rustle of feathers. "But that is beside the point. Will you take my help, Acatl-tzin, if only on this?"

It wasn't safe. Quite aside from the fact that I didn't trust him or his motives, there was also the question of his allegiance. He was of the Triple Alliance, but not Mexica, and Tizoc-tzin would seize on any association between us to make me look worse in the eyes of the Court. I ought to have refused him. I ought to have walked away from whatever he proffered, trusted my instincts and let Yaotl's men continue the search. But the Duality was weak, and the Southern Hummingbird had retreated to safer climes and could not help us any longer.

"Only on this," I said.

His lips curled up for a smile, revealing teeth like the fangs of a snake. "Good."

Night had fallen by the time I exited Nezahual-tzin's chambers, and my fatigue was worsening. My stomach yawned in my body like the blind, gaping mouth of a beast; and the world around me was not as steady as it had once been. I stopped by a carved pillar to catch my breath, waiting for the colours to return to sharpness and the wave of dizziness to pass.

There was little time left. I could rest later; what I needed now was an audience with the She-Snake.

I took the time to shed my blood for the Fifth Sun, to comfort Him in his journey across the night sky, and then detoured through some nobleman's kitchens, to snatch maize and peppers from a passing slave. After that, I headed back to the other side of the palace.

It stood wreathed in darkness, a counterpart to Tizoc-tzin's chambers. The plaintive music of a bone flute wafted from above, like an offering to the Heavens, an unceasing prayer for our continued existence.

The platform was deserted, and so were the chambers behind the entrance-curtain, the only smell that of old incense congealing in the burners. No one stopped me as I stepped through the remnants of a feast, my feet crunching on crumbs of fried food, and torn reed-mats.

The She-Snake sat in the central courtyard, on a coarse reed mat, listening to the music. He dressed in unrelieved black once more, his face a clearer patch in the shadows, his eyes closed, his hands unclenched in his lap.

The clatter of my sandals on the stone floor made him look up. The music quivered, and then stopped as the slave threw a glance at the She-Snake, who nodded, gravely, as if my entrance were nothing more than a minor inconvenience.

"My Lord…" I said.

He shook his head. "No need to apologise, Acatl. It's a beautiful night for an interview, isn't it?"

Overhead were the stars, unclouded, the blinking eyes of monsters, the elbows and joints of they who would tear the world apart. Overhead was the Moon, the incarnation of a vengeful, angry goddess who stirred in Her underground prison.

"I don't think so," I said.

"A pity." The She-Snake nodded, gravely. "Leave us, will you?" he asked the slave, who bowed in return, and left us alone in the courtyard.

The She-Snake did not move, sitting tall and straight on his mat, as regal as if he had been Revered Speaker himself, waiting for me to speak up. The air was cold and crisp, like the breath of the lake at dawn.

"I come because I have no choice," I said, finally. "I have questions–"

He raised a hand, not unkindly. "Priests always have questions, Acatl. Whatever god you serve, you seek and hoard knowledge like jade or turquoise."

It sounded half like a reproach, but I did not rise to the bait. There was too much at stake. "You haven't been exactly enthusiastic about helping me before," I said.

The She-Snake raised an eyebrow. "I am a busy man, but not an impolite one. You can't hope to come to me with any petty requests you might have, and to have me jump up to see that your needs are met."

The words came fast and smooth, with barely any pause in his breath. I couldn't believe any of them. He was too much at ease, as if he had been expecting this conversation all along. "I see. And now that I'm here…"

"I have time," the She-Snake said. He looked up, at the night sky. "Thanks to your trick with the Duality, we have plenty of time left."

"It wasn't a trick."

"Ask Quenami." The She-Snake's face was expressionless, but he sounded amused. "I very much doubt it's on his list of authorised behaviours, even in the absence of a Revered Speaker."

"Quenami is a fool," I said.

The She-Snake nodded gravely. "We can agree on that, if nothing else. Was that the only question you had, Acatl?"

He made me feel like a child, caught in something much larger than myself – like a fish on the ground, twitching and gasping while land creatures ran effortlessly. "Tell me about Tizoc-tzin," I said.

He watched me, for a while. "I could tell you many things about Tizoc. What is it you want to know, exactly?"

"I don't want to influence you."

He laughed; a small, joyless bark. "Believe me, nothing you say will influence me one way or the other. Am I not the supreme judge of Tenochtitlan?"

I knew that; and I also knew what Axayacatl-tzin had told me, that I could not trust him under any circumstances. But did I have any choice? My little "trick" with the Duality, as he called it, would only hold for a time, and I wasn't sure Tizoc-tzin could do as he wanted and call an election here and now. The council had sounded much too preoccupied with their own lives, as if they already knew that whoever was elected Revered Speaker wouldn't be able to protect them. "Tell me. Does Tizoc-tzin have the Southern Hummingbird's favour?"

The She-Snake looked at me for a while. It didn't look as though he had anticipated that particular question. "Probably not," he said. "Are you wondering whether he would be able to channel Huitzilpochtli's powers into the Fifth World?"

If I went ahead, if I spoke my mind on this, then I would move from healthy scepticism into outright treason. "Yes," I said.

The She-Snake did not speak for a while. "I don't know. Quenami would be better placed to answer that question than I. Tizoc is older than Axayacatl was, and he was never the greatest of warriors, or the most fervent of believers in the Southern Hummingbird's might."

"I–" I said. I kept expecting something to happen, guards to burst out, *macuahitl* swords at the ready, to arrest me for sedition.

As if guessing my thoughts, the She-Snake smiled.

"There is only darkness to hear us, Acatl. I don't think you're worrying about the right thing here."

"The preservation of the Fifth World?"

"Quenami is selfish and arrogant, but no fool. He wouldn't back a candidate if he didn't have some plan for making sure of his own safety. He'll know some ritual, or some other trick to make sure that the star-demons remain where they are."

"But it's not–" It wasn't meant to go that way. He was not supposed to cheat. "It's not a game. You can't fix the rules as you please."

"Tizoc wants his due," the She-Snake said. "He's waited most of his adult life for the Tturquoise-and-Gold Crown, ever since he was passed over in favour of Axayacatl. He was promised this by his own brother."

And he was acting like a child denied a toy. Manatzpa was right; he did not have the stature to become Revered Speaker. I took a deep breath, and spoke the greater of two treasons. "The councilmen's deaths…"

If he had nodded, I wouldn't have believed him. But he merely looked troubled, as if I had raised a disturbing possibility he hadn't considered. "I don't know," he said. "But I wouldn't be surprised."

I couldn't trust him, I couldn't. He was a consummate actor; he was playing me for a fool.

The She-Snake must have seen some of the hesitation on my face, for he said, "You don't believe me. I hadn't expected you to. It's one thing to know Tizoctzin for a conceited, self-aggrandising fool, and another to know his true nature."

"Someone told me he wouldn't dare use magic," I said, but I couldn't remember who had said this to me.

"Even if that were true, his allies have no such scruples. But Tizoc himself would do anything to wear the Turquoise-and-Gold crown. Anything."

Such as summon star-demons himself, and throw

the council into a panic so that he could emerge as their saviour? Surely he would not.

"I don't believe you," I said. "You're the only other serious candidate, with the council in disarray and Xahuia in flight. If you're so sure Tizoc-tzin is going to win, why don't you throw your support behind him?"

His lips curled up a fraction. "A matter of principles, I guess you would say."

I didn't believe he had any, but some scrap of self-preservation stopped the words before I could utter them. "Then what are you doing?"

"Swaying the people that matter. Talking to you." He appeared amused, as if at some secret joke. "I will show you something, if you will come with me."

"What?" I asked. "Where?"

"I can't tell you until we are there."

"Then why–"

"Afraid?" He raised an eyebrow again. "Come, Acatl. I have no interest in your death."

I didn't think he would dare, to be honest. A High Priest who vanished after visiting him… It wouldn't be in his favour, no matter how he could disguise it.

I looked at him, and saw nothing in his grey eyes. His face was relaxed and open like a spread-out codex, his skin the colour of polished copper, his traits as in-human as those of a god. In that moment he looked like the carved images of his father Tlacaelel-tzin, the man who had taken us and turned us from a rabble of uncivilised warriors into a great civilisation.

"I know you won't trust any oath I make by the gods," the She-Snake said. "But if you want to send a messenger to your temple and warn them that you're going with me, please do so. I don't intend to make you disappear."

Nevertheless… Nevertheless, accidents could happen, and he was canny enough; and he had his own goals. Axayacatl-tzin's warning still echoed in my head. What need was there to take risks? I was already doing enough accepting Nezahual-tzin's help, why did I need to further abase myself?

But I couldn't shake the memory of the star-demon's taint on Tizoc-tzin, and the way his fear seemed to have eaten him, not only fear for his life, but the annoyance of someone denied a treasure in his grasp.

"I'll send that messenger," I said.

The She-Snake sent for two spiders – not the small harmless ones in our houses, but the ones found in the southern jungles – hairy and twice as big as my open hand. He took them as if they were pets, stroking them gently in a way that made me distinctly uncomfortable. For all that they were Lord Death's animals, connected to darkness and the end of all things, it was no reason to favour them so much.

"I'm not sure I understand," I said, watching him cut into his earlobes to draw a circle on the ground.

He smiled. "We're not invited where I'm taking you, Acatl. Better make sure we're not seen."

"You know a spell of invisibility?" I asked. I had never heard of one. I'd been told by Lord Death that it would cost Him too much power, but I had always wondered whether there wasn't a deeper, more selfish reason for this. Such a spell would have removed the wearer from the sight of all creatures, including the gods and Their agents. And I would imagine the gods wouldn't want to have mortals blundering around where They couldn't see them.

"In a manner of speaking," the She-Snake said. "Come in the centre, will you?" The blood on the ground was already shimmering, as if reflecting the light of the stars above.

Axayacatl-tzin's warning echoed once more in my

head, but I silenced it.

He sacrificed both spiders in a swift, professional way. Of course, he was the She-Snake, and would have taken the lead in the major sacrifices while the Revered Speaker was away on the battlefield. Their blood was not red, but rather an amber ichor that coated his hands like glue, dull and dark, as if it were eating the starlight.

However, when he started his hymn, it was to a goddess I had never heard of.

"*In darkness You dwell*
In darkness You thrive
You of the shell skirt, You of the star skirt…"

Smoke spread inside the circle, rising from the She-Snake's hands – warm and smelling of herbs, a pungent odour that reminded me of something infinitely familiar, and yet that I could not place. What goddess was this? It almost sounded like Itzpapalotl, the large star-demon who had consumed Manatzpa's soul before disappearing under the Great Temple. But it couldn't be. It couldn't possibly be.

"*You of the large teeth, You of the shrivelled mouth*
Darkness Your inheritance, darkness Your kingdom
Darkness that hides
Darkness that smothers."

The smoke thinned, flowing out, but it remained on the edges of my vision. I tried shaking my head, but it was as if it had become stuck to my cornea. Its tendrils shifted on the edges of my vision, and never left no matter what I looked at. Magic crept along the nape of my neck, cold and unforgiving, almost like under-world magic, but without its comforting familiarity. It

247

wasn't the resigned acceptance of a god who took whatever dead souls were left to Him, but the endless hunger of something that lived between the stars, something that had been there since the start, and would be there in the end, that would see the night swallow us all, our hymns and our poems, our flowers and our songs, our fires and our blood-offerings, and make us all as nothing.

What goddess had the She-Snake called upon?

"Come," the She-Snake said, bending his head with a smile. His grey eyes had become bottomless pits in the darkness, a window into the deepest cold, the one that had settled across the world before the Fifth Sun had risen.

I followed because I no longer had any choice; but my fingers clenched around the obsidian knife at my belt, feeling the arc of Lord Death's power, a reassurance that I wasn't alone, come what may.

We walked through the palace, and it was as if we had become ghosts. No one, not a single slave, not a single servant or nobleman turned to look at us. It seemed to me, too, that we were moving faster than we should have been. We passed the House of Animals in what seemed barely a heartbeat, and were in the other half of the palace, the one belonging to the Revered Speaker, before I could even accustom myself to this strange magic.

The She-Snake was already walking ahead, into a courtyard I would have recognised anywhere – Tizoctzin's.

Like the previous time, it was deserted and silent; but this time the palpable smell of neglect became something else, a thin veneer over decay and rot and fear. As I climbed the stairs in the She-Snake's wake, I saw traces of blood clinging like black splotches to the limestone, and the smoke spread to wreathe the whole building, making it seem pallid and distant.

Inside, the same silence, the same smell. The She-Snake crossed between the pillars, hardly looking up to avoid them. He stopped at the back of the room, by a window overlooking the tropical garden. To the left was an entrance-curtain, the bells tinkling out a muted lament.

"Here."

"I don't see–" I started.

"Go inside," the She-Snake said, bowing his head. "And ask me any questions you might have, afterwards."

I threw him a suspicious glance. But if he wanted to kill me this was a singularly complicated way to go about it. Suppressing a sigh, I lifted the entrance-curtain. It slid between my fingers like raindrops; I hissed in surprise, but then took the smarter approach, and merely pushed through it. It was like walking through a waterfall, a little resistance, like the crossing of a veil, and then nothing more.

Inside, the room should have been a riot of colours. Vivid frescoes, and luxuries such as feather-fans and bronze braziers lay piled on reed mats; but they were muted by the smoke, highlighting the impermanence of such a gluttonous display of wealth.

Tizoc-tzin sat on a reed mat in the further corner; and the silhouette by his side, with the blue feather head-dress, could only be Quenami. He wasn't a particularly tall man, but even seated he seemed to tower over the hunched figure of Tizoc-tzin.

I dared not creep too close to their whispered conversation – Quenami, for all his bluster, was High Priest, and might have a way of seeing me – but the smoke was making it difficult for me to hear: it cut their words into four hundred meaningless pieces, carried away by the cold wind between the stars.

"...crown... mine..."

"...Lord of Men... sacrifice... regrettable deaths, but necessary..."

"...that they would dare disobey..."

Carefully, I walked closer. Quenami stiffened. I stopped, my heart hammering against my throat, but he relaxed again, and bent closer to Tizoc-tzin.

Southern Hummingbird blind me, why did he always find a way to thwart me?

Closer... The smoke whirled around me; the world shifted and blurred, a prelude to being torn apart.

"You worry too much, my lord," Quenami was saying, smooth and smiling. I was close enough to see the paint on his face, the jade, obsidian and carmine rings on his fingers, made almost colourless by the smoke.

Tizoc-tzin shivered, and did not answer. He was staring at a cup of hot chocolate; the bitter, spicy smell wafted up to me, not pungent but oddly muted, as if the smoke plugged my nose.

Quenami went on, "Everything is going according to plan."

I didn't like the idea that those two had a plan. "You call this –" Tizoc-tzin's voice was a hiss – according to plan? No wonder priests are such appalling strategists."

Quenami's face went as smooth as carved jade. "You're tired, my lord."

Tizoc-tzin looked up sharply. For a heartbeat I thought he was looking straight at me, but he was merely staring at Quenami, his face tense. "Yes," he said, thoughtfully. "You're right. I grow weary of this nightmare, Quenami." He lifted his cup of chocolate: the bitter smell wafted up stronger, as unpleasant as a corpse left alone for too long. I shook my head to clear the smell; the tendrils moved across Quenami's arms and hands in an unsettling effect. And as the smoke shifted, so did their voices, receding into the background.

"…over soon…" Quenami was saying. "Tomorrow… opposition removed quite effectively…"

What was happening tomorrow? What opposition? I needed to know. I bent further, and all but lost my balance as Quenami shifted positions. My hand passed a finger's breadth away from his head. He stopped, then, looked around him suspiciously. One of his hands drifted downwards, to pick an obsidian knife from his belt.

Time to go. I didn't know whether his spell would be effective, but I had no intention of finding out.

When I came out, the She-Snake was waiting for me, sitting on his haunches on the platform, watching darkness flow across the courtyard, as if it were the most natural thing in the Fifth World.

I said, slowly, "It can't be true. He wouldn't dare–" Do what, exactly? I hadn't heard much, but the little Quenami had said had made it clear those two were no longer playing by any rules I might have known. "It's some trick of your spell."

"No tricks," the She-Snake said. "Do you think me capable of inventing something that complicated? I'm a much more straightforward man than you take me for, Acatl."

"It's not what Axayacatl-tzin thought," I blurted out.

"He had his own opinions; and he had lived for too long in my father's shadow."

"Fine," I said. But I couldn't trust him. I couldn't possibly face the enormity of what he had shown me. "Then tell me Whose protection we are under, tonight."

"Do you not know?" the She-Snake said. "Ilaman-tecuhtli."

"The Old Woman, She who Rules?" I asked. The title meant nothing to me.

"Another aspect of Cihuacoatl, the She-Snake." He smiled when he saw my face. "Did you think my title was purely honorific? I serve a goddess, as much as the Revered Speaker serves Huitzilpochtli."

"The goddess of–"

He smiled again. "There is a temple, in the Sacred Precinct, the walls of which are painted black. Its entrance is a small hole, and no incense or sacrifices ever trouble the quietude. Inside are all the vanquished gods, the protectors of the cities we conquered, kept smothered in the primal night. The name of that temple is Tlillan."

Darkness. "And you–"

He looked at me, and his eyes were bottomless chasms. "In the beginning was darkness, and in the end, too. She is the space between the stars, the shield that keeps us safe."

"And She is on our side?"

"As much as a goddess can take sides."

"Why would she be?"

"I told you. She is darkness, anathema to all light. She holds our enemies to Her withered bosom." The She-Snake rose, staring into the sky above.

"Huitzilpochtli is light," I said. The only light, the one that kept the Fifth World safe and warm, the earth fertile and the rain amenable.

"Every great light must cast a great shadow. And every shadow knows it cannot exist, without that light."

"I still can't–"

"It was not illusion." His voice was grave. "Think on it, Acatl, think on what you have seen. Think on what and whom you believe in."

I didn't know, not anymore.

FIFTEEN

A Prayer to Quetzalcoatl

I walked back to my house in much the same state as a base drunkard, one foot in front of the other, scarcely able to focus on where I was going. The tendrils of smoke were slowly dissipating, taking with them the coldness at the back of my neck. But the memory remained, of the She-Snake's face, pale against the darkness he had summoned, of Tizoctzin, hunched and frightened, of Quenami, plotting the gods knew what magic to dispatch his opponents.

Inside my house I all but collapsed on the reed mat. My sleep was dark and restless; I woke up several times, gasping for air, my eyes hunting vainly for any light that would dissipate the shadows gathering at the edge of my field of view, and fell back again into darkness, oblivion swallowing me whole.

When I woke up for good, the grey light before dawn suffused the room, and the long, pale shadows seemed too distorted and unreal to be much of a threat. I sat cross-legged on my sleeping mat, breathing deeply, until my heart stopped beating like a sacrificial drum within my chest.

"Think on what you have seen, Acatl. Think on what and whom you believe in."

The Southern Hummingbird blind me, this looked to be the worst in a series of bad days.

I made my offerings of blood to the Fifth Sun and to my patron Mictlantecuhtli, then strode into the courtyard, determined to find Nezahual-tzin, locate Xahuia and put an end to the whole sordid business before the council started to vote.

However, I had not expected Quenami, who, by the looks of him, had been sitting under the pine tree in my courtyard for a while. "Ah, Acatl," he said. "We need to talk."

I raised an eyebrow. "That sounds ominous."

Quenami shook his head, annoyed. "Between High Priests, that is." As usual, he made me want to hit something.

"Have you decided to play your part in the order of the Fifth World, then?" I asked, unable to restrain myself. "That would be novel indeed."

"Oh, Acatl." Quenami shook his head, a little sadly. "Such lack of tact. You are so unsuited for the Court. "

"Perhaps," I said. "But I don't intend to shy away from my responsibilities."

"I'm glad," Quenami said.

He seemed a little too eager, a little too easily contemptuous? Something seemed to have changed in him, as in Tizoc-tzin. Perhaps Teomitl was right; perhaps they had pushed back a star-demon, and were waiting for its inevitable return.

Still, they were both planning something. Something large and spectacular, and unpleasant, and I didn't know what.

"What do you want, Quenami?" I asked. The time for subtlety was past, if there had ever been one.

"Merely to know how your investigation was

progressing." He smiled again a little too broadly. "And if there was any help I could offer you."

"I don't think so."

"You'd reject a held-out hand?" He frowned. I felt as if he were playing his part not for my benefit, but for that of some other observer, as if he was doing this only so he could say he had gone through the proper procedures.

"I have enough allies combing the palace and the city." Not effectively or with tangible results, but he didn't need to know that.

"I see." His eyes were dark, narrowed slits. "I see. You are… peculiar, Acatl."

"I'm flattered," I said dryly.

He went on, oblivious, "Alone at Court, you stand for the Fifth World, for the continued balance that keeps us whole. Most people are not so self-effacing."

My hands had started to clench into fists; I controlled them with an effort. Compliments had never been Quenami's strength, if he was being so lavish, he wanted something from me.

But I couldn't see what.

"You're unwavering. Dutiful, a loyal servant of the Fifth World."

"I'm sure you have better things to do than sing my praises," I said.

He shook his head. "Don't be so modest. Things are changing at Court, Acatl, and we need people like you at the centre, who will hold to their convictions no matter what. Loyal servants of the Mexica Empire."

There it was, the true sting. "Loyal," I said flatly.

"Aren't you?"

"Of course I am." I said, carefully detaching every word, "I served the previous Revered Speaker, and I will serve the new one, when he is elected. But I won't play in your power-games, Quenami."

"No." He sounded almost regretful. "You're much too wise for that. But you'll continue your investigation, won't you?"

"Someone," I said, barely keeping the irritation from my voice, "is summoning star-demons. I don't intend to sit still while they do." No matter what Tizoc-tzin or Quenami said.

"I see." Why did he look so pleased all of a sudden?

I decided to hit him where it hurt. "What does tar mean to you, Quenami?"

It was a spear thrown in the dark, but somehow it connected. I saw his face tighten, as if at some deeply unpleasant memory. "Nothing," he said, and that was the worst lie I'd heard him utter. "I have no idea what you're talking about."

Oh, but he had, and we both knew it. "Tar protects against water," I said, aloud. "It's connected with boats and sacrifices."

His face, which had begun to relax, tightened again at the mention of sacrifice. Sadly, it wasn't exactly surprising. Palli had already told me that someone had died in Axayacatl's room. "A councilman went missing," I went on, slowly. "Pezotic. I'm starting to wonder if he's alive at all, Quenami."

His face shifted again. How I wished I could read his expressions, but he had a tight control on them. "What wild tales you spin, Acatl."

It was clear I wouldn't get anything else out of him; not without more evidence. "Why are you here, Quenami?"

He smiled again, about as convincingly as a star-demon. "I told you, Acatl. To offer to assist you."

As if I'd believe him. "Well, I should think I've made my position clear."

Quenami watched me for a while. I got the feeling he was trying to decide how best to handle me.

"Yes," he said, finally. "You have made that perfectly clear."

I was saved from thinking up a reply by Teomitl, who entered the courtyard with the brisk step of a warrior on his way to the battlefield. "Acatl-tzin!"

"Ah, I see your student is here. Don't let me stand in the way of your imparting of knowledge," Quenami said. He bowed to Teomitl, much too little to be sincere. Teomitl's eyes narrowed, but he actually managed to retain his self-control, a fact for which I was eternally grateful.

He waited until Quenami was out of the courtyard to speak, though. "I didn't know you were on speaking terms with him."

"I'm not," I said, curtly.

"Then why is he here?"

"That's the problem." Why had he come here? I thought back to the way he'd acted, much too friendly, much too smooth, in a way that even I could see. Either he thought me not worth deceiving anyway, or he was truly in a panic, unable to master himself. "Has anything happened at the palace?"

"Yes," Teomitl said. "But I'm not sure he would know."

"What?" I asked.

He did not answer at once, he was too busy staring at Quenami's retreating back. "Teomitl!" The Duality curse me, was everyone turning into copies of Nezahual-tzin?

"Tizoc-tzin gathered the remaining members of the council yesterday. They're going to vote in two days."

I looked up, into the clear sky. The stars were pinpoints, barely visible unless one knew that they were here. Two days, eh? And three or four more, for the ritual of coronation to take place. Perhaps we had a chance. Perhaps we could stand until then.

My mind came back to Quenami, and to more mundane matters. "He knows about the vote, no question." I thought again on what he had asked me. "He wanted to make sure where I stood."

"And?" Teomitl asked.

"I told him that I would stand by whoever was elected Revered Speaker." As I said this, I thought of the scene I'd seen the previous night. If my worst suspicions were right, then I had just made it clear to Quenami that I was a liability, a man they needed to neutralise, and fast. "We need to go back to the palace."

"Of course," Teomitl said.

"And to see Nezahual-tzin."

Teomitl's face froze. "That's a bad idea, Acatl-tzin."

"He made me an offer I couldn't refuse," I said. I explained, as best as I could, during the time it took us to cross the Sacred Precinct. It was early morning, and the crowds were there as usual, carrying offerings and worship thorns and leading sacrifices to the pyramid temples as if nothing were wrong. I caught sight of a woman with an embroidered cotton skirt who looked up at the Great Temple, her face frozen in cautious hope. Her earlobes were bloody, and she was whispering the words of a prayer.

As I expected, Teomitl's first reaction to my story was hardly enthusiasm. "I see. And you believed him?"

"I think he's honest." I was suddenly glad I hadn't had time to get into the details of my meeting with the She-Snake. "As long as it suits him to be, of course."

"I'm not surprised," Teomitl said. "He thinks too much of himself, that one."

"You seem to have developed a liking for him," I said, dryly.

"I've seen enough."

"From one meeting?"

"You forget," Teomitl said. "He was here, for a while."

They were much the same age; but somehow, it had never occurred to me that they could have met. From Teomitl's sombre tone, it must have been more than that. "You were still a child when he left Tenochtitlan, and so was he. People change."

Teomitl shook his head. "I doubt he has."

Clearly I wasn't going to be able to make him change his mind, and I didn't feel like arguing at this juncture. What I needed to do was understand who was doing what in this palace – and fast, before I stopped being able to work out things at all.

One of Nezahual-tzin's men met us at the entrance of the palace, by the red-painted columns, and directed us, not towards the boy-emperor's chambers, but to the sweatbaths.

We found Nezahual there in one of the bigger baths, seated on one of the low stone benches. Three attendants stood by his side. The firebox at his feet was already warm, and the feathers of his headdress drooped in the growing heat. His face was mottled, a dark shadow against the vapour, and his arms and legs bore the wheals of the rushes and of the blades of cutting grass the attendants had struck him with: thin raised welts, with blood barely pearling up through the broken skin.

His eyes were closed, and he didn't move when we came in. "Ah, Acatl."

"Impressive," I said. He was deep into his meditation, his eyes still closed; but obviously he saw on another plane than the Fifth World.

"A trick, as the She-Snake would call them." His voice was deprecating. "I see the pup is with you."

I didn't have to turn round to guess Teomitl's hands would have clenched. "Let's try to be civil here," I said, ignoring the fact that I was talking to one Revered Speaker and a man who could very well become one in the future. "As you said, the Fifth World is at stake. Whatever quarrels you have can wait."

Teomitl glowered at Nezahual-tzin, but he said nothing.

"I'm surprised to find you here," I said. "Sweatbaths don't belong to Quetzalcoatl." Several gods and goddesses took an interest in those places of purifications, not least among Whom was Tezcatlipoca, the Smoking Mirror, Quetzalcoatl's eternal enemy.

Nezahual-tzin smiled. The vapour swirled around him, coalesced into the shape of a huge serpent, so much clearer than the one I'd seen in his rooms that I could count every feather, every jewelled scale on the huge body wrapped around the boy-emperor. "Enemy territory is where you prove yourself, where you're most sharply defined against what you're not, what you'll never be."

"Interesting," I said. "Nezahual-tzin, there is something I need to ask you about Tizoc–"

He shook his head. "After the ritual. It can wait."

I wasn't sure it could.

"We're not here to talk." Nezahual-tzin leant back against the wall of the sweatbath. The serpent leant with him, growing larger and larger, its outline sinking into the wall, gaining colour and texture until it seemed a living fresco.

"Into the place of the fleshless, away from the abode of life
You came, You descended
Into the region of mystery
For the precious bones, for men to inhabit the earth…"

The serpent was growing larger; the world was receding, fading into insignificance, the city a child's

map, spread on the ground far, far below us, the Fifth
Sun so close we might touch it.

"You came, You ascended
Into the gardens of the gods, into the place of the Duality
You came, You made them whole
The broken bones, made whole through Your penance..."

Abruptly, everything faded out and I came to in the
vapour-filled room, the unpleasant prickle of an obsidian blade against my back.

The attendants had retreated, Nezahual-tzin had
risen, regal and wrathful. "What is the meaning of
this?"

"You can't possibly–" Teomitl said.

I turned, slowly. Three warriors stood with their
macuahitl swords pointed at me; and Quenami was
with them, smiling from ear to ear. "I don't understand," I said, though I did perfectly. My time had just
run out. "Teomitl is right. You have no authority."

"Oh, I don't do this on my authority," Quenami said.
He smiled even more widely. I hadn't thought that was
possible, but the son of a dog managed it. "Tizoc-tzin is
the one who gave the order."

"On what motive?" I asked.

Quenami jerked his chin in Nezahual-tzin's direction. "Conspiracy with foreigners against the good of
the Mexica Empire should do, for the moment."

Meaning there was another reason, and that, given
enough time, he'd find a way to present it before the
judges, whoever they might be. "I see." I threw a
glance at my two companions who now stood apart,
as if to make it clear they'd have nothing to do with
each other. It might have been amusing in other circumstances.

Teomitl was working himself up to a speech; I silenced him with a brief shake of my head, and hoped

to the gods he'd have the wits to remain silent. It was highly doubtful anyone would arrest Nezahual-tzin, who was Revered Speaker of an allied city, but Teomitl did not have such protections. I didn't think Tizoc-tzin would want any harm to come to him, not unless the fool spoke up for me.

Luck must have been with me, for Teomitl remained silent, his eyes wide in his dark face, as if not quite sure what had happened.

"Oh, don't look so glum, Acatl," Quenami said as the guards took me away from the sweatbath. "We should have a new Revered Speaker to decide your fate."

Oh yes. And we both knew what he would be, and what he would decide.

SIXTEEN
In Enemy Territory

The cell was small, a square of beaten earth surrounded by four adobe walls, with barely enough space
for me to lie down, and a mangy reed mat as its only
furniture.

But still, as far as cells went, it was comfortable. A
year ago my brother Neutemoc, a respected Jaguar
Knight, had awaited his judgement in a wooden cage
on the platform before the palace, out in the midday
sun. At least I was in the shade, and they had even
given me a few maize flatbreads.

The ground under my feet was slightly warm, im-
pregnated with a magic I wasn't quite sure where to
place, faint and distant, like the echo of something vast.

The first thing I tried after they'd drawn the entrance-curtain closed was to cast a spell. The remnants
of that were still on the ground, my blood a duller
shade than the earth, stubbornly refusing to quicken.
It was as if something were blocking me – perhaps the
other High Priests? I hadn't imagined they had that
much power.

With nothing much to do, I sat against the wall furthest from the entrance, watching the quincunx I'd

drawn on the ground recede further into the shadows as the blood sank into the earth.

Everything seemed to grow fainter as time passed. Emptiness crawled across my limbs – a terrible sensation of dislocation like a maize stalk uprooted from the field. I tried moving my fingers, and it was as if my body no longer knew how to answer.

The flatbreads. Was that the same poison that had killed Ceyaxochitl? But no, I was a paranoid fool. Manatzpa had admitted to that, the only thing he had turned out to be responsible for, in the long string of magical offences that had brought me here.

But still…

Still, I felt as if I was rising in and out of consciousness – sleeping a restless sleep, waking up gasping and no longer quite sure of where I was, as if whatever they had put in here was eating at me, gnawing at my spirit little by little.

With faltering hands, I reached for my obsidian knife, hoping for the comfort of Lord Death's power arcing through me, the aching, stretched emptiness that was my province, but they had taken that away from me, too.

The Duality curse me, I needed to focus. I couldn't let it end like this, not with the star-demons the gods knew where, not with Teomitl still vulnerable against the intrigues of his brother. I needed to–

My hand fell back on the ground, limp, and somehow I couldn't muster the strength to lift it again. Shadows flickered at the edge of my vision, like the smoke of the She-Snake's ritual, slowly spreading to cover the world.

There is a temple, in the Sacred Precinct, the walls of which are painted black…

I needed to get up, I needed to…

The name of that temple is Tlillan. Darkness.

Just one moment. A moment's rest, that was all that I needed, a moment with my eyes closed, thinking of nothing but the bare walls, a moment here on the earth, warmed up by its touch. I needed…

The entrance-curtain was drawn aside with a jarring sound. I knew that sound, I thought, but it seemed too far away to be recovered, too much of a struggle to retrieve; like lifting my hands, like clenching my fingers. Like…

Footsteps echoed on the beaten earth, and a dark silhouette came to stand over me, its features moving in and out of focus in the shadows.

"Well, aren't you a sight. Pathetic, Acatl."

Acamapichtli? I'd expected Quenami with more accusations, or promises of what punishments Tizoc-tzin would push for; but why Acamapichtli? He hadn't even been in the palace recently. He was in disgrace, according to the She-Snake. Why?

Dimly, as if from a great distance, I saw him bend over me. Something glinted in the darkness, coming to rest by my side and gradually, as the fog across my vision lifted, I made out its shape – a polished jaguar fang, carved with images of seashells and frogs, shimmering with the blue-green magic of Tlaloc the Storm Lord. A slim piece of paper wrapped around it, steeped in a dark, pulsing colour I knew all too well – fresh blood.

Acamapichtli had withdrawn, was once more towering above me. "I inscribed this with the blood of a human sacrifice before coming here. It won't last. But at least we'll have a more coherent conversation."

I struggled to bring my mind back from the boundaries of the Fifth World, where it seemed to have fled. "I don't understand–"

"You're a fool," Acamapichtli said. "That's all there is to say." He did not move, watching me pull myself into a more upright position. Saliva had run down my chin, staining my cloak and I tasted blood in my mouth. I must have bitten my tongue as I sank into oblivion.

"Tlaloc," I said. My thoughts seemed to be a hundred scattered shards, the pieces of a broken mirror. "Lord Death. I–" I had been stretched out, as thin as though I was deprived of sustenance – dying, perhaps? If they left me longer in here, I would come out a drooling idiot. "What is this place?"

"Finally." In the dim light, I guessed more than saw his smile, as predatory as that of his god. "No longer the Fifth World, Acatl."

A god's world. A land where both my magic, which came from Lord Death, and that of Acamapichtli, which came from the Storm Lord, were uninvited guests. "The Southern Hummingbird," I said. "This is land consecrated to Him."

"Not quite. It's His land, Acatl, a portal into a small part of His heartland. Whatever you've done, they want to make sure you remain silent, badly enough to spend so much power on your prison."

The heartland. The seven caves. Aztlan, the White Place where we had all come from, the centre of Huitzilpochtli's power. "I have done nothing," I said, still struggling to reorder my thoughts. "Yet." Too late, I remembered the snatches I'd heard in Tizoc-tzin's rooms, about removing the opposition. I should have thought a little more on who they'd consider against them.

Acamapichtli smiled again. "That's why they want you in here."

"And I suppose…" I paused, gathering my thoughts. "I suppose you're with them?" I could see no other reason for him to be back at Court so soon.

"Don't be a fool." He snorted.

"You came back…"

He shrugged, a thoughtless, arrogant gesture. "I needed some time to make myself forgotten, but it seems events are moving faster than I foresaw."

"You're out of the game," I said.

"Xahuia-tzin is out of the game," Acamapichtli said, thoughtfully. "That doesn't mean I am. But I don't have Quenami's powers, alas."

His face had the same haughty cast as when he'd told Teomitl the envoys weren't his. "That's a lie, isn't it?" Gingerly, I pulled myself upwards, careful to remain near the jaguar's fang. My head brushed against the ceiling and, up there, further away from the magic, I could feel it, the skittering at the edge of my mind, the force that wanted to erode my whole being. How could Acamapichtli stand it?

No doubt he had his own protections. No doubt he had planned for it. He was not the prisoner here.

He was still watching me. The shadows sculpted his face, made it seem as distant as that of a carved statue in the darkness of a shrine. "That's a lie, isn't it?" I repeated. "You're more than strong enough to blast us all out of the Fifth World."

"Perhaps." He bent his head sideways, as if considering me in a new light. Without a doubt, I was no longer the High Priest that he had seen in the corridors, perhaps no longer his peer. I had no doubt he'd cast me aside without a moment's doubt if I was no longer useful to him.

But still, he had come to visit me. He had spent the power of a human sacrifice to speak with me. Just to gloat? "What do you want?"

"What I've always wanted," Acamapichtli said. "The Fifth World to survive, and our new Revered Speaker to lead us to glory." He cocked his head again. "One that would remember that the Great Temple is more than the Southern Hummingbird's territory."

Finally, we were there, at the crux of the matter. "You had influence before," I said. "Before the Storm Lord tried to seize power."

"I'm not responsible for His actions." He sounded almost annoyed at that, as if he could pretend to control the will of his god.

"And you think I can help you?"

"No," Acamapichtli said. "Of course you can't, Acatl. Let's be honest here. You blunder into Court day after day, doing your best to follow intrigues you are utterly ignorant of."

"What compliments," I said. My vision had started to fade again, but I wasn't fool enough to touch one of Tlaloc's artefacts without any protection of my own. Much like Huitzilpochtli's spells, that magic was opposite to my own.

"You're admirable, in your own way." He snorted, but with much of the usual aggressiveness gone. "Choosing not to meddle in what you can't grasp. You know your own limits."

If I'd had more strength, I wasn't quite sure of what I'd have done. For all his arrogance and hasty judgments, he had a point. I had never been made for politics, or for the post of High Priest; I weathered as best as I could, did my best to rise up to the occasion. But I would never breathe it in as Quenami did, as Acamapichtli did, as all the birth-noblemen did, the ones who had watched their parents and grandparents swim in the currents of politics like children in the waters of Chalchiuhtlicue's streams and lakes. "He who remains bound by his own limits is the worst kind of prisoner," I said.

"True." Acamapichtli shifted. "But you're still a foolish man, Acatl. One does not dive into the bees' hives without knowing where the queen is."

"If that's all you have to say, I wonder why you

bothered to come at all."

His lips curled up, in a smile without sincerity. "As I said, I'm not their ally. With you removed, they'll turn their attention to me. I've come to make sure you last as long as you can."

More than anything, his matter-of-fact tone chilled me. "They've decided, then?"

"They'll find a pretext," Acamapichtli said. He snorted. "They lack imagination, but it won't be hard to concoct something they can blame on you. And then the next Revered Speaker can appoint a High Priest more malleable than you are."

There were two ways to appoint a new High Priest: when the old one was demoted, or when he died. "They won't strip me of my rank," I said. It wasn't a question.

Acamapichtli said nothing. The cold at my nape could have been that of the underworld. Death held no secrets for me anymore, but sometimes, knowing was worse than being in the dark; it left no place for hope, none at all. Like all the souls I guided down into darkness, I would make my way to the throne of Lord Death, and dissolve into oblivion, everything left unfinished forever. There was no recourse. There had never been.

I took a deep breath, refusing to think about the chasm yawning at my feet. "Very well. If that's the way it's going, I'll need information."

Acamapichtli nodded, as one craftsman to another. "You'll have an audience, a closed one, with only Tizoc-tzin and perhaps a few of the faithful in attendance. They planned for you to be insensate long before this, to make it fast and short." He gestured to the fang on the ground. "This won't hold until then, but it should deflect part of the Southern Hummingbird's magic."

"I see." I sat down again, my hand straying towards the fang. The earth was warm underneath, but I wasn't fooled. Like Grandmother Earth in the Fifth World, it was nothing but hunger, and would not rest until all the blood had left my veins. "I'm surprised they let you do this."

He snorted again. "As I said, fools, the lot of them. They think I'm settling accounts with you for my disgrace."

He, too, was a much better actor than he had appeared to be at first. I had underestimated him, perhaps even more so than Quenami. Never again.

"Any defence I have wouldn't be much good, would it?" I asked.

Acamapichtli did not move for a while. "It might. I don't know. You have one chance, Acatl, and one only. The She-Snake will be part of the audience. They won't be able to do anything but include him, since they want to expedite this before the election."

The She-Snake? He was much too canny to be caught doing anything in favour of a convicted traitor. Not much of a chance. The hollow in my stomach wouldn't close.

"What about Teomitl?" I asked.

"He's not in a position to help you. Tizoc-tzin has him confined to his quarters, ostensibly for his own safety."

"And Nezahual-tzin?"

"Too smart to let himself be dragged into something like this," Acamapichtli said.

I hated to admit this, but he was right. Nezahualtzin had known how fragile his position was all along, although ironically his offer to help find Xahuia and clear his name was the one thing that would allow Tizoc-tzin to accuse him of collusion and treason.

270

"I see," I said again, though all I could feel was the abyss yawning under my feet. "It's not much."

"There isn't much I can do." Acamapichtli shifted, slightly.

"Do you know anything about the murders of the councilmen?"

"Do you think this is going to help you?"

"If I have to die, then at least let it be for something I can understand."

He snorted, almost gently. "We all die in the end, Acatl. We all drift out of the Fifth World, our destination determined by the manner of our deaths. But..." He was silent, for a while. "All I know is that the council had a frightful quarrel, five days before Axayacatl-tzin died."

"What kind of quarrel?" And then I remembered what Echichilli and Manatzpa had told me. "Pezotic," I said. The Master on the Edge of the Water, the councilman who had been dismissed for running away. "Pezotic disappeared."

"Yes."

"What was the quarrel about?"

"I don't know." Acamapichtli shook his head in an annoyed manner. "I'm not privy to the secrets of the gods. I never was. But I've heard they were threatened – badly enough to fear for their lives. They'd turned into pitiful wrecks, both of them."

It made me feel as though I had crossed a great lake, only to see mountains ahead of me. "You're right. It's not much help."

"Believe me. If I had any idea what they were up to in truth, I would make sure everyone else knew."

"I have no doubt you would."

Acamapichtli's lips curled up a fraction. "Good. So long as we understand each other. Any other questions, Acatl?" He'd started to move out of the cell, back towards the entrance-curtain.

I couldn't think of any. He went out, leaving me in darkness with not a flicker of light to be seen.

I must have slept again, watching the jaguar fang by my side. I came to with my hand wrapped around it, and a stinging pain in my palm, a trace of the Storm Lord's power engraved into my skin. My mind skittered, refused to hold on to anything.

He had said…

Acamapichtli had said that the audience would be soon, that they wanted this done with before it was too late. That they–

Images drifted across my field of vision, faded into darkness again. The smoky, wavering outline of the entrance-curtain – a faint light I could barely make out – sank further and further out of sight as time passed. I had no way of knowing if it was still day outside or if it was night, and I had missed my devotions.

I made them, regardless, in the encroaching darkness, spilled blood that had no potency, whispered prayers the Fifth Sun or Lord Death might never hear. It was what I had always done.

When they came for me I jerked out of a dreamless sleep to find a Jaguar Knight bending over me, his face framed between the jaws of his animal-shaped helmet. For a brief, timeless moment, he seemed like my brother Neutemoc, but then I saw they had nothing in common.

He hauled me to my feet without ceremony and out into a corridor and a succession of courtyards. Outside, the Fifth Sun's light hurt my eyes and a hundred spots flickered at the edge of my vision like star-demons streaming down. I caught a vague glimpse of noblemen, clustering in a sea of gold and turquoise ornaments, of palace slaves in their wooden collars, of warriors in

272

feather regalia. Banners flashed across my field of vision, a riot of bright colours all merging into one.

I kept my hands clenched, focused on the prayers I had learnt as a novice priest in the *calmecac* school, and repeated day after day at dawn and at sunset, the prayers that kept the world whole.

"As grass becomes green in spring
Our hearts open and give forth buds
And then they wither
This is the truth
Down into darkness we must go…"

Over and over, a familiar litany washing over my broken thoughts, the words I knew by heart, the words that defined me. I thought of Nezahual-tzin, doing his ritual in the sweatbath, under the gaze of the Smoking Mirror, his god's eternal adversary.

"Enemy territory is where you prove yourself – where you're most sharply defined against what you're not, what you'll never be".

Time to see if he was right.

The light flickered, and my captor flung me to the ground. My knees connected with something hard, and the rest of my body followed. I barely had the time to bring up my hands to stop my fall. Pain shot up my wrists, an agony I silently pledged to Lord Death.

Slowly, like a hurt animal, I pulled my hands back, lifted my head to look at my surroundings.

More riots of colours – frescoes against the wall, the painted gods and goddesses wavering as if in a great heat, feather fans negligently propped against the pillars, carvings, rearing into sudden focus and just as suddenly vanishing into blurriness.

Close my eyes… I had never wanted so much to close my eyes, but I couldn't. I needed to see… I needed to…

"We convene here today for the trial of Acatl, High Priest for the Dead. The charge is treason."

Quenami. He stood somewhere to my left and ahead of me. I blinked, struggling to bring the world into focus. I could feel saliva drip down the side of my mouth again. I must have looked like an imbecile. Good. I needed them to underestimate me, even though I wasn't entirely sure what I would gain by it.

Ahead was a dais I recognised from another lifetime. This time it held two people. The one to my left, decked in emerald-green, had to be Tizoc-tzin, and the patch of black, placed slightly lower than Tizoc-tzin, could only be the She-Snake.

"I've read the charges," the She-Snake said. "I'm not quite sure what to make of them." The volume of his voice wouldn't remain steady, it kept hovering between a whisper and a shout. The Duality take me, why couldn't I focus on anything useful?

"I don't see what there is to add," Quenami said. "First Xahuia, and then Nezahual-tzin. There is a definite pattern."

"I admit to not knowing him as well as you do." I couldn't make out the tone of the She-Snake's voice. "But, nevertheless, I'm surprised. His record is impeccable."

"Biding his time," Tizoc-tzin said, sharply.

"Until Axayacatl died?"

"Until such time as he could damage us most," Tizoc-tzin said. "You have seen him worming his way into the court, weaving his webs like a spider for a few years now. First the appointment, then the taking on of my brother as a student, and finally, his sister…"

Mihmatini. I had to do something, I had to… My mouth wouldn't move. The Southern Hummingbird blind Acamapichtli, couldn't he have carved a stronger talisman?

"Much of that seems irrelevant, if not outright defamatory." The She-Snake's voice was mild, but I felt Quenami recoil. "And I don't see the point of this farce, Tizoc. It's also quite obvious he can't speak. I'll remind you that pain is an offering to the gods, not a means to silence people or interrogate them."

"I… " I managed through parched lips. I clenched my hands, felt my skin ache where Acamapichtli's jaguar fang had seared it. "I… can… speak." Every word was a burning stone, charring my windpipe and my lips as it came out.

"Quenami—" Tizoc-tzin snapped.

"It wasn't meant to happen," Quenami said. "I made sure—"

"Of what?" The She-Snake asked, but did not wait for an answer. "What do you have to answer the charges against you, Acatl?"

I had to focus. There had been a quarrel and the council had split, five days before Axayacatl-tzin's death. On the following day, Manatzpa-tzin had gone to a priest of Quetzalcoatl the Feathered Serpent, to buy the Breath of the Precious Twin. "They're hiding something," I said, slowly, carefully.

"You do not have the right to speak!" Tizoc-tzin all but screamed.

"Perhaps they are," the She-Snake said. His face swam into focus, grave and concerned. I could no longer be sure if it was an act or not. "But that has nothing to do with the accusations against you."

"They… they're trying to silence me," I said. "Because I know… you did something to the council, didn't you, Tizoc-tzin? Did whatever it took to be sure you'd be named Revered Speaker, even if you had to sacrifice them one by one."

"That's a lie," Tizoc-tzin said, but I heard the panic in his voice, and the She-Snake must have as well.

"I was the one who ordered Xahuia arrested," I said. I tried to stand, but my muscles wouldn't support me. "How can you call me a supporter of Texcoco?"

There was a moment of silence, but Quenami was not about to be undone so easily. "And the boy-emperor?" he asked. "Nezahual-tzin. Will you also claim to have been investigating him?"

"He offered his help to find his sister."

"And you took it?" Quenami said.

The note of triumph in his voice was all too evident. "Texcoco is a member of the Triple Alliance," I said. "Our ally since the founding of Tenochtitlan."

Quenami snorted. "With one of their princesses involved in a plot against the Mexica Empire? Texcoco is a tribute-paying province, like the rest of them. It has no business meddling in our politics, and you have no business accepting Nezahual-tzin's help."

"For all the help you gave me–"

"I offered," Quenami said. "I offered and you denied me. You preferred the Texcocan boy."

"Acatl?" the She-Snake asked. "Is that true?"

It was true. At least, I couldn't deny it without outright lying, and I refused to sink to Quenami's level.

My moment of silence must have been all he needed. I saw the She-Snake bow down his head. "Then I'm afraid there is nothing I can do. If they are right…"

They were; and they weren't. They were the ones endangering the Mexica Empire, the whole of the Fifth World, but there was nothing I could say. "It's not the point," I said.

"It's the point of this audience." The She-Snake's voice was almost gentle, an apology. I had missed my chance, if I'd ever had much of one. "To determine your fitness as High Priest."

"I stand for the Fifth World," I said. "And for the

Revered Speaker, who keeps us safe. What more do you ask for?" I bit my tongue before I could say more.

"Your loyalty." Quenami's voice was gleeful. "And it's clear we don't have that."

"Not until the Revered Speaker is elected," I snapped.

"The charges stand, then," Tizoc-tzin said.

The She-Snake held my gaze for a while. In his pupils, I saw only darkness, the same yawning abyss that his goddess ruled. "I'm sorry, Acatl. But they do."

Tizoc-tzin made a quick, peremptory gesture. "Then it's settled. Treason carries the death penalty."

"You can't–" I started, but this time, one of the guards slammed the butt of his *macuahitl* sword into my back, sending me sprawling to the ground. Now that the She-Snake had joined them, they felt safe to silence me.

"By the flower garland," Quenami said. I wished I could have smashed the smug smile from his face. "Tomorrow at dawn?"

"Better make it quick." The corners of the She-Snake's mouth had curled up in a disgusted smile. "Put an end to the whole sordid business as soon as possible."

I was hauled up again, all but carried out of the room, to the central platform overlooking the courtyard. The Fifth Sun shone clear and bright on what looked to be my last day in the Fifth World.

The warriors that carried me were halfway across the platform when something leapt up from the stairs, seemingly coming out of nowhere, as black and as sleek as a fish, lifting its wrinkled head towards me, the clawed hand at the end of its tail unclenching, coming straight towards me.

An *ahuizotl*.

SEVENTEEN

Ahuizotl

"What in the Fifth World is that?" one of the warriors asked, but the creature was moving again with supernatural speed. Its tail swept down and sent us all crashing down onto the stone floor.

Another one appeared, leapt over us. I lost it from sight, struggling to pull myself upright on shaking muscles. One of the warriors reached out for his *macuahitl* sword to stop me, but the *ahuizotl* was on him before he could react, its full weight resting on his chest. The tail uncoiled again, plunging towards the eyes.

I turned my gaze away, even as he started to scream.

The second warrior had his *macuahitl* sword, was pointing it in my direction. Given my painfully slow speed, I had no hope of avoiding it. I threw myself to the ground nevertheless.

Nothing happened. I felt the wind of something else's passage and heard the warrior tumble to the ground.

"What is the meaning of this?" Tizoc-tzin asked, from inside.

I crawled away from the scene of the carnage. The *ahuizotls* watched me – and so did the last thing – the huge, ghostly serpent rearing in the air, drops of water and blood shining on its feathered collar – for a moment only, and then it lunged towards me. I couldn't avoid it. I remained where I was, fully expecting something unpleasant, but it twisted at the last moment, knocking me off the ground, and before I could understand what had happened, it was under me, its body supporting me as it rose again.

The *ahuizotls* joined it, framing it like an escort. With a single powerful leap, they leapt up and hung onto the serpent's tail; and the whole assemblage started to glide upwards at a greater speed than a boat in rapids.

Hanging on to the serpent as well as I could, I cast a glance backward. Tizoc-tzin, the She-Snake, and Quenami stood on the platform. Quenami was frantically whispering a spell, dabbing blood on the ground. But the She-Snake… He just stood, watching the serpent glide away through the courtyard. He could have done something, too. Unlike Quenami, he had come fully prepared, but he didn't.

I could have sworn he was smiling.

The serpent flew to a deserted spot outside of the city, in the midst of the Floating Gardens, the series of island-fields that grew our crops. It landed in the middle of a patch of newly-planted tomatoes – the green leaves just opening – and, with a great sigh, it sank back down into the earth.

The *ahuizotls* remained. They watched me with unblinking yellow eyes, as if daring me to put a step wrong. I pulled myself into an upright position, the most I could do. It wasn't only the weakness induced by the heartland – less than an hour ago, I had been convinced this day was my last – to find a sudden reprieve was heartening, but it was the sort of unwelcome episode I'd have been glad to avoid altogether.

Four silhouettes walked towards me from the single hut on the edge of the floating garden, wading through the maize stalks. I wasn't surprised when they turned out to be Teomitl, Nezahual-tzin, and the two Texcocan warriors I had seen earlier.

Wordlessly, Teomitl handed me a couple of obsidian knives which I put back into their sheaths.

"Impressive," I said, slowly.

"Just a trick." Nezahual-tzin smiled.

Teomitl looked more preoccupied. "Acatl-tzin? You don't look–"

"I'll be all right," I said, raising a shaking hand. "I just need a moment to recover."

"See?" Teomitl said, with a scornful glance at Neza-hual-tzin. "I told you it would work."

Nezahual-tzin grimaced. "I've heard better plans. But yes, it worked. Only because they got sloppy."

"I thought you were confined to your rooms," I said to Teomitl, the only thought that occurred to me.

"I broke out." He smiled again – pure Teomitl, carelessly proud.

"Right. Right. So did I, it seems." I stared at the ground under my feet, took a deep breath. The air was clean and crisp, nothing like that of my cell. "What now?"

They both looked at me as if it were obvious that I held the answer. The gods help me, I didn't need another adolescent struggling with nascent responsibility, Teomitl on his own was enough trouble for a lifetime, and I had a suspicion Nezahual-tzin would be even worse.

"We need to move," I said. "We can sort out the rest later. Tizoc-tzin isn't going to let you get away with it for long, and neither is Quenami." I looked at Neza-hual-tzin, who was currently focusing on the water lapping at the floating garden's edge. Ah well. Lost for lost, I might as well get a chance to commit the crime they'd accused me of. "How soon can we be in Texcoco?"

Nezahual-tzin's gaze drifted back towards me. He didn't look surprised in the slightest. "One, two days? We have boats and supplies, but we'll have to get past the dyke as soon as we can."

Texcoco lay east of Tenochtitlan, across the lake of the same name, and a great dyke had been built to prevent the waters of the lake from flooding us. It was manned by a few forts, though its main purpose wasn't military. Any invading army would come by land, which meant one of the three causeways rather than the lake.

"Two days?" I asked.

"A little less if the gods are with us."

"Or the *ahuizotls*," Teomitl said. "But not in Tenochtitlan, we'd stand out too much. Let's wait until we're out of the city."

"And Mihmatini?" I asked.

Teomitl grimaced. "She's gone to the Popocatepetl volcano. On a pilgrimage of, ah, indefinite length."

And I could imagine how much she'd have protested at being taken away for her own safety. "Good," I said. "Let's go. We can sort out the details later."

Nezahual-tzin's boats were two flat-bottomed barges, a slightly larger version of the canoes fishermen steered all over the lake. They looked as if they had been specifically purchased for the rescue rather than brought with him. A Revered Speaker such as him would normally travel with more pomp, and the boats looked more utilitarian than grand and imposing.

The first boat was packed with the supplies he had mentioned – wrapped maize flatbreads and fruit, as well as cages holding owls and rabbits. The second one was packed with men – a dozen Texcocan warriors who all looked old enough to be veterans of Nezahual-tzin's coronation war.

Nezahual-tzin caught my glance, and smiled. "It never hurts to be prepared, Acatl."

I climbed gingerly into the boat, found myself a comfortable spot wedged against a particularly large bale, and determined not to move again in a lifetime.

Two of the warriors took the oars. Teomitl's *ahuizotls* slid into the water with a splash, and swam by our side as we moved away from the floating garden.

We cruised through row upon row of floating gardens, a whole district on a grid pattern, like the rest of the city. Soon the floating gardens thinned away, to become streets where peasants carried cloth and maize kernels to the marketplace and where the steady clack of looms from the women's weaving floated to us through the open entrances of their thatch houses. We were swinging around Tenochtitlan, keeping to the more populated areas in order not to stand out.

In between the houses I caught a glimpse of the Sacred Precinct's tallest buildings – the Great Temple under which the Moon Goddess Coyolxauhqui was imprisoned, and the circular Wind Tower, where I had prayed to Quetzalcoatl for Ceyaxochitl's life. The Feathered Serpent had not answered that prayer, but it occurred to me that perhaps He had given me something else to see me through my hour of need.

Nezahual-tzin stood near the prow, watching the houses go past. He looked much like any other nobleman's son, his cloak of thin cotton, his jade lip-plug glinting in the sunlight, his hair pulled back and caught in the base of his feather headdress.

We swung east into ever-smaller streets. The boats wove their way through the traffic – peasants coming back from the marketplace, warriors standing tall and proud in the regalia they had earned on the battlefield, priests with blood-matted hair on their way to the Sacred Precinct – with preternatural ease. If I didn't have Nezahual-tzin in my sights, I could have sworn that there was more to this than the agility of two warriors.

Teomitl was a little further down our boat, his hand trailing just above the water. His face was furrowed in concentration, his eyes focused on the dark shapes trailing the boat.

We came out into an expanse of open water. Ahead of us was the bulk of Nezahualcoyotl's Dyke, keeping back the saltwater and regulating the level of the lake during the flood season.

I had expected trouble at this juncture, but the few warriors manning the fort on the dyke looked bored, and the boats were carried over to the other side without any major incident. While Nezahual-tzin and I engaged the guards in idle conversation, the *ahuizotls* leapt over the wall and slid noiselessly back into the water, dark shapes gone past in an eye blink.

Behind the dyke were only a few boats, going either to Teotihuacan or Texcoco, merchants with goods to sell and wider barges belonging to noblemen on pilgrimages.

Teomitl moved to stand near Nezahual-tzin. "Time to go a little faster."

The *ahuizotls* dived, two under each boat. I felt a slight jerk as they moved to bear the weight of the keel, and then we were gliding across the water at a greater speed than oars alone could have managed. Teomitl's face shone the colour of jade, the light flickering across his features.

"How long can he hold?" Nezahual-tzin asked, sliding next to me.

"I don't know." Teomitl's eyes were two pits of darkness, and sweat ran down his face. I had seen him control more *ahuizotls*, but it had been for a much shorter amount of time. He had to have summoned these early in the morning for my rescue, and he hadn't released them since.

"I see." Nezahual-tzin stroked one of the owls in the cages, his fingers nimbly avoiding its beak stabs. "You're tutoring him well in magic, but his grasp of politics is appalling."

"So is mine," I said, and it wasn't an admission of shame. "Quenami's, however, is excellent."

"Point taken. But still…"

"You think Tizoc-tzin will be Revered Speaker?" I asked.

Nezahual-tzin's head moved a fraction. "I don't like the idea any more than you do, but we have to face this fact: Tizoc-tzin is likely to have been elected Revered Speaker by the time we come back."

"I know," I said. I hated myself for lending reality to his words, but he was right. There was nothing we could do. "But he won't want Teomitl to succeed him."

"You forget." Nezahual-tzin's lips curled up in a smile. "He's the only one who doesn't get a vote in his succession."

"His opinion matters."

"It does." Nezahual-tzin was silent for a while. "But Teomitl is destined to be a great warrior. He'll honour the Southern Hummingbird much better than I ever did, and the council will see that, in time."

"You're a politician," I said, slowly. To think I was having idle chitchat with the Revered Speaker of Texcoco…

"To each his own. I leave war to those with more heart for strife." Nezahual-tzin smiled. His eyes rolled up in their orbits, as white as pearls. "My face and heart are turned towards knowledge."

A fitting devotee of the Feathered Serpent indeed. "You didn't have to come with us," I said.

"No," Nezahual-tzin said. He watched the water for a while.

"But it was getting a little uncomfortable in Tenochtitlan?" I guessed.

"I'm a fair man, Acatl," Nezahual said. "I know exactly what my faults are, but the Smoking Mirror curse me if I'm going to let Tizoc-tzin run amok. A Revered Speaker may be Lord of Men, but he has a responsibility to them. He is the servant of the people. He is humble and an example of the law he upholds."

Hardly Tizoc-tzin's qualities. "Still," I said. "You can't ask that of everyone."

Nezahual-tzin's eyes drifted briefly towards Teomitl, whose grip on the boat had become so strong it seemed to be eating into the wood. "No. But some people will do it, regardless." He looked down again. "Axayacatl was one of them, but not any more."

He seemed angry or embarrassed. I couldn't be sure. "There was nothing more you could have done," I said.

"No," Nezahual-tzin said. "It's not that." He looked into the water. "I'm Revered Speaker of Texcoco, Acatl. My role is to vote on his designated successor, and to make the first speech at his funeral. That's the only reason I came into Tenochtitlan."

And now it looked as though he would fail at both.

I lifted my gaze against the glare of the sun, watching the shore grow closer and closer. "You'll probably not be in time for the vote. Tizoc-tzin has made sure of it. But, at the rate we're going, you might make the funeral."

And I was startled to see him smile for the first time, surprised and careless, like the boy he was.

We reached Texcoco sometime in the evening. Teomitl was white. As the boats wove their way through the

285

canals of the city, he came down, and sat next to me, his shoulders sagging against my chest. I could hear the thunder of his heartbeat and feel his skin, as cold and as clammy as underwater algae. The Duality curse me, I shouldn't have let him go so far. It was my responsibility to tutor him in magic and to teach him his limits, even if I had a suspicion I would lose that particular battle. Teomitl thought limits were for the weak.

The boat bumped against a dock. Nezahual-tzin stretched himself, looking at the tall adobe houses critically. The warriors in the other boats spread themselves around him in a tight knot. "We're not staying here," he said. "Let's go to the summer palace."

Teomitl did not answer. "He's in no state to walk," I said. I had a dim memory of the summer palace, somewhere in the mountains above Texcoco. It did not exactly sound like an easy trip, and I was in only marginally better shape than Teomitl.

"He won't have to," Nezahual-tzin said. His eyes shone white in the darkness, without pupils or cornea, white as the full moon hanging over us. He had never looked so alien. He shifted aside slightly and two litters loomed out of the darkness, a massive chair of carved mahogany, with a canopy of feathers and gold, and another, simpler one of wood and cloth, with enough sitting space for two. "Get on."

He couldn't have sent word ahead so fast, could he? I didn't know any spells of the living blood to communicate across distances, but he might not have been operating on quite the same rules as most priests. As Quetzalcoatl's servant, his power would come from fasts and vigils, and the occasional sacrificed animal.

Nevertheless, the timing was eerie. I wasn't sure if the point was to disorient us, or whether there was some other, more sinister purpose to his moves, and I had no way of knowing.

'nough. I wasn't Tizoc-tzin, and now wasn't the time for paranoia.

Teomitl did not stir as I set him into the second chair. I climbed on as best as I could, helped by one of the silent bearers. As soon as I was in, the litter started moving with a rocking tilt, away from those few lights I could see.

Nezahual-tzin had climbed in with the ease of someone who had ridden in litters all his life, he sat negligently in his chair, with the casual arrogance of the ruler, and looked at the land around him with the eyes of its owner. The warriors spread behind us, closing the march.

As in Tenochtitlan, the adobe houses gave way to wattle-and-daub, first with triangular, brightly-coloured roofs, and then simple structures of twigs and branches. The road snaked through the mountain, and soon the only lights were those of the torch-bearers by our side as we climbed higher and higher. Scraggly trees went past us in the darkness, the only noise was that of the bearers' feet scattering rocks and gravel on the path.

I dozed off. When I woke up again a huge structure loomed over us, a mass of stone and light clinging to the face of the mountain, with the smell of flowers and copal incense drifting towards us. Slaves rushed to help us dismount and I stood on shaking legs, looking at the sculptures of the Feathered Serpent framing the massive entrance, their jaws open as if to swallow us whole. Above the lintel was carved an image of the Storm Lord, fangs protruding from His lower lip and a snake shaped like lightning in His left hand. His blackened eyes seemed to be following me a little too closely for comfort.

And there was magic on the ground, arcing through my legs and spine, a slow ponderous heartbeat that seemed to link the Heavens and the earth, a compound of spells I couldn't identify. Wards shimmered all over the stone, shivering like a sea of crawling insects. From the ground to the sky above, endlessly renewed, endlessly forged anew. My hand itched where Acamapichtli's talisman had burnt me.

Nezahual-tzin was all but subsumed in a crowd of slaves and servants but he turned towards me, his eyes still rolled up in their orbits, shining like pearls in the murk of the lake, his smile like that of a jaguar. Something cold descended from my throat to my stomach, coiling like a venomous serpent – a sense of disquiet, a pressure against my chest.

I had felt this once before, a year ago, moments before the Fifth World slid all the way into chaos.

Tlaloc. The whole complex was dedicated to the Storm Lord.

"Welcome to my humble abode, Acatl," Nezahual-tzin said. "I'm sure you'll find the stay worth your while."

EIGHTEEN
The Pleasure Gardens

"We shouldn't have come here," Teomitl said. He sat on the reed mat in my room scowling, something he had been doing ever since waking up. Behind him, the columns of the rooms were carved in the shape of huge snakes rising up from the floor, their painted maws closing around the carved flowers jutting down from the ceiling.

"There wasn't much choice," I said. I felt like scowling, too. Tlaloc's magic was anathema to that of Lord Death, just as the Southern Hummingbird's was. So far, it wasn't anything like what I'd undergone in Tizoctzin's cell – a little tightness in the chest, as if I stood atop a high mountain, a sense that every gesture was made through tar; but that didn't mean I felt comfortable here.

"There were plenty of other choices. I was a fool. We could have hidden in Tlatelolco, or Tlacopan."

I shook my head. "They wouldn't have sheltered us. Tlacopan is a member of the Triple Alliance, but their influence has been on the wane for a while. And Tlatelolco…"

Tlatelolco, our direct neighbour on the island, had

been conquered seven years ago, its ruler killed. Now there was only a governor who owed everything to the Imperial Court, and would have no wish to set himself against the future Revered Speaker.

Teomitl grimaced. "I know." He pulled himself upwards in a fluid gesture, and went to stand before one of the carved frescoes. It was early morning, and the scent of flowers was all around us, the smell of the gardens casually spread on the mountain's face through hundreds of aqueducts, of the canals and bath-houses, the luxuries of Nezahual-tzin's father. A summer retreat, Nezahual-tzin had called it. Except that he seemed to have disappeared, and that none of the ever-present army of servants would answer our queries. Why had he brought us here? Obviously, it had been deliberate, but what use could he possibly have for us?

I didn't think he wanted to end the Fifth World. He had sounded sincere when he had said that. But he would have the best interests of his city at heart, like any ruler.

Not Tizoc-tzin, a treacherous part of me whispered in my mind. I quelled it before it could fester.

And, if the best interests of Texcoco were to hand us back to Tizoc-tzin, to smooth over their little "disagreement"... I had no doubt Nezahual-tzin would do it in less than a heartbeat. For all his youth, necessity had made him ruthless.

"Come on," I said. "Let's go for a walk." He needed the distraction, and the gods knew I needed to reassure myself that my legs were still working after my time in prison.

They were none too steady. In spite of my best intentions, we made it through two courtyards before I had to stop, leaning against one of the carved pillars until I stopped shaking.

290

"That was a foolish idea," Teomitl said. He glared at the manicured flower patches, and finally settled on the ground, crouching on his haunches as he often did. Unlike any palace I'd seen in Tenochtitlan, the ground sloped down, and the palace followed it. Water flowed out of a fountain in the centre, cascading downwards along a flight of stairs towards a room with a richly decorated entrance-curtain adorned with a huge stylised frog, splayed on the cotton cloth as if transfixed by a spear.

"No more foolish than breaking me out of prison," I said. "I haven't thanked you properly."

"You don't need to. Anyone would have done what we did."

"You were the only ones," I pointed out.

His gaze didn't move from the flowers. "Perhaps. But I don't do formalities very well, Acatl-tzin."

You're going to have to learn, I thought, but didn't say. "You've gone against your brother now."

"Yes," Teomitl said. His whole body radiated frustration. "It was always going to come to that, in the end, wasn't it?"

"It might not have," I said. There was so much more I wanted to add, except that my resentment and my hatred would come billowing out of me and wreck my relationship with Teomitl forever. Because he was right, blood should stand by blood, no matter how tainted the blood might be. It was what brothers should do for each other, and I had paid the price of that lesson a year ago, when my own brother had almost died because of my prejudices. "He's a paranoid man."

Tizoc was surely a more complex man than the wreck which had sentenced me to death for being a hindrance. He had to be. As our next Revered Speaker, he had to—

But I couldn't shake the She-Snake out of my mind, and the casual, almost instinctive way he had given my worst fears life and blood: *"Are you wondering if he'll be able to channel the Southern Hummingbird's powers into the Fifth World?"*

And I had known the answer, even then.

Teomitl looked up at the star-studded sky. "He was a great man, once. At the beginning of Axayacatl's reign, everyone was glad to have him as Master of the House of Darts. He was the darling of the Court, his acts the fabric of legend. They thought he was going to be as great a warrior as Father, leading the Empire to glory that would endure past the end of this age."

He couldn't have been remembering that, for he had been a toddler at the time Axayacatl ascended the throne. I guessed the warriors or the servants would have told him that as he grew up moody and isolated. Like a wildflower, Ceyaxochitl had said of him, and I wasn't altogether sure he'd ever go back to manicured gardens and clear-cut boundaries. Too much wilderness in him, and far too much knowledge. "Not everyone lives up to the expectations we have of them," I said.

"It ate him from the inside," Teomitl said. "They always compared him to someone: to Father, to Axayacatl, it didn't matter. How long can you live your life in shadow?"

A typical warrior's fallacy, that – that burning need to matter, to be showered with gifts and status, to stand out on the battlefield or in the city, no matter the cost. "Some people can," I said. As when I talked to my warrior brother, I had the feeling of slipping into an alien world, where the rules weren't the ones I'd always lived by. "Some, however…"

"I know." Teomitl made an impatient gesture. "Not everyone is a warrior. But, really, what else could he be?"

Growing up in the imperial family, being goaded to take his place in the Southern Hummingbird's dominion? No, not many paths open to a man whose father and brother had both become Revered Speakers. "He made his choices," I said. "You can understand him, but you can't change that."

"I suppose not." Teomitl shook himself, in a gesture eerily reminiscent of an *ahuizotl*. "Not that it matters, now. I wish…"

That things were different. I knew, and I knew nothing I could say would change anything. But still… "Teomitl–"

I was cut off by the sound of sandals in the courtyard, Nezahual-tzin, followed by a cluster of warriors, striding with his characteristic, thoughtless ease. "Taking some air?"

"As you see," I said. "What's going on, Nezahual-tzin? Why are we here?"

Teomitl had pulled himself upwards with preternatural speed. He stood watching Nezahual-tzin as a vulture might watch a dying animal, waiting for a moment of weakness to swoop down and finish it off.

"Good, good," Nezahual-tzin said, eluding my question altogether. "I had some preparations to make."

"What preparations?" I asked. "For a ritual?"

He smiled. "So impatient, Acatl."

I rolled my eyes upwards, towards the stars shining in the blue sky. "There are pressing matters, and not only of politics." Acamapichtli had said two days. They'd still be gathering the councilmen, fighting for influence. They would surely elect Tizoc-tzin, and start the weighty rituals that went into investing a Revered Speaker with the authority of Huitzilpochtli. The Storm Lord's lightning strike me, there had to be a chance, no matter how minuscule, that we would survive this…

"Of course." Nezahual-tzin bowed his head. "Come with me. There is something you must see."

"I don't play games," Teomitl said haughtily.

Nezahual-tzin's smile was starting to become annoying. "This isn't a game," he said, slow, sure of himself. "Merely an invitation, as your host. A proffered hand."

The last person to talk of proffered hands had been Quenami, and I had no wish for a repetition of what had happened afterwards. "And if we refuse?"

"You do as you wish. It would be a shame, but I have no doubt all of us would recover." Nezahual-tzin started to move away. The warriors followed, one of them holding a large fan to keep his master refreshed.

"Who does he think he is?" Teomitl whispered.

Revered Speaker, sadly, and, secure in the familiar setting of his power a radically different man than the one who had chatted with me on the boat. One more disappointment. I was getting used to those. "Let's indulge him," I said in a low voice. "I don't want to sample the Texcocan cages."

Nezahual-tzin must have had keener hearing than I'd assumed, for he turned, and smiled at me, sweet and innocent like a young warrior just released from the House of Youth.

I was not fooled. Whatever he thought we should see would be to his own advantage. If we were lucky, we would glean useful scraps, but nothing more.

If that was political acumen, then I was glad Teomitl was incapable of learning it.

We went down the mountain, following the flow of the water. It shimmered to my priest senses, a reminder of who the palace complex was dedicated to. It made me slightly uneasy. The last time I'd dealt with the Storm Lord, He had been trying to overthrow the

Fifth Sun. But still, the mark on my hand, an itch that grew strong the closer we went to the water, was a reminder that things were no longer quite the same.

In the canals floated garlands of flowers and wood carvings of frogs and seashells; and everywhere were small reed islands, scattered in the shape of quincunxes, reminders of the harmony of the Fifth World. Power hung over the water, shimmering like mist. I breathed it in with every step, a liquid constriction in my lungs, a heaviness in my throat.

We had been going for a while when Nezahual-tzin stepped into a courtyard, which seemed no different from all the others – save that the adobe walls surrounding it formed a circle, and that reeds had been carved all around the circumference. Dark stains marred the ground – living blood, a maze of power that thrummed in my chest, not the sharp, oppressive beat of Tlaloc's magic, but rather that of another god.

Reeds, and a circle. A circle for the unbroken breath of the wind, and reeds for One Reed: Topiltzin, Our Prince, the man who had ruled the legendary city of Tula as the incarnation of Quetzalcoatl, the Feathered Serpent.

Teomitl took in a sharp, unpleasant breath, and threw a glance at me. I nodded. It was a spell set in a circle wide enough to contain an entire battalion with the blood of dozens of… I paused, then, unsure of whether Nezahual-tzin would be ready to sacrifice so many of his subjects for one ritual. But no, the Feathered Serpent disliked human sacrifices. It had to be animals.

Still, it was impressive.

Shallow steps descended towards the centre of the courtyard, and so did the water too, flowing over them in a wide cascade. In the middle of the water was an island of stone, the part above the water carved over with a mass of serpents, that shivered and danced in the sunlight, almost as if they were alive… I shifted, and saw a yellow eye open and close. The gods take me, it *was* stone, and they were somehow alive.

Slaves laid a bridge to carry us across the water. Nezahual-tzin walked onto it with scarcely a break in his stride

The only building on the island was an awning of cotton, a poor protection against the gaze of the Fifth Sun. Someone sat underneath – shifted slightly when Nezahual-tzin approached, in a way that was gut-wrenchingly familiar. Beside me, Teomitl tensed. "Acatl-tzin."

"I know," I said, having only eyes for her.

"You have visitors," Nezahual-tzin said, in the way of a priest enjoying a secret joke. "See that you behave yourself."

"When have I not behaved myself, brother?" Xahuia-tzin, Axayacatl's missing wife, smiled up at us, as careless and as regal as if she had still been ensconced within the Imperial Palace in Tenochtitlan, but her eyes were dark and hollow, those of a woman already defeated.

A quick, intelligent man would have made a snide remark to let Nezahual-tzin know that his manipulation had not succeeded. A smarter man would have smiled, enjoying the same secret joke.

I was neither fast on my feet, nor smart, nor dishonest. I simply gaped, looking for words that seemed to have fled.

"It has been a long time, Acatl-tzin," Xahuia said.

Nezahual-tzin had retreated slightly, standing near the wooden bridge leading back to the palace, his hand carelessly wrapped around the hilt of his *macuahitl* sword. But, of course, like the She-Snake, he never did anything carelessly.

Teomitl spoke first, his face as harsh as newly-cut jade. "You said you hadn't found her."

Nezahual-tzin smiled. "I would have hated to waste a good ritual. Wouldn't you?" He inclined his head in a way that implied disagreeing with him would be foolish.

"I think a little honesty would have served us all better," I said, more sharply than I'd intended – cutting Teomitl mid-sentence, before he could say something irreparable. Perhaps it was a good thing, after all, that he was far removed from the imperial succession; or he and Nezahual-tzin would tear what remained of the Triple Alliance apart.

"Perhaps," Nezahual-tzin just smiled that smug, annoying smile of the superior. He looked every bit the warrior parading through the streets. "Won't you talk to her, Acatl?"

"I don't see why I should. You've already learnt everything you need to."

"You're assuming I spoke to him," Xahuia said. She threw a glance at her brother that was– no, not hatred, but something more complex, a mixture of reluctant admiration and determination. "I don't see why I should."

It occurred to me that someone was missing from the family reunion. "Your son–"

"My own business," Nezahual-tzin cut in. "Talk to her, Acatl."

Like his suggestion for the ritual, it was an order from a Revered Speaker in his own right. One day, I'd get used to the fact that the person speaking in such a composed, authoritarian tone was a boy, barely old enough to have left *calmecac* school.

But then again… I might as well make use of the opportunity before me, before he did whatever he'd intended to do with us all along. "I'm not sure you'll want to talk to me," I said to Xahuia.

She lifted her head and there was still, in spite of everything, a hint of the same attractiveness I'd seen back in the palace, in another life. Her eyes met mine, held my gaze for a while.

"I'll speak to you," she said. "Alone."

Nezahual-tzin's shoulders moved, in what might have been a shrug. "As you wish. Teomitl?"

Teomitl glared back at him, but they stepped back onto the shores of the islands, unconcernedly.

I remained alone with a woman I wasn't quite sure how to deal with. Her only crime, as far as I knew, had been ambition, but it would have led her to worse if we hadn't intervened. Her sorcerer would have stopped at nothing to get her the Turquoise-and-Gold Crown.

"Things have changed, haven't they?" Her gaze took in her surroundings – the coiled power of Quetzalcoatl the Feathered Serpent, the ground under us, the throbbing stone mass that was composed of living snakes – no, better not to think about that. There were visions I wasn't quite ready for, at least not until I was back on dry land.

"They have." I crouched on my haunches, coming to rest at her level. "They could have turned out another way."

She shook her head. "Very differently, perhaps. And then you'd have been the one coming to me as a supplicant."

"Am I not?"

The corners of her mouth twitched, a little. "So it is that even prisoners and slaves have power, in the form of knowledge." Her hands clenched. "That's what Nezahual would say, at any rate."

"He's not always right."

"He's right in too many things." Her gaze drifted again, coming to rest on Teomitl and Nezahual-tzin, standing side by side like two comrades, if one didn't know any better. "Enough small talk, Acatl-tzin. You have questions. Ask them."

"I'm not sure why you'd answer them," I said, carefully.

"What difference, as long as you have the answers?"

"I'd know how true they were likely to be."

That made her laugh, sharp, bitter, joyless. She had changed indeed, away from power. "Fine. I'm not a fool. I know when to swim into stormy waters, and to stop before *ahuizotls* drag me down. I can play for Tenochtitlan, Acatl. I won't play for the Fifth World."

I looked at her; she returned my gaze, her eyes steady, not a muscle of her face moving. I had heard the same thing so many times, from so many different people; and they had all been sincere. The problem was the line between reasonable risk and endangering the Fifth World, a line everyone seemed to place much further out in their minds than it really was.

"Fine," I said, finally. "Let's say I believe you. For the moment. What did your sorcerer do?"

"Nettoni?" She looked surprised. "He was my bodyguard."

"Bodyguard?"

"As you no doubt saw, it wasn't a safe place to be after dark." Her voice held the lightest touch of irony.

"Yes," I said. "You employed him before the murders started, though."

"One can never be too careful." Her smile was bright, and just the tiniest bit forced, not quite spreading to her eyes.

"I don't think it's that," I said. I was carefully dancing around the subject. What I truly wanted to know was what had frightened everyone in the council. But if I asked directly, I suspected she'd clamp up like a shell. "The palace was a busy place after Axayacatl-tzin's death."

Her lips tightened, her eyes moved away from me. I thought of the tar. "Before his death, too, wasn't it?"

"I was a fool. I came in too late. Axayacatl had told me–" She closed her eyes. "He told me that I need not fear the future. And I believed him." Her hands came up, as if to push me away. "Fool."

He had told her… I thought about it for a while. Unbidden, a memory was rising to the surface of my mind, a deep voice on cold shores, and a shadow that became more and more indistinct the further it walked into Mictlan, and its words to me, a mystery that had remained unsolved.

"I'd always known there would be a rift when I died. But only for a time. I've made sure it will close itself."

"He did something," I said, slowly, carefully, building my sentence in the same way a child will pile wooden blocks in the mud. "To make sure his choice was respected. He and Tizoc-tzin–"

Oh gods. Was I truly sitting here, accusing the former Revered Speaker of colluding with Tizoc-tzin, of arranging the summoning of star-demons to sway the council his way? I couldn't possibly…

"You're wrong," Xahuia said, in the dreadful silence that froze my heart. "Axayacatl was many things, but he was a warrior first and foremost, a servant of Huitzilpochtli. He would have wanted to do the right thing, and preserve the Fifth World."

"Then why–" I hesitated, but now I was standing on the brink, and all my careful dancing had done nothing but bring me closer to the bitterness holed up inside, the raw memories of the past few days. "Why is the council so frightened? Why did so many of them disappear, or buy the strongest protections they could afford? Why…?" What had Quenami and Tizoc-tzin tried to kill me for?

My voice trailed into silence; embarrassed, I hovered on the edge of an apology, but Xahuia went on as if nothing had happened. "You forget. I was one wife among many, and I very much doubt he would have confided in women, in any case." She didn't sound sad, or angry, just stating a fact.

"So you don't know anything?" This was starting to sound more and more like a waste of time, whatever Nezahual-tzin might have thought.

She shook her head. "I didn't say that, merely that Axayacatl's plans were beyond me." She shifted slightly, moving away from the glare of the sun and the pinpoints of starlight in the sky. "But I wasn't completely inactive."

I couldn't see what she was hinting at. "You had spies in the palace," I said slowly, as much for effect as to compose myself. "You saw—" I stopped, then. What could she have seen?

When I didn't speak for a while, she went on, with a tight smile, "I can't give you much, Acatl-tzin. Not much at all that you won't already know. A councilman went missing…" She stopped, raised a hand to her throat as if to remove something lodged in her windpipe.

Pezotic. "And you don't know why," I said, carefully. If that wasn't what she wanted to tell me… "But you know what happened to him."

"I know where he went. Pezotic," Xahuia said, with a quick, fierce shake of her head. "For all I know, it isn't where he is now. But still—"

"Go on."

"I had him followed because he was a coward, and a weakling. A man who could be bought." Her lips curled up, halfway between a sneer and a smile. "He bought passage on a boat headed east."

"East?" I asked. "Into Texcoco?" It would have been convenient, but I was reasonably sure luck was not with us. From the start, it had never been.

"No," Xahuia said. "To Teotihuacan."

Of course. Teotihuacan, the Birthplace of the Gods, a sacred place where the gods had made the sacrifice that had led to the birth of the Fifth Sun, a place of pilgrimage and of worship, a place of safety, the bastion of Their strength.

"He might have moved," I said.

"He might," Xahuia agreed. "But it's all I can give you, Acatl-tzin. Take it and use however you wish."

"Thank you," I said. I rose and bowed to her, in the same fashion as if she still had been imperial consort. Her gaze rested, for a moment, on me; that of a weak, broken woman, grounded by her brother's magic and utterly at his mercy. "I'm sorry," I said.

"Don't be." She did that peculiar half-smile, with no hint of joy in it. "It's a game, Acatl-tzin. That's what you never understood. You have to be ready to gamble it all in order to win. And sometimes, you lose."

"I can't play that kind of game," I said.

"I know. But you'll find that all Revered Speakers can."

Xahuia's words still echoed in my mind as I walked back to Nezahual-tzin, who stood waiting next to a scowling Teomitl with a half-amused smile on his face.

"So, did you find out anything?"

"What you expected me to find. It's all a game to you, isn't it?" I asked.

He watched me, as dispassionately as one might watch a mouse or an ant. "Perhaps. Perhaps nothing is real, after all… just the gods, putting us on the board with the other *patolli* pieces."

"You're the one putting us on the board," I said.

"Why so much anger?"

"Because we've wasted time," I said. "Because we're here in Texcoco, indulging your taste for mysteries while Tizoc-tzin is getting elected."

Nezahual-tzin's shoulders moved in a gesture I couldn't read. "There was nothing you could have done about it, Acatl."

I knew. And the Southern Hummingbird strike me, it hurt, as much as obsidian shards, as much as salt in wounds. He'd disgraced me, sent Teomitl fleeing away from his own city, insulted my sister, who, unlike us all, had no means of defending herself. I hoped she was safe, that Tizoc-tzin hadn't thought to follow her out of the city. "Still," I said, as we walked away from the basin, "still, there was another way."

"Not that I could see." Nezahual-tzin's face was serene.

"And now what?" Teomitl asked.

Nezahual-tzin stopped, looked at us, pondering for a while. His eyes rolled up again, becoming the uncanny white of pearls, of milk and the looming Moon in the Heavens. "It depends."

"On how much we're worth to you?" I asked.

He smiled. "You're learning."

"Not what I wish to learn."

"All knowledge is good." He smiled again.

"You want to sell us?" Teomitl's hand strayed to his *macuahitl* sword. "You'd dare to–"

"Teomitl," I said, warningly. The palace wasn't ours and it was full of warriors, not to mention whatever sorcerers Nezahual-tzin might have in his service. "He'd sell his own sister." He already had, unless I was grievously mistaken.

"Of course," Nezahual-tzin said. "But she'd understand."

"You lie." Teomitl's face was all harsh angles, his skin slowly whitening to the pallor of jade.

The worst was, I didn't think he was lying. He and Xahuia – and Tizoc-tzin, and Quenami, and even the She-Snake – seemed to operate by a different set of standards, as alien to me as the ways of the southern tribes.

"Of course not," Nezahual-tzin said. "You're a fool, pup. I'm ruler of Texcoco. I do what is best for my city, and that includes not going to war against Tenochtitlan. Making, how would you call them, peace offerings to the new Revered Speaker?" His teeth, when he smiled, were the same uncanny white as his eyes.

"Why help me escape then?" I asked, and then realised that he had been caught in the same accusation as I. "Of course. You weren't welcome in Tenochtitlan either, after my arrest."

"No," Nezahual-tzin said. "But it will change, when I come back."

"As long as Tizoc-tzin doesn't find out you helped me."

Nezahual-tzin smiled, in that smug way I was coming to hate. "I'll explain to him it was the only way to get his brother to reveal his true allegiances. And he'll have both of you back; and that will matter more to him than alienating a valuable ally. The forms will have been respected. I will have made my amends for dealing in magic on his territory."

"We're not bundles to be passed on!" Teomitl snapped.

I noticed, from the corner of my eye, the warriors getting closer, circling us like vultures hoping for an easy kill. Teomitl's skin shone with sweat, and with something else – the otherworldly light of Chalchiuhtlicue, Jade Skirt.

"Everyone is a tool, at one point or another. Better get used to it, pup, or your life will be brief." Nezahual-tzin watched the warriors converging on us with the distracted interest of a man pondering the words of a poem. "Briefer than it could have been, at any rate."

Above us were the stars, an oppressive reminder of the stakes if I ever needed one. "You're intelligent enough to know what is upon us," I said.

"Of course I am. As you said, Tizoc-tzin will claim the Turquoise-and-Gold Crown. The Southern Hummingbird's power will once more flow into the Fifth World, and that will be the end of this incident. Meanwhile, I'll have worked my way back into favour at the Mexica Court."

"With our deaths." Teomitl's face was frozen, halfway to divine light. Sweat dripped on his cheeks.

Nezahual-tzin laughed. "Don't bother. The ground you're on is blessed by the Storm Lord, and your goddess won't have any hold here."

He might have been right – and it was my duty to see the Fifth World preserved, beyond any selfish grievances I might have. No, the Storm Lord's lightning strike me, I couldn't do this. "You do know how I escaped."

"With our help." Nezahual-tzin shook his head, contemptuously.

I snorted. "You do have tremendous faith in your abilities."

"I serve a god."

"So does the She-Snake," I said.

"The She-Snake? I don't see what he has to do with anything."

"The She-Snake said…" I swallowed, remembering darkness all around us, the rustle of something large and malevolent which hated all life, all movement, all sound, and wouldn't rest until everything was silent and dark. "He said that Tizoc-tzin wouldn't be able to channel the Southern Hummingbird's favour into the Fifth World." He'd said, too, that Quenami might have a trick, a way of bending the rules to his advantage. But Quenami had miscalculated before.

"You're lying."

I met his gaze head on, staring into the numinous white of his eyes. "I'll swear it by my face and by my heart, or by any god you name."

Nezahual-tzin didn't move for a while, his eyes still on me. There was a chasm, deep inside them, colours, swirling amidst the white like oil on water, a spiral that opened and drew me in…

I came to with a start, the air burning in my lungs. Nezahual-tzin was standing next to me, one hand on his *macuahitl* sword, another holding up my chin. His touch was as cool as shadowed stone; and I could barely hear his breath. Teomitl had shifted, caught by surprise; but he'd been too late, his sword barely drawn.

"All right. I believe you." Nezahual-tzin released my face, and took a step away from me. I fought the urge to reach for the knives at my belt. It would only show weakness.

The warriors remained where they were, while Nezahual looked up into the sky, his eyes on the largest star, the Evening Star, which belonged to the Feathered Serpent, the only one which would not fall upon us, when the time came.

"From here to Teotihuacan, it's a two-day trip." The Birthplace of the Gods was on the same side of the lake as Texcoco, but much further to the north, on the banks of a large river that descended from the nearby mountains.

"By land." Teomitl's voice was defiant.

"You almost collapsed on the way here."

"You're accusing me of weakness?"

It might have been comical in another context. "Look," I said, fighting to control the mad beating of my heart. "This isn't the best time to quarrel."

"I'd like matters to be clear," Teomitl said. He looked straight at Nezahual-tzin, who equably returned his gaze.

"You're right, let things be clear. I think you're a naive, impulsive fool who keeps overstretching himself. You no doubt think me arrogant, manipulative, and heartless."

That, if nothing else, shocked Teomitl into momentary silence. "It changes nothing to the original offer."

"The *ahuizotls*? I'll apologise for not wanting to be in the middle of the lake when you falter."

I finally managed to intervene. "Then we'll make regular stops. Nezahual-tzin, this isn't time for tarrying."

"A day," Teomitl said, defiantly. "A day and a half, at most."

At length, Nezahual-tzin nodded. "You're right. The lake it is, then. I'll have boats prepared. Come."

Teomitl and I exchanged a glance as we walked between the warriors. His gaze was still the murky colour of the lake's waters, in which flickered the distant radiance of the goddess. "Acatl-tzin…"

"I know," I said, curtly. Nezahual-tzin might be on our side for the moment, lending us his resources. But all of that wouldn't prevent him from selling us, once he was sure the Fifth World was safe.

We needed an escape plan, and we needed it fast.

NINETEEN
The Fifth Sun's Birthplace

The journey to Teotihuacan was tense, but mostly eventless. When we stopped for our first and only night, Teomitl, pale-faced, glared at Nezahual-tzin, who glanced aside elegantly as if whatever Teomitl thought of him didn't matter. Of course, it only made Teomitl glare all the more fiercely.

Meanwhile, I kept my hands on my obsidian knives, wondering how to escape Nezahual-tzin's vigilance. A distraction would serve us well, but the only distraction I could think of was summoning a creature from the underworld, and with the balance of the universe already skewed, there was no telling what that would do. Most of the other spells I knew were either for tracking or for examining a dead body, neither of which would be any use in the current situation.

I managed to catch Teomitl while Nezahual-tzin was preparing for his evening meditations. "How are you?"

He shrugged, in what was meant to be an expansive way but soon turned pained.

"You overreached again," I said.

"I've been better," Teomitl admitted reluctantly. He crouched on his haunches in the dry earth by the riverside, watching the water flow across his outstretched hands. "Not that I'm going to give him the satisfaction of seeing that."

"He probably already knows."

"I'll take my chances. What are we going to do next, Acatl-tzin?" He looked up at me, a student waiting for his master's instructions.

"We might need the *ahuizotls*," I said, slowly. The beasts frightened and repulsed me, and I'd have taken any other solution, but it looked like we had little choice left.

Teomitl grimaced. "So far from the lake… I don't know, Acatl-tzin. They're not river creatures."

"I know." They feasted on the drowned within the lake, lived within murky waters, not the clear clean ones of the mountain streams. "But I can't summon anything from the underworld, not at this juncture in time."

"Hmm." Teomitl looked at the river water for a while, as if he could discern starlight within its depths. "We'll have to see, then. Hold ourselves ready."

I glanced at Nezahual-tzin, who sat cross-legged near our campsite, his eyes closed, his face relaxed and inert, like a mask of flayed skin. There was a good chance he knew exactly what we were going to do, and a small but not insignificant one that he was somehow listening to every word we said.

"Yes," I said finally. "We should be ready."

We arrived in Teotihuacan, the Birthplace of the Gods, the following morning as the Fifth Sun crested the nearby mountain. The first thing we saw looming out of the morning haze were the pyramids, the towering monuments left by the gods in the beginning of this age. They were massive, as large – or even larger – than the Great Temple, mounds of ochre stone dwarfing their boundary wall, their white steps like a beacon of light.

The city itself was away from the religious complex, in a curve in the banks of a river. It was a much smaller affair than Tenochtitlan or even Texcoco, a profusion of temples and houses of adobe, with barely any ostentation. The streets were narrow but straight, set in the same grid pattern as all the cities of the valley. I kept expecting to see canals, but we were on dry land, and the only water was in the mud squelching under our sandals.

It was, and had always been, a place of pilgrimage, and as a result many residential complexes had been turned into temporary accommodation. Nezahual-tzin settled us into a mid-sized one – two courtyards, seven rooms spread around them – before dragging us out again to the nearest temples to ask if anyone had come looking for a powerful protection spell.

When we came back empty-handed, he snorted, and retired into the adjoining sweat-bath.

"The same ritual?" Teomitl asked.

"Why waste energy trying something else?" I couldn't quite keep the sarcasm out of my voice.

"Acatl-tzin?"

"He's not thinking properly," I said. "There is a much easier way of finding our missing councilman."

Teomitl looked at me blankly. I sighed. "Think on it. Whatever happened at the palace, it had them all frightened for their lives. Pezotic came here looking for safety–"

"Oh," Teomitl said. He walked to the gates of the compound, and stared at the pyramids in the distance. "The safest place is the religious complex, isn't it?"

The complex was mostly pyramids, but not only that. Under the massive limestone structures the gods had buried Their physical bodies, the ones they had sacrificed to give the Fifth Sun His nourishment in blood. If any place in the Fifth World was brimming in magic, if any place was safe, under the gaze of every god in the universe, it was that complex.

"It's huge," Teomitl said. "We can't possibly–"

"Magic could help." Not the huge, strenuous magic that came straight from the gods, and that either Teomitl or Nezahual-tzin practised almost as a second nature, but the small spells, the ones anyone could learn, the faithful tools that had served me so well over the years. One in particular…

I could have waited until Nezahual-tzin was more advanced in his meditation. But, with such heavy stakes, I couldn't afford to play games. I was no Tizoc-tzin, and no Quenami. I had sworn to uphold the balance of the universe, and so I would.

"Come on. Let's go see him," I said.

To say that Nezahual-tzin was less than taken by the idea would have been an understatement. His grimace grew more pronounced as I explained myself, until I came at last to a faltering halt.

"That won't work," he said.

"I don't see why not."

"You're counting on the complex being mostly empty."

"It is," I said. "Except for pilgrims, and it's not the season for them."

"Still…" Nezahual-tzin scratched his chin, as if his beard were bothering him. "The death-sight doesn't work like that, Acatl."

"You've never cast it," I pointed out. He had so much power he didn't bother with such small spells.

"I know." Nezahual-tzin said. "You'll be able to see all living beings within the radius of its effect, but that's not going to allow you to discriminate."

I had my own idea about this, too, but I saw no need to explain. He would have found it mad. Our Revered Speaker had grown too used to magic coming with barely any cost, to the point where he barely could envision functioning without it. As High Priest of a god who interfered very little with the mortal world, I'd learnt when to use spells, and when to refrain from shedding blood.

"Fine. If you don't believe it will work, will you at least allow us to try?"

His eyes narrowed. I could tell what he was thinking: was this our ploy to escape him? And, as a matter of fact, it was our best chance yet, though the main purpose wasn't escape at all. "Look," I said. "I'm just trying to make this as fast as possible. It's in none of our interests to have the star-demons come down."

Nezahual-tzin's gaze rested on Teomitl, thoughtfully. "You can try," he said at last. "It should keep you busy until I'm done. But I don't expect any results." He gestured to four of his warriors. "Go with them."

Not unexpected. We'd have to see about those later.

The wall around the complex was lower than the Serpent Wall which circled Tenochtitlan's Sacred Precinct. It had familiar elements though, the same snakes' heads on top of it, the same dark green carvings along its length.

The warriors had deployed to form an escort around us and Teomitl, who, judging by his dark face, could hardly wait to attack them.

We passed under a wide arch, and found ourselves in the religious complex. Before us stretched a long alley, bordered by dozens of smaller buildings like primitive shrines, and from every one of them wafted only silence, a heavy, oppressive atmosphere I knew all too well, the silence of the grave.

The alley was called the Avenue of the Dead, and each of the small edifices held a body, the physical remnants of those who had once been gods, before They offered up Their blood to the Fifth Sun and gave up Their mortal nature.

About halfway up the avenue was a pyramid, a huge, massive thing made of uncemented stone, every section of its construction visible. Even under the cloudy sky it shone like limestone in sunlight, like polished obsidian or chalcedony, the light pulsing to a slow, fierce rhythm like that of sacrificial drums. "That's where…?" Teomitl asked, seeing the direction of my gaze.

I swallowed. "Yes," I said. Even this far, I could feel I wouldn't be welcome there. "That's where the Fifth Sun rose into the sky from His pyre."

I tried to keep my eyes from the end of the Alley of the Dead, all the way past all those tombs, to the smaller but still massive pyramid which shone with a colder light, the one where the Moon, who was She of the Silver Bells, who was our bitterest enemy, had risen into the sky, hoping to challenge Her brother's radiance and dominion.

"Right," Teomitl said. He shook his head. "And now?"

"I'm not sure." I eyed the Alley of the Dead. Someday, I would know the place better, but I hadn't been High Priest for long enough to have come there for a formal celebration. On the other side, a white-and-ochre wall surrounded what looked like a complex within a complex. A procession was exiting through the main gates, priests in green and red, their hair matted with blood and their earlobes torn from years of penance, carrying a feather standard in the direction of the tombs. Priests of Quetzalcoatl, the Feathered Serpent; the pyramid looming over the complex, not quite as grand as that of the Moon or that of the Sun, looked to be dedicated to the Feathered Serpent.

I could have chosen this place for the spell, for Quetzalcoatl was neutral to me, unlike the Southern Hummingbird or the Storm Lord. But the Feathered Serpent was also Nezahual-tzin's god, and I had had quite enough of the boy's peculiar brand of magic for the time being.

"Come on," I said to Teomitl, and headed towards one of the tombs.

As I walked, it grew larger in my sight, and yet still remained small and pathetic, diminished like a corpse in death. Silence spread around me, the chants of the priests receding in the background, meaningless snatches in a language that no longer seemed mine. It wasn't the silence of the grave, but something different, something indefinable, like the quiet after a battle, like the calm after a death, when the priest for the Dead has just arrived, a sense that something of large import had happened here and wouldn't take place again, it was a memory of a moment like a held breath, now vanished into the depths of this age, a moment that wouldn't happen again until Grandmother Earth split apart and the Fifth Sun tumbled from the heavens.

I bypassed the first such tomb, and the second. At the third, however, the silence was a little heavier than it should have been, and twisted a little more in my chest, like a hooked spear.

Carefully I climbed to the top of the platform, standing above the earth with only bare limestone under me. There was only silence, stretching over me like flowing cloth, a familiar aching emptiness in my breast. And a little something, nagging at the back of my mind, an ache I had forgotten, something that wasn't quite right.

But of course things weren't right. It was Mictlante-cuhtli lying underneath that shrine, buried in the chamber under the steps of the pyramid, Lord Death, my own god, as unmoving and as powerless as the corpses I did my vigils for. There was something wrong about the thought. The gods might have been capricious and arbitrary, but They were still more than us, and, although none of this was new to me, to see Them as former mortals was... disturbing, to say the least.

"Acatl-tzin–" Teomitl said.

I raised a hand to silence him and knelt on the platform, drawing one of my obsidian blades. With the ease of practise, I opened my veins, letting the blood drip on my knife – and drew a quincunx on the platform. It pulsed, gently, as if to the rhythm of an alien heartbeat, the air above it shimmering as if in a heat haze.

Then, standing in the centre of the quincunx – in the place that might as well be the centre of the universe – I started the invocation to Lord Death.

"We all must die
We all must go down into darkness
Leaving behind the marigolds and the cedar trees..."

Light blazed, outlining the quincunx in radiance; the wounds on my hands tingled, like coals in a brazier.

"We all must die
We all must leave our flowers, our songs
All jade breaks, all feathers crumble into dust
Nothing is hidden from Your gaze."

In my previous spell of death sight, a veil had gradually descended over the world, until everything material seemed to grow dim and meaningless. But here, the only thing that seemed to happen was that the air grew sharper, burning in my lungs, and the shrines suddenly loomed larger, the inset black stones shining like inverted suns amidst the larger structure of limestone. And under my feet, under the stone, I could *see* the corpse in the pyramid, its bones as green as jade, its heart a shrivelled, bloodless lump amidst the exposed ribs, my patron god's mortal remains, from before He became a god, unnervingly small and pathetic.

No, better not think about *that*.

Teomitl was waiting for me at the top of the stairs, the magic around him shimmering, a beacon of jade light strong enough to blind. "And now?"

I looked down. Dust shimmered over the Valley of the Dead, which had become an opalescent path like a spider's web. The procession of priests left a trail of magic, green with a red core, writhing like the tail of a snake, going towards the pyramid of the Moon at the end of the Alley, a looming mass of pale, cold light emitting rays like the thorns of a maguey.

Aside from the priests, there was no sign of any human presence near the pyramid of the Moon. I looked towards the pyramid of the Sun, which had become an almost unbearably strong radiance, but could distinguish no sign of life, either.

Odd. If I were Pezotic, our missing councilman; if I were so afraid of the star-demons I'd sought the protection of the Fifth Sun himself, then I'd have expected him to be near the pyramid of the Sun, which was the focal point of the complex. But there seemed to be no one there.

So much for that brilliant idea. It looked like I was going to go back to Nezahual-tzin like a beaten coyote, my tail tucked between my legs. I didn't quite have Teomitl's level of contempt for him, but still... still it would rankle.

Unless…

I looked at the procession of priests again, and back at the third pyramid, the one dedicated to the Feathered Serpent. The priesthood was a long and difficult calling, and Pezotic wouldn't have been able to invent himself that kind of identity. However…

I watched the procession for a while – feeling, again, that subtle sense of wrong, which had nothing to do with graves or with the rise of the Fifth Sun. One of the last priests, though he wore the same red-and-green clothes, didn't seem to fit in. I had noticed it, but in a vague, unfocused way, and it had bothered me. And now that I had the death sight on me, I could see that the trail of magic ignored him, the translucent, writhing snake going right through him, instead of rippling as it did around the other priests.

"That's him," I said to Teomitl. "Our missing councilman."

Teomitl was down the steps, obsidian-studded sword drawn, before I could stop him.

TWENTY
The Missing Man

To his credit, Teomitl approached the procession silently enough, but Nezahual-tzin's guards, trooping after him with no stealth or subtlety, gave him away. The procession came to a swaying stop, the priests turning with angry looks on their faces, the magic of the Feathered Serpent gathering around them.

Pezotic just ran. He must have known that we were after him, and that there was no easy escape.

Teomitl sprinted after him. The guards stopped to argue with the priests, waving what I assumed was Nezahual-tzin's authority. In the time it took me to finish rushing down the stairs, I could see that it seemed to be working, or at least to be mollifying the priests. They had stopped looking threatening, and the trail of magic was back to its original state.

Since matters appeared well in hand, I went after Teomitl.

By the time I caught up to him he had Pezotic down in the dust of the Alley of the Dead, and was standing over him, his *macuahitl* sword resting on the other man's chest, the obsidian shards just cutting into the skin.

"Acatl-tzin, there is your suspect." He stood as rigid as a warrior before his commander.

"Teomitl, I don't think this is necessary…"

"He's a coward," Teomitl said. "He's shown this clearly enough. I'm not letting him escape."

I got my first good look at our missing councilman. Pezotic was a small, hunched man, with a face not unlike that of a rabbit, round and harmless, with soft features that made it hard to notice him at all. He wore the priests' green-and-red clothes uncomfortably and his hair was matted haphazardly with blood, not the regular offerings of a priest, but the panicked gesture of a man seeking to blend in.

And he smelled of fear – reeked of it, from his shaking hands to the sallow tint of his skin, from his sunken eyes to the subdued, almost broken way he moved. Something, somewhere in the past, had touched him, pressed on him, and he had snapped like a bent twig.

"I don't know what you want," Pezotic said. "But you don't have the right–"

Teomitl pressed on the *macuahitl* sword, enough to draw blood. I could see it pulsing along the obsidian shards embedded in the blade, blazing like water in sunlight. "We want to know what's going on," he said. "And don't lie. We know you ran away from the palace. We know you were frightened for your life. We know something happened."

Pezotic's eyes widened, and the fear grew stronger. I hadn't thought it was possible, but in the death sight, I could make out a yellow aura around him, exuded from his body like noxious sweat. "You don't know anything," he said.

"People are dead," I said, and saw him flinch, not in surprise, but because he was imagining what could have happened to him had he stayed behind.

"Three councilmen. Ocome, Echichilli. Manatzpa."
And Ceyaxochitl, but that was a wound I carried on
my own, an event like a cold stone in my belly, but
one that wouldn't affect him.

"This has nothing to do with me," Pezotic said. I
wasn't surprised, not even disappointed. My opinion
of him hadn't been high to start with.

"Then why did you leave?"

"I go where I wish."

"You're a councilman." Teomitl shook his head. "You
don't."

Pezotic's lips stretched, in what might have been a
smile if fear hadn't washed away every distinctive feature of his face. "I approve new buildings in
Tenochtitlan. I have no doubt they can find someone
to replace me, Teomitl-tzin."

So he knew who Teomitl was, but hadn't admitted it
beforehand. "We're not here on petty errands of who
does what and who replaces whom. What I want to
know is who is summoning star-demons in the palace,
before the whole council dies."

His lips moved, a smile again, but I'd never quite
seen the like. Sick pleasure, and some kind of vindica-
tion, and... "What do you know, Pezotic?"

Teomitl's face shifted, became the harsh one of Jade
Skirt again, as distant and uncaring as the goddess Herself. "He knows exactly what's going on."

"I don't," Pezotic said, far too quickly and smoothly
to be the truth. "I swear I don't – let me go, please."

I glanced behind us. Nezahual-tzin's guards were still
arguing with the priests, but it was only a matter of
time before they solved their mutual problems and
turned their attention to us.

I cast my stone in the darkness, then, hoping it
would strike water instead of dry, sterile ground. "The
Emperor and Tizoc-tzin were onto something, weren't

they? Some plan to make sure Tizoc-tzin got the full approval of the council."

His eyes moved away from me. "You understand nothing, priest."

For some reason, it rankled that he couldn't even see who I was – to be sure, I attended Court only irregularly, and had never claimed to be indispensable. But still…

"Show some respect," Teomitl said. His eyes were green from end to end, the irises and pupils subsumed in the tide of Chalchiuhtlicue's magic. "Acatl-tzin is High Priest for the Dead."

Unsurprisingly, it didn't seem to faze Pezotic. I looked again. The conversation between the guards and the priests appeared to be winding down. We were running out of time. Not that we'd had much to start with.

Time to give up on subtlety. "Fine," I said. I pointed to the guards. "Do you know who they belong to?"

"Who you choose to ally yourself with is none of my concern."

"Oh, it's going to be. Do you know Nezahual-tzin?"

"A mere boy," Pezotic said. "Even if what you said was true, why should it frighten me?"

"Because, boy or not, he's got the means to make sure you go back to Tenochtitlan."

His face twisted then, opened up like a diseased flower. "You have no authority–"

"You'll find Nezahual-tzin has. Teotihuacan would be wise not to anger one of the rulers of the Triple Alliance."

"That's a lie. I'm here as a citizen of Tenochtitlan and a pilgrim devoted to Quetzalcoatl, and you can't take me away." Pezotic was speaking faster now, words merging into one another with barely a pause. "You or Nezahual-tzin, or whoever you claim to be speaking in the name of."

The guards were coming our way now. Their leader called out to me. "Is that the man we're looking for?"

I cursed under my breath. I didn't want Nezahualtzin involved in this more than he had to, but I had little choice over the matter.

On the other hand, as a means of pressure. "Yes," I said. "Let's get him back."

Pezotic looked back and forth from me to the guards, from the guards to the priests, who stood still with carefully guarded faces, waiting to see how it would all play out. "You can't," he said. "You can't take me back there. You have to leave me here..."

"Then talk." Teomitl withdrew the *macuahitl* sword, considered the guards with a cocked head. "Should I slow them down, Acatl-tzin?"

I held up a hand to tell him to wait. They were strolling nearer, taking their time, secure in their numbers and might.

Pezotic looked up at me, his eyes pleading in a sickening manner. I was no warrior, but the craven way he made himself the centre of the universe was disgusting. "Please–"

When I didn't answer, he whispered, "If I go back to Tenochtitlan, I'll die."

"Death comes to us all," I said.

"Don't give me that, priest," he spat. "Death is nothing but oblivion, but what will happen to us all is worse than that. You know it. Those killed won't dissolve before Lord Death's Throne, or ascend into the Heaven of the Sun. We'll serve Him forever. That was the price."

I signalled to Teomitl to go speak to the guards, hoping that he'd interpret my gestures correctly and not rush into attacking them. "What price?" I asked. "Manatzpa-tzin spoke of duty..."

"Duty?" Pezotic spat again. His saliva glistened on the ground between my sandals, as disgusting as the trail of a snail. "We weren't asked, priest. None of us. It's not duty at all. That old clawless buzzard Echichilli got it into his head that he was going to help Tizoc-tzin, and Axayacatl-tzin agreed... and we weren't given a choice."

Tizoc-tzin and Axayacatl-tzin. And Echichilli. The tar. The ten jars of tar Palli had tracked into the Revered Speaker's rooms. And the old, old death that was there, hanging over the place like a pall.

Surely– A hollow was forming in the pit of my stomach, as cold as ice on Mount Popocatepetl, opening deeper and deeper with every one of his words. "What kind of help?" I asked. "Summoning the star-demons?" I stole a glance backwards. Teomitl looked to be arguing with the guards. Jade Skirt's magic wreathed him in green, watery reflections, but so far no one seemed to be attacking anyone. Good. The Duality only knew how long this could last.

Probably not long.

"Of course not. That would have been too dangerous." Pezotic looked up at me as if I were the worst of fools. I felt like shaking him.

"Then what?"

His lips narrowed. He closed his eyes, as if accessing a memory that was too much to bear – not hard to imagine, given what I'd seen of his mettle. "Axayacatl-tzin wanted to make sure that he'd leave a strong empire behind. That what Moctezuma-tzin had started, and what he'd continued, would go on for another reign, that of a strong Lord of Men, of a strong warrior."

Unless he replaced Tizoc-tzin with another kind of man altogether, I couldn't see what could be done about this at all. "You're not making any sense."

Pezotic smiled, that slimy expression again, of someone who knew the position of all the beans on the board and was intending to profit from the situation for all it was worth. "He wasn't a fool, and neither was Echichilli. They both knew that Tizoc-tzin's biggest problem wasn't the lack of support, or his unwarlike disposition."

"Go on." The pit in my stomach was large enough to fit several levels of Mictlan in by now. I glanced at the guards, thinking we would be rounded up and arrested at any moment – but they stood gaping, watching Pezotic as if trying to make sense of his words.

"What makes a good Revered Speaker, Acatl-tzin?"

I could see only one thing which didn't relate to any of what Pezotic had mentioned before. I said, very slowly, hardly daring to breathe, "The Revered Speaker is the agent of Huitzilpochtli on Earth. He makes sure that we are safe from star-demons and the myriad other creatures trying to overthrow the established order." And, very slowly, because I remembered what someone – Acamapichtli, or perhaps the She-Snake – had once told me. "Tizoc-tzin doesn't have the Southern Hummingbird's favour. I still can't see–"

"Favour can be gained," Pezotic said, bitterly. "With the proper tools."

"I thought the Southern Hummingbird was weak– Oh." It had been before Axayacatl-tzin's death, and the jeopardy that had ensued.

"Echichilli couldn't give Tizoc-tzin any human support. He was much too honest to bribe or threaten the council, no matter how great his influence with them might have been. But he thought he could plead with a god."

He thought he...

Oh no. But Pezotic was going on, regardless of what discomfort he was causing me; or was he all too aware of it, and glorying in the horror he could see, shocked into every feature of my face?

"Echichilli gathered us all one night, in the Imperial Chambers, the whole council save Tizoc-tzin. He had traced a great glyph on the floor, that of *Ollin*." Four Movement, the name of the current age. "We all disrobed, and offering priests painted us with tar."

Tar. Boats, Ichtaca had said, but I'd failed to make the logical leap. A boat implied a journey, and not necessarily one contained within the Fifth World.

It had been a slow process – the tar spread over the skin, cutting the flow of air to the body – the hallucinations starting, the feeling of floating above the room and slowly going away, like a flock of birds released into the sky. Pezotic was scarce on details. I guessed he had no wish to remember the whole ordeal. Of all the painful ways to rejoin the world of the gods…

"You didn't know," I said, slowly.

"Not until we came back. But we should have known, shouldn't we?" His voice was bitter. "You can't have that kind of magic. You can't travel into the heartland of the Mexica Empire without sacrifices. And we were the sacrifices."

Oh gods. I had been so wrong about this, from the start. I'd thought the star-demons were summoned by a devotee of She of the Silver Bells, and all the while I had ignored what was staring me in the face. She was trapped under the pyramid of the Great Temple; and the Moon, Her heavenly body, was nothing more than a pale parody of the Sun. She wasn't the one controlling the star-demons, not anymore.

Her brother was.

Huitzilpochtli, the Southern Hummingbird. The youthful, hungry god, dreaming of spilled blood, of row upon row of captives split open and offered up to Him, of barges of tribute following from the five directions of the universe. All that Tizoc-tzin, so wrapped up in his self-aggrandisement, would never be able to give Him.

I closed my eyes. "The embassy failed, didn't it? Huitzilpochtli refused to grant Tizoc-tzin His favour."

"Of course." Pezotic smiled again, and for the first time it eclipsed his fear. "Tizoc-tzin was the only member of the council who didn't come. Of course the future Revered Speaker couldn't be sacrificed like a common victim. And of course Huitzilpochtli didn't like that." He shivered again. He hadn't told me anything of what had gone on in the heartland itself. I wondered what could be more unpleasant than slowly suffocating to death – and decided I could live without knowing.

Tizoc-tzin hadn't come. He hadn't been willing to offer himself up like the others – raw cowardice. I'd never had any personal contact with the Southern Hummingbird, but I could imagine how He would feel about that.

"And the star-demons?"

Pezotic shivered again. "Sacrifices," he said. "Itzpapalotl."

Gods, I could have kicked myself. Itzpapalotl was the Obsidian Butterfly, the living incarnation of a sacrificial knife. And her underlings the star-demons were the same, tools for claiming blood and souls.

It occurred to me that I hadn't heard from the guards in a while; or, indeed, much of anything. I looked back, and wished I hadn't. Teomitl was facing the leader of the warriors, while the other three sat on the ground, looking dazed.

I forced my attention back to Pezotic. "Why come here? It's Fifth Sun territory, isn't it?"

Pezotic shook his head. "Not that. It's the place where order was shaped out of darkness and chaos. The place where the Fifth Sun called the world into being. No destructive influences can come here. I'm safe here." He hugged himself, as if he didn't quite believe it.

"And that's all you know?" I asked, but saw the gleam in his eyes, the unmistakable hints of joy. Something else...

Oh no.

He must have seen the horror dawning in my eyes, the clutch of ice tightening round my heart. "It's not the council that's the problem," I said, slowly. "Their fate is already sealed, the price has already been paid. It's not... " Not the council, but those who had sent them here, those who had to pay for their presumption. Echichilli was dead, and so was Axayacatl-tzin, but there remained the main instigator of all of this, the man to whom the Southern Hummingbird had refused to grant his favour.

The man who, by now, through cajoling and threatening and bribing and the gods knew what else Quenami could come up with, would have been elected Revered Speaker of the Mexica Empire.

I couldn't remember an instance of a Revered Speaker killed within days or hours of being elected. But, the Storm Lord's lightning strike me, I couldn't even dwell on the consequences. If nothing kept the Southern Hummingbird in check, if nothing sheltered us, if we didn't have His favour anymore...

There were dozens of city-states watching us, waiting for any sign of weakness to launch themselves at our throats like vultures finishing off dying animals, to say nothing of the magical consequences...

We had to get back to Tenochtitlan, and fast, before the worst happened.

Sorting out the conflict between Teomitl and the guards was tricky, but not impossible. It did end up with both of us being "escorted" back to Nezahual-tzin, all but prisoners. They grabbed Pezotic, too, in spite of his protestations. He looked even uglier than before, all hunched back on himself like the Aged Fire-God.

"I'm not sure I understand," Teomitl said. They had confiscated his *macuahitl* sword; and his face was back to normal, although some of the divine light still seemed to be clinging to his features, a fact I'd once have considered as faintly worrying were it not for the urgency gnawing at my entrails like a fanged snake. "You said we had to keep ready for our escape."

"Yes," I said. "But this isn't the point anymore." The point was getting back to Tenochtitlan as fast as we could, and only Nezahual-tzin could ensure that.

I could foresee a long argument, though.

In the courtyard of our residence, Nezahual-tzin was seated cross-legged in the shade by the columns of the porch. He smiled at us when we came in, with a faint hint of irony. "Welcome back. I can see your day has been fruitful."

"Unlike yours," Teomitl snapped.

"Oh, I should say it has been most fruitful indeed." He pointed to Pezotic, and then back to us, neatly grouping us together.

"This can wait," I said. "We have to get back to Tenochtitlan as soon as possible."

"I don't see why." Nezahual-tzin looked puzzled. "There's hardly anything that would –"

"Tell him," I said to Pezotic. He shook his head, refusing to meet my gaze. Fine. I could do the telling myself.

It was a long story, but Nezahual-tzin didn't interrupt me once. Neither did Teomitl, although his face grew darker and darker as I progressed.

"You're sure about this?" Nezahual-tzin asked, to my welcome surprise. I'd expected him to protest or argue with the same usual enigmatic expression on his face. Instead, he unfolded his lanky frame, and walked closer to Pezotic, who all but hung between two of the warriors like a children's boneless doll. He studied the man for a while. I couldn't see his expression, but I knew he'd be showing nothing of what he felt.

"I won't ask you whether this is true." There was an edge of contempt to his voice I'd never heard before. "Seeing that you'd probably twist the truth any way you saw fit. This is your source, Acatl?"

I nodded. Nezahual-tzin turned back to me. "And you trust him."

"Not at all," I said. "I wish I could discard everything he's told me. But it fits the facts all too well."

Nezahual-tzin cursed under his breath. "I don't see how getting to Tenochtitlan is going to improve matters."

"If we can arrive before Tizoc-tzin is formally invested..." Before they finished the ritual, cemented the link between the Revered Speaker and Huitzilpochtli.

Nezahual-tzin shook his head. "Not going to happen." He raised his gaze heavenwards; his eyes rolled up, revealing the whiteness of nacre. Neither Teomitl or I said anything, all the pawns were on the board now, all the bean dice thrown down, and all that remained to see was how we'd move.

After a while, Nezahual-tzin said, "I still don't see

what we can do about it, but you're right. Being at the centre of things is the most important matter right now. We can argue over what to do when we get there."

He looked young and bewildered, an unsettling reminder that, like Teomitl, he was about half my age. For all their connections with their patron gods and goddesses, they had power, but not the wisdom that came with living.

But nevertheless they were my only allies, and the only hope of staving off the Southern Hummingbird's anger.

I caught up to Teomitl on the way to the boats. "You're intending to summon the *ahuizotls* again." A statement, not a question.

"Yes. It's the only way we'll go back to Tenochtitlan in less than a day." He looked at me, curiously. "Why do you ask?"

I bit my lips, hating what I was about to say. I should have been ruthless, caring for nothing else but the survival of the Fifth World. But– "Last time exhausted you far more than normal. You can't–"

"I know how far I can take it," Teomitl said. "Don't mother me, please, Acatl-tzin. This isn't the time."

"We might not have time any more, anyway," I said. "Nezahual-tzin is right. We might not make a difference."

"We might not. And we might. I'll take that chance. If we don't believe in ourselves, who is going to?"

Even with such grave dangers hovering over our heads, he was still unchanged, still holding himself to exacting standards, still trusting in me as his teacher. "I don't know." It occurred to me that there might not be much more I could teach him, not anymore.

"Then let me try. Or I'll feel I've done nothing use-ful."

"You've done plenty. I'm the one–"

Teomitl shook his head. "You and Nezahual-tzin are going to be sitting in that boat, working out a way to salvage what we can out of this situation." He smiled, utterly confident, though I could still see the darkness in his eyes. "I'm sure we'll manage."

I hoped so. But I couldn't find anything like his confidence in myself, and by Nezahual-tzin's sombre demeanour I could tell he didn't have any, either.

Somehow I doubted Teomitl's enthusiasm was going to be enough for all of us.

TWENTY-ONE
The Lord of Men

The journey back seemed to take the whole of an age. Teomitl was at the prow, growing paler and paler; Nezahual-tzin by my side, looking thoughtfully into the water, his group of warriors at our back scowling at us, and the shores of Lake Texcoco never seemed to be growing closer. Before us was Nezahualcoyotl's Dyke. Once there, we would be almost in Tenochtitlan; but it remained a thin grey line against the clear blue skies, never solidifying into anything familiar.

We had left Pezotic under guard in Teotihuacan. As Nezahual-tzin had put it, he couldn't bring much in the way of proof, and he would have been a decidedly unpleasant travel companion.

"You know," Nezahual-tzin said, thoughtfully, "I probably won't be any more welcome in Tenochtitlan than you."

What – oh, the arrest. I stared at my hand again, at the mark there that seemed burnt into it, remembering the wet, unpleasant feel of saliva running down my chin and neck. "I know," I said. It shouldn't have mattered. I was High Priest for the Dead; I kept the

Fifth World in balance with the heavens and the underworld. I was not supposed to matter this much.

But neither was Quenami, and he acted as though he did, taking charge over us all, steering the Empire in the direction of his personal gain. Acamapichtli was annoying and arrogant, but at least he was honest about his motivations. Quenami would smile and make it seem as though everything would work out in the end for the best.

Which, clearly, it wasn't going to.

"Acamapichtli could help us," I said.

"The High Priest of the Storm Lord?" Nezahual-tzin looked sceptical.

I couldn't help feeling the same way. Granted, Acamapichtli had helped me escape, but he had done so for his personal gain. And, like Quenami, he believed we would pull through with the blessing of the gods, forgetting that it was human sweat and human blood which kept the Fifth Sun in the sky and Grandmother Earth giving forth maize. The gods were no longer the keepers of the universe: They had relinquished that right and duty along with Their ultimate sacrifice, and even my patron god, Mictlantecuhtli, Lord Death, was nothing more than a corpse under a shrine. "I don't like it," I said, finally. "But we don't have much choice."

"True." Nezahual-tzin looked up. The sky overhead was blue and clear, but the stars shone, hundreds, thousands of malevolent eyes waiting for an opening. A thin veil of clearer blue marked the boundary of the Duality's protection. "Whatever you did to slow them down–"

The ritual with Teomitl and Mihmatini. "I thought it would keep She of the Silver Bells out of the Fifth World," I said.

"Yes," Nezahual-tzin. "That's not the question."

My cheeks burnt with embarrassment, or anger. I wasn't quite sure how to react to a fifteen-year-old who acted as though he was my mentor. Did he have so much knowledge, or was he just pretending? "The Duality is the source and arbiter of all gods. The Southern Hummingbird falls under Their purview as well."

"Meaning it will work?"

"Meaning I don't know how long it will hold. But yes, it should work."

I hoped so. It was a little more complex than what I'd told Nezahual-tzin. If Pezotic had told the truth – and much as I would have liked to, I couldn't doubt him – then the deaths of the councilmen were sacrifices. The spell for which they'd given their lives, the journey into Huitzilpochtli's heartland, had already taken place; now the price for it had to be paid. The balance had to be kept. The intrusion of the star-demons into the Fifth World was no worse than that of the Wind of Knives dispensing justice in the name of the underworld. That was why the star-demons had so easily penetrated the palace wards, for it wasn't a summoning, merely a counterbalance mechanism.

The irony was that the one thing we had achieved so far – extending the protection of the Duality – was preventing only one thing, the murder of Tizoc-tzin, the one thing I could, perversely, almost look forward to.

Nezahual-tzin sighed. "Not much of a plan."

"All we have." I looked at Teomitl, who stood rigid at the prow. The dark shapes of the *ahuizotls* were under the keel and beside it, a spine-tingling escort I could have done without. Ahead, the dyke seemed to have grown slightly larger, but the sun was past its zenith, and plunging towards the murky waters of the lake.

There was still time. There had to be.

• • •

We passed the dyke without trouble, and soon found ourselves navigating the canals on the outskirts of Tenochtitlan. As we left the vicinity of the Floating Gardens and found ourselves in the city itself, it soon became clear that something was wrong. The canals should have been bustling with activity, from merchants to water-peddlers, from noblemen being ferried to their friends' houses to priests on errands – but there was none of this. Just the gates of houses, closed against the heat, the boats still at their anchor, bobbing on the rhythm of some huge, unseen breath, the sunlight shimmering in and out of focus on the water like a god's smile.

"We're too late," Teomitl said. He'd let go of the *ahuizotls*, which we'd assumed would attract too much attention, and was sitting against the prow, breathing heavily.

"That's not possible," Nezahual-tzin said.

Teomitl's eyes narrowed in anger, and then he rested his back against the reeds of the boat wearily. "Do you see any other reason why no one would be here? They're burying Axayacatl, that's what they're doing. If we're lucky. If not, the council has already started debating."

The debates were a matter of form, the real persuasion and ritual preparation having taken place beforehand. Teomitl was right, we were late.

"I'm calling the *ahuizotls* back," Teomitl said.

"No," I said, at the same time as Nezahual-tzin.

He looked at us, defiantly. "You have a better solution?"

"We'll be at the Sacred Precinct before you know it," I said. "And it's going to be packed with people." And the canals around it, in all likelihood.

"We're–" Teomitl started.

"I know. We're late. That's not the point." As if to

prove me that someone, somewhere, was listening, we turned one more canal, straight into the largest mass of boats I had ever seen, a sea of vibrant colours, of flower garlands and feather-fans. The air smelled of incense and pine essence; the streets were packed with a tight mass of people, laughing and jostling each other, all wearing the colourful clothes of festivals.

Teomitl cursed under his breath. His gaze roamed from the boats, so close together they seemed an extension of the land, to the crowd on the nearby street. "Let's get out."

"On foot?" Nezahual-tzin said, but Teomitl was already leaping from boat to boat, elbowing his way through the crowd with the thoughtless arrogance of the noble-born. He was hard to refuse when he got that way, the gods knew I'd experienced it often enough.

Nezahual-tzin threw me a glance, hoping, I guessed, that I would contradict my hot-blooded student. But, much as I hated to admit it, Teomitl was right. There was no way we would manage to get a long, pointed reed boat through that kind of jam.

Not being as athletic as Teomitl, I disembarked and pushed my way through the crowd on land instead. I didn't have my High Priest regalia anymore, but my grey cloak, embroidered with owls, still marked me as a Priest for the Dead, and Nezahual-tzin and his warriors acted with enough arrogance to part the crowd. Together, we elbowed our way through the throng, into street after street filled with people. I had never seen so many. The gates of houses were open, and the courtyards full, the streets jammed, the boats on the canals so close we couldn't see the water any more. I could hear drums and the plaintive sounds of flutes, and shell-conches, blown in the distance like a call for the Fifth Sun to rise.

I could see the stars too, could feel the pressure above us, like a giant hand pushing through thin cotton, the cloth drawn taut, on the edge of tearing itself apart. It would hold, I'd told Nezahual-tzin, but I wasn't so sure any more.

The crowds got worse as we approached the Sacred Precinct, men and women brandished worship-thorns stained with blood, held up their children, grinning and laughing, priests played drums and flutes, shouting their hymns to be heard over the din.

Nezahual-tzin grabbed my cloak. "Where?" he asked. "You're the local."

I almost snapped back that I hadn't been there for the previous imperial funeral, and that as Revered Speaker of Texcoco he had to know as well, but then memory flooded in, almost at an instinctive level. "They'll start at the temple for the Dead, where the High Priest of Lord Death will formally relinquish Axayacatl's body over to…" I paused. The rest depended on which god was watching over Axayacatl, whether he would be buried under the auspices of Tlaloc or Huitzilpochtli. Most emperors chose Huitzilpochtli, since the Southern Hummingbird was the most important god of the Empire. But Axayacatl meant "water face", and he had been born under Tlaloc's sign. "I don't know," I said at last. "But they'll be heading to the Great Temple anyway."

"Hmm."

I pushed my way closer to the Serpent Wall and used one of the friezes to gain some height over the crowd, whispering an apology to Quetzalcoatl the Feathered Serpent for defacing His effigies. Through the mass of headdresses and coloured garments I could make out the wake of the procession, a slightly emptier space that people were just starting to fill in again. They were almost at the stairs of the Great Temple.

"Let's go," I said. The smaller empty space in front of us could only be Teomitl, he would arrive ahead of us, but not by much.

I was almost at the Great Temple, close enough to see the priests gathered on the bloodied steps, and Acamapichtli and Quenami up there with the rest of the council, when the wards caved in.

Darkness descended across the Sacred Precinct as surely as if a cloth had been thrown over the Fifth Sun; for a moment – a bare, agonising moment of stillness – everything hung in silence, and I allowed myself to believe, for a fleeting heartbeat, that Teomitl was right, that Acamapichtli was right and that we would survive this as we had survived everything since the beginning of the Empire.

And then the stars fell.

One by one they streaked towards the Fifth World, leaving a trail of fire in their wake, growing larger and larger, pinpoints of light becoming the eyes of monsters, becoming the joints on skeletal limbs, becoming small specks scattered across the dark-blue skirts of star-demons as they plummeted towards the Great Temple.

I heard screams, but I was already running, elbowing my way through the press of bewildered warriors. I turned briefly to see if Nezahual-tzin was following, but could see nothing but a heaving sea of headdresses and garlands.

Most of the crowd ahead of me was going in the opposite direction, away from the star-demons, and soon it was impossible for me to move at all, pressing against the current. As they flowed around me, I reached out for one of my obsidian knives. I brought it up in a practised gesture, and, rubbing my own warm blood against my forehead, whispered a small invocation to Lord Death. The cold of the underworld spread from the sign, and the press around me grew a little less dense. I pushed and pulled. I had to get there, had to warn Acamapichtli before it was too late, had to...

Faces frozen in grimaces of fear, my elbows connecting with someone's chest, sending them tumbling to the ground, someone pushing back at me, me, stumbling, catching myself just in time, screams and moans, and the sour, sickly smell of fear mingling with that of blood.

I was on the steps of the Great Temple, looking up into the faces of two Jaguar Knights. "The She-Snake–" I breathed, every syllable like fire in my throat. "Get... the She-Snake..."

When they turned to look at the twin altars above us, I ran. The fire in my lungs spread to my midriff, and then to my legs and feet until everything burned, but I pushed on. They must have been going after me, too, but the aura of the underworld around me would be slowing them down, I hoped, they must be...

And then, abruptly, the Fifth Sun was back, beating on my exposed back like the wrath of the gods. I cleared the last of the stairs, stumbled, out of breath, almost into the arms of another Jaguar Knight, who made no move to support me, or even raise his *macuahitl* sword against me. What...

The world lurched back into sharp, painful focus, like a blow to the face, the limestone platform and its two altars was slick with blood, overflowing in the grooves. Darker masses punctuated the white stone, slumped in the unmistakable stillness of death. Further away, at the entrance to the leftmost shrine... I walked on, slipping several times in the mass of blood, more spilled power than I had ever seen, and yet curiously dry and empty, offered up to no god, sacrifices that had already taken place, prices that had already been paid, without meaning or magic within.

Several people stood in the doorway – the quetzal-feather headdress of Quenami, the heron-plumes of Acamapichtli, the unrelieved black tunic of the She-Snake, and Teomitl, breathing heavily with his hands on his knees, shock etched on every feature of his face.

Across the threshold was a last, bloody mass, and even from where I was I could see the Turquoise-and-Gold crown, its radiance washed away by the gore, lying forlorn and scattered, the discarded remnants of a man who'd believed himself destined to rule us all.

Tizoc-tzin – invested Revered Speaker of the Mexica Empire, Lord of Men, the Southern Hummingbird's agent in this world – was dead, and we were as children lost in the wild, teetering on the edge of utter extinction.

TWENTY-TWO
Sacrifice

I could tell that Quenami was none too pleased to see me. By the frown on his face, he was currently debating how best to proceed with my arrest.

We all stood on the wide platform of the Great Temple, in the middle of two altar-stones encrusted with blood. On the right hand side was the shrine of Huitzilpochtli, painted the colour of blood, with carved skulls on the mantel above the door; on the left hand side, the shrine of Tlaloc, with a simple vertical pattern carved in green. Everything seemed deserted, only a handful of people amidst all that blood, the pitiful few living among the dead.

Acamapichtli's eyes flicked from Tizoc-tzin to me, and then to Quenami. "Don't be a fool," he snarled. "At least, not a bigger one than you've already been."

"He… " Quenami said. "He killed…"

How dare he accuse me of that? "You did that yourself," I said. "You and your schemes to put an unworthy man on the throne." I turned to the She-Snake, who was watching me with an ironic smile on his face, possibly the only person on the whole platform who seemed somewhat happy to see me. "Please tell me that he hadn't been crowned."

The She-Snake shook his head. His gaze was expressionless, as if the slickness, the animal smell of the blood around him didn't matter at all. "That was his dearest wish, the one for which he had sacrificed everything. Did you think he wouldn't put on the Turquoise-and-Gold Crown as soon as he was able to?"

I didn't know. I couldn't think. I could just stare at the damage, at the sky above us, and the lack of anything to protect us any more. In the space of days we'd lost two Revered Speakers, the last one killed by the god Himself, the god who had now withdrawn His protection from us.

Absurdly, incongruously, I remembered a time a year ago, when the Storm Lord had attempted to seize power, when I'd sat in Ceyaxochitl's temple and wondered whether Tlaloc's rule would be any more gentle than the Southern Hummingbird's. I'd said no. I'd believed the Old Ones, the gods of the corn and of the rain, would be worse than the Southern Hummingbird.

But now, standing on this platform where the whole council had just died, under the warm, merciless gaze of the Fifth Sun, I couldn't be so sure anymore.

If Acamapichtli saw what was going through my mind, he said nothing of it.

Footsteps echoed beside me. Nezahual-tzin, out of breath, had just finished crossing the platform. He leant against the largest altar-stone, the one dedicated to the Southern Hummingbird, his eyes rolling up, shifting to the white of nacre. No-one paid him more than a cursory glance. My stomach lurched, and I fought off a wave of unease. I felt like a fisherman's boat adrift in a storm, the shore masked by veils of rain and fog, and no other landmarks than the heaving waves rising to drown me. Nothing was right, not anymore.

"There has to be something we can do," I said. "Something to–"

"Crowning a new Revered Speaker would take days. There's nothing we can do, not in so little time." Quenami looked at Tizoc-tzin's body, the flesh of his face heaving up as if he was about to retch. "Nothing, Acatl. We played and lost."

You played and lost, the Storm Lord's Lightning strike you. Your own fault…

No. No. That wasn't the way forward. I needed to think, to find a solution.

But I had spent most of the journey to Tenochtitlan trying to think of precisely that, and found nothing.

"I fail to see the difficulty." Acamapichtli's voice was harsh and cruelly amused.

"He can send the star-demons any time–" Teomitl started.

"Silence, whelp," Acamapichtli snapped.

Teomitl's face contorted. "You–"

"I am High Priest of the Storm Lord." Light was coalescing around him, a soft grey radiance like a torch seen through the gloom. "One of the three highest powers in the Mexica Empire."

"You're nothing."

"Teomitl!" I snapped. "Now isn't the time. What do you see that's so amusing, Acamapichtli?"

He smiled again. "As I said. I fail to see the difficulty. The Southern Hummingbird has withdrawn His favour from the Mexica Empire, and taken the life of our Revered Speaker into His lands. All we have to do is convince Him to relent."

Convince Him to– "You're mad," I said. Even a hint of the heartland had been enough to tear me to pieces; surely he wasn't suggesting that we go down into it. "He's a war god. They're not known for their forgiveness." Not many gods were, to be honest, but I very

343

much doubted the Southern Hummingbird had any mercy at all.

"It's not forgiveness. It would be in His best interests." He said it as though it was just a matter of strolling into a garden to speak with a senile relative. And, with a stomach-churning flip, I saw that Quenami's head had snapped up, like that of a man being offered a lifeline.

"It wouldn't achieve anything," I said.

Acamapichtli laughed, a hollow, mirthless sound that grated on my nerves. "We're the High Priests of the Mexica Empire, the keepers of the universe's order. If there is a chance, any chance, that we can achieve something, shouldn't we try?"

He'd have had a point, I might have felt shamed, even, if he hadn't been spending so much of his time angling for personal gain. "You've both taken far too many risks with the Empire as it is."

"They might have," the She-Snake's voice was deceptively soft. "But still… Quenami?"

Quenami had risen, his face turned away from the bloody mass on the threshold, his eyes narrowed to give him the air of a vulture considering a kill. "Acamapichtli is right. There is still a chance."

"You tried this once," Teomitl said, taking the words from my mouth. "Remember, when you sacrificed the whole council as a price of passage? It didn't work."

I should have been arguing with them. But, as time passed, I found myself more and more ill at ease, nausea welling up in my gut, a strange, acrid taste filling my throat and mouth, as if I were going to retch. Unsteadily, I walked to Tizoc-tzin's remains, and, laying my hand in the warm blood, whispered the first words of a litany for the Dead, the familiar words a reassuring anchor to the Fifth World.

*"We leave this earth
This world of jade and flowers
The quetzal feathers, the silver…"*

I was on the floor, doubled over in pain The She-Snake's face loomed over me, swimming out of the darkness, mouthing words I could barely make out, something about funeral rites and evening falling…

"Acatl-tzin?"

I could *feel* it, the growing hole in the Fifth World, the yawning chasm waiting to devour us all – darkness and fire and blood, and everything out of kilter, everything as wrong as flowers in the underworld.

"Acatl-tzin!!" Hands steadied me as I rose. Teomitl, his face distorted by fear.

"It's nothing," I said. Acamapichtli was watching me with an ironic smile, and now that I knew how to look for it, I saw the slight tremor of his hands, the grimace of pain on Quenami's features, swiftly hidden as he turned his gaze away from me.

"You're right," I said, each word coming out like a stone, cold and heavy on my lips. "We need to go into the heartland."

"You said–"

I pulled myself up, fighting another wave of nausea. "I know what I said. But Acamapichtli is right, it's going to get worse unless we do something. The Fifth World is stretched to breaking point already."

Teomitl's lips worked soundlessly for a while. "Then I'm coming with you."

"You're not. There has been enough imperial blood shed as it is."

Teomitl's eyes narrowed. "And what will you do when you're in the heartland, Acatl-tzin? Someone needs to plead Tizoc's case. Someone needs to make apologies. I'm his brother." He said it simply, with no

345

arrogance, and yet it carried an authority worthy of a Revered Speaker.

"You're my student," I said. "I can't..." I stopped. We'd already had this conversation so many times. Ceyaxochitl had been right, he was an adult, and this was his own family at stake, and the Empire he might one day rule. I couldn't keep him forever. "It's not my decision to make."

"Then I'll come." His smile was like a rising sun, the same one, I thought with a pang of regret, he had displayed when I'd taken him as a student and given him permission to court my sister.

"You should take me as well." In the gloom, Nezahual-tzin's skin shone the same milky colour as his eyes, and the mane of the Feathered Serpent spread around him like a cloak.

"Out of the question," Quenami snapped. "This is a desperate attempt, not a wedding banquet."

Nezahual-tzin's eyes narrowed. "I am the representative of Texcoco, and wield the Feathered Serpent's magic in the Fifth World. Do you think it's wise to set me aside?"

"You're also under suspicion of interference in Mexica affairs," Quenami said. "And there's nothing we want of the Feathered Serpent now."

Oh, but we did: knowledge and safety, and compassion, all that gods like the Southern Hummingbird or the Storm Lord would never understand. But, nevertheless, there were far too many of us as it was, and this didn't concern Nezahual-tzin any more.

"I don't make it a habit to offer advice," Acamapichtli said, "but I'd follow Quenami's lead, if I were you. This is a Mexica problem."

Nezahual-tzin's white gaze moved up, towards the heavens. "Not any more."

"Then we'll need you here," I said. "To hold things

together." I didn't say "if we fail", but the words hung in the air all the same.

Nezahual-tzin grimaced.

"There are far too many of us going to the slaughter as it is," I said.

He wavered, looking at me and Quenami and Acamapichtli, and at the She-Snake, who had remained silent all the while. "I suppose." He didn't sound as if he believed much of it.

"Then it's settled." Quenami looked at us as if we were foolish subordinates, and I fought an urge to strangle him. "Shall we go?"

I'd expected Quenami to take us to the Imperial Chambers, the place where the council's journey had started. But instead, he took us downwards, to the small room under the pyramid where She of the Silver Bells was still imprisoned.

"There's a wound in the Fifth World," Acamapichtli said, almost conversationally. He'd changed out of his finery, into clothes sober enough to belong to a peasant, though he still bore himself regally enough to be Emperor.

"The star-demons come here to drag souls back to their master. The door's been thrown open, which makes it much easier to reach on our side." He sounded amused. "A good thing. Sacrificing two dozen people for this would have taken too much time."

And been a waste. I bit down on a sarcastic comment, and rubbed instead the amulet around my neck, a small silver spider blessed by Mictlantecuhtli, with the characteristic cold, stretched-out touch of Lord Death and of Mictlan. I'd sent to my temple to retrieve it rather than trust Acamapichtli to provide me with one.

Quenami was going around the room, around the huge disk that featured the dismembered goddess, mumbling under his breath, dipping his hands into the blood that dripped down from the altars high above us. The air shimmered with power, and a palpable rage, a deep-seated desire to rend us all into shreds, a feeling I wasn't sure any more whether to attribute to She of the Silver Bells or to Her brother, the Southern Hummingbird.

"Here is what we're going to do," Quenami said at last, turning back towards us. "You'll stand here in the circle, and not move until this is over."

Acamapichtli shrugged in a decidedly contemptuous way, and moved to stand on the stone disk, right over the torso of the goddess. Teomitl, who had remained uncharacteristically silent the entire time, moved to join him. Something shifted as they crossed the boundary of the disk – a change in the light or some indefinable quality that made their faces appear harsher, closer to stone than to flesh.

When I stepped onto the stone I felt a resistance, like the crossing of a veil, and my skin started to itch as if thousands of insects were attacking me. The pendant around my neck became warmer, pulsing slowly like the heart of a dying man.

Quenami was on his knees, smoothing out the blood to create a line around the stone circle. Unlike Acamapichtli he still had his full regalia, the yellow feathers of his headdress bobbing up and down as he worked, the deep blue of his cloak in stark contrast to the blood dripping in the grooves and pooling in the hollows of the disk.

"Feathers were given, they are scattering
The war cry was heard… Ea, ea!
But I am blind, I am deaf
In filth I have lived out my life…"

The blood spread, slowly covering the distorted features of the goddess until nothing was left. Under our feet the earth trembled, once, twice, and a deep, huge heartbeat echoed under the stone ceiling, growing faster and faster with every word Quenami spoke.

"The war cry was heard... Ea, ea!
Take me into Yourself
Give me Your wonder, Your glory
Lord of Men, the mirror, the torch, the light..."

Quenami withdrew to the centre of the disk, still chanting. In his hands he held a small maize dough figure of a man which he carefully laid on the ground. Blood surged up to cover it from the legs up, as if sucked into the flesh. Quenami withdrew and the manikin seemed, for a brief moment, to dance in time with the quivering all around us, standing on tottering, reddening legs before the pressure became too much, and it flew apart in a splatter of red dough.

"With blood, with heads
With hearts, with lives
With precious stones
In the service of Your glory..."

And then, as abruptly as a cut breath, we were no longer alone. Itzpapalotl, the Obsidian Butterfly, stood in the centre of the room at an equal distance from each of us, huge and dark and towering, Her clawed hands curled up. Her wings spread out behind Her, glinting, hungry angles and planes, all shining with the blood She had shed.

"What a pleasant surprise." Itzpapalotl's voice was low-pitched, strong enough to start an uncontrollable shiver in my chest. The itch on my skin redoubled in intensity, until it was all I could do not to scratch myself to the blood. "Three High Priests and a Master of the House of Darts, all for myself." She smiled. Her teeth were obsidian knives, glinting in the dim light, their edges stained with blood.

"I'm not Master of the House of Darts," Teomitl said.

She smiled again, held his gaze until he started to shake. "You will be, soon."

Quenami threw Teomitl an irate glance, and launched into another incantation. "O Itzpapalotl, Obsidian Butterfly, Goddess of War and Sacrifice. We come before you as supplicants."

Acamapichtli snorted, and I bit back a sarcastic remark. Even when summoning gods, Quenami was his old pompous self, as if it would make Her more likely to heed him. She was a goddess, and Her whims and desires would rule Her far more effectively than any human.

Itzpapalotl cocked her head, staring at Quenami as one might stare at an insect. "Supplicants? It's not often that I have those." Her eyes, the two small yellow ones in her face, and all those scattered across Her joints, opened and closed, and She made a noise which might have been a contented sigh. "Unless pleading for their lives."

To his credit, Quenami did not let that slow him down. "We have need to enter the lands you guard."

"I should imagine." Her smile was malicious, but she said nothing more. Silence stretched across the room, broken only by the dripping sound of blood as it ran down from the altar platform, high above us.

"Will you let us pass?" I asked, slowly.

Her gaze turned to me, held me transfixed until a tremor started in my hand. I felt a pressure in my head, as if someone were driving a nail between my eyes, my heartbeat became distant and far too quick. "Will I?" Itzpapalotl asked. "I should think... Not."

"There is need–" Quenami started, but She laughed, a harsh, scraping sound like stone on stone that drowned the rest of his sentence.

"You mortals are so amusing. There is always need."

She was Goddess of War and Sacrifice, the altar on which warriors were destined to die, the blade that would cut hearts from living bodies. I dragged my voice from where it had fled. "What is your price?"

Her smile would have sent a grown man into fits if She hadn't been half-turned away from us, looking at the disk and the dismembered limbs under Her feet. "The price of passage. You're a canny one, for a priest."

"Everything requires sacrifice," I said, slowly. I shouldn't have been the one doing this, the one giving Her obedience and proper offerings. I was a priest for the Dead, and She was out of my purview.

"Sacrifice." She rolled the word on Her tongue, inhaling once or twice like a man enjoying a pipe of tobacco. The eyes on Her joints opened larger, their pupils reduced to vertical slits. "Yes. Sacrifice."

I said, haltingly:

"I will offer You sheathes of corn taken from the Divine Fields
  Lady of the Knife
  Ears of maize, freshly cut, green and tender
  I will anoint You with new plumes, new chalks
  The hearts of two deer
  The blood of eagles..."

She listened to the hymn, nodding Her monstrous head in time with my inflections, Her lips shining dark red under the obsidian of Her teeth. But when I was done, She shook Her head, in a fluid, inhuman gesture; and the itch on my skin grew stronger, as if hundreds of ants were climbing up from the ground.

"You take living blood," Quenami said. It sounded almost like an accusation.

"There are – other sacrifices. More potent ones."

"A human heart?" Acamapichtli looked around him, at us all, as if pondering who would resist him least.

"You wouldn't dare." Teomitl's hands tightened.

"For the Fifth World?" Acamapichtli spread his own empty hands, a pose of mock weakness that fooled no one. "You'd be surprised what I can do."

"Fools." Itzpapalotl's voice echoed under the ceiling, coming back to us distorted and amplified, as if a thousand star-demons were speaking. "Grandmother Earth wants to be watered with blood, to replenish what She lost when the gods tore Her apart to make the world. The Fifth Sun feeds on human hearts, for His own crinkled and died in the fires of His birth. I…" She laughed, and the sound sent me down on my knees with my hands going up, as if it would diminish the sensation of my ears tearing apart. "I am what I always was, and I only take what pleases Me."

I stared at the floor, at the outline of She of the Silver Bells, blurred and distorted. "What… is it… that pleases You?" Beyond me, I could see just enough to know that everyone else was on their knees.

She laughed again. I managed to drag my gaze upwards, to see her move, come to stand before Quenami. "A true sacrifice, something that will be missed."

The price of passage, determined by a goddess' whims. My chest felt too tight to breathe. What would she ask for?

She moved faster than a warrior's strike – reaching out in one fluid gesture, towards Quenami, hoisting him up in the air as if he weighed nothing and enfolding him in the embrace of Her wings. The jagged obsidian shards seemed to open up like cruel flowers, and swallowed him whole. There was a brief splatter of blood, and then he was gone without so much as a whimper.

Somehow, that made it worse.

Itzpapalotl turned to us, considering. "From him, I have taken my price. Now…" She'd have looked like a peasant's wife at the marketplace, considering whether to buy tomatoes or squashes if she hadn't been so large, Her features too angular and too huge to be human, Her eyes deep pits into which we all endlessly fell.

She lunged towards Acamapichtli before any of us could move. Teomitl, the faster among us, was only half-rising from his kneeling stance, but Acamapichtli was taken and gone before we could stop Her.

And then there were only the two of us remaining. The goddess stared between us, for a moment that seemed to stretch on forever, and then…

I had a vague impression of speed, of something huge pulling at my body – not strongly, but with a dogged persistence that would never stop come fire or blood. The itch flared up, engulfed me in flames, and there was the face of the goddess, looming up amidst a headdress that wasn't feathers or gold, but hundreds, thousands of obsidian knives, her eyes yellow stars that opened up to fill the whole sky.

I landed with a thud on something hard. The pain and the itches were gone. When I pulled myself up shaking I saw a land that seemed to stretch on forever, scorched and blasted. Overhead hung two huge globes of fire – I couldn't stare at them long, for my eyes burnt as if someone had thrown chilli powder in them – and the ground under my feet was dry and cracked, an old woman's skin. No–

The cracks weren't just superficial: they crisscrossed the whole of the land, went in deep. The ground wasn't cracked, it was broken.

"It has been broken for a long time," Itzpapalotl said, beside me.

She stood at my side, looking much as She had in the Great Temple. We were the only two living beings in this place. I couldn't see either of the other two priests, or even Teomitl. "What is this place?" I asked.

"The first sacrifice." She smiled. "The greatest."

"The Fifth Sun…"

A low growl came up. Startled, I realised it was coming from the earth itself.

"Oh, priest." She shook her head. "For all your knowledge, you're still such a fool. In the beginning of time, the Feathered Serpent and the Smoking Mirror fought the Earth Monster, and broke Her body into four hundred pieces. To appease Her, the gods promised Her blood and human hearts, enough to sate any of Her appetites. Do you not hear Her, at night, endlessly crying for the meal She was promised?"

Grandmother Earth. But She had never been… She was remorseless and pitiless, but She wasn't a monster. She wasn't against the gods. "I didn't know–"

"You mortals are very clever at rewriting what was," Itzpapalotl said. "And the Southern Hummingbird even more so."

A chill ran though me. "You don't serve Him–"

"I am His slave." She smiled again, like a caged beast, waiting for its time to strike. "But even that will end, someday. Enough talk. It's time for your sacrifice, priest."

"I don't understand–" In my hands lay my obsidian knives, and my amulet – and there was something else, a sense of absence, as if a part of me were missing.

Her voice was almost gentle. "This was what you brought, to fight your way to the god. Set it aside."

"But I can't –"

"Then you won't pass."

"What about the others?" I asked.

"They all made a sacrifice, according to their natures and their beings. Now it is your turn, priest."

Without them, I would be naked in the heartland, worse than that, a dead man walking with no protection that would keep the magic of the Southern Hummingbird from destroying me. It would be like the imperial jails, only a thousand times worse.

Without this…

I thought of Acamapichtli, of what he had said about risks and acceptable sacrifices. The Duality curse the man, he was right, and admitting it cost me.

"Take them," I said.

Her hands became a round ball of grass, into which my obsidian knives slid, one by one. The amulet went last, hissing as it went in. The grass turned a dull red, the colour of fresh blood, and something ached within me, more subtle than the pain of slashed earlobes or pierced tongue: a sense that I was no longer whole, no longer surrounded by protection.

She parted Her hands again and they seemed different than they had been before, more sharply defined, the obsidian a little less hungry. "Pass, priest," She said.

There was a gate, by Her side, a half-circle of painfully bright light, as if a piece of the sun had descended into this strange world. It flickered, and grew dimmer, until I could stare into its depths, and catch a glimpse of lakes, and verdant knolls dotted by houses of adobe.

I walked up to it. My body shook, and I couldn't command it properly. My whole sense of equilibrium seemed to have been skewed, my perception of myself no longer accurate.

What had She taken from me?

The light grew bright again as I crossed, searing me to the bone. Before I had time to cry out, it was over, leaving me with nothing more than a slightly painful tingle all over. I was kneeling in a circle traced on grass, the blood that had been filling it slowly draining away, sinking back into the mud. Then the circle was gone, and I stood in the middle of grass and reeds, under a sky so blue it was almost painful, with a gentle breeze caressing my skin.

"Acatl?"

It was Quenami, but I hardly recognised him. His hair was dishevelled, his face stained by mud, his finery all gone, replaced by the torn loincloth of a peasant, his gilded sandals faded and broken. There was nothing left of the authority he'd effortlessly commanded.

"Where is–" I started, but then saw Acamapichtli lying at his feet in a widening pool of blood. I hobbled closer. The feeling of something missing receding as I breathed in the air of the heartland. It was warm and pleasant, though I wasn't fooled. It would gradually wear me down, as it had done in the imperial jails.

Acamapichtli looked as if he had been mauled. Streaks of red ran down his arms and his back, lying parallel to each other, like the wheals of a whip, or the claws of some huge feline. His clothes were tatters, heavy with the blood he was losing. Mud had seeped into his feet, as if he had been running barefoot in a swamp.

I looked up at Quenami, but saw nothing over me but the face of a frightened peasant. "The Duality take you!" I snapped. "We need cloth. Is there anything out there that can help us?"

"We're alone, Acatl." Quenami's voice quavered, but he finally controlled it, coming back to some of his usual smoothness. "No villages or any habitation I can see."

Stifling a curse, I took off my cloak and tore it to make bandages. With the help of Quenami, we managed to bind the worst wounds. If only we'd had maguey sap, or dayflower to cleanse them with. A pity Teomitl–

Teomitl? I looked around me, and saw, as Quenami said, nothing but the blades of grass around us, and a hill rising above us. "Where is Teomitl?"

"I don't know." Quenami finished binding the last of Acamapichtli's wounds, his distaste for such a menial task evident on his face. "I was the first here, and then you came one after the other. But since then–"

Since then, nothing. I could hear Itzpapalotl's laughter in my mind as she took my knives and my amulet, all the things I'd been counting on to fight my way to the god.

And I'd been counting on Teomitl's magic, too. That was what I'd been missing since the start.

"He won't come," I said. I didn't know if it was part of my sacrifice, or if it was the thing She'd asked of him in exchange for our safe passage. But he wasn't there, and that was what mattered. I hoped he was safe. I hoped She had not taken his life, or even a small part of him, as a price in Her games. But I couldn't be sure, and there was no point in regrets or fear; not now, not here. It was too late for that, the game was set, and we would have to play it to the end.

I knelt and lifted Acamapichtli. He was heavier than I thought, his limbs unresponsive, continually sliding out of my grasp. Carefully I slung him over my back, and wrapped his arms around my shoulders. It was the best I could do, on my own.

Quenami had been watching me all the while. "He's not coming? But–"

"I know," I said. And, without looking back, I set out towards the top of the hill – unprotected and unwarded, alone with a wounded man and a coward – knowing that each moment that passed brought me closer to unconsciousness.

I could have spared a prayer, had I believed any gods but the Southern Hummingbird were listening.

TWENTY-THREE
The Heartland

It was, as far as the lands of the gods went, a pleasant land. I had been in Tlalocan, the paradise of the Blessed Drowned, only briefly, but this seemed very much like it. Verdant vegetation covering the land, flocks of white birds disturbed by our approach, and the small ponds we passed teemed with fish and newts.

Acamapichtli grew heavier as time passed, his arms bearing down on my shoulders, his legs dangling closer and closer to the ground until it felt as though I were dragging mud.

The sky, too, changed, the only thing that seemed to change at all in this endless succession of hills and lakes. Clouds slowly moved to cover it, and its blue darkened, the air turning as crisp and as heavy as that before a storm.

The sun, though, never stopped shining.

One step, and then the next; mud and grass and water, everything merging and blurring together. I felt Acamapichtli's touch, burning into my skin like the jaguar fang he'd once given me, but it was far away, an inconvenience in some other world. What mattered was walking – one hill after another, one pond after another, feeling the air grow cooler, seeing the light grow darker.

My throat was parched, and soon everything seemed to burn. Was there no end to this land, nothing to bring us closer to the Southern Hummingbird and the souls He had stolen?

Was there–

"Acatl!" Quenami called, from some place faraway.

I came to with a start, almost throwing off Acamapichtli. The right side of my face was wet. Saliva had run down my face, staining what little was left of the cloak, and my mouth was completely dry. I felt like a sick man waking up from a long illness – weak and dazzled, and unable to align two thoughts together. "What is it?" I asked.

He pointed. The landscape had opened up ahead of us, a larger lake lay ahead with a single island at the centre; and, on the island, a larger hill with a stone structure at the top. It seemed familiar, but I couldn't place it for a while.

"A smaller version of the Great Temple," Quenami said. His voice was lower, almost subdued: the loss of his regalia must have cut deep. That said... his arrogance and effortless dignity had been his only edge, just as Acamapichtli's strength had lain in his raw power, and mine in the mastery of Lord Death's magic, and in Teomitl's assistance. The sacrifices Itzpapalotl had asked from us were far from trivial.

By the lakeside was a small village, huts of adobe, clustered together. We descended towards them. By then it was all I could do to hold Acamapichtli and keep my thoughts from fragmenting. Something was going to have to yield, and I wasn't altogether sure my mind wouldn't go first. It had, after all, already done so once in this land, back when Quenami had imprisoned me.

The lake grew larger, reflecting the sky above which had darkened to the grey of a storm with the sun at its centre like a malevolent eye. Its depths would be cool, away from the burning sensation that seemed to have filled me up from the inside – fire in my lungs, in my belly, in my manhood…

"Acatl!"

Quenami was coming back from the huts, and I could not remember having seen him depart. "You have to see this."

The huts were little more than awnings of wattle-and-daub over beaten earth – a shelter against sunlight, and nothing more. There were seven of them, arrayed in a circle around a focal point, and, where the centre should have been, a group of men sat, engrossed in an animated conversation.

"The flowers come from the heart of heaven…"

"That is accessory. What good are they, if they wilt and perish…"

"All the more reason to enjoy the vast earth…"

"They are–" Quenami whispered.

Carefully I set Acamapichtli on the ground, wincing as the weight left me. I stretched, ignoring the fiery pain that flared up my body again, and hobbled to the circle.

They were familiar faces: Manatzpa, Echichilli, all the members of the council I'd interviewed. One gave me pause, it was Pezotic. The last time I had seen him had been in Teotihuacan, under the guard of Neza-hual-tzin's warriors. It seemed that the last inrush of star-demons into the world, which had taken both the council and Tizoc-tzin, hadn't spared him.

They all sat as if nothing were wrong, discussing minor points of philosophy like matters of life and death. But their faces were different, their skins stretched over the pale shape of their skulls, their eyes sunk deep into their orbits.

And Tizoc-tzin wasn't among them.

"Excuse me," I said, pitching my voice to carry. "We're looking for Tizoc-tzin."

"The Revered Speaker," Quenami interjected.

Manatzpa's face rose towards us for a brief moment, but then he turned back to his neighbour. "As Neza-hualcoyotl said, we are nothing more than feathers and jade…"

"I should think we're more than that…"

"Echichilli!" Quenami said. "We need your help. Surely you know what's happening." He grasped the old councilman by the shoulders, and forced him to look his way. "Surely–" He stared into Echichilli's eyes for a while, transfixed, before releasing him, horror slowly stealing across his features. "Let's go, Acatl. It's not here we'll find the answers."

"I–" I said, and then I caught Manatzpa's gaze. A film seemed to have covered his eyes. His pupils were dull, like those of a fish dead for days, and nothing remained of the fiery, driven man he had been in life, the one who had killed Ceyaxochitl, the one who had almost killed me. Husks, that was all they were, what was left after the corn had been harvested – nothing of value, nothing that was real.

Shivering, I hoisted Acamapichtli on my shoulders again, and followed Quenami down to the lake.

He was pushing a reed boat into the water; when I arrived he looked up at me, all arrogance and impatience. "Well? Help me."

"You're something," I said. "I've been carrying Acamapichtli all the while, and you're the one complaining." I didn't mention the fact that every moment we spent there weakened me, because he'd find a way to use it against me.

Quenami snorted. "You could have left him behind."

"And I could have left *you* behind." I wasn't quite sure why I'd been carrying Acamapichtli along all the while. We might have needed him at the end; even unconscious and wounded, he might have had some use. But–

The Duality take me, I'd had a debt to him, and never mind that it was being repaid to more than its value.

"Help me with the boat, will you?" Quenami insisted. Not for the first time, I fought the urge to shake some sense into him.

"Ask politely, and perhaps I'll consider it." I put Acamapichtli into the craft, and moved to push with Quenami.

"It's for our survival, Acatl. If you can't see past that…"

If you can't make an effort, I thought, but didn't say. There was enough with one of us being petty.

Of course, I rowed. Quenami probably hadn't lifted an oar since the day he'd entered the priesthood; the way he wrinkled his face made it clear even the fate of the world wasn't enough for him to demean himself.

I said nothing, but it was hard.

I had been rowing since childhood and it should have been easy, but the wood of the oar quivered in my hands and I felt more and more light-headed with each oar-strike. Every drop of water against my skin seemed to burn, and the island in the centre seemed to blur and shift with every passing moment.

We were perhaps halfway across the lake when Acamapichtli woke up. "Where–" he whispered.

"The heartland," Quenami said.

"What happened?" I asked, but he shook his head, and closed his eyes again. It didn't look as though he was going to be much use, after all.

If I had thought the heartland was bad, the central island was worse. The moment I set foot on it, I felt a jolt travel through my chest, a particular tightness, growing steadily worse. There was something in the ground, something in the air, something that didn't want me, that would wash me away like a flood washed away boats and nets. Acamapichtli seemed to weigh as much as a slab of stone, and I could barely focus on the path, for there was a path this time, snaking upwards around the hill. I watched the earth, step after step, I watched the water that filled the footsteps of whoever had come before us clawed and monstrous, a trail I had seen before but couldn't seem to focus on...

Step after step, agonising breath after agonising breath, fire in my lungs, rising up to fill my brain, confused images, of seven caves gouged into the hillside, torn open by some giant beast, of fountains where herons bathed in a blur of white, of an old woman in rags, sweeping the threshold of her house and watching us pass by with bitter satisfaction in her eyes, and then the scene shifted, and her face was that of a skull, her hands were claws, and the broom she held was made of human femurs, bound together with thread as red as blood.

Up, and the seven caves faded away, and small shrines appeared by the hillside, mounds of earth with pyramids on them, shimmering with light, their staircases dripping with blood even though the altars were empty...

Up, and a flock of herons took flight, cawing harshly, shedding white feathers as they went, and then skin, and then blood-red muscles, until only their skeletons remained, and darkness in the hollow of their eyes...

There was a sound on the edge of my hearing like the buzzing of flies on a corpse, the grating of bones.

After a while, I realised it was my name, coming from infinitely far away, but it didn't matter, not anymore…

That sound again, and everything scattering, fading into darkness.

"Acatl!"

I lay on something hard, and my cheek hurt. I moved, my hand coming to rest against my skin, it felt like stretched paper, nothing living anymore. "Quenami?"

He still had his hand up, braced for a further strike against me, and Acamapichtli was lying prone at his feet. His eyes were open, his mouth working around words I couldn't recognise. Raising my gaze, I saw that we were on a stone platform with a simple altar, encrusted with so much blood the stone seemed to have turned red. "How–"

"I dragged you here." He sounded exasperated. "That's not the point."

"Then what is?"

And then I saw Her. Itzpapalotl stood waiting for us at the entrance of the shrine – casual, relaxed, Her claws flexed, Her obsidian wings in repose. And behind Her…

He was tall, impossibly so, with the body of a youth, tanned skin and raised muscles, and a face streaked with deep cobalt blue, coming up so high it seemed to merge with the sun in the sky. In His left hand was a huge snake, and, every time it writhed, flames flared up, licking its scales; in His right hand was a *macuahitl* sword decorated with paper banners, the same ones carried by warriors during the annual sacrifices, and the feather headdress that stretched behind him was a circle of yellow feathers, pale and blinding.

I flattened myself against the ground in the lowest form of obeisance, ignoring the dizziness that flared up again in me. The floor was blessedly cool, a steadying influence. I didn't have to move after all, just to focus on speaking out. Beside me, Quenami abased himself as well. Acamapichtli attempted to move, but fell back with a groan.

"Priests," Itzpapalotl's hollow voice said. "You have come in the presence of the Lord of Men, the Southern Hummingbird, the Slayer of the Four Hundred, He who makes the sun rise, He who follows the path of war. What do you have to say for yourselves?"

There was silence, for a while. We slowly raised ourselves up, remaining on our knees, our gazes turned away from Huitzilpochtli. One did not meet the eye of a Revered Speaker, much less that of the god who had invested him in the first place.

"My lord," Quenami's voice quivered at first, but then he appeared to gain confidence, stretching himself up as if he still had all his finery. "We have come for the body of our Revered Speaker, that we might not find ourselves cast in darkness with the star-demons."

I recognised the tone and cadence of a ritual, and fell in step with him. "We have come for the body of our Revered Speaker, that it might be restored to its rightful place on the sacred mat."

Acamapichtli coughed. When he spoke, his voice was so low I had to strain to hear it. "We have come… for the body of our Revered Speaker… that it might…" He stumbled there, closed his eyes and went on, a grimace of pain stretched across his features. "… that it might wear the Turquoise-and-Gold Crown… and lead us all to glory…"

He fell silent. I heard nothing but our own breaths, smelled our fear. By coming into a god's land, we had placed ourselves at His whim. Nothing prevented Him from killing us with a thought.

The air grew warmer, and tighter. Already in a weakened state, it was all I could do to breathe. "I took your Revered Speaker's life," Huitzilpochtli said, "and I had ample justification for it. Why should I restore him to you?"

"My lord," Quenami said, "are we not your people? Long, long ago, you made us emerge from the caves in this hill, you led us to Tenochtitlan, to await with our bellies, with our heads, with our arrows, with our shields. You led us to found a city of battle, where the eagle flies and the serpent is torn apart."

"I did." The god's voice was pensive, but I could still feel His anger. "And look what you became. Look at you, priest, and all your frivolous finery. Look at the luxuries you take for yourself, and look at what you'd do to keep them."

Quenami fell back as if he'd been slapped in the face. He might have been, too. The anger of a god in His own territory would be strong. "Will you judge us on my character alone, then?"

Huitzilpochtli made a sound like drums beating a charge. It was only after a while that I realised it was laughter with nothing of joy, but merely cruel amusement. "Of course not. It's the Revered Speaker we are judging here, are we not? That poor, pathetic wreck of a man with no taste for war, who dares to imagine himself wearing the Turquoise-and-Gold Crown? Who thinks he can buy My favour to get it?"

The air was that before a storm, quiet and breathless, as if the whole Fifth World hung suspended. Quenami swallowed audibly. "My lord, Tizoc-tzin seeks only Your blessing, as is proper. He would not have dared to ascend to the Revered Speaker's mat without Your approval."

"Of course he wouldn't." Huitzilpochtli's voice was dark, thoughtful. "I made the Empire, from its earliest days to the bloated monstrosity you have become. You would do well to remember that. And your master, too, that pathetic, gutless man unproved on the battlefield."

"Tizoc-tzin knows the value of war—"

"Your master sees war as a tool," Huitzilpochtli snapped. "As something that he can use to rise in power and to increase his prestige. He understands nothing. War is the gift I gave you, priest. War is the struggle of life and death, and the shedding of blood to keep the Fifth Sun in the sky, and Grandmother Earth satiated. War is everything."

Of course He would say that. Of course He would think that. It was His nature, nothing more, nothing less. That was what Quenami couldn't understand.

"I assure you," Quenami said, in a calm and measured tone. How could he speak thus, in the face of this? "Tizoc-tzin knows the value of war, and the debt and service we owe You. We all do."

"Do you? Will you show me, then?" Huitzilpochtli's voice was cruel. "You who pretend yourself my High Priest, you who speak for all men, will you show me that you are a warrior?"

From the corner of my eye, I saw Itzpapalotl's wings open, with a snick-snick sound like dozens of obsidian knives unsheathed at the same time.

Oh no.

Quenami said, flustered, "My lord…"

"Acatl…" Acamapichtli was pulling at my cloak, weakly but insistently. He was lying on the ground, but his face, cut and bruised, was turned towards me, as pale as muddy milk, his eyes sunk into hollows deeper than the way into Mictlan. "The fool's going to do it."

"It?" I asked, as stupidly as Quenami.

He shook his head, with a shadow of his old impatience. "The last time Quenami fought in earnest was boys at the *calmecac* school, when he was a student. Look at him. Do you really think he can win anything?"

"But why?" I asked.

Acamapichtli smiled again, that mirthless expression I hated. "Why not? Because he does care, in the end? If it makes you happier, consider he's found the only way he can turn things to his gain."

I couldn't imagine why that should make me happier. "And what do you expect me to do about it?"

His eyes were on me, mocking, as cruelly amused as those of the god. I'd forgotten that he was my enemy, that he had almost seen my brother condemned to death, that he had intrigued for his own benefit, that he despised Teomitl and would be glad to see him gone. "I don't–"

He grunted, shifted, and slid something towards me on the blood-stained stone of the platform: a single obsidian knife still in its sheath. I felt nothing of magic within it, not the touch of the Storm Lord, not even a minor spell to keep the blade sharp. It was as mundane as they came, the kind of knife used to extract the heart from a sacrifice's chest, polished to a cutting edge, but as brittle as fired clay. Carefully, I reached out for it. My hand closed around it, and the jolt of power from Mictlan I expected didn't climb up my arm. It felt wrong.

I looked at Quenami again, who stood with his face unreadable, his hands clenched, and an expression I knew all too well – that of a man on a chasm, about to take the plunge.

I would have loved to see him brought down and defeated; but, if that happened, we'd have failed. "My Lord," I said, rising, carefully, with the knife in my hand. The world spun for a bare moment, settled back into the bloodied limestone and the grey sky overhead. "I will take his place."

I wasn't looking at Him, but I felt the moment His attention shifted from Quenami to me, a vast movement in the air, with the hissing crackle of flames as He hefted the fire-snake in His hand. "You, priest?" Laughter, like thunder overhead. "The least among them, and you fancy yourself a warrior?"

Least among them – I could see where Quenami had got his ideas about me. I swallowed the wave of bitterness that flooded me. Now was not the time.

In answer I lifted the knife. "If the least among us is a warrior, doesn't it prove our worth?"

There was silence for a while, that before a lightning-strike. The fire-snake hissed, as if climbing along wood, charring bones and flesh on a funeral pyre. At length, Huitzilpochtli spoke. "It might, at that." He sounded a little calmer, but the cruel amusement was still there, the inhuman pleasure He'd take from seeing us fail. He had resolved to withdraw from us; it wasn't something that could be changed in an instant. "Very well. Prove your worth, and I'll give your Revered Speaker back to you."

Itzpapalotl moved, impossibly swift, to come before me, on the same side of the altar. "Priest," She said. She raised Her hands, unfolding Her claws one by one. They glinted in the sunlight of the heartland, drinking it in as they'd drink blood.

In answer, I raised my own, pathetic knife, a knife that wasn't magic, that didn't have even the meagre powers of Lord Death, that couldn't protect me from the corrosion of the heartland.

If my brother Neutemoc could see me like this, he'd appreciate the irony – that I, the failed brother, the shameful priest, should be the one to fight Her.

From afar came a blast of conch-shells, and a slow beating of drums, and a din, like a thousand voices shouting the names of a thousand different cities at the same time. The air wavered, and the battle was joined.

She was upon me almost before I could move. One wing brushed against my arm, opening up a flower of pain, and I was on my knees, one hand scrabbling to stem the flow of blood. Then She was gone, watching me from afar.

"Pathetic," She whispered. "Is that the best among you?"

"You should know," I said through clenched teeth, fighting the darkness that quivered at the edge of my vision. "You took one, and incapacitated the other."

She laughed. "All is fair in war, as you should know."

No, I didn't. I didn't know the rules of the battlefield or even of the training-ground. My world had been the *calmecac* school, the penances and the night-runs to watch the stars in the sky, in another lifetime where the stars were pinpoints of light faraway, unable to harm us.

She moved fast, far too fast for me to outrace Her, especially in my current state. My only hope was to be ready for Her when She came. I hefted the knife carefully, watched Her, the way Her wings spread around and behind Her, larger than those of a bird, with obsidian knives hanging from their thin bones like obscene fruit...

The wings merged into Her desiccated shoulders almost seamlessly; but there had to be some junction, some point of weakness I could exploit.

She was upon me again, the breath of Her passage the only warning I got, about an eye blink before Her wings slashed me again. This time, instead of trying to remain standing, I threw myself to the floor, and rolled under the thin shape of Her legs.

There.

A small bump, where the obsidian blades sank back

into the bones, a raised area of yellowed flesh, as taut as the paper of a codex.

She was gone again, watching me, toying with me like a jaguar with its prey. "I've fought worthier opponents."

"Teomitl?" I asked. "What have you done with him?"

"Taken my sacrifice, what else?"

A fist of ice closed over my heart. But no, I couldn't afford it, not any more weakness, not any more ways for Her to reach me. "He's alive, isn't he?"

She didn't deign to answer me. But this time I caught the slight shift of Her skirts which announced Her move, the muffled rattle of seashells that heralded Her, as it did all star-demons.

When She came upon me, I was already down, and rising to meet Her, my knife blade sinking into the flesh of Her back.

She shrieked, raising Her hands to the sky, her cry steadily rising in intensity until I thought my ears were going to burst. When She turned back towards me, Her pupils had become vertical slits, Her eyes windows into chasms.

"So... not so foolish after all, priest." So... not so foolish after all, priest." Her smile was wide, cutting – the obsidian blade of her tongue shone in the light.

Her next attack knocked me on the floor. The knife, torn from my hand by Her left wing, skittered on the floor. As if in some distant nightmare I watched it totter over the edge of the platform and fall down with the inevitability of a heartbeat. I tore myself from Her embrace pain blossomed on my arms and chest as Her knives sliced against my flesh.

I was on the ground, bleeding and dizzy, dizzier than before, though I hadn't thought it possible, watching, with a distant, nagging sense of worry, my blood pool into the grooves of the platform, quivering with a power that was denied to me, for the only god present here would not accept my sacrifice. The world was folding back onto itself like a rolled-up sacrifice paper. The air was almost too tight to breathe, searing my lungs, and darkness hovered at the edge of my vision.

I heard – something, a buzzing of flies, a grating of bones against bones, my name, spoken in a low but insistent voice. Dragging my gaze upwards, I caught a glimpse of Acamapichtli's pale face, turned towards me, one of his hands extended, pointing at something, the place where the knife had gone over the edge?

He was gesturing to me, but understanding him was too much work, and Itzpapalotl would be back, anyway. I had to–

It came to me then with preternatural clarity, that it was indeed the knife he was pointing to, that he carried a second one with him, and meant to give it to me. But he was too far away; and I knew, with the certainty of those about to die, that I would never make it.

I tried to move towards him, as if through tar, even though I knew it was futile.

Itzpapalotl laughed, Her voice infinitely distant, echoing in what little remained of my mind. "You delay the inevitable." Her shadow fell over me and I felt the shift in the air; She was moving to pick me up, to throw me over the edge.

Over, it was over. Why had I ever thought I could be a warrior, that I could fight a goddess with no weapons and no rules, nor hope to win?

That I could–

She had said–

No rules.

She had said everything was fair on the battlefield.

And She had Her back to Acamapichtli, whose hand

was holding a second knife.

In the moment She bent over me, the moment Her claws dug into my skin, deeper into my wounds, I did the only thing I could, putting what little strength remained into my voice, I screamed.

"Acamapichtli! Throw it – now!"

As She swung me up like a broken doll I heard the hiss of the knife and prayed to whoever was listening – to the Duality, to Lord Death, to the Feathered Serpent – that it would fly true.

It did.

There was a thud and Itzpapalotl screamed again, a sound that seemed to echo in the bones of my ribcage, filling my lungs and stomach with a buzzing like a knife against bone. The world spun and spun as She lost control, and faded into darkness.

It seemed to last but a moment, but when I regained consciousness I found Acamapichtli propped over me. "What... happened?" I tried to pull myself upwards, and gave up. Everything ached, but I couldn't feel the searing pain of wounds. Gingerly I touched my arms and felt nothing but my skin and the scars that had been there before the fight.

"A trick," Huitzilpochtli said, but He didn't sound displeased. "It seems priests can still surprise."

Itzpapalotl was sitting on the stone altar, nonchalantly staring at Her hands. She, too, appeared unharmed, and in the gaze She directed towards me was nothing but the wary respect between warriors.

"I don't understand," I said, and then it hit me. "Nothing was real."

"Everything is as real as I make it," Huitzilpochtli said. "It is My world, after all."

It wasn't a comforting reminder, though I guess I appreciated the knowledge that I wasn't going to bleed to death. "Does this satisfy you?"

His attention shifted from me to Quenami. "A smooth speaker, a fighter and a resourceful man. I see." There was something like amusement in the air, but more that of a parent for a child. "Yes, I suppose it does. A bargain is a bargain."

I let out a breath I hadn't even been aware of holding. As He had reminded us, we were in His world, and the rules were what He made them, if He had wanted to break His promise, He could have done so without trouble.

Something landed on the ground beside me, but before I could see what it was the platform and the shrine were fading away, and everything grew intolerably bright.

We were back under the pyramid where everything had started. Itzpapalotl was with us, a dark, amused presence at our backs, and Teomitl too, rising from his crouch at the edge of the stairs. "Acatl-tzin!"

He was there and he was whole, thank the Duality. I looked around at the other High Priests. Acamapichtli's wounds had closed, though he remained pale and moved with the stiffness of the unhealed, and Quenami had recovered his finery. My knives appeared to be back in their sheaths. Just to be sure, I laid a hand on one of them, and felt the familiar emptiness of Mictlan arc through my whole being, a comfort that I'd thought I'd never have again.

I looked down, then, at what the god had given us, but even before I did, I already knew that the immobility at my feet, that peculiar, dry and stretched smell, could belong to nothing but a corpse.

TWENTY-FOUR
Creation

"He's dead," Quenami said, accusingly. He turned to Acamapichtli, as if the priest of the Storm Lord held the answers to everything. "You said–"

I knelt, touched it – felt not skin, not even the cold, clammy one of a corpse, but something that might as well have been cloth or leather – nothing beat underneath, nothing warmed it from within. It gave slightly, under my touch. "It's not real," I said.

"Of course it's real," Acamapichtli said. "It's a soul. What did you expect, flesh and blood?"

It didn't look like the sad, bedraggled spirits I conjured, not even like Axayacatl-tzin's soul, which I had conveyed down into the underworld. Just like something that had once been alive, and from which all life had been stripped.

"It's still a corpse," Quenami said. "However you look at it."

I felt a hand on my shoulder, claws, resting lightly on the skin, though not breaking it. Itzpapalotl. "This is a place of power, priest. The heart of the Mexica strength in the Fifth World."

Quenami stared at Her for a while. "Surely you're

not suggesting–"

"What was broken can be made whole, given enough blood."

I thought, for a moment, on what She was offering us. "We can't," I said. To put back together a body and soul…

"*You* can't," Itzpapalotl said. "You send the soul down into death, and only you can call it back. But Huitzilpochtli is the one who severs the thread of life."

And the one who could knit it back together.

Quenami closed his eyes. "It is one of the forbidden rituals."

"And with reason." Itzpapalotl inclined Her head. "But permission has been given, just this once."

Teomitl looked from Her to Quenami, and then back to me. I shrugged, having only a vague idea of what he was talking about. Acamapichtli, too, seemed to be waiting for clarification.

"We already have plenty of human blood," Quenami said. "We'll need hummingbirds for Huitzilpochtli, owls for Lord Death, and a heron for the Rain Lord…"

"And explanations for us," Acamapichtli cut in, with just a hint of sarcasm.

"We can put the soul back in the body." Quenami grimaced. "Actually, make a new body beforehand, too. But it's going to take the three of us." He turned to Teomitl. "Go get the remains, some maize dough, and the animals."

"Acatl-tzin?" Teomitl asked. "Outside isn't the best place to be, right now. It feels as if something awful is going to happen."

I had no doubt. The Southern Hummingbird might have put aside some of His grievances against us, but we still didn't have a Revered Speaker, we were still as vulnerable as we had been since the start.

I sighed. I could have argued about Quenami's impoliteness, but I couldn't muster the energy. "Go. Take guards if you need them. We'll deal with this later."

Quenami lifted his eyebrows. Clearly, he had no intention of discussing anything with me. He knelt in the disk again, and looked over the blood.

Which left Acamapichtli and me, and I certainly didn't feel up to small talk.

"How do you know all this, anyway?" I asked Quenami.

He shrugged: a particularly expansive gesture, indicating I was barely worthy of his time. "I am High Priest of the Southern Hummingbird. I've had the secrets of my order handed down to me."

"One does wonder why," Acamapichtli said, voicing aloud what I thought.

Quenami turned, glaring at us. "For situations such as this, where a lighter – touch, shall we say? – is needed. Now let me work."

"By all means," I said, not wishing to talk to him any more than I had to.

By the time Teomitl came back Quenami had rearranged everything. What I thought of as the body of Tizoc-tzin – even though it had no material reality – was at the centre of the disk surrounded by a large quincunx drawn with the endlessly dripping blood of the chamber. A further circle surrounded the quincunx, encasing it within the grinning face of the Fifth Sun.

Teomitl was followed by two slaves who carried a wrapped-up cloth from which came the smell of offal. He held the cages with the animals; the hummingbirds a blur of speed, obviously unhappy at being disturbed from their rest. The rabbits were more sedate, curled up at the bottom of the cage as if sleeping.

"Put it here." Quenami pointed to one end of the circle, the one furthest away from the stairs. "And those here." He didn't bother to thank Teomitl or the slaves.

He had given us the explanations in the meantime. Acamapichtli had pulled a sour face but had said nothing. He did not look as though he had much energy left to argue either.

Quenami opened the cages and grabbed the hummingbirds before they could fly away, slicing their heads off with a practised gesture. Blood splattered on the ground. He smeared it into the circle, drawing the symbols for Four Jaguar, the First Age, ruled by the Smoking Mirror, the god of War and Fate.

> *"O master, O lord, O sun, O war*
> *We ask of You Your spirit, Your word*
> *Your blessing…"*

Acamapichtli, meanwhile, was sacrificing the heron, and filling in the symbols for Four Water and Four Rain, the Third and Fourth Age, ruled by the Storm Lord and His wife.

> *"For he who was bequeathed the turquoise diadem*
> *The earplug, the lip plug,*
> *The necklace, the precious feather*
> *He who was crowned Lord of Men…"*

I came last with the owl, drawing the last symbol, that of the Second Age, Four Wind, ruled by the Feathered Serpent, the age of knowledge and wisdom, now passed into legend. The symbol pulsed under my hands, as if seeking to stretch itself into something else.

> *"Give him Your torch, Your light, Your mirror*
> *The thick torch that illumines the world*
> *Your heat, Your fragrance*

We place our trust in You,
We the untrained, the ignorant…"

Next came the maize dough, which Acamapichtli fashioned into the life-sized shape of a man. His hands shook, and the limbs of the figure came out crooked, a fact which made Quenami's face contort with anger, but he said nothing. I fully expected we'd pay for it later.

The face was two holes punched into the dough, and something that might have been a smile: an incongruous sight, given how seldom Tizoc-tzin had smiled when he was alive. It ought to have looked sad and pathetic, this child's figure of a man, but it didn't. Light fell over it, swathing it in the colour of stone and blood; and the face, wrapped in shadows, seemed almost alive, some monster come from the underworld to devour us all.

I'd expected Itzpapalotl to go away but She still leant against the wall furthest away from the stairs, out of the circle. If She'd been human, I'd have said She was curious, but I think it was something else that kept Her there – perhaps further orders from the Southern Hummingbird?

"I give my precious water, I give my blood
To the maize in the fields, to Grandmother Earth that was
broken
I give my spirit, I give the sun…"

Acamapichtli sliced both his earlobes, and let the blood drip into the eyes and the mouth of the dough figure.

"Eyes to see the Fifth World, the five directions
A mouth to give thanks
A mouth to fashion the flowers, the songs…"

In the chest cavity, where the heart should have been, there was only a small hole, like that of a flute. Acamapichtli moved away to stand at the base of the body, and left the way wide open for me.

Quenami inclined his head. I walked through the circle to the dead soul and carried it back to the dough figure. Then, bending over, I carefully laid one atop the other. Tizoc-tzin sank into the dough like a man swallowed by quicksand, and the dough shifted, the manikin taking on his features, the bloodied mouth closed in a scowl, an eerie resemblance to the man's favourite expression. It almost seemed as though he was going to speak up; to accuse us all of slighting him. But the only sound was that of our breaths, slow and regular, and Itzpapalotl's claws raking the stone to the rhythm of some unheard hymn.

Quenami placed himself over the opening in the chest, Acamapichtli near the crotch, and I at the head, over the blood-filled mouth.

"We leave this earth
This world of jade and flowers
The quetzal feathers, the silver
Down into the darkness we must go..."

The words that came to me were the ones I had spoken to the She-Snake a lifetime ago, and they were out of my mouth before I could call them back.

"Let the Revered Speaker be no exception."

I bit my lip, but it was too late. Quenami hissed, his gaze narrowing in my direction, but he couldn't speak for fear of breaking the ritual.

I went on regardless, less assured. I hadn't thought it was possible, but I was shaking as hard as if Itzpapalotl had been looking at me with the full force of Her gaze.

"But some return
With sunlight shining on them
With moonlight and starlight to show the way
Some return, some go back home
To the three-legged hearth, to Old Man Fire's face
And the song of maidens, and the laughter of children…"

I knelt and pressed my lips against the dough. It was cool, like something that had rested in the shade for far too long, with the faint, acrid taste of rot. I was vaguely aware of Quenami and Acamapichtli getting ready for the rest of the ritual, for giving the body life, and tying the soul back to it, but even that faded away, as the dough breathed back into me, and harsh light flooded the chamber, until the underground room seemed but a memory.

Over me towered the round, grinning face of To-natiuh the Fifth Sun – bloodied tongue lolling out, His red hair framed by the signs of the calendar, giant stone glyphs arrayed around Him like a crown. His gaze, His endlessly burning gaze, rested on me, and I slowly became aware that I held Tizoc-tzin's soul in my arms.

It was small and misshapen, like the body, and the light of the Fifth Sun made it seem transparent, as if it would wash it out of existence at any moment.

Somewhere beyond me was Acamapichtli, carrying the living body. Quenami stood in the centre, waiting for us. "Now, Acatl."

I walked, or flew, to him, and so did Acamapichtli, and we were as one. They were pressing against me, Quenami with his insufferable arrogance and conviction that the universe owed him everything, and Acamapichtli, already thinking of ways to turn the situation to his advantage. There was an over-ambitious priest in his temple that he needed to get rid of, and this would be the perfect opportunity...

And Tizoc-tzin.

Small and pathetic and made of fears, of envy, of an uncontrollable ambition that had, as Teomitl had said, eaten him alive. I sought for a man, cowering behind that mask, and could find nothing. No face, no heart. Doubts and fears and suspicion, was this the man we had raised as Revered Speaker? No wonder Itzpapalotl was still waiting, waiting for the Empire to fall, for Her mistress to be free. There was no other place he could take us, he and Quenami and Acamapichtli, all working for their own gain.

Something was wrong. Something...

They were calling my name from far away, and I still held the soul clutched tightly in my grasp, in the Fifth Sun's light, a light that was growing in intensity, promising the heat of the desert, the scouring touch of pyres. What was I thinking? It was the Fifth World at stake. Surely I could force myself to–

But I couldn't. Here, in this time, in this place, in the heart of our strength, no lies were left. I couldn't be one with the other priests, for they were my enemies, and I couldn't bring Tizoc-tzin back, for I had despised him beyond words when he had been alive.

I thought of Ceyaxochitl, making her slow way into darkness. It wasn't fair. Why was Tizoc-tzin – as unworthy of an exception as they came – chosen to be lifted out of death, while she remained in Mictlan? Why did he get to have everything he wanted, in spite of all the damage he had done, all the lives he had carelessly spent, from Ceyaxochitl's to Echichilli's?

Why?

I couldn't.

"Acatl!"

I–

Surely there had to be a way, something I could do. I tried to release Tizoc-tzin's soul, but it wouldn't budge. I tried going to Quenami and felt everything that separated us, every reason I despised him, he who had intrigued and schemed and thrown me into jail and almost executed me. I tried going to Acamapichtli, and saw his power-games and how little he cared about human life, that he would sacrifice anyone and anything standing between him and what he wanted, including my own brother. And I couldn't forgive either of them, or even claim to understand their acts.

In that place, in that time, I sank to my knees with Tizoc-tzin cradled against me, watching as if from a great distance, watching the Fifth Sun's grin grow wider and wider, as if He had always known I would fail, feeling, distant and cruel, Itzpapalotl's amusement, and Teomitl's frantic attempts to understand what was going wrong.

Surely I could set my feelings aside, for the sake of the Fifth World?

Surely.

But I had no lies or accommodations left, and my contempt was destroying everything. All I had to do was to believe in what I was doing, to see Tizoc-tzin as our worthy Revered Speaker, Quenami as our leader, and Acamapichtli as a peer. Only that, and I would rise, I would give back the breath that was in my body, and everything would be as it should with the world.

But Tizoc-tzin had cast my sister aside as nothing, Quenami had thrown me in jail, and Acamapichtli had tried to kill my brother. In the end, it was the pettiest things that defined me.

The Fifth Sun's light washed over us, strong and unforgiving, like a wave in a storm. I dug my heels in, but I could feel its strength, and knew that it was going to throw me out of the circle.

Too late.

My whole body tingled in the wash of light... No, that wasn't it. There was something that ached more, a dull pain throbbing in my hand. I looked down at Acamapichtli's mark, grey and diminished against the light's onslaught. A jaguar fang, perfectly formed, and the blood of a human sacrifice, all freely given to me. It had been for his own gain, as he had blithely admitted, but still, he had helped me. Still...

I saw again Quenami, his fists clenched, about to get himself killed against Itzpapalotl. He had dragged me to the top of the hill, I and Acamapichtli, even though he'd laughed and suggested we leave the weak behind.

Acamapichtli was smiling in my mind. "We will endure," he whispered. "We will do what needs to be done. We will–"

I hated them. I despised them for their beliefs, and for everything they had done in the name of gain and greed. But, in the end...

In the end, Teomitl had allied himself with Nezahual-tzin, and I with Acamapichtli. In the end...

In the end, they were my peers and my equals, and the only ones who could see this through. In the end, when push came to shove and the Fifth World tottered on the brink of extinction – when even they could see the price of failure – I could trust them to do what needed to be done.

And that was the only truth.

"Acatl!"

"I am here," I whispered, and, gently, very gently, breathed out Tizoc-tzin's soul, back into the Fifth World, before joining my fellow High Priests for the rest of the ritual.

TWENTY-FIVE
The Fifth World

Tizoc-tzin's formal designation was a small and subdued affair. With his brother's funeral over, and him still in a state of weakness, he simply opted for a quiet ceremony with the governors and the magistrates. The Revered Speakers of Texcoco and Tlacopan, his fellow rulers in the Triple Alliance, offered him congratulations, and sacrificed quails to mark the beginning of an auspicious reign.

Tizoc-tzin wasn't quite yet crowned, of course. That would come after the coronation war, when he had brought back enough prisoners and slaves for a true celebration. But, nevertheless, he was already invested, with enough power to keep us all safe.

After the ceremony he received us in his private quarters. There were no slaves and no noblemen, just Teomitl, Acamapichtli, Nezahual-tzin and I, standing barefoot amidst the luxurious decorations, and the exquisitely carved columns. Fine feathers fans and gold ornaments were casually strewn across the room.

Quenami was beside his master, richly attired, with coloured heron plumes at his belt, blue-and-black paint, and a stylised fire-serpent winding its way across the hem of his tunic. The air smelled faintly of pine needles and copal incense, and there was the faintest hint of smoke, causing my eyes to itch.

"I am given to understand that we owe you a debt," Tizoc-tzin said. His eyes were sunken deep, his skin a pale brown, almost waxy, and he stumbled a little on his words. I wasn't sure if it was because something was wrong with his speech, if my delay in the ritual had cost him something, or if it was simply because he disliked uttering them. By the scowl on his face, there was at least some of the latter.

Nezahual-tzin shrugged. "I'm glad to see proper diplomatic relations restored between Tenochtitlan and Texcoco. I shall look forward to your coronation, my lord."

"I see." Tizoc-tzin bent to look at Nezahual-tzin, as if not quite sure what to make of him. "Perhaps you do," he said grudgingly.

"It's in our best interests." Nezahual-tzin's smile was wide and dazzling, that of a carefree sixteen year-old. I wasn't fooled.

"And you." Tizoc-tzin turned his attention back to Acamapichtli and me.

"We did our duty," Acamapichtli said. "To the Revered Speaker and to the Empire." One of his arms, the one that had thrown the blade at Itzpapalotl, was a little stiff, and I didn't think it would ever move smoothly again. My own legs ached whenever I rose. Whatever Huitzilpochtli had said, there had been a price for entering the heartland. There was always a price.

Tizoc-tzin was silent for a while. His gaze moved from Acamapichtli to me and back again. "Then I am assured of your loyalty."

Not surprising, I guessed. A little saddening, but then I had known when we had brought him back to life.

Death had changed nothing in him, no lessons had been learnt.

"You've always had our loyalty," Acamapichtli said effortlessly.

"I have pledged service to the Revered Speaker of the Mexica Empire," I said.

He noticed the omission of his name, that much was clear. His eyes narrowed. I fully expected him to demand something more of me, some show of obeisance, but he didn't.

"I see," he said, again. "So that's how things are." He leant back, his back straight once more, and turned back to Quenami. "The council is still empty, and we have to see about appointments. Teomitl?"

Teomitl rose from his crouch. For a moment, he and Tizoc-tzin faced each other, and I wasn't quite sure what I read in their gazes. It wasn't love, or even respect. Perhaps simply what my brother Neutemoc and I shared – the knowledge that, no matter how distant we might be, how difficult we might find getting on together, we still shared the same blood.

At length Tizoc-tzin nodded. "I need a Master of the House of Darts."

"I don't think–" Teomitl started.

"Nonsense. You'll do fine," Tizoc-tzin said. "If I can't trust family–"

"That's not the problem." Teomitl's face hovered on the edge of divinity again. "You know what's wrong."

"Do I?" Tizoc-tzin looked at him for a while more. His pale face was unreadable; his skin pale and translucent, enough to reveal the bones and the shape of the skull. He'd died. He'd come back. We couldn't pretend things were normal. "We'll have to see about another appointment for her. Some gift of jewellery or perhaps a grant of land. It would be unseemly for my brother to marry beneath him."

What? I looked at Tizoc-tzin. I had misheard. But, no, Teomitl still stood, as if struck by Tlaloc's lightning. "Brother–"

"You have objections?"

"No, no, I don't. But–"

"Don't get me wrong." Tizoc-tzin was still scowling, like an unappeased spirit back from the underworld. "I don't like this. I don't approve of this. I'll stand by what I think of your priest."

Always pleasant, I could see. But as long as he agreed...

"But you're my brother, and there will be no war between us."

Because he couldn't afford it, or because he loved Teomitl? I couldn't tell, not any more, what those two felt for each other. It seemed to me that something had broken in the hours before my arrest, when Tizoc-tzin had cast doubts on Mihmatini's reputation, something had come apart then, a mask broken into four hundred pieces, and things would never be the same.

Teomitl stood straight, as if to attention. "Thank you."

Tizoc-tzin scowled. "But you're getting the other appointment as well. Don't flatter yourself. It's time you took part in imperial affairs."

"I know," Teomitl said. He bowed, very low, a subject to his Revered Speaker, but I could feel the impatience brimming up in him.

"That will be all," Tizoc-tzin said. "You may leave."

"Don't look so sad," Acamapichtli said, as he raised the entrance-curtain in a tinkle of bells. We walked down the steps into the courtyard – deserted at this hour of the afternoon – almost companionably.

"I'm not," I said, stiffly. "We got what we wanted, didn't we?"

He looked at me, a smile spreading on his face. "Of course. Because we worked together."

I wasn't in the mood for a moral, especially coming from him. "It's not an experience I'm anxious to repeat too often. Still, I suppose I don't have a choice."

Acamapichtli smiled. "You're learning." He clapped me on the back, like an old friend. "We'll meet again." And then he was gone, striding down the stairs as if nothing had happened, ready to play his little games once again.

Learning? I supposed, in a way, that I was, but not lessons he'd ever have understood.

Teomitl caught up with me at the exit to the courtyard under a fresco of butterflies and moths, a stream of souls rising up from the ground towards the huge face of the Fifth Sun. Nezahual-tzin fell in with us, casually and innocently, though he never did anything without cause. "So, I take it I'm invited to the wedding?"

Teomitl scowled, an expression reminiscent of Tizoc-tzin at his best. "You're the Revered Speaker of Texcoco. I don't think I could leave you out if I tried."

"How nice," Nezahual-tzin said. "I'll come with pleasure."

"I have no doubt." Teomitl shook his head, as if to scare off a nagging fly. "Acatl-tzin –"

"Yes?"

"He hasn't changed, has he?"

I shook my head.

"People seldom change," Nezahual-tzin said. We passed the imperial aviary where the birds pressed themselves against the bars of their huge cages, the quetzal-birds and the parrots, the herons and the quails, everything laid out for the Revered Speaker's pleasure. "They think they do, but in the end most change is an illusion. Perhaps the greatest one put in the Fifth World."

I knew. I knew that Quenami was going to continue grating on my nerves, that Acamapichtli would support me only as far as his own interests, that I would never be able to rely on them.

But, the Duality protect us, I was still going to work with them. "He's granted you a wife," I said finally. "Don't ask for more than that."

"It would be arrogant to. Not to mention out of place." Teomitl puffed his cheeks thoughtfully. "He'll deal with you, though, in the end. Quenami will convince him to."

"He has what he wanted," I said. "The Turquoise-and-Gold Crown. He should be more amenable now." So long as we didn't contradict him in anything. It was going to be a difficult reign. Thank the Duality I had the rest of my clergy with me.

"I guess so," Teomitl said, but he sounded unconvinced. "I'm not sure–"

"He's your brother. And the Revered Speaker."

"I know. I guess… I guess he's not who I thought he was." He smiled, suddenly carefree, pure Teomitl. "But it's not so bad, in the end."

This from a man who had just become heir-apparent to the Mexica Empire. I stifled a smile. "I'm sure you can live with it. Come on. Let's find Mihmatini and tell her the good news, and then I'll go back to the Duality House and finish Ceyaxochitl's vigil."

We strolled out of the Imperial Palace, past the Serpent Wall, and into the familiar crowd of the Sacred Precinct. The Fifth Sun was overhead, beating down upon us, the heavens bright and impossibly blue. Blood ran down the steps of the Great Temple, going underground to settle into the grooves of the disk, sealing again and again the prison of She of the Silver

391

Bells, and the star-demons were gone. Everything was right with the world, or as right as it could be.

Except…

Except that, at the edge of the sky, I could see them, the same storm clouds as in the heartland, slowly closing in, grey and swollen and angry, a reminder of the god's presence. And I didn't need Mictlan's magic to see the skeleton beneath Tizoc-tzin's skin. We had put a dead man on the throne, an empty husk, animated only by magic and the blessing of a god.

When Huitzilpochtli's blessings and magic ran out – and they always did – what would happen then?

ACKNOWLEDGMENTS

No novel is written in a vacuum, especially a research intensive one like *Harbinger of the Storm*. Accordingly, I would like to thank the livejournal communities *ancient_americas*, *ask_a_historian* and *little_details* for helping me narrow down the date of Axayacatl's death. Traci Morganfield, as usual, was a stupendous help, both with sources and with general support – her continued faith and enthusiasm for the series was a great help to keep me going through the terrible middle of this volume. Likewise, Marion Larqué's enjoyment (she read both books in record time) kept me writing throughout.

Dave Devereux, whom I met in 2009 at Eastercon in Bradford, turned out to be a dab hand at murder methods, and provided me with several poisons for causing the symptoms I wanted for Ceyaxochitl's death (though I do wish to note that I find his expertise slightly worrying and am not entirely sure I want to have dinner with him, in spite of his obvious culinary skills).

Justin Pilon read both the synopsis and the novel, and provided awesome feedback on both – not to mention provided awesome advertising for book one.

Rochita Loenen-Ruiz, in addition to being a fabulous writer herself, provided me with much-needed space to unwind and fascinating discussions on culture and cultural identity.

The writers of the Villa Diodati workshop provided interesting conversations on novel writing, novel promotion and general brainstorming, as well as great food and great company: Deanna Carlyle, Nancy Fulda, Stephen Gaskell, Sara Genge, Floris Kleijne, Chance Morrisson, Ruth Nestvold, John Olsen, Ben Rosembaum, and Jeff Spock.

The members of my writing group Written in Blood read the second draft of this and helped me fix several broken moments, as well as cut down on the number of characters involved in court intrigues. Many thanks to Keyan Bowes, Dario Ciriello, Janice Hardy, Doug Sharp, Juliette Wade and Genevieve Williams for making this a smoother and easier read.

A humbling number of people promoted book 1 online and offline (in addition to those mentioned above): Kevin J Anderson, Elizabeth Bear, Lauren Beukes, Blackwatch, Dave Brendon, Tobias Buckell, Stephanie Burgis and Patrick Samphire, Seb Cevey, Andy Cox, Electra aka starlady38, Emmanuel Chastellière, Tom Crosshill, Pat Esden, Roy Gray, Dave Gullen, Rob Haines, Colin Harvey, Caroline Hooton, Chris Kastensmidt, J. Robert King, James Maxey, Lucas Moreno, Cara Murphy, Nik aka Loudmouthman, Gareth L. Powell, Stefan Raets, Julia Reynolds, Roxane aka edroxy, Angela Slatter, M.J. Starling, Rob Weber (alias Val online), Sean Williams, Russell Wilcox, Maria Zannini at Online Writing Workshop, the T-Party writers' workshop, Danie Ware and the Forbidden Planet staff involved with my signing and bookselling there, and to everyone else who talked about the book, reviewed it, or was kind enough to let me blather about my writing in their corner of the web. In the promotion department, special thanks go to Janice Hardy, who in addition to having a sharp eye for structure and conflict, is also an awesome graphic designer and provided me with *Servant of the Underworld* bookmarks and business cards.

As always, many thanks to the AR crew, Marc Gascoigne and Lee Harris, and to my agents, John Parker and John Berlyne at Zeno Agency, for the enthusiasm, the responsiveness, and for putting up with my more naive questions on the world of publishing and deadlines.

And finally, to my family: to my paternal grandparents, whose house was always a treasure-trove of books; to my maternal grandmother, my *bà ngoai*, who took care of me as a child, and still does; to my parents, for always being there; and to my sister, who promoted the book to all and sundry across Europe, from Spain to Finland.

And, last but not least, thanks to my husband Matthieu, who, not content with being dragged to London to see a (wonderful) exhibition on the Aztecs, cheerfully suggested suspects, brainstormed rituals and plotted bloody murders with me, in addition to reading the first draft of this with his usual critical eye.

ABOUT THE AUTHOR

French by birth, Aliette de Bodard chose to write in English – her second language – after a two-year stint in London. Though she has trained as an engineer (graduating from Ecole Polytechnique, one of France's most prestigious colleges), she has always been fascinated by history and mythology, especially those of non-Western cultures. Her love of mysteries gave her the idea to write a series of cross-genre novels which would feature Aztecs, blood magic and fiendish murders.

She is a Campbell Award finalist and a Writers of the Future winner. Her short fiction has appeared or is forthcoming in venues such as *Interzone*, *Realms of Fantasy*, and *Fantasy magazine*, and has been reprinted in *The Year's Best Science Fiction*. She is now hard at work on her third novel – the next in the *Obsidian and Blood* series.

She lives in Paris, where she has a job as a computer engineer.

www.aliettedebodard.com

AUTHOR'S NOTES

As I mention in the afterword to *Servant of the Underworld*, writing a book set in Aztec times carries with it a number of challenges, not the least of which is reconstituting a history we know little about. As usual, any egregious mistakes are my own, and not those of the sources I consulted.

The other challenge is how to make the civilisation intelligible for modern readers. Most Aztec names are long; for the longer the name was, the most prestigious it was. They are also replete with a number of phonemes barbarous to English ears such as "tz" or "tl". Accordingly, I took the decision to simplify matters somewhat. The inhabitants of the city of Texcoco are in fact the Acolhuas (much as those of the city of Tenochtitlan are the Mexica-Tenochca); but given how little they were referred to, I used the word "Texcocan", which has the merit of having a clear common root with "Texcoco".

Similarly a number of names were simplified. I chose to refer to the She-Snake by his title rather than by his name, the rather long and unwieldy "Tlilpopoca-tzin"; and Nezahual-tzin's full name is in fact "Nezahualpilli-tzin", quite a mouthful. Most other names chosen were deliberately short, useful for us but something that would have been highly disrespectful in Aztec times.

I twisted history in several respects, perhaps the most notable being the addition of the High Priest for the Dead to the highest level of religious hierarchy. The histories only mention the High Priest of Tlaloc and the High Priest of Huitzilpochtli as supreme religious authorities, but I needed a triumvirate in order to justify Acatl's presence at Court.

And, while it is true that the Great Temple, the centre of religious life in Tenochtitlan, was rebuilt and enlarged multiple times (one of the most notable expansions being the one started by Tizoc and continued by his successor Teomitl), the huge disk I describe underneath the temple was not, in fact, in this location. The disk, which showed the dismembered body of Coyolxauhqui, She of the Silver Bells, was in fact set at the bottom of the Great Temple steps. The bodies of the sacrifices would tumble down the steps, and fall onto the disk, re-enacting the primal sacrifice of She of the Silver Bells, and ensuring Huitzilpochtli remained dominant.

Harbinger of the Storm is set a year and a half after its predecessor, *Servant of the Underworld*. It concerns itself with the matter of the imperial succession, a thorny problem in a society which had no formal system of inheritance and relied instead on a group of elders and important noblemen (the council) to designate the man they thought fit to rule the Mexica Empire.

We have little record of what actually happened around Axayacatl-tzin's death, save that the year of his death coincided with a total eclipse of the sun. I chose to situate the eclipse in the days following his death, which puts his death in the winter season, towards the end of the Aztec year. Obviously, given the symbolism of the Revered Speaker as representative of the Southern Hummingbird Huitzilpochtli, and the latter's ties with the Fifth Sun, the proximity of an eclipse to his death would have seemed deeply ominous to the Aztecs.

The She-Snake is worth a brief mention here; he was part of the duality which underpinned most Nahuatl thought. Just as most gods had a female counterpart, the Revered Speaker, the representative of Huitzilpochtli, had his counterpart in the *Cihuacoatl*, the She-Snake. The former was in charge of what we would call external policy, such as making war; the latter handled internal matters like order in the city, the Sacred Precinct and the palace. This is the same duality we find at the lowest level between husband and wife, the husband taking care of external affairs like going to war and taking care of the fields, while the woman was the one responsible for running the household. At the time of the Spanish conquest, the She-Snake had his own palace, I chose to have Axayacatl's She-Snake take his quarters in the Imperial Palace in order to keep him closer to the plot.

The very first She-Snake was Moctezuma I's brother Tlacaelel, the man who is credited with rewriting the history of the Mexica Empire to give them their divine destiny to conquer the world, as well as restructure the religion around the mass sacrifices to their tribal god Huitzilpochtli. Many sources have him live well into the reign of Teomitl, but I have taken the more likely explanation offered notably by Nigel Davies, that he died in Axayacatl's reign, leaving his son Tlilpopoca to ascend to the position in his place.

The ritual to access the Mexica heartland was inspired from the one described in Fray Diego Durán's account (in *The History of the Indies of New Spain*, as collected in The *Flayed God*), in which the wise men of Moctezuma's reign go to beseech Huitzilpochtli's guidance, and are berated by the god's mother for having forgotten their humble origins. Part of the mother's speech I used as an inspiration for Huitzilpochtli's angry questions in the heartland.

Another character is worth a mention, Nezahual is perhaps most known as the wise old man who announced the arrival of the Spanish to the then-Aztec Emperor Moctezuma II. Revered as a sorcerer, Nezahual is also known for being a great lover: he had 2,000 concubines (though only 40 bore him sons). His reign was the golden age of Texcoco. I therefore chose to give him as a patron god Quetzalcoatl, who was most often associated with knowledge and benevolent progress.

Finally a brief note on geography. This volume sees Acatl and Teomitl stay mostly with the Imperial Palace, with two notable exceptions. The pleasure gardens they visit in chapters 17-18 are those of Texcotzingo, built by Nezahual's father. Their ruins are still extant in Mexico. The other place, Teotihuacan, is much more famous. The ruined pyramids bear witness to a civilisation that flourished around 150 BC-700 AD, dominating the Basin of Mexico. By the time the Aztecs came, only the ruins of the temple complex remained, which the Aztecs believed to have been built by gods. The Aztecs believed Teotihuacan to be the place where the sun had risen into the sky, hence its name, which roughly translates as "The Place Where the Gods Emerged". The ruins themselves were walled off and became a place of pilgrimage. In the shadow of the wall a busy city-state flourished. It is in this newer city that Nezahual, Acatl and Teomitl find sleeping quarters.

The Historical Setting

Like its predecessor *Servant of the Underworld*, *Harbinger of the Storm* is set in late fifteenth-century, near the apex of the Mexica (Aztec) Empire. Unlike its predecessor, it is far more concerned with the political intrigues of the court. The Mexica Empire had a very peculiar, semi-hereditary system of leadership, as evidenced in this book. We don't have many records of how the deliberations went, but I suspect they were much shorter and less protracted than in the book, as the next Revered Speaker was often chosen in the wake of the funeral for the latest.

Though the choice was theoretically between all members of the imperial family, the eleven Revered Speakers the length of the Mexica Empire were mostly chosen from the brothers of the previous title-holder or from those of fraternal descent – ¬ if they weren't the brother of the previous one, they were a nephew or great-nephew. The She-Snake, who could claim a line of descent from the brother of Moctezuma I (the Revered Speaker before Axayacatl) would have been an unlikely but possible candidate, particularly if Tizoctzin had been found unworthy. Xahuia's son would have been a possibility also, but still more unlikely. Ironically, the second-best candidate would have been Teomitl, as Manatzpa himself proposes, though he would have been considered very young for the position. Five years later, when Teomitl acceded in turn to the Turquoise-and-Gold Crown, the annals note that he was specifically chosen for his youth and dynamism.

I took some other liberties with the setting. I added Acatl, High Priest for the Dead, to the duo of High Priests at the apex of religious hierarchy (the histories mention both the High Priest of the Southern Hummingbird and that of the Storm Lord). And you will probably have guessed that Teomitl's planned first marriage with Mihmatini is entirely fictional as well. In reality, as Acatl mentions, the first marriage would have sealed a diplomatic alliance. It's not impossible that it would have involved one of Nezahual-tzin's sisters or daughters, giving these two a further reason to remember each other.

The town of Texcoco plays a large part in this book. By 1481, the Triple Alliance formed between Tenochtitlan, Texcoco and Tlacopan was mainly spearheaded by the first two cities. The inhabitants of Texcoco were actually the Acolhuas (just as the inhabitants of Tenochtitlan are the Mexica), but I stuck with "Texcocans" so as not to muddy the waters in a book already loaded with characters and factions.

The gardens Acatl, Teomitl and Nezahual-tzin visit in the course of chapter 18 are those of Texcotzingo. They were built by Nezahual-tzin's father and dedicated to the god Tlaloc, and were said to be a true wonder, though very little remains of them today.

Teotihuacan, the Birthplace of the Gods, plays a particular role in Mexica mythology. the ruins of the rich civilisation which had built it were mistaken by the Mexica as the work of the gods. The huge pyramids were deemed to be the tombs of the gods, who had given their lives at the beginning of the age so that the Fifth Sun might rise (hence the renaming of the central alley as the Alley of the Dead). By the 15th Century, Teotihuacan had become a centre for pilgrimages – the ruins fenced off by a great wall, while the bustling, new city was further west.

Nezahual-tzin is actually Nezahualpilli-tzin (his name means the Fasting Prince/the Hungry Prince, and the name of his father, Nezahualcoyotl, means the Fasting

Coyote). I shortened it for ease of reading. Nezahual-tzin is best remembered in Aztec history as a canny old sorcerer ; it was he who prophesied to Moctezuma II the arrival of strangers from beyond the seas, though he did not live to see the Spanish arrive. Aside from his mysterious powers (which I attributed to Quetzalocatl, god of Wisdom and Knowledge), Nezahual-tzin is mainly remembered for the size of his harem (around 2000 concubines, and 144 children), and for his unbending sense of fairness. He executed his own son for adultery, and one of his Mexica concubines for multiple murders, almost sparking a Mexica-Texcocan war. Many historians, including Nigel Davies, have suspected Nezahual-tzin of being less than eager to wage war, preferring to stay at home and indulge in the luxury of his palace, which would have annoyed *Ahuizotl*, a strategist always eager to campaign with his soldiers.

The interplay between *Ahuizotl*/Teomitl and his brother Tizoc is, again, the stuff of speculation. What we do know about Tizoc is that he had the shortest and most lacklustre reign of the Mexica Emperors. His coronation war was a dismal failure, and his reign one series of mediocre campaigns after another. There is a hypothesis that his death after only five years of rule was the work of sorcerers, possibly in the pay of his over-eager brother *Ahuizotl*. What he is best remembered for is for starting a large-scale rebuilding of the Great Temple, which would later be completed by his brother and successor *Ahuizotl*, a dedication mainly remembered for the scale of human sacrifices offered at this occasion, as if to truly make clear the Empire's domination, or to imprison again a great goddess...

As to the occult stuff... The disk that Acatl and Teomitl discover underneath the Great Temple in chapter 2 is a much larger version of an existing work of art which lay at the feet of the pyramid; each sacrifice would tumble down the steps and come to rest on the dismembered image of She of the Silver Bells, re-enacting the Southern Hummingbird's primal sacrifice and sealing again the alliance of the Mexica with their tribal god.

It's also worth noting that although we do not know the exact date of Axayacatl's death, we do know that it was the same year as a total eclipse of the sun – which, to a culture so obsessed with the warrior sun, would have been a disaster, a sign that the Fifth Sun/the Southern Hummingbird were withdrawing their favour or losing their power against the forces of the night. I chose to have a (sudden) solar eclipse happen at the tail end of chapter 21, as Tizoc, the anointed Revered Speaker, dies torn by a star-demon, a sign that the gods have indeed abandoned the Mexica Empire.

Other date-related tidbits: the year Two House is of particular significance, since it would have been the anniversary year of the foundation of the Empire, which had also started in a year Two House (1325), a round number of "bundles of years" (or fifty-two-year intervals, the Aztec equivalent of centuries in terms of significance). Just as the Christians were afraid the world would end at the turn of the first millennium, so the Aztecs would have been worried as such as a juncture approached. This is one of those bonuses I didn't actually plan for, but which was pretty cool to find out.

The idea for the heartland comes from the Mexica migration myth, which sees them wandering in the marshes for generations until they finally reach the bountiful place promised to them by their god. Depending on the version of this myth, the Mexica either come from Atzlan ("the White Place", from which comes the name "Aztec") or from one of seven caves at Chicomoztoc. The description of this mythical place, where the Southern Hummingbird still dwells, was drawn from the inspiration for this journey in the annals of Diego Durán. Under the reign of Moctezuma, sages go on a journey back to the heartland to find their god, and are berated for losing sight of their humble origins. Most of those myths are conflated together within Acatl's delirium in chapter 23 – he sees the seven caves, as well as the flight of the herons which are said to be plentiful in Atzlan, and the woman sweeping the floor with a broom of femurs is Coatlicue, the Earth Goddess who is the Southern Hummingbird's mother (and who fell pregnant with him while sweeping the floor of a mountain temple).

Further Reading

Manuel Aguilar-Moreno, *Handbook to Life in the Aztec World*, Oxford University Press, 2006

Frances F. Berdan and Patricia Rief Anawalt, *The Essential Codex Mendoza*, University of California Press, 1997

Warwick Bray, *Everyday Life of the Aztecs*, B.T. Batsford Ltd, 1968

Elizabeth M. Brumfiel and Gary M. Feinman, *The Aztec World*, Abrams, 2008

Roy Burrell, *Life in the Time of Moctezuma and the Aztecs*, Cherrytree books, 1992

Inga Clendinnen, *Aztecs: An Interpretation (Canto)*, Cambridge University Press, 1991

Aurélie Couvreur, "La Description du Grand Temple de Mexico par Bernardino de Sahagún (Codex de Florence, annexe du livre II)", *Journal de la Société des Américanistes*, 2002

Nigel Davies, *The Aztecs: A History*, University of Oklahoma Press, 1973

William Gates, *An Aztec Herbal: The Classic Codex of 1552*, Dover, 2000

Christopher P. Garraty, "Aztec Teotihuacan: Political Processes at a Post-classic and Early Colonial City-State in the Basin of Mexico", *Latin American Antiquity*, 2006

Ross Hassig, *Aztec Warfare: Imperial Expansion and Political Control*, University of Oklahoma Press, 1988

David M. Jones and Brian L. Molyneaux, *Mythologies des Amériques*, EDDL, 2002

Roberta E. Markman and Peter T. Markman, *The Flayed God: the Mythology of Mesoamerica*, HarperSanFrancisco, 1992

Jacques Martin and Jean Torton, *Les Voyages d'Alix: Les Aztèques*, Casterman, 2005

Colin McEwan, *Moctezuma, Aztec Ruler*, The British Museum Press, 2009

Mary Miller and Karl Taube, *An Illustrated Dictionary of the Gods and Symbols of Ancient Mexico and the Maya*, Thames & Hudson, 1993

Charles Phillips, *The Complete Illustrated History of the Aztecs and Maya*, Hermes House, 2006

Jacques Soustelle, *Daily Life of the Aztecs*, Phoenix Press, 2002

G.C. Vaillant, *Aztecs of Mexico*, Pelican, 1965

Online Sources

Aztec Calendar: *http://www.azteccalendar.com*

Sacred Texts: *http://www.sacred-texts.com*, and most particularly the "Rig Veda Americanus" by Daniel G. Brinton

A BRIEF PRONUNCIATION GUIDE TO NAHUATL

The present pronunciation guide comes from a phonetic transcription of the Nahuatl language made in the 16th century by the Spanish friars.

Nahuatl words usually have no accent mark, and bear the stress on the penultimate syllable.

Vowels

The vowels are pronounced as in Spanish

a is pronounced "ah", as in "ash" or "park"

e is pronounced "eh", as in "ace"

i is pronounced "ee", as in "seek"

o is pronounced "oh", as in "old"

u is pronounced "oo" as in "wood"

Consonants

All consonants save ll and x are pronounced the same as in Spanish, and therefore the same as in English, except for these notable exceptions:

c is pronounced "s" when it comes before e or i

cu is pronounced "kw" as in "query"

c is pronounced "k" when it comes before any other vowel

h is pronounced "w" as in "wild"

ll is pronounced like a long English "l" as in "fully"

que is pronounced "kay" as in "case"

qui is pronounced "kee" as in "keep"

tl is pronounced as a unit like the "tl" in "battle"

tz is pronounced as in "pretzel"

x is pronounced "sh" as in "shell"

z is pronounced a hissy, soft "c", halfway between "zap" and "cite"

LIST OF CHARACTERS

Acatl: Protagonist, High Priest of the Dead
Acamapichtli: High Priest of the Storm Lord
Axayacatl: Revered Speaker of the Mexica Empire (deceased)

Chalchiuhtlicue (Jade Skirt): Goddess of Lakes and Streams, Teomitl's patron
Ceyaxochitl: Guardian of the Empire, agent of the Duality in the Fifth World
Coyolxauhqui (She of the Silver Bells): Southern Hummingbird's rebellious sister, imprisoned beneath the Great Temple

Echichilli: Eldest member of the council; respected magician.
Ezamahual: Novice priest in Acatl's temple

Tlilpopoca: The She Snake, vice-emperor of the Mexica

Huitzilpochtli (Southern Hummingbird): God of War and of the Sun, Protector of the Mexica

411

Ichtaca: Fire priest of Acatl's temple, second-in-command of the order
Itzpapalotl (Obsidian Butterfly): Goddess of War and Sacrifice, head of the star-demons

Manatzpa: Member of the council, Teomitl's and Tizoc's uncle, Axayacatl's brother
Mihmatini: Acatl's sister, courted by Teomitl

Nettoni: Xahuia's sorcerer
Neutemoc: Jaguar Knight, Acatl's brother
Nezahualcoyotl: Former ruler of Texcoco, father of Nezahual-tzin (deceased)
Nezahual: Ruler of Texcoco

Ocome: Councilman

Palli: Offering priest in Acatl's temple
Pezotic: Master on the Edge of the Water, councilman

Quenami: High Priest of Southern Hummingbird
Quetzalcoatl (Feathered Serpent): God of Creation and Knowledge

Teomitl (Ahuizotl): Brother of Axayacatl and Tizoc
Tezcatlipoca (Smoking Mirror): God of War and Fate
Tizoc-tzin: Brother of Axayacatl and Teomitl, Master of the House of Darts, heir apparent to the Mexica Empire
Tonatiuh (the Fifth Sun): Huitzilpochtli's incarnation as the Sun God
Tlaloc (the Storm Lord): God of Rain and Lightning

Ueman: Fire priest, second-in-command of Quetzalcoatl's Wind Tower in Tenochtitlan

Yaotl: Ceyaxochitl's head slave

Xahuia: Princess from Texcoco, Axayacatl's wife
Xochipilli (the Flower Prince): God of Youth and Games

Zamayan: Son of Xahuia

A BRIEF GLOSSARY OF AZTEC TERMS AND CONCEPTS

Ahuizotl: A beast living in Lake Texcoco, feasting on the eyes and fingernails of the dead.

Calmecac: (Lit. House of Tears) a school where the children of the wealthy and those destined to the priesthood were educated.

Calpulli: Clan. In reality, a clan had both a geographical extent (the calpullis owned their land, and Tenochtitlan was split along the lines of calpulli lands), and a political and religious one (the elders of the calpulli were responsible for basic justice as well as for worship).

Chinamitl: (Also chinampa, Floating Garden), an artificial island used to grow crops.

She-Snake (Cihuacoatl): Mexica equivalent to viceroy. Symbolising the female order, he was in charge of domestic affairs. When the Emperor went to war, the She-Snake ruled the city in his stead. The two of them never left Tenochtitlan at the same time.

Iyac: (Lit. Leading Youth), a warrior who has proved his worth in combat by taking a prisoner, either singly or in combat.

House of Youth: The counterpart to the calmecac. Trained warriors not of the nobility.

Knights: elite corps of warriors, reserved for those with strong prowess in battle. Includes the Jaguar Knights, the Eagle Knights and the Arrow Knights.

Macuahitl: A wooden sword with an edge made of embedded obsidian shards; the traditional Aztec weapon.

Master of the House of Darts: the House of Darts was an armoury (the darts referring to the throwing spears kept inside). There were actually several of these in the capital: one in the Imperial Palace and three around the Sacred Precinct at the entrance of the causeways that were the only link between Tenoctitlan and the mainland. The Master of the House of Darts was the commander of the armies, a step below the Revered Speaker. He coordinated the movement of troops, decided tactics and planned the campaign once the Revered Speaker had decided to declare war on a city.

Mictlan: The Aztec underworld, destination of most of the dead. In Aztec mythology, those who had died in peculiar circumstances – battle, sacrifice, drowning or in childbirth, for instance – went to various heavens. The remainder went into Mictlan.

Nahuatl: Language spoken in the Basin of Mexico. The dominant Nahuatl dialect was that of the Mexica, but their neighbours such as the people of Tlacopan and Texcoco spoke other dialects.

Patolli: Aztec board game, played with beans as dice.

Priests: The priestly hierarchy had various ranks, the lowest ones being those of priestly aspirants and of calmecac students. Then came the novice priests, who served a particular god in a particular temple. With time, they could be promoted to offering priests. Those cults which offered human sacrifices had a higher rank, that of fire-priest, responsible for choosing the victims and for lighting a fire in their chests. Finally came the High Priests.

Tlatoani: Revered Speaker; the Mexica Emperor

Triple Alliance: formed by the cities of Tenochtitlan, Texcoco and Tlacopan, the Triple Alliance was the main military body of the Valley of Mexico. A mostly military alliance, it had very few political ties, and each city remained independent, but they sent joint armies to war and shared in the tribute that came back.

Tzin: Aztec honorific, equivalent to "Lord". I have taken the liberty of using those as marks of reverence (much in the way of the Japanese "sama"), and not as actual titles.